VENGEANCE BETRAYED

Also by **P.D. LaFleur**

In the Company of Strangers

To Richard Keenan

P.D. LaFleur

VENGEANCE BETRAYED

P.D. LaFleur

I hope you enjoy reading this as much as I did writing it.

RGI
Press

The Ramsden Group, Inc.
Punta Gorda, Florida

This is a work of fiction. Names, characters, places and events are products of the author's imagination or are used fictitiously. Any resemblance to actual events, locales or persons, living or dead, is entirely coincidental.

Vengeance Betrayed

ISBN 0-9792597-0-3
CIP data available

Cover design © Vivid Invention (vividinvention.com)
Author photo © John Zawicki (jzstudios.com)

Printed in the United States of America

RGI
Press

For Madison & Scott

PROLOGUE

May, 1958
Rostrevor, Northern Ireland

With a sharp pull upwards on the heavy knotted rope, the young boy reached the thick branch of the alder that was his goal. The branch was broad and ran nearly parallel to the ground for several feet when it split and made a dense canopy of the deepest green. From this vantage point, not far above the front door of his grandparents' cottage, he could scan east and nearly see the deep cold waters of Carlingford Lough and pretend to be a mate aboard a grand sailing ship. At ten, he had only recently finished Stevenson's *Treasure Island* in which he identified closely with young Jim Hawkins. Like Jim, this lad craved travel and adventure. He reached the crotch of two strong branches and imagined himself perched in the crow's nest of the Hispaniola. He probed the horizon and determined it was a fine day for sailing.

Comfortable in his fantasy, he plucked a leaf and stuck the

stem between his teeth. Below him, separated from his perch by a scant six feet, was the gray slate roof of the cottage, and a lone pigeon sat at the edge of the painted bricks of the chimney. There was no peat fire today, it being a rare day of relative warmth and sunshine in Rostrevor, and no wisps of smoke escaped the flue and curled its way into the sky as it did on typical damp and foggy mornings. The dull gray pigeon became a bright green parrot and the slate roof the rolling deck of the Hispaniola. If the voices of his grandparents had not been so plain and clear through the open door and windows, the reverie might be more complete. Their conversation in their sitting room about the vagaries of Irish weather and the rising price of good beef certainly didn't sound like that of coarse adventurers seeking pirate gold.

The nearest neighbor was the ancient widow Kibroney far to the north. A narrow brook ran past his grandparents' home, and a crude wooden bridge spanned it and led to a narrow path. Widow Kibroney's cottage sat alongside the path several hundred yards away and over the crest of the hill. It was a mean affair with untended gardens surrounding it, and it reflected the character of Mrs. Kibroney herself. Narrow, with a pronounced list to one side, lonely and unwelcoming.

His grandparents, he was proud to note by comparison, maintained a bright and cheery home, with colorful and aromatic patches of wild gentian and fennel clustered about it, and a garden promising various melons, tomatoes and luscious other payback. His grandfather, recently retired from his professorship at Queens College in Belfast, enjoyed the mornings with his coffee, rolls and newspapers. Grandmother, who had once owned a coffee house in Rostrevor, filled the house with the aromas of baking breads and muffins. The couple was as gregarious as they were gracious and he thoroughly enjoyed the time spent with them and in their care. Friends and relatives were frequent visitors, and he learned as much about horsemanship and dog training as he ever would by simply being in the presence of their conversations.

He only wished that his grandparents would stop calling him "Linny" or "Young Lins", but this was a small price to pay for the fresh air and trees he enjoyed, the cracking wit and wisdom of his grandfather, and the delicious food and rich desserts his grandmother prepared for him. Except for the silly name, Linny felt like a young prince during his holidays here.

The green hills of Rostrevor and the welcoming warmth of his grandparents were a stark contrast to his own surroundings in London. There, his home was narrow, tall and built of gray granite, sited on a street of nearly identical houses. Gracious in their own way, the buildings reflected a Victorian perspective: Solid, and sound, but simultaneously cold and uninviting. With few trees and fewer grand vistas, London afforded him scant opportunity to exercise his imagination, which he fed with voracious reading. That's why he leaped at the unexpected opportunity to visit his mother's parents in Ireland. His father had been called once more to exercise his considerable skill in important negotiations relative to the Middle East, and his mother, as was customary, would accompany her husband on the mission. This was, after all, a summons from the highest authority.

He and his parents rarely took advantage of the country estate of his paternal grandparents in Cumbria. It too was a naturally inviting place with rolling hills and profuse gardens, but it was to his mother's parents that he was sent of occasions such as this. And in truth, he preferred Ireland to Cumbria, and his mother's family to his father's. In Cumbria, grandfather and grandmother furnished a less carefree escape. They were more austere in their approach, more stern in their manner, and more reserved with their emotions. They expected their grandson to dress formally for dinner each evening and to maintain a demeanor appropriate to his family's standing in society.

While he felt affection for his father's parents, they were so unlike his Irish kin who would eagerly trot off to their local for a pint and the crack of conversation and debate. The youngster looked forward to those times when he's join his Gran and Granda at the pub and absorb the sights and smells and sounds of enthusiasm that regularly engaged his every sense.

Still scanning the Lough from the "Hispaniola", he thought he spied two figures on bicycles riding in his general direction across the fields. Unusual, he thought, but not unheard of, with so few cars on the area roads. Rostrevor had nothing in common with the crowded, smoke-choked streets of London. He studied their forms as they neared: One of marked breadth, and the other much taller but with sloped shoulders and much thinner. Workingmen's clothes. He thought of Mutt and Jeff from the comic pages and noted that the broader of the two carried a rucksack. They were perhaps a quarter mile away when they reached a white wooden fence and dismounted their cycles. They parked their bikes against the fence facing downhill, the direction from which they had ridden, and began to cross the field on foot. There was no doubt now that they were heading directly to the cottage. They moved unhurriedly and uncommunicatively. This looked like it might be a business call rather than a visit from two friends.

He kept silent as a fly in the tree above when the two men reached the cottage and he rested there not six feet above their heads when they rapped at the door frame. The noise stopped his grandmother mid-sentence. "Yes?" she called to the doorway. Her voice was as bright as a bird's. "Who is it?"

The bright sunshine outdoors kept the two visitors in deep silhouette. They did not respond at once, and after a moment or two of silence the shorter of the two slipped his arms from the rucksack and opened it while he remained standing just outside the cottage doorway.

"Well, who might you be?" It was his grandfather speaking now. "Come in if you've a mind. It's so bright out there I can't see who you are." He could hear his grandfather's shuffling feet as he made his way across the flagstone floor and approached the front door.

He heard his grandmother say, "Who is it, Ian?"

The shorter of the two visitors removed a long black pistol from the rucksack and calmly handed it to his taller colleague who accepted it and held it waist high. The shorter one then reached into the rucksack and slowly withdrew a long knife, its blade glinting in the sunshine. To this point, neither had uttered a word. The youngster almost gasped aloud when he saw the knife and the pistol and his eyes were wide in alarm as the visitors entered the cottage. He heard a rush of breath and a sucking sound and could only guess that the long knife had been put to use on his grandfather. A low groan, surely the voice of his Granda', confirmed this, and his ears told him that he was slumping to the hard stone floor of the cottage entry. "Why, why?" It was his grandfather in a weak voice.

Again the sound of knife entering flesh. A scream . . . his Gran just coming to understand that her husband of forty-seven years was mortally hurt. Then a loud pop . . . the gun. Less explosion than a sharp crack, and he heard a body hit the floor hard. Only now did either visitor say a word.

"'Tis done. Let's just give them a quick neck slice to send them to their reward in hell."

"Aye", the other responded. Some shuffling about the cottage and the two men walked out as indifferently as when they arrived. Without any evidence of rushing, they made their way to their bicycles, walking them a ways as they came; no rush and no conversation. The whole scene took perhaps fifty seconds from the first rap at the doorway to their exit.

Young Linny waited until he was certain the men were pedaling their bicycles and heading down the hillside and away before he dared scramble down and enter the cottage himself. Breathing was difficult, coming in short bursts. He stood at the door at the exact spot where the visitors stood and made their presence known. In the semi-darkness of the interior, Linny could see his grandfather lay, head nearly severed, in a thick pool of blood. There was no movement, but his eyes and mouth were wide open in a fixed state of surprise. Not five feet away, his grandmother lay crumpled in the middle of the room, eyes closed, blood still pulsing in dribbles from her neck, her legs quivering once and then again, a flutter of movement from her eyes, both still twitching, but even to the youngster, death a certainty and in short order; there was no saving her. Upon the white wall of the kitchen, directly above the table, a single printed word in still warm blood: "Harvest."

ONE

Massachusetts, Last Summer

It was late Thursday afternoon in Cambridge. Across the Charles River, where earlier several small sailboats glided on light breezes in bright sunshine, lay Boston. Charles Whyte sat alone in his office at the British Consulate and looked across at the city, its skyline now casting long shadows in the late afternoon sun. Clouds were scudding quickly from the west though, and soon the shadows would disappear to be replaced by light rains. A freshening wind caused the river to ripple, and a few whitecaps began to chop its surface.

Whyte checked his watch, the dual time Tag Heuer his wife had bought for him for their fifth wedding anniversary. It had cost a small fortune, one they didn't have, at least at the time. Barbara's eyes lit up when he unwrapped the gift and slipped it on his wrist. "See, Charles? You'll know exactly what time it is here and back in London. No more adding or subtracting hours to figure out the right time." Right now it read just after nine o'clock London time, but his specific and very firm instructions were to call at midnight and no earlier. The telephone sat in the middle of his desk reminding him of the evening's chore. He whispered to himself in near despair: "Barbara, do you have any idea what you've done?"

When she finally addressed and sealed the oversized manila envelope, Barbara Whyte inhaled deeply. Only one step left before the cheerless errand was complete. This is, she hoped in spite of the wretchedness and despair she felt inside, the best course to take. Betrayal was not a notion she took casually, but in these circumstances, she could see no other reasonable choice. She thought of her husband, her child, her mother, her entire life as it existed, and finally slid the envelope onto the Post Office counter. The clerk picked it up and placed it on the scale. "First Class?" Barbara nodded approval. "Anything liquid, perishable, food or agricultural products?" Again she nodded, this time in the negative. "One eighty-eight." Barbara slid two dollar bills across the counter, accepted her change and her receipt, and watched as the clerk tossed the envelope into a bin. In a voice low enough not to attract the attention of anyone nearby, she said, "There, I've done it."

"Something's wrong," his superstitious side told him.
Andrew Fortin stood alone and silent at his office window and looked out. The predicted wet weather began with a hovering mist quickly thickening to a drizzle that coated the window-panes and presented a softened view of the ill-tended landscape below. A lonely clump of white birch at the edge of the parking lot appeared to shiver and welcome the dampness on its leaves. He checked his watch: After four. She should have been here at three thirty.
Barbara Whyte, he recollected, drove a Honda sedan. Red. And she was always on time. If she had to cancel, as she did two or three times in the past, she always called in advance to let

him know. Ever responsible and thoughtful. "You know, you are my most considerate patient," he once told her. "Not everybody calls to say they have to miss an appointment or show up late."

He'd give her a few more minutes before calling her home. He rarely felt as disquieted when other patients missed their allotted spots on his schedule; there were always excuses ranging from "I was sick" all the way to "I just completely forgot." In most instances, a blown appointment would simply give Fortin some extra time to review a patient's file, or to catch up on his reading of the professional journals. But this patient's absence caused him greater concern. She did not look well the last time he saw her, and her decline over the past weeks was disturbing to him. In her file after their last session, he'd remarked on her appearance: "Gaunt, frail, agitated. Consider MD referral for med adjustment." He would wait for a few more minutes. Hers was the last appointment of the day anyhow.

The parking lot below was beginning to empty. Offices in the small complex were winding down for the day. His part-time office assistant, Karen Larrison, left for home an hour ago. From this distance, three floors up, he could easily make out the relaxed smile of Frank Wendt, his dentist neighbor across the hall, climbing into his canary yellow fifty-nine Cadillac convertible with the continental kit. It was Frank's pride and joy and the product of two years of careful restoration. "No joy in keeping it in a garage all the time," Frank once told him, "so I drive it every day, rain or shine."

Candace Allan, at fifty-five still supple and capable of drawing the attentions of men far younger than she, was walking purposefully towards her Mercedes coupe, and Fortin admired the fine curve of her legs as she entered. Candace ran a successful financial planning business in the office directly below his own, and Fortin had established a comfortable friendship with her since he began his practice here three years ago.

Fortin saw his own vehicle parked in the last space in the lot, an aging Nissan pick-up, and brushed off the passing thought of replacing it with something newer and nicer. But his solo practice as a psychotherapist was still in its early years and was not so flourishing that it afforded him more than a modest lifestyle. His bank account was not in any condition to yield the kind of capital he'd need to consider acquiring anything better at the moment. In another year or so, when his professional calendar was more crowded and personal bank account more extensive, perhaps he'd consider it. For now, he paid scant attention to what he drove and considered his battered pick-up, like himself, a survivor; it complained once in a while but never succumbed.

Candace engaged him once on the subject of finances in general and vehicles in particular. A veteran of starting a small business, she appreciated the weight of incoming bills versus limited income in the early stages. But she suggested that he look to improving his mode of transportation when his cash flow could afford it, even before investing in anything else. "Sitting in a fine car improves your self image and makes the simple task of going to work and returning home more pleasant; even if you're flat broke, you'll look successful to those around you, and you'll feel more successful inside." Whatever, he thought. He'd think about it when the time came.

He looked down at his desk calendar and saw plenty of open space. The practice was building slowly based on referrals and it still had plenty of room to grow. The potential patient population was plentiful, but he turned down many cases, usually because the patients were either two old, too young, too violent or too indifferent to therapy. There were pediatric and geriatric specialists around, and he'd had his fill of the truly violent when he worked on staff at McLean Hospital in Boston, and later, to a lesser extent, at Leonard Morse in Natick. He preferred to deal with people whom he believed would respond to talk/drug therapy, and he was building what he hoped were long term relationships with practitioners in the area who agreed with this approach and made referrals to him. Today had been fairly crowded by his standards; six patients, all one-hour sessions.

He opened Barbara Whyte's file and copied the telephone contact information on a slip of paper that he slid into his breast pocket. Reluctantly then, Fortin placed her file into the top drawer of his desk and locked it.

Still bothered by her failure to appear, he took a last glance at the parking lot before he reached for the telephone and placed a call to the private line of his good friend, sometimes mentor, sometimes colleague, Dr. Janet Chapel. Chapel, a psychiatrist who specialized in children and psychopharmacology, regularly referred patients, usually parents of her patients, to Fortin, and was once his patient herself. Fortin and Chapel developed a warm friendship and enjoyed each other's company. While she was no longer his patient, they shared an enthusiasm for fine eating and fine wines. Fortin loved to play chef; Chapel loved wines. Together they indulged their passions of gastronomie.

Chapel picked up on the second ring. Without a greeting she said, "Are we still on for tonight?"

"Absolutely. Tell me the time and I'll be ready for you. Can you stop for wine?"

"Six thirty-ish, and sure. I'll be driving by the Village Winery on my way to your place. Just give me hint . . . what are you looking for?"

He knew Janet's palate to be highly refined. She and he had spent many hours over the past few years enjoying the discoveries of the subtle textures and aromas of fine wines, and she had taught him to sip with his eyes closed, to let the bouquet fill his nostrils and allow the wine to make its way slowly down his throat. She was, he was certain, incapable of presenting a foul beverage at his table. "Something red and coarse." he said. "I'm thinking maybe sausages and garlic tonight."

Janet's husky snicker came across the line. "That must mean no sex after dinner, right? See you at Hovelton around six-thirty."

Fortin hung up the phone, amused at how a few moments conversation with Janet could lift him from the deepest regions of his soul. He rose from his seat and turned off the office lights. He felt somehow reassured as he locked the door behind him that Barbara Whyte would be just fine.

Fortin brought his pick-up to a stop directly in front of Carlo's Italian Restaurant. Washington Street in Wellesley was a horrid place to be driving at this time of day. It was particularly jammed with the thick and anxious traffic of home bound commuters this evening, and Fortin considered himself undeserving of the good fortune he enjoyed at finding a parking space, a legal one at that, directly in front of his destination. He knew that Carlo's would have a line of customers out front in less than an hour, it being one of the finest Italian restaurants in the area.

Fortin opened the front door of the restaurant and inhaled the full, warm and delightful aroma of basil and garlic and tomatoes and oregano. Carlo's daughter Francina was putting the menus together at the front counter and looked up at the psychologist with a broad smile. Francina, twenty-two, single, and with the dark alluring eyes of Sophia Loren, was a patient of Fortin as well, but not one with any regular schedule.

"Hi there, Francina. How have you been?"

"Doctor Fortin. It's good to see you." Francina, he knew, had taken to him, perhaps too strongly. He always felt as if she was sizing him up for a steamy session between the sheets, in spite of the fifteen-plus years of difference in their ages. She eyed him with more than casual interest as she reached under the counter for a paper bag. A young healthy woman gifted with perfect, generous breasts, Francina tended to wear scoop necked tops that presented her assets in all their Mediterranean glory. Francina's was a body blessed with flawless olive skin and sufficient curves and just enough jiggle to catch every breathing man's attention. Fortin had some difficulty looking away, and instead succumbed willingly to the view.

"My sausages are ready?" Fortin reached into his pocket and withdrew a thin cluster of dollar bills.

With a smile and, Fortin thought, even a wink, Francina responded. "You bet, Doctor Fortin. Nice big sausages." She stretched out the words. She handed him the bag and held on for a half second longer than she needed to. "Two mild, two hot and spicy. Just like you wanted." It was a game with her, he knew, but he was accustomed to her coy attempts at teasing. "Five even."

Fortin placed the cash on the counter, knowing that he'd spend much more elsewhere for inferior sausages. Francina never glanced away from his face.

"Thanks, Francina. Tell your father that I think his sausages . . ."

". . . Are the best this side of Palermo," she interrupted. "I will tell him, and it always makes him happy to hear it. You know, he doesn't sell anything else out of his kitchen, except to you, Doctor. He thinks you are just wonderful. I think you must have bribed him with that Palermo stuff." Francina's expressiveness was the kind that could make her eyes and lips smile with wit and allure simultaneously, and she used it now. "But if he finds out you told somebody that you get your sausages here," she said with mock seriousness, "he'll make sure your knees are suddenly out of commission. Capisce?" She went back to her menus. "By the way, if you have any openings, I need to see you." Much more serious now, her smile was instantly replaced with the sober expression of someone more emotionally delicate than she cared to be. Her twin brother's death last year from cancer had rocked her sense of good and evil, and she was still grieving. Periodically, she came to talk to him about it. It was that time once more, he thought.

"Certainly. Call me tomorrow, Francina, and we'll set up a time."

She walked in front of him and opened the front door, Fortin admiring her every step. She waved to him as he left the restaurant but kept her head down. This, Fortin knew, was a woman of extreme emotional intensity. Mercurial was an appropriate description. She could be radiant and enthusiastic one moment; ominous and disheartened the next. A woman of stunning beauty, she would someday make some man's life alternately magnificent and miserable, with barely a moment's notice between one and the next. Theirs would be a marriage filled with brilliant highs and dismal lows, a roller coaster ride from mood to mood. Life with Francina would be challenging and fascinating, and never, ever, dull. While he wasn't aware of any long-term boyfriend in her life, he hoped that he'd be invited to her wedding, and he'd wish her new husband well, whoever he was, most sincerely.

Fortin climbed in to the front seat of his pickup and pumped the gas twice before starting. It was a custom he and the truck had become used to. The choke never functioned properly since he bought it third hand from the younger brother of his landlord three years ago. It started predictably and he was off, this time heading for his apartment in Wayland. He wanted to get supper started before Janet arrived. He would simmer the sausages and slice some vegetables for a salad. Janet would bring two bottles of wine, he knew. A glass or two apiece before dinner. Another with their meal. She almost always left a half bottle for him to enjoy alone, either after she was gone or with his meal the following day.

Fortin pulled into the gravel driveway of the gray shingled

two-family home where he lived. "Hovelton" was his one-bedroom apartment on the second floor. His landlord, Todd, lived alone in the first floor apartment. Fortin had the entire second floor for himself. He parked, walked to the front and picked up his mail from the roadside mailbox. Returning to the side of the house, he climbed the stairs to the second floor and picked up the newspaper on the landing. When he unlocked the door to his apartment, the interior was deep in shadow, punctuated by the blinking red light of his answering machine.

He turned on the kitchen light, set his mail, the paper and the bag of sausages on the table and walked to the answering machine at the end of the counter. The machine had recorded three messages. He pressed the replay button and took off his jacket and loosened his tie as he listened.

"Andy, it's just Todd downstairs. I'm going to be away this weekend in New York and I just wanted to let you know. If you'd just pick up my mail on Friday and Saturday and hold it for me, I'd appreciate it. I should be back Sunday night, assuming everything goes well on Amtrak. Thanks." A pause. Then, "Oh, Andy, I should have asked if you were going to be around first. If you're not, or if it's a problem, let me know. And, by the way, there may be some ripe tomatoes on the plants out back, so pick what you want. Enjoy. Thanks."

The second caller was a hang up. He didn't know if it was a reluctant patient or a wrong number. Maybe a thief, casing his apartment to see if anyone was home. Outside of a few scratchy albums and a thin collection of jazz CD's, he doubted if he had anything worth a good thief's trouble. Caller ID said "Unknown Name/Unknown Number". The time of the call was four-twenty, about an hour ago.

The third caller caught his attention. It began with the short-cropped sounds of hurried breathing. "Doctor Fortin. It's Barbara Whyte. I'm sorry about missing the appointment, but I tried to call your office. I need to see you. You're the only one around here I can trust." The voice sounded afraid and rushed. He could hear noises in the background, sounds of street traffic. More hurried breathing. "I've got to go. I'll try you again later." Then a dial tone.

He slipped his jacket over the back of a chair and replayed the last message: ". . . I need to see you. You're the only one around here I can trust." He checked caller ID: "Unknown Name/Unknown Number." The time of the call was just twenty minutes ago.

Fortin reached for his phone and called his answering service. He didn't recognize the voice. "Yes, Doctor Fortin?"

"Any calls?"

"No, I don't think so. Hold on for a sec." She sounded as if she was reaching for something. "No, Doctor Fortin. No calls."

"Can you double check for me? I'm expecting an important call."

"Hold on." Fortin heard her call someone else in the office. He heard his name mentioned.

"Hi Doctor, it's Marion. There was one call at 2:45, but she didn't leave a name. She wanted to be put through to you directly, but Karen said you were with a patient. She said she'd try later, but never said who she was, and didn't call back. Sorry."

"Thanks." Fortin placed the phone slowly down on the cradle. Almost absently, he replayed the message from Barbara Whyte. ". . . the only one I can trust."

He reached for the slip of paper he put in the breast pocket of his shirt and read Barbara Whyte's home telephone number. He picked up his phone and punched in the number. Three rings. Same voice on the recorder. Still no one home to answer his call. He tried her cell phone with the same result. He hung up without leaving a message and considered his options.

He could wait and call again later. That seemed a sensible choice, but he didn't want to settle right away.

She sounded anxious, agitated. Afraid even. He could call the Framingham police and ask them to drive to the Whyte's home and just make sure she was OK. But that seemed a bit too much of the alarmist.

Perhaps a middle road. Wait another hour or two. Call her again. If there's still no answer, then consider calling the Framingham police. He thought that option over as he unwrapped the sausages and placed them on a griddle. Yes, he decided. He would choose door number three.

The smell of the sausages filled the kitchen as he poured corn meal and salt into a pot of boiling water. Cooking, especially Italian cooking, brought him back to his youth when he'd spent hours in the kitchen watching his mother and grandmother stirring, paring and sautéing, and all the while talking. His grandmother had come to the country as a young woman and brought with her a passion, almost a lust, for good food and how to prepare it. This she passed on to her daughter and grandson, both of whom were students of great dedication.

'Nona' was gone now, and his mother as well, but the love for good food, well prepared, never left him. From his mother, he learned of more French Canadian foods, given her marriage to Louis Fortin, and the tradition of the kitchen in which he was raised. Fortin felt blessed to share blood with the two heritages, both with foundations firmly planted in the enjoyment of eating.

Tonight's would be a rustic meal, simple and sturdy. He stirred the cornmeal and turned his attention to another pot holding the sauce. He checked the clock above the stove and saw that he had another forty minutes or more before Janet Chapel arrived.

On his CD player, he had Miles Davis and 'Kind of Blue.' He poured himself a glass of mineral water and sat on the sofa, glancing at his hodgepodge collection of pictures, mementos, and other relics of his past. His two bookcases housed a few current novels, a dog-eared dictionary, and two rows of travel books. Above the bookcases were two display shelves.

On one shelf sat his father's old Bulova watch, some worn rosary beads and a breviary from his days in the seminary, and two railroad spikes from the Boston & Maine line that ran near his childhood home. On another sat his grandfather's bent stem pipe. Seeing the pipe and inhaling the aroma of tomato and garlic brought him back to his grandparents' house, and then to a conversation he'd had one day there with his mother:

Jack Fortin had finally died. Eighty-seven and all angles, a face cast in some forge, way up in Vermont where men still sat around in front of wood stoves at the local general store and told stories. When Andrew was just a child, old Jack or "Pepère Jack" as Andrew always called him, would take him by the hand and place him on a short stool at the edge of the taller chairs where Jack and his friends would sit. A pickle barrel sat in the corner, its sour fruit speared by the shop owner for a quarter. Andrew would have the run of the penny candy counter on those days, sometimes chewing through a dollar's worth in one visit.

Pepère Jack was born 'Jacques' in St. Agapit, some thirty miles southwest of Quebec, and moved to St. Albans as a child with his parents and thirteen brothers and sisters. There were no borders then; families crossed into and out of the United States with barely a whisper of concern. Most of the old men spoke French or some variation of broken Franglais as they smoked Camels or Lucky Strikes or Chesterfields and drank from small bottles . . . most without labels . . . that smelled razor sharp to the little boy. They cursed and spat in brass jars.

On the way home one day in early winter, Pepère Jack said something that stuck with Andrew: "I got six grandchildren, you know. But you're the only one that's like me." Andrew's face turned up to his grandfather with a question. *"Don't let it take you where it took me."*

After the funeral, Andrew helped his mother bring cold cuts and cheese and mustard to the dining room table. There were jars of olives and small rounds of bread and Andrew, nearly twelve by then, looked at the faces of his aunts and uncles and some of the cousins who accompanied them to the services. When the day turned to evening and the last of the relatives had left, Andrew carried the nearly empty trays back into the kitchen where his mother was washing everything by hand and setting plates and utensils in the drying rack.

"Pepère told me once that I was the only one that was like him." He had never said anything aloud about the conversation until today. His mother stopped and turned to face him, eyes turning deep into the young boy's. *"He said I shouldn't let it take me where it took him."*

His mother dried her hands quickly on her apron front and grasped Andrew by the shoulders. *"Don't ever say that stuff again, Andrew. Your Pepère was a good man sometimes, especially when he got old like you remember him. But he could be a mean man, and he could be a very bad man, too. I just hope that God took him into heaven anyway."* She turned back to her task while Andrew stood, still a little stunned by her reaction. *"Your father is nothing at all like Pepère Jack, and I think that's good. I don't think you're anything like your Pepère either, if that's any consolation."* But Andrew sensed that his mother didn't really believe her own words.

TWO

_____

Barbara Whyte checked her watch. Six-thirty, so she still had some time. She'd raced home from the post office and made an important phone call. Could her friend take care of her eight-year-old son, James, for the night and bring him to Logan Airport in Boston tomorrow? She was fairly certain that the answer would be yes; they'd been friends for so long, and Barbara knew that she would do the same if the tables happened to be turned. But the tables were right where they were right now, with Barbara on the wrong side and needing help. The answer was "Yes" and no reasons were requested or offered. Neither was required. That's the way they had always been. Even if they didn't spend as much time together as they would have liked, they maintained clear and solid connections that kept them bound to each other.

The message Charles left on the answering machine earlier said that he'd be home late. No particular time given; just "Late." Since she'd made arrangements with a neighbor to look after her son for a couple of hours and she needed to get moving if she wanted to get everything done. First she went to the front closet where her son's luggage was already packed and ready to go. Tomorrow young James Whyte would be heading to England to spend some time with his grandparents in North Yorkshire. James loved his grandparents thoroughly and was looking forward to the trip. Plus, James had made a friend last year on his annual visit, and for the past several months had been communicating via email with his British friend. The airline tickets and James' passport were on the kitchen table and she grabbed those as well. The car was in the garage and she stowed the luggage in the trunk and the travel documents in the glove compartment.

Then she found her own empty luggage in her closet and began stowing an assortment of her own clothes. She had no idea where she'd be headed later on after she dropped James off, nor how long she'd stay away. She just knew she needed time away from Charles, and with James headed to England for three weeks, this was the right time. She just wished she'd had an opportunity to visit with her therapist first, at least to explain what she was sending him through the mail. Not that she knew exactly what was going on with her husband. Her suspicions were sufficient to reach the conclusion that Charles was involved in a scheme that was illegal, dangerous and potentially disastrous. The fact that Barbara now knew something about the scheme . . . that it existed at all . . . could put her own safety in jeopardy.

She had not planned to get Dr. Fortin involved, but she saw little choice. Charles didn't want to talk about the situation; her friends would likely contact the police, and that could jeopardize any future that Charles and Barbara might have together. Dr. Fortin was bound by the rules of confidentiality, at least to a point, and she felt she could trust him. She felt immensely relaxed in his presence and confident in his capacity as a therapist. He'd look through the packet of papers and know what to do. She hoped she was right.

She loaded her luggage in the trunk of her car and checked her watch once again. She needed to double check everything and collect James at the neighbor's and head to her friend's house in New Hampshire. She said she'd pick James up before eight-thirty. Before she did, she decided to leave a note for her husband. Sitting down at the kitchen table, paper laid flat and pen in hand, she began to cry.

In a dark tavern in South Boston, the tall man drank alone and went over his progress in silent contemplation. It had been a lovely day before the drizzle. Early in the morning, he took the subway to downtown Boston and walked along several streets near the Public Garden, enjoying the abundance of flowers and the serenity of the pond. He walked through the area and across the granite bridge to Arlington Street and paid particular attention to the area at the foot of Newbury Street. With a digital camera, he took several snaps and appeared to be, like many others enjoying the area, just another tourist admiring the scenery. He bought a coffee and bagel from Dunkin Donuts and sat on a park bench to assess his opportunities and his challenges.

Just before noon, the man walked into the bar at the Ritz Carlton and ordered a chicken salad sandwich and a martini, relishing every bite and drop of his lunch. He overheard some days earlier that such a luncheon was considered *de rigueur* to Boston's elite who frequented the Ritz. When he left, he returned to the park bench and removed a cell phone from his pocket. He punched in a series of numbers and waited. On the third ring the call was answered. In calm, level tones, he described what he saw and the plan he devised.

"It's Keough. The site's selected. From the top of the Ritz. When our guest arrives at Burberry's. It's wide open with good sightlines and angles."

From the other end of the line he heard, "Fine. I just spoke with his secretary and as I suspected he'll make that his very first stop when he arrives. How about your young ranger?"

"He's prepping and he'll be ready to go. It's so easy here. Just a word or two in the proper ears and there's always a name comes up. This one's trash with the right genetic connections and a propensity for being, shall we say, a bit thick."

"So he won't be missed?"

"Mother's dead. Father's in Limerick. Long history over there. A real hero for the Republic. This chap would love to earn a merit badge from his da'. Do I mention anything to Charles?"

"About the site, fine. But not a word about your ranger."

"I'll keep that bit to myself then."

"Good. Charles is good for some things but not others. What we're talking about would cause him more distress than we want or need. So when do you get him ready?"

"He'll be ready to go once we do a walk through. That will be tomorrow or the next day at the latest."

"Excellent. He sounds like he'll make a wonderful dead man."

The aroma of the sausages caught Fortin's attention and he rose from his seat to turn them over. Janet Chapel would be arriving anytime, and he wanted to make sure the meal was ready to go. He saw Barbara Whyte's telephone number on the counter and recalled the events of the first session five months ago with Barbara as being fairly routine. As usual, the first session consisted largely of some basic questions and answers: Family history, health history, very general for first time patients.

Born Barbara Anne Chicoine in central Maine thirty-six years ago. Father, Marcel, professional photographer, mostly weddings and portraits. Emigrated from the province of Quebec as a child. Died suddenly when Barbara was just six years old. Myocardial infarction at forty-five.

Mother, Liddy, seventy-two, who, like her husband, had family ties to Quebec. A nurse who'd spent time in the military before marrying, she recently retired and lived in the same home where Barbara grew up. One brother, Leo, six years older, divorced and childless, teaching physics at Bowdoin. A sister, Mary Ellen, the 'free spirit' of the three, two years older and living with her boyfriend on a houseboat in the Bahamas. No children.

Barbara herself was married and the mother of an eight-year-old son, James. She lived in Framingham, about a thirty-minute drive west of Boston and only twenty minutes from Fortin's office. Her husband, Charles, was in diplomatic service for his home country, Great Britain. He worked as a Consul at the British Consulate in Cambridge near the MIT campus.

Barbara met Charles and fell in love during her junior year of college, which she spent overseas at Oxford. After returning to Maine and graduating cum laude from Bates, she married Charles at the school's grand college chapel on the edge of the quad and moved to London where they lived for three years. A series of assignments for the Foreign Service found Charles and Barbara Whyte living for a time in Rome, then Bangkok, and later in Tokyo, where their son, James, was born. Four years ago, Charles accepted a transfer to the Boston consulate in Cambridge, and Barbara was delighted to finally be posted so close to home and to her mother.

Life was going along rather evenly for Barbara until the past five or six months. She had lived through several moves around the globe without any seeming problems, and the fact that she was encountering some rough times lately bothered her sense of self. Barbara considered herself to be self reliant, and she was proud of that quality. She expressed resentment more than once to Fortin that she had lately felt a need to reach out for someone else's help, that she could not effectively handle her own problems, especially problems with no apparent physical cause.

She suspected that her continuing insomnia, fatigue and weight loss were connected to some form of psychological depression. But she hoped that a thorough exam by her family physician would reveal something more tangible she could grasp onto and attack, something organic to discover, treat and overcome.

When a psychiatric evaluation was first suggested, she told Fortin in that first session, she felt her body become tense. "After all," she related, "I climbed Mount Katahdin alone when I was fifteen. I've traveled around the world and lived in at least half of it. Damn it, I know the daughter of the Japanese Prime Minister like a sister. I love my husband. I have a wonderful child. There's every reason to be thrilled with my life . . . and I'm feeling so miserable and lost."

Fortin saw the despair and the frustration in her eyes. He asked her some questions about her life over the past four years. Moved to a nice apartment on Marlborough Street in Boston at first. Great location. Lots of things to see and do. Museums, theater, restaurants, a wonderful city for strolling. Charles could walk across the Massachusetts Avenue Bridge into Cambridge and be at work in twenty minutes. But raising a family, they found that space would be a problem for them in the cramped confines of their apartment, and they found a nice single-family house for rent in Framingham.

She made the house a home for herself, Charles and their son, James. Charles held a wonderful position at the consulate, and except for the odd trip every five or six months back to London, or to Washington or New York for meetings, he was able to establish a reasonable pattern to his life. Home most evenings for dinner. An occasional round of golf with friends on the weekend. Raking leaves. Quiet nights in front of the fireplace. Things, in general, seemed quite nice, all in all.

Barbara did feel some urge to become more professionally productive, and when James started kindergarten, she was thrilled to be asked to fill in as a teacher occasionally at St. Francis of Assisi High School, just a short drive from her home. When a permanent teaching position came open at the school, she gratefully accepted the offer, and she charged into the job with enthusiasm. English Literature. World History. These were passionate subjects for Barbara Whyte and she relished the challenge of bringing them to life for her students.

The compensation was low and the benefits nonexistent, but Barbara leaped into the job headfirst and loved every minute. Her students reacted warmly to her, and her enthusiasm for language and thought was infectious. Without question, this was a peak in her life.

So when the news came from Monsignor Lambert last spring that her position would not be funded for the coming school year, Barbara's fall was steep and swift. She completed the school year with a flourish, only to withdraw into herself during the summer. Her appetite languished. She found herself waking at two in the morning, unable to fall back asleep. Charles expressed concern, but he was certain that she would burst out of her "funk", as he called it, soon enough.

She didn't, and by the end of the year, she had dropped twenty-one pounds. She was gaunt, hollow eyed, and excessively tired. On a visit to Maine at Christmas, her mother cried when Barbara stepped out of the car. It was she who urged Barbara to see her physician, and when she returned home to Framingham, she did.

Her physician conducted a thorough exam and several tests, ending with the suggestion that she was suffering from depression. He recommended that she see Dr. Janet Chapel at Bradley-

Bourne hospital for a psychopharmacology consult. From there, she'd be referred to a psychotherapist, and that's when she started seeing Fortin on a regular basis.

Fortin agreed with the diagnosis of depression and the prescription from Doctor Chapel for Paxil should help. It would take a few weeks to see any noticeable difference, Fortin assured her, and he knew that Janet Chapel would monitor her progress and consult with Fortin from time to time. A therapeutic level of the antidepressant might require adjustments in the dosage amount; individual metabolism, diet, body mass and other factors could influence the effects. In spite of all the scientific efforts brought to bear upon the disease, treating it effectively was still largely a guessing game.

Meanwhile, Fortin would conduct "talk therapy" with Barbara Whyte, and that, in combination with drug therapy, had proved most effective for most patients most of the time. "This is not an exact science," he often reminded himself and his patients, and he even wrote the aphorism on an index card that he taped to the inside of his desk drawer.

Barbara appeared to be responding favorably to the treatment, and after four weeks her appetite had improved and she gained three pounds. Nights of uninterrupted sleep remained elusive, however, and Janet increased the dosage of Paxil in gradual steps.

Depression as a response to a major loss . . . the death of a loved one . . . divorce . . . retirement from an active work life . . . was common enough. At first blush, Barbara Whyte appeared to exhibit the classic response to the sudden loss of her teaching position at St. Francis of Assisi, especially given the joy she derived from the job.

But Fortin heard other clues in her words, and they were not solely related to being laid off from her teaching position. Barbara could be confident and composed, and Fortin would attempt from time to time to hold her gaze steadily. She tended to look him straight in the eye. But occasionally, her eyes would dart away to a corner of the room, and usually when the subject was her husband, Charles.

Barbara described Charles Barr Whyte as handsome and recollected that at their first meeting she thought of him as her "knight in shining armor." She remarked once that his weight was unchanged from the day they married, in spite of the gobs of caviar and Brie that would be placed before him at frequent consulate receptions.

The second child of an insurance broker father and librarian mother, Charles was raised in the small market town of Thirsk in North Yorkshire. He was a studious boy, excelled at three A-levels, and entered Oxford. Both parents were alive and well and remained in the home in which they had raised Charles and his younger sister.

At Oxford, where he was admitted to Wadham College, Charles found his footing in the study of politics and history. Not one who was naturally gregarious, he made few close friends. When Fortin probed, Barbra explained that Charles might be better described as more serious than stern. He relished the spirited conversations in the university pubs, but was just as likely to be found alone with his studies in his room or at the library.

He made the acquaintance of a professor of political science, Geoffrey Ramsden, who made an enormous impression upon Charles in a seminar program on international relations. It was Ramsden who later advised Charles regarding his course selections and who further suggested that Charles consider a career in public service. Sir Geoffrey, whose lineage was prominent and traceable through several centuries, was a well-regarded peer, knighted at the relatively early age of forty, and a few years later stood successfully for election to Parliament. Born and raised in London's Mayfair section, he was about as far from the market village roots of Yorkshire as an English man might be. With his relative affluence, family background ("He's the sixth Earl of something," Barbara noted), and academic credentials, Ramsden was among the "Great and the Good" of his country. "He's quite well known in Britain," Barbara told Fortin. Indeed, Fortin recognized the name as Ramsden was a very strong figure in British politics, and the Prime Minister didn't step too far afield without first getting Sir Geoffrey's counsel. "Without his influence on Charles' behalf," Barbara went on, "we'd probably be posted to some barren outback. Instead, when Charles asked about the opening at the Boston Consulate, Sir Geoffrey made certain that Charles would be offered the position. We're fortunate to have him on our side."

Barbara's attempts at smiling nonchalance when she spoke of Charles and his work at the consulate were of late betrayed by her eyes, for it was on these occasions that she would cast her glance elsewhere, anywhere else but directly at Fortin.

Fortin probed, but gently. Barbara revealed little, but Fortin increasingly sensed that part of her depression arose from some change in her relationship with her husband. He had no clear evidence of that, but Barbara's inability to look him in the eye when the subject was Charles concerned him.

During her most recent therapy session, she seemed particularly on edge when the subject was raised. Fortin had asked her about her attendance at various consulate functions. Did she find them enjoyable? Did she find them tedious? He wanted to try these relatively innocuous questions to lead into a gradually deeper discussion.

Her responses were a forced smile and focusing her eyes on a colorful paperweight on his desk. She said that she used to find them enjoyable, but that lately . . . she trailed off. When he waited for her to continue, the prolonged silence was broken with her looking at her watch, standing up and feigning tardiness for a missed appointment elsewhere. "Oh my goodness, I forgot. I have to pick up James at the sitter. I'm sorry, but I have to go." Fortin saw that there were nearly ten more minutes to her session, but didn't stop her. She left his office that day in a rush.

Something more lay beneath the surface. Fortin made a note in her file and stood by the window. He saw Barbara hurry across the parking lot to her car in the approaching darkness of the early evening. The lights in the parking lot were on, and she held her purse in the glow as she fumbled for her keys. She entered her car and closed the door. She didn't leave immediately, though, and instead held her head in her hands for some time. She didn't look like a woman in a hurry to pick up her son. She looked like a woman weeping.

THREE

Janet Chapel arrived at Fortin's apartment a few minutes later, entered as usual without knocking, and was immediately seduced by the food aromas. Before she set the wine on the table, she leaned, eyes closed, over the kitchen range, breathing deeply and taking in the bouquet of garlic, basil, tomatoes and spices.

Fortin, who had been setting the table in the dining area when she entered, stood behind her. "Looking and smelling is OK, but don't you dare touch a thing."

"And good evening to you, my fine friend," Janet said in mock indignation. "Are you always this uncivil to your dinner guests? Especially guests bearing gifts of fine wine?"

"What kind of rude medicine did you bring over this time, Doctor Jekyll?" Fortin leaned over and pecked her cheek.

Janet smiled and removed the two bottles with mock flourish from the paper bag and placed them on the table. "A simple Chianti Classico, Signore. Warm and friendly, but with a little bit of a bite. Just like me."

"I'll go along with 'bite', but I'll pass on 'warm and friendly'. Should I open one up?"

"Why not open both. We can let one breathe a bit while we sit and talk."

Fortin opened up a kitchen drawer and rattled around the clutter until he found the corkscrew. He spoke while he worked at the corks of the two bottles. "I picked up two mild sausages and two hots from Carlo's on the way home. You're the guest so you get your choice."

Janet was walking to the living room and turned her head back to answer. "One of each would be wonderful."

Fortin took two stemmed glasses from a cabinet and followed her with one of the opened bottles. He poured and sat in the heavy club chair across from Janet who sprawled across his couch. "Tough day, Jan?"

"Oh, the usual. Too many patients. Too little time. And I swear I'm taking my telephone off the hook from now on."

Fortin knew that her days were filled to the brim. Even cutting back on her patient load as she'd done in the past year didn't give her much relief. She was working on a paper she would present at an upcoming conference in her "free" time, and he asked her about its progress.

"Progress? Well, let me ask you, Fortin. If I read at a normal pace, how long would it take to read a typical page, double spaced?"

"Probably a minute and a half, I'd guess. Why? How long is your talk?"

"Three minutes."

"Not coming along as quickly as you hoped, huh?"

"I actually thought I'd be able to put the concept on paper with no problem. It's on adolescent behavior studies, and I deal with those all the time. But it's a lot tougher than I thought. I could probably wing it for a while, but I don't trust myself doing that. I agreed to do this presentation as a personal favor to an old professor of mine, and it's important to me to make it a good one."

She sat up and reached for her glass. A long sigh. She raised her glass, swirled it around, and waited for him to raise his. "Let's put that bullshit aside for a few minutes. Here's to friendship." He reached and they clinked glasses.

"Wonderful," he said when he finished his first sip. "Nice rich color. Good aroma." He swirled the wine in his glass and studied it in appraisal. "Lousy legs, though."

Janet affected horror at the suggestion. "Legs? You want legs? In a Chianti Classico?"

"Wrong, huh?"

"The only nice legs in the room belong to me, and that's the way it should be." She was right about that. At five-ten, Janet Chapel had a model's figure with the legs to go with it.

She smiled and took a second sip. "So tell me something about yourself. What's happening in your life? What's up for the weekend?"

"Nothing special. My landlord's going away for the weekend, and the only certain things on my calendar are picking up his mail and bringing my shirts to the cleaners."

"Where's Todd going? Did he say?" She met Todd when Fortin first moved in and the three had enjoyed an occasional dinner together.

"New York. Sometimes he goes to visits friends. Takes in a play. Why?"

"Just wondering." She took a sip and lounged back on the sofa. "I like the idea of getting away on weekends. It sounds sort of civilized. It must be nice."

"Why not try it yourself, then? It would do you some good." This was not a new suggestion. She rarely took time off, even on weekends. He once proposed a joint vacation, but she never found enough time. "You know, some people, as unusual as this may seem to you, take a whole week and go away to different places. Just for fun. Seven whole days. In a row! It's called a vacation."

"The world hates a wise ass, Fortin."

"I mean it, Janet. You need time off. I'll bet you tell patients that all the time. Relieves stress. Refreshes the soul. All that."

"All the time." In a resigned tone, "I know you're right. I do say it all the time to my patients. Maybe I should take my own advice for a change. Any suggestions?"

He pondered the question before answering with his own. "Where's the conference where you're delivering your paper?"

"Jackson Hole. I love to ski, but August is a lousy month for that. The conference board likes to book nice places but they always do it in the off-season. Makes it a lot cheaper. So I'm planning to fly in and out as quickly as possible. No possibilities there."

"So what? There are dozens of other conferences. I'm sure you're on every mailing list in the world for all the professional associations. You're always facing another round of continuing education requirements, so just pick one that fits your specialty and sign up."

She drained her glass. "You're right. Vienna's always big for psych meetings and it's a beautiful city. Freud and all that penis stuff. But the idea of getting away just to spend time with a bunch of other shrinks isn't very appealing. We're not a particularly fun group."

Fortin stood and went to his desk in the corner of the room. He riffled through stacks of mail and magazines until he found one with some promise. He returned to his seat with a recent copy of the Journal of the American Society of Psychotherapists. He flipped to the rear of the journal and skimmed the ads. As he expected, the pages were brimming with travel ads, most of them tied in to some psychologists' seminar or another. "Here's one. Three days. Rio de Janeiro in November and it carries a bunch of CE credits. A symposium on pedophilia and other sexual deviance."

"What a place for that meeting. Tits and ass everywhere outdoors and all that frustration working itself out indoors. Give me another one."

"Okay. Scottsdale. Same week. The subject of the meeting is geriatric medications and counseling."

"Nah. Too depressing."

"It's at the Scottsdale Princess. Great place!"

"Nah. Give me another one." She was beginning to enjoy this. The two of them daydreaming about faraway places.

"London. Early December. Fourth Annual Symposium on Psychotherapy for AIDS or HIV-Positive Patients."

Janet looked up with mild interest at that one. When he saw her face, he connected that many of her patients at Bradley-Bourne were gay men with the disease. The London seminar might have struck a nerve.

"What were the dates again?"

He told her.

"London, huh? Shitty weather, though."

Fortin considered it. "It has to better than Boston. More like Seattle. Damp and a little foggy. Cool at night."

"What about the Cratchet kids in *A Christmas Carol*? Sliding on the ice, knocking Scrooge's hat off with a snowball. Or did Dickens set the story in Oslo?"

"Let me check my travel guide, Miss Skeptical." Fortin loved to travel, even though his limited financial resources didn't permit him to indulge the passion with any frequency. His bookcase was crammed to overflowing, with the bottom row devoted to dog-eared travel guides of every sort and for most destinations. He scanned the row and found the one he sought. He flipped through the first several pages and stopped. "Listen to this. 'Roses blooming in December are no rarity in London.

Warm winter days are apt to be rainy. Cold days may bring some occasional sleet.' Now, I don't have a travel guide for Boston, but I'll guarantee that if I had one it wouldn't be so generous about our winter weather. Ice. Snow. Brutal winds. I'll take London."

"OK. I'll think about it. I've got some time coming that I need to use before the end of the year. It's far enough away that I think I can work out some coverage. How much?"

Fortin knew that Janet had too much money to spend. She lived in a modest condo in Newton and drove a leased Saab sedan. She rarely spent money on herself. He checked the ad again. "Seven seventy five for the seminar alone. Or there's a package for seventeen fifty. That covers the plane, the hotel and the seminar. Breakfast and lunch, too."

"Mmmm, homemade British cooking. Boiled eggs, boiled herring, boiled beef. And all that wonderful British wine. What a treat for the gourmand."

At her sarcasm, Fortin stood up, remembering the dinner simmering on the stove. "I almost forgot!"

"I didn't. What else do you have besides sausages? I smell tomatoes and garlic."

"Polenta tonight. With marinara sauce."

"Great." She rose from the sofa and brought the nearly empty bottle of wine with her to the table. She poured the remnants into her glass and brought the second bottle from the kitchen. "Need any help?"

"Salad's in the fridge. Dressing's on the counter. You can bring it over."

Fortin took two plates from the cabinet and placed them on the counter while Janet carried the salad to the table. The telephone caught his attention and he decided to give one more try at reaching Barbara Whyte before serving dinner. His instincts said she wouldn't be home, but he waited for the third ring and the recorder. "Hello, Barbara, this is Doctor Fortin. It's seven thirty. Please call me when you return home." He recited his number before hanging up.

He returned to the dish of warm polenta and placed healthy slabs on both plates. He was reaching for the sausages when Janet stepped into the kitchen. "I heard you on the phone, Andy. I thought you were the guy who jumped all over me about leaving my work at the hospital."

"A patient missed an appointment this afternoon, and I was just calling to make sure she was OK, but she's still not home."

"Afraid she might do something stupid?" Janet's concern was evident in her wrinkled brow.

"It's Barbara Whyte, Janet. I'm concerned, but I don't read her as suicidal. It's just not like her to skip without calling first. And her last appointment left me a little uneasy."

"How so?"

As fellow professionals dealing with the same patient, confidentiality wasn't called for. It was Chapel who first met with Barbara Whyte and gave her a prescription for anti-depressants before referring her to Andrew Fortin. He described her behavior when Charles Whyte was brought into their conversation. How she averted his eyes and left the session abruptly. Then, most troubling, the phone message on his recorder today. He went to the answering machine. "Listen to this and tell me what you think. The message was on my recorder when I got home." He pressed the replay button and they both listened as Barbara Whyte called Fortin "the only one around here I can trust."

Fortin looked at Janet, and Janet's face was screwed up in a puzzled frown.

"What do you think?" he asked.

"That's my question."

"I'm not sure. I figured I'd let it set for a little while and then call the police if she doesn't call me by nine. Just to drive by her house. Check it out."

"You're afraid?"

"A little. I don't want to alarm her if she turns out to be out shopping or something. But her phone message bothers me. I think she's very disturbed about something involving her husband, but we hadn't got into anything yet."

"Like what? Is he unfaithful? Do you think he's abusive?"

"No. It's as if she's sitting on something she doesn't want to talk about just yet."

"You know what I think of your instincts, Fortin. Your hunches are so good, I still think of you as my own personal Quasimodo."

Fortin knew exactly what she meant. Janet's own situation was one in which Fortin's instincts probably saved her life. When she first met him and discussed the possibility of his being her therapist, Fortin sensed that here was someone who was being battered. Which turned out to be true. Battered by herself.

He saw a Janet Chapel as a woman who was extremely tough on herself. Who was driven. Who was hiding from herself. And who was struggling to present a cool exterior persona in spite of herself and the turmoil within.

A natural beauty, she was tall and slender, but with curves in all the right places. She wore no makeup and usually tied her thick blond hair into a ponytail. She disdained fashion and formality, and he could not recall her dressed up in anything fancier than a simple blouse and skirt. More often, like tonight, jeans and a sweat shirt was her typical wardrobe. Andrew knew she'd be striking dressed in a potato sack.

Her eyes were extraordinary. Pale gray one moment and sea green the next. Flecked with shards of sky blue. And extremely expressive. He'd once heard that the eyes were the windows to one's soul, and he was never more convinced of this than when he met Janet Chapel.

At their initial meeting, Andrew was taken by her easy manner and general good humor. While she initially approached Fortin on the basis of wanting therapy as a means of maintaining her "equilibrium disturbed by her professional demands," he rarely took any patient's self analysis on its face, even one made by someone as grounded in the profession as Janet Chapel.

He noted at once Janet's distinct ability to intellectualize most issues, and he elected to pursue an avenue which challenged her and dared her to internalize and, hopefully, express her feelings. Janet, he could see, was comfortable and expert at viewing and assessing complex and difficult issues when there was professional space between the issue and herself, but woeful when the issue was herself. Not that she harbored no feelings about herself. Rather, she could accept conditions of imperfection in others, but she set impossibly high standards for herself.

In those early sessions with Janet, his attention was drawn to the marked change in her eyes when he'd press her on her feelings toward herself. It was more than the usual discomfort he might have expected, and her responses were carefully worded, as if she were attempting to answer a test question for which she was unprepared.

"You are damned direct when you focus on matters at a distance," he said to her in an early session. "But you talk in meandering circles around the subject when I ask you to get close to your core. Do you see that tendency in yourself?"

They both knew that this disposition was not particularly unusual. In fact most people build protective barriers of varying dimensions to guard their souls from intrusions and threats. In Janet Chapel's case, her strategy, whether she recognized it or not, included deflecting penetrating questions. Sometimes she'd use humor, make a small joke and manipulate the conversation into a different and safer direction. Fortin's persistent attempts to get Janet Chapel to look inward and describe what she saw met no progress. She willingly spilled her brains, but not her guts.

He told her of his frustration. After her fourth session, he confronted her. "Janet, everything you've said to me makes perfect sense. But I have to tell you that I think you're being dishonest with me, or at least deluding yourself and others."

She looked puzzled and uncomfortable, but said nothing.

"I hear you speaking to me, Janet, answering my questions. Leading me along. But I feel like I need a third ear." He looked her square in the face. "Do you know what I mean?"

Fortin detected a flash of anger in her eyes as he continued. Janet Chapel was not in the least comfortable by his observations.

"You're speaking to me on several levels most of the time. Much of the time, I think I can take what you say literally. Other times, I sense that you're speaking to me in riddles and hints. Some are subtle and some are not so subtle. I feel manipulated. Don't misunderstand me, Janet. I don't think you're intentionally lying to me. I'm sure you're not. But you do a lot of dancing around and daring me to guess what you really mean."

Janet's eyes narrowed. "I'm dishonest? You've known me for what . . . a few goddamned weeks? And you're calling me dishonest? You're an ass, Fortin."

He ignored her assault and pressed forward. "Intellectually, you're way out in front of me, Janet, and I'm struggling to keep up."

"Don't patronize me."

"If you slow down a little, and listen to yourself, listen to what you're telling me, we'll both have half a chance to grab hold and maybe even accomplish something positive."

"And you're telling me you feel manipulated?"

"Yes. You're real good at it."

"No shit, Sherlock!" She reached for the sweater on the edge of her chair and started to rise from her seat. "You're a real fucking genius."

"I know that I'm asking you to do something difficult."

She leaned forward and her eyes burned with fury. "Kiss my ass, Fortin."

"You've got too much at stake to continue deceiving yourself, Janet."

"Who died and made you Freud?"

"I'm asking you to be honest with me."

"You should have stayed in the seminary if you wanted to hear confessions, Fortin."

"To be honest with yourself."

"I don't need this shit."

"You're letting yourself off the hook."

She stared him straight in the eye. Neither would yield. He waited. The silence was building in crescendo.

"I'm gay," she said flatly.

Fortin's mouth snapped opened in a grin. "Well, that's a relief."

Chapel was taken aback by the smile and apparent flippancy of Fortin's response to her innermost secret. She felt a loss of composure and was momentarily speechless and her eyes began to fill. When she regained her bearings, there was fury in her voice.

"What the hell is that supposed to mean, asshole?"

Fortin leaned forward in his chair and addressed her eye to eye. "You finally said something about yourself that was direct and forthright. No equivocation." Fortin gave the appearance of someone who had just reached the top of a mountain. He was openly pleased.

Janet Chapel, on the other hand simply held his gaze, searching for some judgment, some denial. There was none.

"Look, Jan," Fortin went on, "You're as methodical a thinker as I've ever met. Set aside the issue of being gay for a minute: Do you see how well you can weave and dodge around issues? You can really make a therapist work his ass off to get any-where."

She remained silent, processing his remarks. They had found purchase. Finally, she nodded her agreement.

"Look, you've been here for an hour, and I'm tired. I'm sure you are. What do you say to calling it a day and grabbing a Coke or something?"

Chapel was stunned. She'd just revealed her deepest secret from the most protected corner of her self, one she'd guarded for years. One which had threatened her well being like an evil troll, patient, waiting for a momentary lapse so it could leap from the shadows of its swamp and clamp its teeth into her being, relentlessly attacking and draining her of her strength, killing her. She hated herself for it."

She was benumbed. Fortin rose from his chair and watched her eyes following his. He took one step toward her and Janet rose slowly, never breaking the gaze. Her eyes filled and she began to shake, trying to stifle the sobs rising from her belly. Fortin opened his arms and she fell into them, convulsing, tears freely streaking down her cheeks onto his shoulders. He held her close and let her weep. When she stopped, he reached for the box of tissues that he kept on his desk and handed it to her. He was smiling a comforting smile.

"I'm sorry."

"It's OK," he said, voice low and reassuring. "It's OK."

Over the next several weeks, Fortin met frequently with Janet Chapel, and she spoke freely and openly. As if a dam had ruptured, Janet poured herself forth in waves of tears and reve-lations. She felt an overwhelming sense of alleviation in disclos-ing what she had worked so long and hard to conceal, she told him. Free from the pain of harboring her fears alone.

"Revealing one's self to somebody else takes courage, Janet, the rawest kind of courage."

"I was afraid," she said to him, "that I'd let you in, and then you'd reject me. I didn't want to tell you who I was . . . who I am . . . because if you didn't like me, what else would I have to give?"

She told him a story from her youth. "I remember going to confession once . . . I was fourteen. I told the priest that I was falling in love, and that I couldn't get sex off my mind. Well, you'd think I had just confessed to killing JFK. This priest raised his voice and told me I needed to pray for my own salvation starting right this minute." In a mock dialect of the angry priest she said, 'Imagine . . . a young girl like you . . . Mary Mother of God.' He railed on about chastity and virtue and virginity. "I started to cry, and finally I just left. When I stepped out of the confessional, I saw everyone staring at me. I just left by the back door and never went back."

Fortin listened patiently. He knew she wasn't finished with the thought.

"I can't imagine what he would have said if he knew I had the hots for Cheryl Maloney."

Being gay, she acknowledged, was behind a good deal of her increasing workload at Bradley-Bourne. If she worked hard enough, she had negotiated with herself, she could keep the issue at bay. "Quiet times, when I'm not busy, are the worst," she told Fortin. "I try to keep active, and working seems to help."

"How many hours a week do you work, typically?"

"Well, my hospital coverage at Bradley is a standard forty hours. I see a few private patients in my office for about another ten hours a week, sometimes twenty-five. Consulting on other cases? Say a couple of hours a day."

Fortin had been making notes as she walked through her

schedule. He finished and asked her, "What about meetings or reading professional journals?"

She looked at the ceiling, silently counting the hours. "I'd say I spend no more than five hours a week reading journals and papers, usually at night before I go to bed. Most of the meetings are during my regular hospital hours, but sometimes they'll run long."

"OK, that leaves a handful of hours a week, assuming you take eight hours a day at home for sleeping and such. What about emergency room coverage? You must be on the hospital's schedule sometime during the week."

They went back and forth like this, adding hours here and there for different tasks. At the end, Janet Chapel had a total of about four hours each week unaccounted for.

"Is there anyone in your life right now?"

"Are you kidding? You know what my schedule's like. I don't have time for somebody else right now."

"I'd say, Janet, that if staying active seems to help, then you don't need me. And besides, if you needed to see me, you wouldn't have the time for it."

"I understand that. I see my work for what it is. I don't happen to like it. I mean, I thoroughly enjoy what I do for a living. I just don't like the fact that I've allowed it to consume me to such an extent."

"And it will probably kill you at the rate you're going. You've filled your days so full of other people and your work that it simply has to take a toll. You have to eat. You have to put some distance between you and your work, or you'll fall apart at the seams. You need to connect with somebody other than just your patients. Or me." He kept his eyes fixed on her.

"What is your greatest fear, Janet? That your homosexuality will become an issue at the hospital? That it will ruin your career?"

"That's part of it."

"But you know that there are other physicians who are gay."

"Sure."

"But being gay yourself . . . ?"

"Scares the hell out of me. I mean, I'm a psych. I've worked hard to be a good one. Do you think my patients would still come to me for therapy if they knew I was gay?"

"I don't know, Janet. Why would they need to know anything about that aspect of your life?"

She ignored the question. "Or the other psychs who use me as a consult? Or the MD's who refer patients?"

"I can't say, Janet. But are being gay and a good psych mutually exclusive?"

She didn't respond, but Fortin could see her working through mental images. He waited before he spoke again.

"Tell me, if I was a gay man, would you still come here for therapy?"

She considered the question and locked eyes with him. "Are you?"

"Don't cop out; just answer the question."

"Yes, I would. It wouldn't bother me if you were gay. But are you?"

"Do you routinely answer patients' questions about your personal life? Many patients want to establish personal relationships with their therapists. Some are just curious. If one of your patients asked you the same question, would you answer?"

"I think it's inappropriate and dangerous. And besides, I'm not interested in being the 'gay' shrink."

"So I guess you're answering your own question."

"So you're saying you won't tell me."

"What does it matter?"

"It doesn't, but I know some of my patients would freak if they knew about me."

"Are you concerned that if your patients found out, which is doubtful anyway, that you won't have enough patients?"

"There are plenty to go around. But that's not the point."

"And do you really think your referrals would drop off if your colleagues learned of your sexuality?"

"Maybe some. But, I'm turning patients away as it is."

"So if some physician who currently refers patients to you turned out be homophobic, you wouldn't suffer a loss of patients."

"Correct."

Fortin looked at Janet but said nothing. He could see wheels turning.

Therapy with Janet Chapel became a once a week routine, then once every other week. Over time, she did indeed trim back her working hours and, with Fortin's encouragement, reestablished her love affair with wines. Always having a sensitive and discerning palate, Janet confided that she sometimes wished she could have been a sommelier and have the opportunity to taste and furnish wines as part of her everyday life. Fortin asked what kept her from doing so. She had lost her faculty for wine tasting, she said.

While she still enjoyed an occasional fine wine, she was no longer the student of the subject she once was. Medical school at Columbia's College of Physicians and Surgeons, her internship at George Washington, and her residency at Beth Israel consumed her life. She had time for little else. Since coming to Bradley-Bourne, she made time for little beyond her work.

Fortin was a fine, self-taught chef, and he dined as often as his wallet would allow at better restaurants. He appreciated the passion that great sommeliers had for their trade. On a hunch, he approached his friend, Carlo, whose restaurant was gaining a strong reputation in the vicinity. "Could you use a sommelier on your staff, Carlo?" The response was met with waving arms and a flood of broken Italian-English, the sum of which was: "Are you kidding? Do you have any idea how much it would cost me to put a wine steward on my payroll? Are you out of your mind?"

Fortin repeated the question, but added the words "at no cost to you" into it. It would be a volunteer.

"If he's good, and if he doesn't cost me money, of course I would. Are you crazy?"

Fortin thanked him, never revealing whom he had in mind for the position. He presented the notion to Chapel. Since then, every Tuesday evening from seven to ten found her in a black tuxedo at Carlo's. Three hours not a physician. Three hours a sommelier.

Fortin also encouraged her to enroll in a night course at Harvard on the subject. She did, and she now taught one session every other month herself.

Wine was more than a hobby to Janet, and she felt grateful for Fortin's persistence in making wine more a part of her life.

Her new involvement in wine, besides taking her away from the single focus of her work, was an escape valve. It allowed her to shift into another mode, to meet new people, to discuss things other than the subjects of her psychiatric career. To Fortin she said, "I feel like a more interesting person," and Fortin agreed with her.

Dealing with being gay remained an issue for her, but the fear of disclosure no longer ruled her life. She didn't advertise her lesbianism. She had no current partner, nor was she interested at the time in establishing a relationship with one. She did, however, appear to be more accepting of herself as time passed, and Fortin reinforced this perception.

Janet Chapel had also grown to establish a closer friendship with Fortin, and became, at his urging, the patient of another therapist. They both agreed on the need for a greater degree of professional distance between patient and therapist, more than either considered possible if they continued in their roles without a change.

So tonight, they were personal friends and professional colleagues, currently co-managing the potentially difficult matter of Barbara Whyte.

Fortin placed Janet's plate of polenta, sausage and sauce in front of her. He sat down with his own and they conversed between bites.

"Andy, if your instincts tell you she could be in danger, you ought to consider acting on them. Even if she is out shopping, safely making her way around the mall. Besides, you won't sleep tonight if you don't know what's going on."

"I think you're probably right, Jan."

"Mmmm. This is heavenly. I've haven't had polenta for years, but I remember it as being corn meal mush."

"That's really all it is. It's a staple food in a lot of countries, but it's basically plain old corn meal, poor man's food. It fills you up, and you can alter its flavor depending on what you serve with it."

"The sauce is heavenly. Your own?"

"Sort of. I buy baskets of tomatoes at Haymarket at the end of the season, super cheap. Not good for slicing but great for sauce. So I froze tons of it last fall. Todd has a huge freezer in the basement he lets me use. Half of this sauce tonight is the last batch from my storehouse of frozen chopped tomatoes. Then I combined it in an old family traditional recipe. I take a jar of Prego spaghetti sauce, remove the cover and put it in a saucepan."

"You are a prize, Fortin. This is great."

"Thanks."

They ate without speaking for a few minutes.

"I think I'll call when we finish."

"The police?"

"That's probably my only good choice short of driving there myself."

FOUR

Frank McCarty usually enjoyed being the senior officer breaking in the rookie cops. He fancied himself an elder statesman, of sorts. In nineteen years on the Framingham police force, he worked with dozens of eager, fresh-faced kids. Some washed out; some took bigger jobs in the department, the current chief among them. Frank knew his limitations, and understood that he was never going to be among the senior management of the force; he'd been a sergeant for twelve years, and he'd probably retire a sergeant. That was OK with him.

He considered himself fortunate to be where he was, considering how close he was to becoming a roaring drunk, a druggie, or even a convicted felon. He had three brothers, and each one had made it to the Framingham police force. Frank was the only one of the four still on the force.

His oldest brother, Jimmy, was now the unofficial town drunk of Framingham. Unemployed, unemployable, and living off a small disability check in a dirty one-room flophouse on the south side of town.

Gerry, the second son, had the current good fortune of

working now as a truck driver. Frank had recommended Gerry to a neighbor who was a shipping manager for a metal stamping firm in Ashland, but Gerry was in danger of losing that job just like he had his last one. Drugs. Cocaine last time. Heroin this time. And Frank knew from Gerry's wife that Gerry was using again.

And Frank's younger brother, John. There was a case for the books, Frank thought. Bright. Full boat scholarship to Holy Cross. Good looks. Scored highest in his class at the academy. But lazy as sin and greedy as hell. When the FBI pulled a sting operation involving the theft of computer hardware from a local firm working a government contract, John was indicted as the cop who made sure there'd be no one around when the trucks pulled away from the loading dock. Five years, two served. Felony theft. That counted for hard time in Danbury. He'd run through five or six jobs since his parole, but Frank was convinced that John would see the inside of a cell again one day.

If Frank McCarty wasn't lucky, at least he wasn't stupid. Tonight, the rookie beside him in the front seat reminded him of his little brother. Smart and sometimes a little cocky. McCarty got the feeling the kid had potential, but, like John, he might be too smart for his own good. The kid needed some humility, and McCarty would work on that.

The call came to his car at seven fifty-six. He listened to his lieutenant explain the situation. Check out a house at 19 Woodland Road. See if Mrs. Barbara Whyte is present in the home and not in danger. If she's home and everything is cool, she should call her doctor; McCarty wrote down the doctor's phone number. If she's not at home but her husband is, relay the message from the doc, but get a feel for the situation and make sure he knows you'll be checking back later on. If no one's home, take a look around and report what you see.

These calls came in all the time. Mostly they involved kids, but sometimes, like this, they involved adults. Usually because the subject failed to show for an appointment and the subject was possibly in some danger. At least it didn't look like a domestic call. Those were the worst. Screaming, crying, usually a lot of drinking going on. You could never tell when you got there what the story would be. Once, he knocked on the door and the boyfriend answered the door with a thirty-eight in his hand. The girlfriend was screaming from the back bedroom, two black eyes and all beat to hell, and she's the one who comes after McCarty with a kitchen knife. Defending her loving boyfriend from the menacing police officer.

The rookie in the front seat with him this time, Scott Mendes, was only on the job three weeks. McCarty knew his father, Ray Mendes, from the fire department. There was no emergency tonight, so no flashers and no siren.

When they reached the end of Woodland Road, McCarty slowed the cruiser to a crawl. Quiet residential street. Only a few street lights, but the full moon helped. Lights on in most of the houses. Nobody walking around outside. Number nineteen was a white Cape Cod style home with dark shutters and an attached garage. Neat and clean looking. No car in the driveway. No lights on inside. McCarty pulled in to the driveway and used his two-way radio to report his activity. Mendes was already out of the car and waited for McCarty.

McCarty walked to the front door and rang the doorbell. He heard the chimes inside but there was no movement. He knocked on the door. Still nothing. He tried turning the doorknob. Locked.

McCarty then went to the side door and tried the bell, then knocked. No response. Door locked. Mendes remained three paces behind him and scanned the scene in all directions.

McCarty walked to the garage and looked in the window. "Kid, you got your flashlight?" he asked Mendes.

"No, but I'll get it."

McCarty's flashlight was under the front seat, but he knew from experience that the rookies always had the freshest batteries.

"Put the light on the garage. See if there's anything in there." Mendes did, and they saw nothing inside.

McCarty then walked to the rear of the house, speaking to Mendes in an even voice. "Let's look at the yard while we're here. I don't want to miss something obvious just because we're focused on the house."

McCarty went to one corner of the rear lot. Fenced in. Nice, small lot. There was a wooden swing set in good condition. Nothing out of place. Mendes walked from the other corner of the lot. "Nothing," he said.

They walked toward the house, but the moonlight wasn't bright enough to see indoors. Mendes asked, "Want me to use my flashlight to look in the windows?"

"Look where you can, but keep the flashlight off. We don't have a warrant. No evidence of any crime. Let's just see what we can see without getting the neighbors upset."

Mendes looked into the kitchen window by standing on the bulkhead door to the basement. Nothing to see. McCarty peered into the living room from the front steps, but nothing looked out of place there, either.

When they returned to the cruiser, McCarty told Mendes to call the lieutenant and tell him what they found. "Nothing to report, lieutenant. No one home. No sign of anything wrong. No windows broken. No car in the garage. Everything appears to be in order, sir."

The lieutenant thanked Mendes and ended the transmission. McCarty pulled out of the driveway and started down Woodland once more. It was a quiet night in Framingham.

Whenever Charles Whyte got especially nervous, his mouth would go dry and his armpits would go wet. Barbara called it

"Flopsweat," and it was no truer than this moment. Tonight, as he sat in his office in downtown Boston, telephone to his ear, his mouth was especially dry, and his armpits especially wet. He'd been on the phone for one hour and thirty minutes already, and the conversation was not going well. It was a reflection of his life in general lately.

"But, sir, I must tell you once again that there's no way I can manage that issue. I've tried several times, and I've gotten nowhere at all."

Whyte was alone in his office, his door closed and locked. "I'm afraid she knows about Shamrock, or at least parts of the plan, but short of a confrontation, I have no certainty of that." His perspiration penetrated his shirt and his jacket, making dark half circles on his pale gray suit. "Of course. I understand that fully. If she does tell someone else, we're knocked out. Completely knocked out. But as I said, sir . . ."

Whyte was cut off mid sentence once again. He wanted to crawl through the telephone wires all the way to London and shake the caller by the lapels.

"I'm terribly sorry. Of course. Yes, I'm aware of that. He's arriving in just a few days. Yes. I'll expect your call tomorrow night."

He waited until he heard the click on the line signaling that the caller had indeed hung up. Then he placed the phone on its cradle and pressed the switch attached to the base of the telephone set. The switch activated a scrambler, standard devices on most telephones assigned to those in the British diplomatic corps. Whyte could not afford to have a secretary or other passer by pick up another line and listen to his long distance conversation. For most of the daily mundane calls, no scrambler was necessary, unless, of course, security could be breached by someone learning that caviar and white Bordeaux would be served at some terribly boring reception in honor of this mid level visitor from Helsinki or that representative from a trade ministry in Manila. But tonight's call, as were every communication from this caller, were not for anyone's ears but his own.

Whyte sat erect in his seat and folded his hands on his desk. He needed time to compose himself. The caller was losing patience with Whyte. Either he confirmed that the information in question remained secure . . . that is, beyond the possibility of his wife's reach . . . or his wife would have to be silenced. That was the word Ramsden used: 'Silenced', and upon it Ramsden did not elaborate. Not one whose service to Great Britain involved deep cover or Bond-like intrigue, Whyte's only conclusion was based on his own limited experience. Did Ramsden mean "silenced" as in, 'dispatched'? As in 'terminated', 'sanctioned', 'downed'? "Barbara, Barbara," he said to himself in a voice barely above a whisper.

Whyte sat immobile for several minutes. With a heavy sigh of resignation, he stood up and took purposeful strides to the east wall of his office. There, he admired the pen and ink drawing by the architect and designer Inigo Jones, matted beautifully in ecru linen and framed in dark cherry. It was a gift from his parents when he completed university, and he carried it with him on every assignment since then. The drawing depicted in intricate detail the scenery of William Davenant's masque, Salmacida Spolia. When he first moved in to this office and hung the drawing, he was reminded of the irony that it was Jones, an Englishman, whose translation of the works of the Italian Palladio inspired and instructed the American architect, Thomas Jefferson. Now stationed in the U.S., it had crossed Whyte's mind that perhaps he would influence America in as meaningful and in as lasting a fashion as Inigo Jones.

He brushed the frame with his fingers. Then, glancing back to the entrance door to his office to reassure himself that it remained secure, he slid his fingers to the top of the frame and pressed a metal lever. The frame swung away from the wall, revealing a small wall safe with a combination lock. Whyte dried his fingers with a handkerchief and carefully spun the dial. In seconds, the tumblers were in position and he pulled the handle. Inside were three file folders, a single large white envelope and a dark green velvet sack. Whyte reached for the sack and gently removed it and its weighty contents and placed it on the corner of his desk. He loosened the gold braided cinch and pulled the plush fabric to open its end. He removed the contents. A dull charcoal colored nine millimeter pistol, lightly coated in oil, and a single container of fifty hollow point bullets.

Whyte stared at the weapon moving his head slowly back and forth, wanting to deny what might well become inevitable. Obtaining the weapon had been relatively easy, given the immunity of the diplomatic pouch. His patron in London had insisted that he have it, and there seemed no reason at the time to object, considering the remoteness of its ever becoming necessary.

As if suddenly struck by some fresh idea, Whyte shook his head and replaced the weapon and its ammunition in the velvet sack, placed it inside the safe, closed the safe door and spun the dial. He swung the frame and thus exposed the Inigo Jones drawing, and he did so with a combination of resolve and grief.

Andrew Fortin and Janet Chapel were finished washing the dinner dishes, and Janet was preparing to leave. Her days started early, and she liked to be home and asleep before eleven.

"Look, I hope you get a call from Barbara Whyte, or at least from the Framingham police telling you everything's OK. I don't want you to be up all night worrying." Just then, the telephone rang and Fortin reached over and picked it up.

"Hello?" His tone was urgent.

"Doctor Fortin?" It was a man's voice, not Barbara's. And

not accented like Charles' would likely be. Fortin looked at Chapel.

"Yes, this Dr. Fortin."

"This is lieutenant Siemasko from the Framingham police. You called earlier about checking out the home of a patient, Barbara Whyte, on Woodland Road?"

"Yes, I did."

"We just sent two officers to the house, and there's no one home at the present time. No lights on. No sign of any foul play or anything."

"Nothing at all?" Fortin didn't know what to ask, but he didn't want to end the call so quickly. He wasn't satisfied with the report. He tried to think.

"Was her car at home? She drives a red Honda."

Fortin listened as the lieutenant checked something. "Let me see. No, no car in the garage. I wish I could tell you more, Doctor, but there's nothing more to report."

Fortin was about to thank the lieutenant and hang up when he thought of another question. "I don't want to be a pest, lieutenant, but do you think it would be possible to send an officer to the house tomorrow morning? Early?"

The lieutenant evidently read the anxiety in Fortin's voice. "I don't want to promise that, sir, but I will leave the request for the supervisor of the next shift. You know, maybe she went away for a couple of days. Family emergency. It could be anything."

Fortin wasn't convinced, but he thanked the lieutenant and hung up.

Janet caught the gist of the conversation. "Nothing, huh?"

"Nothing. No car in the garage. There were no lights on in the house, so Barbara and her son are out." Fortin chewed on the words as he spoke them. "The husband. I'll call the consulate. See if he's there."

"It's late, Andy. The place must be closed up for the night."

"Not if there's a function going on there tonight." He was already pushing the telephone keypad for Cambridge information. "Can you give me the number of the British Consulate, please?" He waited and jotted down the number. He pressed the switch hook for a moment to disconnect and punched in the Consulate's number.

Charles Whyte descended the great polished oak staircase of the British Consulate and was about to open the enormous door fronting the building when the telephone at the receptionist's desk rang. He stopped mid step and turned to see if anyone was at the desk. It would be unusual to see anyone around at this hour, save a security guard, especially when no reception was held this evening. Whyte considered letting it ring. Probably some tourist who lost his passport. Or a wrong number. From the corner of his vision, Whyte saw Edgar, the security guard, walking from one of the side hallways towards the phone. In a quick, impatient tone, Whyte barked, "Let it ring, Edgar."

Edgar, a long time employee of the Consulate stopped and looked at Whyte. "But, sir, I always answer the night calls. I can take a message and leave it on . . ."

Whyte suddenly stepped to the desk and picked up the phone himself. If the phone would be answered, he would do it. "British Consulate. May I help you?"

"Yes. I hope so. My name is Doctor Andrew Fortin. I know it's very late, but I'm trying to reach Mr. Charles Whyte. Is there any chance that he's still there?"

Whyte could taste the cotton in his cheeks. His temples throbbed and his sphincter tightened up into a knot. His briefcase suddenly weighed two hundred pounds. "Uh, no, sir. Uh, he's not in at the moment. Uh, gone for the day. Can I take a message for him?" Whyte could see Edgar looking at him. Maintaining a cool demeanor was a struggle.

"Will he be in his office in the morning?"

"Yes," Whyte said, with some relief. "I believe he'll be here by nine o'clock. Um, are you sure there's no message?"

"No, thank you. I'll call him tomorrow."

Whyte hung up. Why is Barbara's psychologist calling me? At this hour? Whyte recovered sufficient poise to nod and say an unruffled good night to Edgar on his way out the front door. When the cold night air struck his face, Whyte shivered. Why is he calling me?

Perhaps she's . . . no. He wouldn't call me in that case. Did she have an appointment today? Yes. Wednesday. So why is the bloody shrink calling me?

Whyte walked briskly to the parking lot and his car, a black Ford Taurus, parked at the front edge. The weather had turned that day from just damp to icy. The wind was in his face and Charles pulled his scarf higher and tighter. He opened the trunk and slid his briefcase onto the floor. When he sat behind the wheel and started the car, the radio blasted loudly. "Damn!" he said as he turned the radio off and pushed the heater controls to high. He usually liked to listen to news in the morning and music at night. But tonight, he wanted silence to consider the events of the evening. Barbara has really fudged the gears, he thought. She should have kept her curious nose to herself. Damn it to hell! Why is she so intent on putting herself, and me as well, in peril? Leaving the computer turned on was my fault, I agree. But we were drinking and anxious to make love. If I had shut it down and placed the disk in my briefcase as I usually did, this never would have happened. She never would have seen the computer screen still glowing on my desk when she arose in the middle of the night to use the loo, and she would not have been tempted to satisfy her curiosity.

Damn it all to hell!

Whyte negotiated the narrow side streets of Cambridge that never failed to remind him of London, with its haphazard intersections and the odd angles. Except that even some of the narrower streets of this city would be considered quite substantial by London standards.

He crossed Memorial Drive and the Charles River, entered the Turnpike and drove west towards home. His mind and heart were heavy with the burden caused by the light night breeze last week. Barbara may have read the bloody notes on his disk. That was probably correct, he presumed, given the change in her nature since then. True, she has been melancholic for some time, and the doctors seem to agree on her depression. But that matter seemed to be moving ahead rather nicely. Her sleep seems to be improving, bit by bit. Her appetite has certainly improved, and she's added a pound here and there.

The only rational explanation for the current malaise: She read the notes. She knows. She's probably been suspicious for a while; the bloody notes on the disk only sealed the matter. And maybe her fate.

When he reached the exit for Framingham, he turned off and headed north toward the neighborhood of compact, tidy houses that held Woodland Road and his home. He had no plan as yet. He could draw Barbara away from their son's bedroom, perhaps down to the basement. James was surely asleep at this hour. There, he could confront her about the papers and determine what she had put together on her own. Most important, he could force her to reveal the name, or God help me, the names of those to whom she revealed anything at all connected with the proposal known simply as "Shamrock". Whyte couldn't think beyond that point.

In his entire life, the only weapons he ever fired were small caliber rifles at a shooting range. Purely recreation. Even the small pistol he kept hidden at home had never been fired. It remained in its original carton under his shirts in the dresser.

When he first moved to the U.S., a colleague at the consulate advised him to keep a weapon at home just in case of a break in. Barbara dismissed the notion as foolish; she didn't want guns in the house, especially with a youngster in the house. Over her objections, Charles arranged to acquire a small silver plated pistol. He wasn't even certain of its caliber. Better to be safe, he thought.

He had loved Barbara and thought theirs to be a blessed union. Many of his co-workers in diplomatic service were either never married or divorced. The likelihood of transfers to all corners of the earth, plus the customary evening receptions and frequent travel put enormous strain on the best of marriages. Theirs, however, seemed to weather the storms of separation and adjustment, thriving through their years together. Until this year. The loss of her teaching job had been a severe blow to her, he knew. Perhaps he didn't sympathize sufficiently at the time, but he did try to make light of the loss, telling her another position would appear soon enough. He saw now the folly of that strategy. Barbara had begun her slide downward, and before he knew it, she had sunk into blackness and despair.

He sensed her growing detachment and her isolation, watching her disappear into a corner of the spare room where she would sit alone in the dark, sometimes weeping, but always alone. Dr. Chapel's medical prescriptions seemed to help, as did her sessions with Dr. Fortin.

The image of Dr. Fortin jarred Whyte from his rambling thought. He was approaching the intersection of Woodland Road, and would be at number nineteen in less than a minute. Dr. Fortin. Why on earth was he calling the consulate? Whyte turned into his driveway. He frowned at what he saw. Total darkness. Unusual. No interior lights on at all. He and Barbara had argued once about her use of electricity; she liked the house lit up, he considered it wasteful and certainly expensive. She said the lights made their house look inviting. She added that she was the one who was home every evening, and he was often staying late at the consulate, or away in London, so she would do with the lights as she wished; he said it was. . . . Charles lost that minor skirmish.

He pressed the button on the remote garage door opener and watched the door rise in front of him. Very odd. Barbara's car is gone. He parked his car and walked to the side door, fumbling for the correct key in the darkness.

Entering the kitchen, he turned on the lights. In spite of the absence of Barbara's car and the fact that all the lights were off when he arrived, he called Barbara's name. His voice echoed in the hallways. He walked to the foot of the stairs and called once again. Still no answer. He called his son's name as he walked up the stairs. He looked in the bedrooms and the bath. The beds were made. Even her habitually cluttered nightstand was in order.

He went back down to the first floor quickly and opened the cellar door. He flipped on the lights and rushed down. No sign of Barbara or James. In the corner, the laundry was dry and folded. Tomorrow was the day that James was going to England to spend some time with Charles' parents. He and Barbara were going to drive to the airport together in the afternoon.

He walked back up to the main floor puzzled. Nothing appeared out of place except for the gaping absence of his wife and child. If anything, the house seemed particularly orderly as if Barbara had taken extra care this day to put everything in its place. He walked to the kitchen table and leaned against the counter. He felt warm and noticed for the first time that he hadn't removed his heavy wool coat. He considered checking outside but dismissed the thought. She was not going to be outside. She was not indoors. Her car was gone.

It was then that he saw the envelope in the center of the table. On the face was written "Charles" in Barbara's hand.

He picked it up and opened it hurriedly. Folded neatly was a handwritten note. In his throat, bile burned a hole.

"Dear Charles. I've taken James with me; I'll make arrangements for him to get to the airport tomorrow. But I will be away for a while. I don't know how long. I have so much to think about, and I need this time away. Please don't try to contact me. And please forgive me for what I've done. I have always loved you, Charles. Barbara."

Whyte was frozen in place. *"Please forgive me for what I've done."* He read that sentence over and over, swirling through her words. His chest heaved periodically, acid rising from his gut. Minutes passed and the only sound within was the rhythmic ticking of the hallway clock. Possibilities sprung from the darkest doors of Whyte's mind. None were pleasant, and most were terrifying. The workable realities ran to only two results: One spelled Barbara's demise, and its sad irony jarred Whyte as he laid her note atop his briefcase; the other spelled his own.

FIVE

It was nearing ten o'clock when Fortin hung up the phone but his hand was reluctant to leave its grip on the receiver. He wanted to feel more assured by the conversation than he did, but something about the call gnawed at him. He picked up his phone and punched in the numbers for Janet Chapel's private number. There was no answer, and he left her a message. He waited only a few minutes when she called back.

"I guess I was worried over nothing," he said without conviction. "I just got a call from Charles Whyte. He said that Barbara went to Maine. Apparently her mother is ill."

Janet listened, sensed an unfinished thought.

"He said it was quite sudden." Fortin's voice was flat and did not resonate with confidence.

"You're not relieved?" It was more of a statement than a question.

Fortin considered the question. She was right. His concerns over Barbara Whyte were not allayed. "I'm not sure why, but I got an uneasy feeling talking to her husband. He sounded on edge, but I guess that understandable. After all, his mother-in-law is ill and his wife rushed up to take care of her. But something about him . . ."

"Her mother lives in Maine?"

"Auburn, I think. I'd have to check the file. It's about an hour north of Portland. At least that's where Barbara grew up. She's talked about her mother once or twice, and I guess I just assume she still lives there. It made an impression on me because that's where my father lived when he was growing up. I still have a few cousins there."

"Maybe you could call her mother."

Fortin considered the option for a moment but shook his head. "No, I think maybe I'll let it go for now. I'm probably reading too much into this; after all, it's just a matter of a missed appointment."

"And a very unusual telephone message, don't forget."

"I know. And there's something about the husband. He sounds a lot like the person who answered the phone at the British Consulate, the one who told me that Charles Whyte was gone for the day."

"But why would he say that, if it was in fact Charles Whyte who answered the phone."

"I don't know." He could hear papers being shuffled on Janet's end of the phone. "Look, Janet, you're not doing work at this hour are you?"

"This paper you hear me rummaging around with? This is B.S. work. But," she went on with her thought, "set the call from her husband aside for a while. Do something else. Read a good book. Or, if you're still in therapist mode, read through some case files or something. Go to bed. Sometimes I do my best thinking on a subject when I'm unconscious."

"I understand. That's good advice and I probably ought to take it."

"Really, Andy, there is such a thing as over analysis. Like Sigmund said, 'Sometimes a cigar is just a cigar.' "

"You're right. And you should take your own advice and get some sleep yourself. Like they say in the movies, 'fugget-aboutit'."

"I'm sending you a hug, okay?"

"Thanks. It helps."

"You know, Andy, you got me thinking about London and that psych conference. I put a good deal of stock in your advice, and maybe a few days away from the daily grind will do me some good."

As they said their good-bys, Fortin smiled at the joy he felt at having Janet Chapel for a friend. That was a stroke of good fortune.

Charles Whyte sat at his kitchen table, sweating profusely and pondering his predicament and the workable options. Barbara was gone. To her mother's home in Maine? Perhaps. That would be predictable. But Barbara had many friends throughout New England, and Charles did not feel any sense of certainty when he considered the range of possibilities.

Since Barbara's bout of depression was diagnosed, he'd read as much as he could find about the condition and knew that one of its dangers was the possibility of suicide. Would Barbara kill herself? He shuddered and cursed the thought. The irony of his anxiety struck him bluntly: "Damn the bloody Shamrock," he muttered to himself, taking another sip of Laphroaig. "Damn the bloody Prince of Wales. Damn the whole lot." He stopped short of damning his benefactor, probably on his way at this same moment from his Mayfair flat to his offices at Parliament at this hour, thousands of miles away and safely removed from Charles Whyte and this whole pitiful scene.

Charles loved Barbara, as much as he could love anyone, but he was also owed his professional life and good fortune to Ramsden, and he could not dismiss the loyalty he felt in that regard.

"Shamrock", for all the time it consumed in Charles life over the past several months, and all the turmoil it generated in the past few days, was a noble exercise, and he felt privileged to be a crucial part of the plan. Success with Shamrock would most surely put the current Ulster Dialogues in fatal disarray, sealing the fraud and the empty sentiment of appeasement for at least another generation and perhaps more. The Northern Counties would stay just that; there'd be no more hollow calls for conciliation. Sinn Féin would shrink in its effectiveness and once more be lashed unequivocally to the IRA standard, right where it belonged. Orangemen throughout Ulster would be reinvigorated and the UK would remain just as its name implied, "united".

Ramsden had made clear the simplicity of the proposed plan. Its value was in its extreme high drama, according to Ramsden. It would be nonetheless, assured Ramsden, a matter of relative harmlessness. Its success would all but guarantee that the ongoing discussions between the factions would not only cool but be placed so far on the back burner as to be out of sight, and therefore out of mind, while the opposition scrambled to reestablish its veracity as a willing and worthy partner in any so-called "peace accord".

For everyone's benefit, the matter required extraordinary secrecy. Nothing could be exposed under any circumstances. The plan would be developed and then unfold with an absolute minimum number of participants. All communications were to be secure and in code. Telephone calls between Ramsden and Whyte were to be made on secure lines. A simple code would make communications swift and effective.

Exposure would not only ruin Ramsden in every way, but also Charles. Hard jail time would likely ensue; Ramsden's ultimate hopes to lead the party and Great Britain would end in flames; shame would fall on Ramsden, Whyte and everyone associated with them.

To add insult, any exposure would certainly result in the

peace process inherent in the Ulster Dialogues being enhanced instead of scuttled. Utter, absolute secrecy was necessary.

I need to confront Barbara, to speak with her, Charles thought. I need to learn what she's done with the information I left unprotected. If my worst fears are true, if she's shared her findings with anyone else, then I have to make some decisions. The thought of discharging her from this universe with a single blast to the brain was more than repulsive, but such a course of action was called for by Ramsden.

And what of James? Their son was consummate joy, a magical addition to their marriage. Would he have been capable of robbing James of a mother? Charles shook his head to clear it of its dissonance. No. There'd be no guns. No death threats. What was called for was a sane, rational discourse. With James on his way to spend three weeks in England at Charles' parents' home, he'd be safe from the turmoil that would surely ensue when he and Barbara finally sat down together and . . . what? . . . had their "rational discourse".

He turned his attention to the telephone, considered calling Ramsden. What would Sir Geoffrey have to say should he learn that Barbara had disappeared? If he knew that the plan could be fatally compromised by a suburban U.S. housewife? How composed would the usually unflappable M.P. become? Would his polished poise be fractured by the notion of a renegade wife of a mid level Foreign Service employee possessing knowledge that could potentially disturb and destroy the most careful plans for only days hence, and with it the career and reputation of Sir Geoffrey Ramsden and perhaps a dozen others highly placed in the government of the United Kingdom?

Whyte threw back a solid gulp of the heavy whiskey and grit his teeth at the jolt the fluid caused as it burned its way to his insides. And James? Can't forget James.

Whyte put his head on the table and began to snore a sour

sleep, perforated by nightmares, but salved by the numbed stupor that the Laphroaig afforded.

Her car's digital clock read "10:51" as Barbara approached the driveway just outside Portsmouth, New Hampshire. She pulled in, shut her headlights off and shut the engine of her Honda. It wheezed to a halt after a few misfires. James was sleeping in the back seat, slouched against the door of the sedan. She could hear a faint snore and regretted that she'd be waking him in only moments. James was not a quick and easy one to wake. Like Barbara, James needed ten minutes or more to get the sleep out of his eyes and the air into his lungs. Charles was the bright and cheery one of the family, bounding out of bed refreshed every morning and full of life and energy only moments after his alarm sounded.

The side door of the house opened and Barbara saw her best friend standing there in a heavy bathrobe, shivering and waving for her to come in. Barbara knew that Nancy would keep a confidence and also knew that she'd care for James as if he was her own. Nancy Clowder had been Barbara's closest friend since high school where they both graduated with honors from Edward Little High School in Auburn. They both attended Bates and kept their friendship active via letters, phone calls and email ever since. But while Barbara was the ethereal 'right brain" of the pair, Nancy was the technologist. With her aptitude for analysis and logic, she had taken her accounting firm from one person (herself) operating from the basement of her home in New Hampshire, to a seventeen member business planning and consulting firm operating in three states. In the course of developing her company, she'd also found time to raise two beautiful children, maintain a household that she shared with her artist-husband, Richard, and earn a fortune.

In her earlier phone conversation, Nancy asked few questions. Barbara was her best friend; she had a sudden and unexpected problem; could Nancy take care of James for tonight and bring him to Logan Airport in East Boston tomorrow? There was a need and Nancy would fill it. She was only too happy to see Barbara again, in spite of the circumstances, and would gladly take care of James for as long as Barbara wanted or needed.

Barbara opened the trunk of her car and removed James' suitcase. She then roused James sufficiently to get him moving in the general direction of Nancy's house where a warm bed would be waiting for him. Barbara was sure that when James woke the next morning, he'd be stunned to learn that he'd been at Aunt Nancy's house most of the night. Little boys, Barbara was convinced based on her experience with James, seemed to travel through life in a sort of semi-coma.

She gave her son a great big hug and a kiss. She wouldn't see him for three weeks, and with the recent discovery of Charles' papers and his computer files, there was some virtue to be gained by putting James at some distance.

There was little conversation in Nancy's house after James was safely and surely asleep in an upstairs bedroom. Nancy understood that this was not a social occasion, and gently urged Barbara to sip her hot tea with honey. Certainly, Nancy would look after James; don't worry for a minute. Richard was home almost every day working in his studio, and he'd be delighted with the company. The flight to London was late afternoon tomorrow, and they'd be certain to get him there in plenty of time.

The conversation was casual and reflected the sense of understanding, and of love, that had been born and nurtured over the past twenty years. Nancy sought no explanation, and Barbara offered little in the way of one. Instead, tacit communication was sufficient and more so. Barbara would be at her mother's for at least two days; she'd call Nancy tomorrow; if Charles does happen to call, admit nothing . . . not having seen or heard from Barbara ... not, especially, that James is staying at her house for the night. There were hugs and some tears before Barbara, who hadn't even removed her heavy coat, squeezed Nancy's hand and left by the side door. Her car's engine was still warm when she seated herself behind the wheel and began the next leg of her journey to Maine and her mother's house in Auburn. The engine started easily but she knew the aging Honda was due for an overhaul. She slipped the gearshift into drive, crossed her fingers, and was on her way.

In a large office at Buckingham Palace, Richard Panel stood at the great paned window overlooking the gardens. As usual, upon his entry this morning, a cassette tape lay on his desk. Now a recorder on his desk was playing and the uninflected voice of the Prince of Wales drifted across the room from its place on the enormous oak desk. Panel pulled the heavy drape and saw a pair of rail thin laborers pulling dead leaves from the bases of handsomely trimmed shrubs where they had blown. He recognized one of the workers as the father of the young woman who kept this wing of the Palace supplied with hot tea and warm biscuits. Emma, he thought. Emma Phillips.

He listened half consciously to the recorded drone of the Prince deliberating over his scheduled attendance at the Royal Scottish Guards reception tomorrow evening. Most of the daily tapes from the Prince were similar in nature if not in precise content. Notes to someone or other in stiff acknowledgment of various courtesies. Amending schedules to accommodate personal whims, such as a stop at an old schoolmate's home on the way to a visit to the crippled children's hospital in Leeds. In between the niggling complaints about a particular newspaper account, or the lack of proper starch in his shirts.

As the assistant secretary to the Prince of Wales, Panel considered himself the recipient of vast good fortune mixed with the empty charge of tidying up after an individual whose importance in the scheme of the planet was illusory to most observers. The compensation was grand, he would acknowledge to his proud parents, but the daily routine was truly less than satisfying. And as to the sense of purpose . . . Panel shrugged as he let the drape swing back across the glass. In three days, the Prince would visit the U.S. and Panel had prepared matters precisely and well in advance. His assignment was narrow, to see to the Prince's daily needs. Schedules had been arranged separately by the Secretary. Speeches had been written elsewhere, crafted to the Prince's wooden style and devoid of almost anything of substance. Any issues of substance devolved to the responsibility of the Prime Minister.

Panel would serve, well, as the Prince's servant, more or less. He would be present at the rising hour, at the Prince's pleasure during the waking day, and with him before retiring to, no doubt, listen patiently to the Prince's review of the events of the day. It would be a long five days for Richard Panel.

The saving portion was the simple fact of traveling to America. Richard Panel took comfort in this as he continued his effort to pay attention to the painfully prolonged recording. How Panel wished that the Prince would inject some passion in his voice. As someone who spent many hours at the side of Royalty, Panel understood the stultifying nature of the Prince's life. He knew the Prince privately to be engaging, well-read and a delightful joke-teller. But Panel's duty was not to promote the air of excitement, to present the Prince as a bon vivant. Instead, the Prince's speeches were usually empty and the world would only get to see the man in the most polite and ineffectual of circumstances. He took a sip of tea and continued gazing on the gardens outdoors.

The night was moonless and the sky ink black. The roads at this hour . . . just past midnight . . . were nearly empty, which suited Barbara. Her overnight bag rested on the seat beside her. She had no idea how long she intended to stay away, and she packed only a few days worth of clothing and some toiletries.

The noise of the shifting gears gradually yielded to a steady, dull monotone as the car reached the interstate. Alone with her thoughts, Barbara guessed that she'd be at her destination around one in the morning. She wondered if she was doing the right thing, lobbing arguments pro and con from the corner reaches of her mind. She thought of the cartoon angel and devil, each perched on a shoulder and whispering their enchanting songs, each presenting as rational an argument as the other.

Maybe I should have waited for him, to confront him and have him tell me that the whole affair was a harmless misunderstanding. Perhaps the scheme was but someone's bent attempt at fiction, a fantasy peopled with living characters.

Or was her darkest suspicion on target? Had he in fact bartered his soul to his mentor, to a Mephistopheles whose inherent evil lay hidden beneath the polished glaze of gentle civility and good humor?

Sir Geoffrey Ramsden was among the brightest and most fascinating men she knew. Well read, a renowned and published scholar of European history and a marvelous conversationalist, he had captured her attention from the start. It was no wonder Charles could become so attached to the man; Sir Geoffrey was ambitious, urbane, sharp-witted and passionately and entirely British to the bone. To a young student like Charles, impressionable and eager to please, Ramsden represented all that was keen and positive, a true model of civil living.

He was a hero to Charles Whyte, and the admiration was returned with kindly, sound advice and the delectable promise of future reward. "You can have the wonderful career ahead of you, Mister Whyte. But beware those who suggest that the only path weaves through one's boot straps." Sir Geoffrey spoke tangentially on his way to a point, always using the carom to reach his target. "No, use your British sense of fair play and fair commerce. That's the way you'll reach greatness, young man."

She played the scene over and over. It was early spring, not long before graduation, and the three of them were enjoying the sunshine and premature warmth of a convivial afternoon picnic on the green at Cambridge. Barbara had fond memories of those times. The dons striding along the paths dressed in their robes. Students rushing to classes or in clusters chatting and sharing words and laughs.

That day held little promise at daybreak, with rolling dark clouds scudding across the gray English skies. Another bleak day of drizzle. Not atypical for spring, but it made her more anxious for the warmth of the sun and the energy of its shine. Barbara had been hoping to spend a day outdoors for a change. She'd even bought a wicker basket the weekend past in hopes that she and Charles would soon put it to its intended use.

So when the sky suddenly cleared before midday, Barbara ran to the courtyard to bathe in the rays of the sun, simultaneously taking psychic inventory of the ill equipped larder in her small room: Some leftover chicken, half a loaf of fresh bread, some boiled eggs and a wedge of Stilton. She raced back into her room and called Charles.

"Have you looked outside? It's absolutely glorious. I can almost hear flowers blooming!" Charles was equally anxious for a chance to step outside without a warm coat or umbrella. They planned to meet near the great oak at two o'clock. There, they'd share the food, drink in the sunshine and explore each other's personal wishes on a red wool blanket. The reawakening of the earth signaled by spring was seducing Barbara into a welcomed acceptation of freshness and joy.

Barbara was a few minutes late in arriving, having detoured from her intended path to buy a bottle of wine for their private celebration. When she turned the corner of the great central hall and looked for Charles near their appointed meeting place, she saw Charles and Ramsden sitting together on the lawn engaged in animate conversation.

As she neared the pair, she caught details of the discussion. The subject today was Rome and its collapse as an empire. Did the Romans simply fail to pay attention to their borders? Were the Romans spread so thinly that they could not pay such attention? Did unusually hard freezes in central Europe early in the fifth century contribute to Rome's woes by providing unhindered access for the hordes of barbarians over the Rhine and the Danube?

Deliberating world history was not what Barbara had in mind for this rarest of afternoons. Instead she hoped she and Charles could just enjoy each other's company. Maybe talk about the coming month when she would leave Cambridge and England for her return to Maine.

Nevertheless, she joined the debate and vigorously defended her position that the substance that was Rome had disappeared, and that its demise was self-inflicted with a sword of overabundant leisure and lawlessness. Charles took the position that the Christianizing of Rome contributed to its collapse as a world power. And Ramsden played champion to every intellectual position, enjoying the controversy and planting bits of cerebral fuel to each side periodically to keep the contest going. To him it was a game, one he'd played often and well.

The conversation continued over cold chicken and wine. Eventually, lengthening shadows and a cooling breeze reminded the three of the late hour. As Barbara collected the bits of tissue and empty cups from the lawn, Ramsden begged Barbara's forgiveness, but could he and Charles chat privately for a moment. "Only a few moments, I promise," she remembered him saying. "Of course," she answered. "I'll be in my room, Charles."

Charles stood and walked with Ramsden. It was apparent to Barbara that this was a most serious discussion, for Ramsden put his arm over Charles shoulder in a fatherly gesture as he spoke. She recalled Charles' expression, perplexed as he searched Ramsden's face for some specific direction.

Barbara waited only ten minutes for Charles to join her. Finally, she thought, we'll spend some time together, just the two of us.

But Charles seemed preoccupied. A position had been presented, in a manner of speaking, he said. Lots of promise, but a good deal of hard work and probably some hardship as well. Diplomatic corps, he said. Not great wages, but an attractive career opportunity nonetheless.

She wondered now: Did Charles make a deal with the devil that day? Or was this simply the most innocent of beginnings, and did Ramsden seduce Charles gradually over the course of time, guilefully bartering for Charles' ingenuous soul as the years of loyal service to the Crown progressed?

She had no answer, shivered unwillingly at the recollection, and jarred her senses back to the present. The lights from oncoming vehicles reflected from the highway, now lightly coated with rain.

She sighed as she drove, vanquished by nagging self-doubt, and incapable of translating the maelstrom within into a sensible deliberation. Should I have taken James with me instead of leaving him with friends? What if my suspicions are correct? Would James be endangered, even in the company of his own father?

Amid the disquiet of her thoughts and the low hum of the engine, she came to no conclusions and watched for the exit from the Maine Turnpike to Auburn.

Sergeant Frank McCarty yawned as he turned onto Woodland Road, alone in the cruiser and marking time until his return to the station to end his double shift. He was getting too old for sixteen straight hours, he thought to himself as he drove slowly past the darkened houses. At five o'clock on a winter Friday morning, all was calm and serene. It had been a quiet couple of shifts, and Frank McCarty was grateful. At seven thirty, he'd head back to the station and get ready to turn the town's safety over to the hands of someone younger and more eager. By eight thirty, he intended to be home, in bed, and sound asleep.

He passed number nineteen and took a quick mental note. The house he was sent to check out last night with the new kid, Mendes. Lights on somewhere inside the house. Nothing unusual to the naked eye. He reached for his notebook and marked down the time and his observations when he reached the end of the street.

SIX

————————

Charles Whyte stared at the telephone. The small mantle clock, a wedding gift, ticked relentlessly as it marked the approaching dawn and the sky was beginning the cast a smoky light into the dining room where he sat motionless. While his throat was stale with the taste of too much whiskey and too many cigarettes, his mind was sufficiently clear to recognize that he could not forestall the inevitable.

It would be early morning in London; he must speak with Sir Geoffrey at once. Charles removed the phone from its cradle and punched in the series of numbers that would connect him with Sir Geoffrey's private line at his Mayfair home. He visualized the scene there, having spent many convivial hours in that home. Elegant, highly polished furnishings to match their owner. Everything made a statement, and that statement was one of tradition, strength and power. A series of blips and whistles over the line told him the call was going through.

One ring. No answer.

Before the second ring was completed, the phone was picked up and Charles heard the voice of Sir Geoffrey, bright with nonchalance and self-assuredness. "Good morning, Ramsden here."

Charles' voice was but a croak: "It's Whyte, sir. I'm calling from my home." Charles wanted to be certain that Sir Geoffrey would invoke greater prudence in the conversation knowing it was not a secure line.

Sir Geoffrey returned with lower tones: "Understood, Charles. Go on, but . . . you understand."

"Yes, I understand. We have a problem, I'm afraid. With the plan."

Sir Geoffrey maintained his calm, but a growing urgency was evident as he spoke. "If this problem jeopardizes our plans, our plans for the future, perhaps you could contact me from your office and we might discuss it then." The meaning was clear. A secured line with scrambling devices at either end would permit the communications to be carried on much more directly.

"Yes, it very well could cause our future plans to go awry. But . . ."

"Very well, then. Let me hear from you when you arrive at the office. I'll wait for your call."

"Please, sir. It's Barbara." Charles did not want the call to end. "I'm afraid that she's gone away very suddenly. Unexpectedly."

There was a lengthy pause before Charles heard any response. "Is there any reason why you are unable to call me from your office?"

In spite of Charles' more desperate wish to linger in a hot shower and gather his wits, there was none, and Charles said so.

"Call me in forty-five minutes."

The line went dead.

Charles stared at the telephone, not wishing to believe that he'd been put off so abruptly. Did Sir Geoffrey not understand the urgency of the current situation? Barbara was gone. Without compromising the extreme need for secrecy, he'd done his best to convey the gravity of the matter.

He looked at his watch. Three ten in the morning. He slipped on his jacket and made for the garage. If he drove into Cambridge to his office, he could call Sir Geoffrey, have their discussion over the scrambled line, and return before eight for his shower and a change into fresh clothes.

Barbara felt comforted after the phone conversation with her mother. She called her from a service station on the Turnpike. "It's Barbara, Mum, and I need you." Without a question, her mother told her that a pot of hot tea and a warm bed would be waiting for her arrival. Barbara knew, as well, that her mother's soothing embrace and unconditional love would await her as well.

In the deepest part of the night, the kitchen glowed warmly. Together with the smells of muffins, baked as usual from scratch, the sense was calming and reassuring. Barbara Whyte sat at the kitchen table as her mother rinsed dishes at the sink.

"If you gave me three hours, Mum, I'd never get these muffins baked. You're incredible."

The early hours were spent sitting at her mother's table, telling her the story of the past few days. The discovery of Charles' papers was innocent enough. She happened to see his laptop computer left on one evening and went to shut it off. She never intruded in Charles' business matters. Besides the issue of respecting his privacy, she genuinely found his work at the consulate uninteresting. Charles rarely discussed his work at home anyway.

But she caught a few key words as she sat down and prepared to shut the computer off. And she was mystified. The messages from London. Crazy plans. Guns. Plots. All directly from Sir Geoffrey Ramsden.

Liddy Chicoine listened patiently to her daughter. This was all too fantastic for words, but she maintained her composure. A nurse by training and with years of experience watching patients for symptoms, she was stunned by the news that her son-in-law could be anything but the caring person she'd come to know. Charles might be a bit reserved and formal at times, but he had never been anything but a fine husband and father. He'd even learned enough about baseball that he played catch with James during the warm months, and attended several Little League games when James played.

She knew that her daughter had recently been suffering from depression, and had been placed on medication. But she spotted nothing in Barbara that suggested anything irrational in her daughter's current behavior. This was a reasonable person with all her wits about her; only the facts of the story were bizarre.

"And then," Barbara went on, "just after I picked up James and we drove away, I saw a police cruiser come down our street. I saw in my rear-view mirror that they were stopping right front of our house. Mum, I thought I was going to throw up."

Liddy didn't know what to say.

"I mean, maybe Charles called them to check up on me, but I don't know. Why would he do that? This whole mess with Charles and Ramsden has my stomach in knots."

Liddy remembered Sir Geoffrey Ramsden as a charming man of remarkable grace. They had met only once, but she was taken with his elegant speech, his genuine conviviality, and, not least, his dashing good looks. Tall, straight, gray at the temples, pearls for teeth . . . Cary Grant. She remembered telling Barbara that at the time.

"And James," Barbara was saying. "I just know Charles would never hurt him. But I'm so afraid."

Liddy poured herself a fresh cup of tea and held the pot up with a question.

"No thanks, Mum."

Liddy sat at the table and put her hands on her daughters'. "I think you've done the right thing, Barbara. Charles may be in over his head, but he'd never harm James. You need some time to sort things out. Your bed is ready any time you are, by the way."

"Thanks, but I'm too wound up right now. I feel like I've got to do something, but I don't know what to do first. I've got all these notes from Charles' disc stashed in my overnight bag. I mailed a copy to Dr. Fortin before I left. I wanted to see him personally, but I didn't have time to get everything done before Charles came home, so I just jotted him a note, slapped a bunch of stamps on an envelope and mailed the package."

Barbara looked at her mother as if for approval, and seeing it, continued.

"I'm hoping I did the right thing."

Liddy asked the first question since her daughter arrived. "Who's this doctor you sent the notes to?"

"My psychologist. I felt I had to put a copy someplace, and I tried to think of the safest place I could. He's someone I can trust."

"What about the police, Barbara? I'd think they'd be the first place I'd turn."

"I thought about the police and even the FBI. But that would just get Charles into enormous trouble; I could lose a husband; James could lose a father; and right now, it's Charles' move to get himself out of this mess. He knows everything about this foolish plan and he can call it off. If he wants."

"And this doctor friend of yours. You don't think he'll go to the police or the FBI?"

Barbara considered before answering. "I don't think so. I really don't. In the note I sent him with the papers, I told him it was important not to call them."

Liddy could see that Barbara wasn't entirely convinced of this but elected not to pursue the matter now. Her daughter was operating on nerves alone. Barbara was right: She was filled with fear, uncertainty and faint hope. She didn't need her mother to probe even further, not right now. She stood up and began removing her apron. "What about a nap, Barbara? It's four o'clock in the morning, we've been up all night, and we're both going to fall flat on our faces if we don't catch a few winks. We can talk again when you get up."

Barbara was ready. Her eyes were sunken and red. She looked up at her mother, turned a grateful smile, and began a slow but comforting march towards the bedroom upstairs, her bedroom when she was a child.

In a few moments, Liddy was certain she could hear Barbara softly snoring. She climbed onto her own bed and tried to sort through her daughter's saga. In seconds, she was asleep.

"Ramsden here."

"Charles Whyte, sir. I'm in my office at the Consulate."

"Hold for a moment, Charles."

Charles could hear Ramsden closing his door. In moments, the phone was picked up again. "So tell me, Charles, what is the situation? And spare me no details." Ramsden's impatience traveled clearly across the Atlantic.

"It's Barbara. She's gone. She left a note. When I arrived home last evening, I found it on the kitchen table. I'm sure she knows about Shamrock." Charles voice was filled with panic.

"This isn't entirely new turf, Charles. You were quite certain earlier that she was more than just a bit suspicious. Where did she go?"

"I don't know, but I would suspect she went to Maine to her mother's house."

"Also not terribly unexpected. Was she expecting you to

confront her?" He didn't wait for an answer. "Do you have any idea if she's told anyone?"

"I don't know. She didn't say anything in her note except that she was going to do something."

"Something? What?"

"She asked me to forgive her for what she was about to do. That's all."

"And she hasn't called?"

"No, sir. She skipped her appointment at her therapist's and left. No word since."

"How do you know she missed her appointment? And what's this about therapy? Has Barbara shown signs of instability?"

"She's been depressed ever since she lost her teaching position, and she's been seeing a psychologist for some time now. It's had an effect, sir, and she's improved. She had another appointment yesterday afternoon."

"And this psychologist called you?"

"Dr. Fortin, yes. He told me he was worried when Barbara didn't appear for her appointment. I told him her mother was taken suddenly ill, and that she went to her home."

The ensuing silence over the line told Charles that Ramsden was considering several options. Charles silently wished he was still posted to Afghanistan.

"Listen, Charles. She's certain to have told her Mother, if she did go to her. That's entirely logical. I want you first to determine if she went there, straight away. If she is with her mother . . ."

The pause begged Charles to interject, to object, but Ramsden went on.

". . . Listen to me, Charles. I have a task for you." Ramsden's voice had taken on a smoother, less anxious tone, but Charles' fear was not allayed. "The stress must be unbearable for you. And your busiest days are just ahead of you. You need to be fresh to face this challenge and to press on with Shamrock, don't you agree?"

"Yes, sir."

"I'm asking you to make a list of every possible place you believe Barbara may have gone. Her mother is an obvious choice, and I suggest you try there first, even if you think she may be elsewhere. And consider the possibility that she dropped James with a relative or a friend. Then call me back. I'll see what I can do from this end. Now, Charles, do you think you can make that list for me and call me back in fifteen minutes? Time is, of course, of the essence. We need to make sure James is safe."

Charles was numb. First by the discovery of the papers and the disc by Barbara; then the first conversation with Ramsden; Barbara's running off with James; and now, with Ramsden giving instructions. Barbara was gone.

"Barbara." It was a statement and not a question, but Ramsden pushed on.

"Yes, Charles, Barbara. We've already discussed the matter. If she knows about Shamrock, she must be convinced to remain silent."

"I'm sure she knows, Sir. The note . . ."

"Yes, Charles, the note said she wanted your forgiveness. And as far as you can be certain, she has let on to no one as yet."

"Her mother." Another statement. Flat, without emotion.

"Perhaps. Perhaps Barbara hasn't said a word, Charles. So, get to it. Get me the list in fifteen minutes. I'll be waiting for your call. We must move quickly, Charles."

"Yes, sir."

The line went dead while Charles still held the phone to his ear. Several moments passed as Charles slowly cleared his mind. He looked at his watch. Fifteen minutes.

At least he had something productive he could do. He took

a sheet of lined paper from a pad on the corner of his desk and began to think and write. In twelve minutes, he'd assembled thirteen names, thirteen people whom he suspected might, just might, be likely people to whom Barbara would turn in an emergency.

The first name, of course, was her mother, Elizabeth; the second, her brother Leo, who lived in a restored farmhouse in Pennellville, not far from the Bowdoin campus; the third, Barbara's sister, Ellen, in some godforsaken houseboat in the Bahamas . . . scratch that one; an aunt, Alice, Liddy's sister, also in Auburn; a cousin, Lucy, who operated a bed and breakfast with her husband in Camden; and assorted friends: Carol Oliver, an herbalist somewhere around Portland; Nancy Clowder, an accountant in Portsmouth; Phillippa "Pippa" Goldman, a librarian somewhere north of Bangor; Beth Daniels, who worked at a hardware store in Ogunquit and made pottery as a sideline; Ruth Kirk, a pilot for American Eagle out of Portland; Carolanne Coulombe, a housewife somewhere around Freeport and working part-time at L.L. Bean; Lydia Kurowski, somewhere in New Hampshire selling real estate; Jill Ephraim, also in New Hampshire and just divorced for the third time; Ingrid Barlow, once notorious for the part she played, nude, in the Sabbatus Community Theatre revival of *Oh! Calcutta!*, and now waiting tables at a diner in Rumford. He could check Barbara's Christmas card list when he went home, but he felt reasonably sure that he'd hit the major names. He called Ramsden with the list. After answering a few questions about some of the names on the list . . . how close are they to Barbara? How long have they known each other? . . . Ramsden appeared satisfied and told Charles to go home and rest.

Charles rose hurriedly from his seat and left the consulate; it was still early, and he wanted to be on his way home when the first consulate employees arrived. As he drove from the parking lot, Sarah Marsh, his secretary, entered the front door of the consulate using her magnetic security ID and walked briskly up the stairs to the second floor. Strange, she thought idly, but Mr. Whyte's office door is open. He usually locks it up when he leaves. Unless he's arrived early this morning. Not like him to be here so early, though. She stuck her head in his office and looked about. A few untidy papers on the desk, also not like Mr. Whyte to leave clutter anywhere at all, but unoccupied nonetheless. Sarah Marsh wrinkled her nose at the stale odor of perspiration and cigarettes, and closed the door to Charles' office before going to her own desk in the hallway.

No time to spare. Ramsden barked to his secretary that the balance of his Friday appointment calendar was to be rescheduled, and that he was not to be disturbed. A most busy day ahead of him. Ramsden used the mouse to point to the appropriate names on the screen and clicked to highlight the ones he wished to explore further. God bless the internet, he thought. He was hurrying, but remained very deliberate as he assembled a series of addresses and telephone numbers based on the information he was gleaning on line. When he was finished, he checked his watch: almost one o'clock in the afternoon in London, still very early in the US. He spun his chair so that he faced his telephone and made his first phone call

Ramsden's travels to the U.S., and his having seen countless movies from the states, made mimicking the accent easy for him. For the immediate task, he was quite sure that the regional twist he sought would require an almost unnatural stretching of the vowels. "Nawth" instead of "North", he recalled. "Ayuh," instead of "Yes". He remembered Henry Fonda in On Golden Pond. That was Maine, wasn't it? Oh well, close enough. Besides, this call shouldn't take but a few seconds. He stretched his jaw and his lips while he waited for the connection to go through. After three rings, he heard a woman's voice, as clear as if the call was being made to an office down the street. It was an older voice.

"Hello?" With a question. A slight crack of fatigue. Maybe suspicion as well.

"Ah, is this Mrs. Chicoine?" Ramsden had settled on middle class New England. His tone was unhurried and deliberate.

"This is Mrs. Chicoine. Who's calling?" Definitely suspicious, Ramsden felt.

"Ah, is there a Mrs. Whyte there, by any chance. I'm trying to locate Mrs. Barbara Whyte." Ramsden could have been anyone. The point, to Ramsden, was just to avoid being somebody.

"Can you tell me who's calling?" Liddy was suspicious; this could be Dr. Fortin on the line, but she had no way of knowing.

"It's a friend, Mrs. Chicoine. I just want to make sure she's OK."

But what he heard next caused his voice to catch in his throat.

"Dr. Fortin? Is this Dr. Fortin? Hello?" Liddy was asking the caller.

Ramsden slowly replaced the receiver in its cradle, stunned by the response his call elicited, and at least momentarily paralyzed. Dr. Fortin . . . Barbara's bloody therapist. She actually expected a call from Dr. Fortin. Ramsden used a pencil to almost mindlessly draw circles, boxes and arrows on the pad of paper before him.

He then made a second phone call, also to the US, but this time to an apartment in South Boston occupied by a man of rare and special talents, Patrick Keough. The phone rang four times and the line was picked up by Keough's recorder. Ramsden was at first aggravated that Keough wasn't there to take his call. Keough would return the call without delay, Ramsden felt certain. Ramsden left a message for Keough to return the call at once. He'd use the meantime to organize his thoughts and formulate a plan of attack. Then, when Keough returned the call, the wheels would be put in motion.

Liddy waited for Barbara to rise on her own. It was a painful wait. Liddy was edgy enough, what with all this talk about Charles and Ramsden and a crazy assassination plot. But the phone call pushed her right to the brink. Damn, she thought. Who was it and why didn't he identify himself. If it was Doctor Fortin, as she suspected it to be, he wouldn't have hung up as he did. She paced the hallway and gathered her thoughts.

The caller wasn't Charles; she would have recognized the voice. Liddy slowly opened the door to Barbara's room and looked in. Barbara was snoring lightly, curled up on her side on top of the bedspread. Liddy closed the door and returned to pacing. She tried to imagine what the person on the other end of the phone looked like. It was a man. He was a man of some maturity, not a youth, she was sure. He had no discernable accent, short of being slightly nasal.

Libby entered the kitchen and poured cold water into the coffeepot. In moments, the fragrance of brewing coffee made its way through the house, and Barbara arose from her nap. Liddy heard the footsteps in the hall, then saw her daughter emerge from the shadows, hair mussed, eyes still red and swollen. Liddy had never felt so helpless.

"Coffee?" she asked Barbara. A nod said yes. "Barbara," she said, "there was a call a while ago. It woke me up." She placed the cup on the table in front of Barbara who was now seated. "He didn't say who it was, Barbara, but he wanted to know if you were here."

Barbara looked up at her mother with a question in her eyes.

"He just asked if you were here. I thought it was this Doctor Fortin at first. But I don't think it was, because he just hung up."

"Did you tell him I was here?"

"No, not in so many words, but I'm sure he knows you're here."

"Charles. Are you sure it wasn't Charles?" Barbara said his name with a dull edge of loss in her voice.

"No, I'd recognize his voice, and the line was clear as a bell. It wasn't Charles. What does Dr. Fortin sound like?"

Barbara thought about it for a moment. She called up Dr. Fortin on her memory bank and replayed bits of conversation. Nothing unusual. Lower than average voice, maybe. No real accent. She told her mother, who shrugged.

Barbara sipped her coffee and tried to assemble her thoughts. "I have to leave." She met her mother's eyes. "Whoever it was wants to know where I am. And I'd better leave before he gets here."

"But Barbara, let's think this through. Where would you go?"

"I don't know. Just away." Barbara was already gathering her purse from the table and looking for her shoes on the floor.

"And what if someone calls again?"

"Tell them I was here and that I went back home. Anything. The less you know right now, the better off you are." Barbara turned to face her mother.

"Here, Barbara, take this with you." Liddy handed her a paper sack filled with sandwiches, fruits and juice. Barbara smiled and gave her mother a hearty squeeze.

"I'll call you and let you know where I am." Barbara was halfway out the door when she turned and hugged her mother once more. With a kiss on her cheek, she added, "I love you, Mom," and was gone. Liddy stood on the steps and watched her daughter walk to the driveway, throw her satchel and the supply of food in the back seat, and start the car. Or try to. In the damp cold of the overnight, Barbara's car would not turn over. After some minutes of frustrated observation, Liddy turned back into her kitchen and reappeared with the keys to her own car, a twelve-year-old Chevrolet with a complexion problem. Barbara was still trying to get her Honda started when her mother tapped on the window.

"Take mine. I'll call the garage and get yours fixed in the meantime." Barbara accepted her mother's car keys gratefully.

"I won't be needing it right away," she told her daughter. "It needs gas, though. And check the oil before you go too far."

Barbara blew a kiss on a smile to her mother and stepped into Liddy's time worn Chevy. She faced her first choice five minutes later at the highway on ramp. Left to Augusta and points north. Right to Portland and points south. She let up on the gas and eased left.

Janet Chapel was wrong. Sleep did little to allay Andrew's concern for Barbara Whyte. He awoke from an unsettled sleep at seven, made coffee and called his answering service. No calls.

He drove to his office at eight fifteen and checked with his answering service once again. This time, there was one. "Yes, Doctor Fortin, I just had a call a few moments ago. Francina Ficociello called. She said she was a patient, and she wanted an appointment to see you. I have her number here."

Andrew marked it down. It was only yesterday that he chatted with her at her father's restaurant. He called her at once. She sounded tense over the phone.

"Thanks, Doctor Fortin, for calling me so soon. I need to see you as soon as possible." Andrew had his calendar open and in front of him. He had time later in the day but Francina's work schedule kept her at the restaurant then getting ready for the dinner hour. They agreed on nine thirty Saturday morning.

SEVEN

Fortin's attention was focused on the patient file that lay open on his desk before him. In it were his notes and observations from six previous sessions with a thirty-seven year old insurance adjuster who was in the midst of a traumatic divorce and trying desperately to avoid using his usual method of dealing with difficulties: Drinking himself into a stupor and punching anyone unfortunate enough to be within arm's length. So far, he had been successful. He would be coming for his once a week appointment with Fortin in another forty minutes, and Fortin found that ten minutes reviewing his patient files in advance helped him distill his thoughts, form his questions, and generally make the most of his sessions. He had finished jotting some notes and closed the file when his phone rang.

"This is Doctor Fortin."

"Andy, it's Janet. Gotta sec?"

"Sure. What's up?"

"I made reservations for London this morning. What do you have to say to that?"

Fortin leaned back in his chair and smiled. "That's super news, Janet."

"I even added an extra day there just to goof off by myself. No patients. No meetings. No bureaucrats."

"You deserve a lot more than just a day, but I know better than to suggest a longer vacation."

"Damned right. I'm already surprising myself with one extra day." Janet's tone changed and she became serious. "Look, the reason I called is I have a patient I'd like to refer. Female. Forty-one. Widowed a few years. Just found out her son is the biggest dealer in his high school. Feeling inadequate and over-whelmed. I'd like to give her your name and have her give you a call. She a strong lady, but she needs to talk."

"Sure. What's her name?"

"Laura Douglas. Nice lady. I think you and she'd be a good fit."

"Meds?"

"Nothing yet, but I'm considering Ativan for a start. Or Paxil. She's had some anxiety episodes, and she's coming in around ten. If she's still shaky, I'll give her a script."

"OK. I'll wait for her call and let you know how we make out."

"Great. And thanks, Andy."

"Thank you, Janet."

"No problem. I'm doing it because I know she'll be getting a great therapist. See you later."

Fortin hung up the phone and stood up. Out his window he could see the postal truck pulling out of the parking lot. He looked at his watch: 9:30. He decided to check his mailbox on the first floor and reached into his jacket pocket for his keys. As he locked his office, he saw Frank Wendt walking down the hall.

"Mail call, Andy."

"Hi, Frank. It's good to see you. I thought your receptionist usually got your mail."

"She usually does, but she came in this morning on crutches. Ankle sprain. So I get to do all the dirty work for a few days."

They walked together to the first floor. "A. L. Fortin, PhD, LICSW" was directly below "F. S. Wendt, DDS PC", and Fortin let his dentist neighbor go first. Wendt removed a fist full of envelopes, most presumably with checks inside. He riffled through the envelopes as Fortin opened his mailbox. Fortin expected the usual, which included very little in the way of envelopes with checks.

Inside were four envelopes: One advertisement from the Chevrolet dealership in Wellesley promised "Huge" discounts on its line of new pick-up trucks. Another was an envelope from a patient; he recognized the return address and hoped it had a check inside. This particular patient was getting a little behind, and a payment would certainly help. Fortin detested the financial necessity of having to dun the occasional bad paying patient. In conversations with other colleagues, including Frank Wendt, who had his share of bad payers like anyone else, the most common suggestion was to turn the matter over to a professional collection firm. "They go at these bills like a pit bull on red meat," according to Frank, who was happy to cede a good percentage of the collected balance to the collection firm. "Half a loaf, Andy. Half a loaf."

Fortin wasn't ready for that yet, but he had to admit he was getting close. Janet Chapel didn't have these same problems; she had an in-house collection staff as part of her hospital connection.

The third piece of mail was a 'special invitation' to join other professionals in learning about various investment options. It would include a free lunch as part of the seminar. Under the meager circumstances in which Fortin currently found himself, he decided to forgo the opportunity.

The fourth piece of mail was a bit more intriguing. It was a regular business-size envelope from his alma mater, Texas Wesleyan. It was probably another solicitation for donations, and Fortin usually responded with a check for $100. But the envelope probably enclosed an alumni newsletter, and Fortin always took some pleasure in reading through that news.

Fortin walked back to his office and dropped the mail on his receptionist's desk. She had been in earlier to pick up her check and was scheduled to come in for an hour or two later on to do some filing, and she could take care of the patient envelope at the same time. The Chevy ad and the financial seminar information hit the round file. He checked his schedule once more. Two more patients today, but nothing for another hour and a half. He also noted that his secretary had left him a pink post-it note to remind him of an appointment tomorrow morning with Francina Ficociello, Carlo's daughter from the restaurant. He didn't like to schedule Saturday appointments, but he knew that Francina's schedule kept her at the restaurant most days.

Fortin sat at his desk and opened the Texas Wesleyan envelope, and as he predicted, it was a combination of a request for money along with a newsletter. He began reading. He recognized only a few names; one was of a recently published professor, a teacher Fortin had found among the most boring speakers he'd ever heard. Another was the notice that a classmate had recently become a member of the President's Task Force on Human Rights. Good for him, he thought.

He reflected on his three years in Texas and recalled the sky as he stood on the bluffs in Fort Worth. He was preparing to head to a new job in Boston soon, and enjoyed driving around the city to cement the memories in his brain. He parked his car at the side of a rural road west of Fort Worth and saw a storm start in the west, perhaps two hundred miles away, like a giant's black fist rising from the horizon. Watching it reach up slowly into the pale sky until its dark anvil overcame the light. It roared to the east. Blackness surrounded him like a shroud. Lightning flashed gold and red in a maelstrom of pelting noise and violent rain. The soil sucked the water from the blackness and the storm passed quickly, leaving a wake of crystal sky and freshening wind. Birds sang, and Fortin felt renewed.

His thoughts traveled in time back to Texas Wesleyan University in Fort Worth. He had just a few criteria for the school he'd attend once he left the seminary: It had to be far away from his small-town home in Massachusetts; it had to offer psychology as a major subject; and it had to be not at all connected to a Roman Catholic education.

At Texas Wesleyan, he found his solution. As the crow flew, the school was almost 1,600 miles from his home. It offered a major in psychology. And, in spite of the school's religious backdrop as a Methodist institution, the environment was secular, and had no connection to the Roman Catholic Church.

Fortin found a small apartment in Euliss, east of Fort Worth. It was an undistinguished studio unit in a featureless beige building and fronted a busy roadway with a raft of fast food restaurants on either side. The apartments appeared to house primarily people who commuted to their jobs in the bulging metroplex of Dallas-Fort Worth. By nine o'clock, the parking lot was almost empty. It wasn't a place to forge lasting relationships. After a month of classes, he had a few acquaintances at the campus but no close friends. He tended to bury himself in his textbooks and to find his amusement at either Joe T. Garcia's on the north side of the city, or the Stockyards area where there were dozens of small bars. He enjoyed the anonymity that came with living in a city setting and spent much of his time just watching the patrons come and go as he sat, almost always alone, reading his books and sipping draft beer. Not a naturally outgoing person, he tended to get involved in conversations only when he was approached. Then, he found that he could engage in conversation quite readily. He was troubled, though, by his discomfort in beginning the dialogue.

On one such an occasion, he sat alone at the end of the bar with a textbook flipped open in front of him in the White Elephant Saloon in the Fort Worth Stockyards area, wondering to himself what he was doing in Texas and where he'd go from there. It was still early in the evening and the place was still nearly empty. He didn't miss his past, and certainly not his time in the seminary, but he craved some connection, and especially the means of making one. He was nearing the bottom of his beer mug and raised his head to motion to the bartender for a refill, an undertaking he found more daunting than most of the other patrons appeared to suffer. He felt weak and ineffective at even the simplest tasks. His eye caught not the bartender's but the eyes of a woman who sat a few empty seats away and who was staring directly into his eyes. She held his gaze and moved to the adjacent bar stool. "Jessica," she said, holding out her right hand. "If you're a nice guy, you can call me Jess. You look lonely."

He shook her hand which was warm and soft. She was, he guessed, roughly his age, twenty-four, maybe a few years older, and not at all unattractive. On the contrary, Jessica . . . or Jess . . . was 'maht-a-fahn', as he'd heard good-looking women described by his fellow male students. "I've seen you here a couple times. Always by yourself. Why's that?"

Fortin didn't avoid her eyes and answered. "New around here."

She glanced at his textbook. Social Psychology. "A student. And darned near out of beer." She turned towards the bartender and raised her hand in a weak wave. Instantly, it seemed to Fortin, the barkeep responded. "My friend here needs another beer."

He was stunned by the quick confidence with which she

commandeered both his attention and that of the bartender. In one moment, a fresh beer appeared; in another, he'd told her his name. People began coming in and the jukebox was cranking up. He closed the textbook. In ten minutes, they'd shared something of their backgrounds and shared a dance.

"It's called a two-step, and it's easy, if y'all pay attention." He tried to follow her steps but stuttered about the floor in a less than graceful manner that drew the attention of several other patrons, all of whom appeared born to dance smoothly and without effort. "Watch my eyes, not my feet, for at least a second. Let your body feel the music down in your feet. This ain't the cha-cha-cha." And he did, and he could feel the rhythm and the downbeat and she held him by the arm and walked . . . that was it . . . it was to him more a style of walking than dancing . . . and by the end of the song (he never could remember the titles or the words, only the melodies), he was gliding with Jess across the floor. "See?" she said as the music ended. "It's not hard at all."

A country western trio was setting up in a corner of the saloon when Jess suggested they move to more quiet surroundings. "There's a little garden area out back. What do you say to buying me a Margarita . . . rocks and salt, please?" They took their drinks and sat at an outdoor table. The next hour was spent chatting about Fort Worth, college life, her background as a commercial artist for a local magazine, and his as a seminary drop out. She was from Grand Prairie, another DFW suburb. "Pretty much plain vanilla, but there's a pool at the apartment complex, and it's kind of nice." From Galveston originally, she'd graduated from UT Dallas as a Visual Arts major and decided to stay around the city where the jobs were more plentiful than back home. "Besides, you see one hurricane, you've seen them all."

She was intrigued by his experience in the seminary. "I was raised Southern Baptist, so it's a little difficult to relate. We don't have this celibacy thing going on. We're not really supposed to drink, either. You've heard of Demon Rum? Well, we got a saying that the Moslems don't recognize the Jews, and the Jews don't recognize the Moslems; and Southern Baptists don't recognize each other in a liquor store. It's all a charade, you ask me."

She studied his face for some reaction. When he didn't show any, she asked, "Is that why you left? I mean, was it just a charade for you, too?"

Fortin considered the question and answered. "Sort of, I guess. There's just as much hypocrisy in my church as there is in yours, and I wasn't real happy with what I was seeing on the inside. But it was more than that. More fundamental."

"More fundamental than being a Baptist? That's hard to believe."

"No, not that way. I mean more fundamental when it comes right down to my faith. I have a lot of questions, and my faith isn't maybe quite as blind as it once was. I sort of miss that. It was comfortable to just accept things like they were taught."

They continued their discussion and Jess seemed genuinely intrigued by the seminary life and the entire subject of religious belief. She, for one, no longer went to church, except for the rare occasion when she was visiting her mother in Galveston. Fortin, on the other hand, still attended Mass, but infrequently. He explained that he had always believed that God existed, but grew unconvinced that He was moved by the worship of man or by the tribulations and extraordinary vagaries and antics of the creation He had set into being.

Around ten o'clock, Fortin checked his watch and said that it was time for him to go. Early class tomorrow. Jess said she understood and that she, too, was scheduled for an early appointment with an advertising client in the morning. They both rose together and she surprised him by taking his hand. "Walk me to my car, would you?" Fortin felt a little like a teenager on a date. He hadn't held a girl's hand since high school, and it felt unusual, and very good.

When they reached her car, she unlocked the door and climbed in. "Come on in and set a while." Fortin sat in the passenger seat and Jess smiled at him. Her right hand moved simultaneously to his thigh where she rubbed and slid her hand to his crotch. She held his gaze as she unzipped his fly and then moved her head to his lap. Fortin couldn't believe what was happening to him but as he felt her warm mouth on him, he lay back in his seat and stroked her hair. In moments, he erupted in an orgasm that caused his hips to buck and his shoulders to shudder. When she finished, she tucked him back in and zipped him back up.

Jess looked at him and leaned over to kiss him on the lips. "I don't know what brought you to Fort Worth and to the White Elephant tonight, but welcome, soldier. I like you a whole lot, and I hope we can see each other again."

Fortin was still speechless, still replaying the events of the past three minutes and catching his breath. "She took a card from her pocket and placed it in his shirt pocket. "Give me a call, would you. And don't get all conflicted and everything. That was what we call sex, Mr. Priest. It happens to most people, and it's actually not a bad thing at all. Now get on home and get some sleep. You've got school in the morning."

Sir Geoffrey Ramsden stood and surveyed his audience in Parliament as a landowner might survey his holdings. Debate had been alternately fiery and tepid for the past weeks as the "Ulster Dialogues, as the Northern Ireland peace talks were most commonly described, were continuing in Belfast. Representatives of Sinn Fein, recognized as the political arm of the Irish Republican Army, and the largely Protestant government of Northern Ireland, had been meeting in Belfast's City Hall for several weeks. The discussions inside City Hall were kept in confidence by both parties, but some news had developed that progress was being made.

After centuries of Protestant Catholic discord and especially "The Troubles" of the most recent decades, observers on both sides were increasingly restless. Prominent Protestant spokesmen were publicly convinced that any resulting agreement between the parties would be injurious to their continued dominance and they decried what they saw as the hypocrisy of Sinn Fein and its inability to control the violent activities of its IRA membership. Catholic leaders lashed out in response and complained bitterly at the inequities of the current system and the duplicity to which they believed the Protestant leaders were predisposed. Most people, as is true of most populations, found themselves somewhere in the middle.

There was little question as to where Sir Geoffrey Ramsden was positioned. While most of the key party leadership in the UK expressed hope for progress at the Ulster Dialogues, Ramsden was wary of any concessions that might be developed in the struggle for progress in Belfast. In his view, the United Kingdom ought not to be compromised by the rabble and violence he saw as endemic to the Catholic minority in the northern counties. England had ceded more than enough; it was time to remain resolute in the face of the demands of the noisy and aggressive few. All eyes and all cameras were trained on him and he measured the moment. Without raising a hand or even an eyebrow, Ramsden commanded absolute silence and he began.

"My fellow members, it was Edmund Burke who once wrote that "A great empire and little minds go ill together" and Mr. Burke was absolutely on the mark. Of course, during his years of service to the empire, the subject of greatest import to the realm was the uprising in the North American colonies. That was a period that threatened the

very concept of the British Empire, and it proved to be a period that presents us with lasting lessons.

"There were, historians have argued almost continuously since Burke's era and the eventual separation of the colonies from Great Britain, countless reasons for the disaster that eventually ended on the battlefields of Yorktown. Let me remind you that the eighteenth century saw a divided parliament with many factions just as we have here in these chambers today. The causes may have had different names, but the principles of diversity and divisiveness are much the same now.

"We can, if we train the ear, hear the echoes of the arguments that took place then. And one of the loudest and most forceful arguments presented was one of appeasement. That word is certainly loaded, and shall we and our descendants ever hear the name Neville Chamberlain without raising the empty promise of appeasement simultaneously.

"Now many of you here may be saying 'we never said the word!' But you are wrong, and your error, as Chamberlain's in 1937, will only serve to raise your names in shame when, generations hence, the histories of our United Kingdom and Northern Ireland are discussed in classrooms.

"You use the word "peace" to describe your aim, and for that you deserve an award ... an advertising award ... for what you are trying to sell is nothing more than appeasement dressed in a prettied up fashion.

"To paraphrase Mr. Burke, your 'proposition is peace. Not peace through the medium of war; not peace to be hunted through the labyrinth of intricate and endless negotiations; not peace to arise out of universal discord, fomented from principle, in all parts of the empire; not peace to depend on the juridical determination of perplexing questions, or the precise marking of the shadowy boundaries of a complex

government. It is simple peace, sought in its natural course and in its ordinary haunts.'

"*The pursuit of peace is such a noble cause and it deserves to be so, but peace to be achieved at what price? I suggest to my detractors and supporters alike that there is always a price to be paid when one party seeks something from the other.*

"*We are now engaged in another period of threat to our empire. We as an empire have strived to be a great nation, and we as an empire should recognize the trust that has been placed in us by those who have served the empire well. We ought to elevate our minds to the greatness of that trust to which our nation has been called. By facing the dignity of this high calling, our ancestors turned a savage wilderness into a glorious empire, and have made the most extensive and the only honorable conquests, not by destroying, but by promoting the wealth, the number, the happiness of the human race. Let us not acquiesce, let us not appease, and let us keep our nation and our empire whole. The English have made it all that it is; the English alone will make it all it can be.*"

Charles Whyte watched Ramsden's address via satellite in his offices at the consulate. In spite of Barbara's disappearance and the threat that came from the knowledge she had accidentally gained surrounding "Shamrock", he saw no lack of composure in Ramsden and took some comfort in that. Hoping that Barbara kept the information to herself, he wanted to believe that her leaving was simply done in a fit of pique and that she'd return soon. He'd been wrong before; he'd be wrong again.

EIGHT

Patrick Keough snuffed out his cigarette and swallowed the last of his coffee. He detested Pall Malls, but they were one of the few remaining unfiltered brands he could buy here, and the closest he could find to his regular brand. The Friday morning sun was climbing high, and he'd enjoyed the day so far in Boston: A jog around the streets of South Boston; a light workout at the local Gold's Gym; a thorough reading of the Boston Globe; finally, a cup of coffee and a croissant at Dunkin' Donuts new outdoor café. His watch said that eleven was fast approaching, and it was time to get to work. He'd miss Boston when his work here was complete. If all went as planned, he'd be gone in just a few more days. He'd especially miss his apartment on H Street in South Boston more than anything. Much larger than the flats to which he was accustomed back home, it also had a dozen good pubs within a ten minute walk.

To anyone passing Patrick on the sidewalk, he looked unremarkable. A bit taller than average, he received little notice from passers-by. That was fine with him. More than anything else right now, he didn't want to stand out from the crowd.

Carrying a tan leather briefcase and clad in a navy blazer, light blue shirt, tan slacks and loafers, Patrick Keough could have been anyone. He took the subway from Broadway southbound. The train was less than half-filled. A few elderly people, a few college students, a shopper or two. Keough nodded to a young woman as he took a seat opposite her own. Four stops and sixteen minutes later, the train reached its last stop, Braintree station. Keough walked directly to a line of waiting buses, found the one he wanted and climbed aboard. In twenty minutes, at precisely three minutes before noon, Keough walked in the front door of the South Shore Rod & Gun Club.

The Club was reserved for members, but a rather precise forgery of a membership card from another reciprocal club in Florida had appeared one morning in his mailbox and assured him unencumbered access to the range.

His orders were explicit. Get entirely familiar with the weapon. Practice. Adjust the sight. Practice some more. Readjust. Practice. There would be no margin for error. Not that Keough's line of work ever allowed for any such margin. But this was the job of a lifetime. THE job.

Keough assembled the weapon. It was as high-tech as high-tech can be. Everything snapped into place with no effort at all. A perfect piece of equipment. And absolutely legal under the laws of the United States. This fact amazed him, for in nearly every other corner of the earth, possessing such a weapon was among the most serious of crimes.

The barrel latched in place. He checked the magazine once more. Twelve rounds perfectly seated and awaiting his command. The target hung from its wire at a distance of twelve yards. He raised the weapon. Balanced and fine like a work of art. And aimed. And squeezed the trigger.

The paper targets were standard black and white bulls eyes, and after the first three rounds, Keough saw that he was one inch to the left and a half inch low. He adjusted his aim and squeezed off three more rounds; a half inch too high, but directly in line. The last six shots tore the center of the target to shreds. He moved to another target, this one twenty yards away. Reloading his weapon, he aimed and fired, repeating the process. At the farthest distance, seventy-five yards, he was placing six rounds in a circle two inches across.

After thirty minutes of sighting, firing, adjusting, firing again, fine-tuning and firing again, Keough spent another fifteen minutes carefully cleaning and oiling the weapon. He placed it carefully, almost lovingly, into its fitted case before he left the club and strolled to his bus stop. He would stop at his apartment, drop off his weapon, and then make his way to an appointment at three o'clock at Amrhein's restaurant on Broadway.

John Murphy would be waiting there, probably on his third or fourth pint by the time Keough arrived. Murphy would be dressed in his usual black tee shirt with the arms cut off at the shoulder, exposing his massive biceps. He'd also be clad in a pair of bib overalls and a faded Scally cap. To Keough, Murphy reminded him of photographs of John L. Sullivan, the Boston-born prizefighter from another century. Murphy combined enormous physical strength with nominal intellect and a long history of aiding the cause by collecting and shipping money and arms to the old country. A perfect package.

Keough knew that Murphy's father remained active as a warrior for the IRA, and was, at this moment, living near Limerick. Murphy was easy to engage when the subject was his father, and from the stories, Keough would have concluded that Murphy's father had single-handedly run every IRA operation since the early sixties. Keough knew of the man well, though never met him. Rogan Murphy was noted for his curly red hair and fiery temper, and he'd certainly been involved in various IRA activities over the past decades. But to hear John Murphy tell it, his old man Rogan was a candidate for Irish sainthood.

Murphy's maternal uncle was Mossy McDonough, another semi-legend in the IRA underground. Dead of multiple gunshot wounds as he left a pub in Monaghan twelve years ago. Murphy had plenty of reasons to be part of the grand plan that Keough was about to put in motion. He was motivated, and until now, had played only the smallest of roles in 'the cause', so here was his chance for vindication and a place of honor among family and friends.

Keough had earlier supplied Murphy with a lovely weapon, a Beretta M501 sniper rifle, difficult to find outside the Italian military. The rifle was not new, and in fact had played a role in the 1992 roadside shootings of three men in Portadown, some forty miles or so southwest of Belfast. The Beretta had the timeless lines of almost any machine of Italian design and manufacture. It was sleek, with a stock of the finest hardwood. It wasn't particularly lightweight, and it featured an old-fashioned bolt action. But inside, a harmonic balancer reduced the vibrations one would otherwise expect. The Zeiss-Diavari-Z 1.5-power x 6-mm zoom telescope assured astonishing accuracy. He'd personally trained Murphy on its use and Murphy, using another gun club, had been practicing. Keough wanted a report, thus today's meeting at Amrhein's. Then he'd present Murphy with the immediate task at hand.

He exited the subway station closest to his apartment and walked up the street. His telephone message recorder was blinking and Keough thought it prudent to respond; two calls . . . both with a great urgency expressed in the caller's voice . . . from Ramsden in London. It would be eight o'clock in London already, but Keough knew that Ramsden would be there to take his call. He might be a few minutes late for his meeting with Murphy, but he dialed Ramsden's private number and waited.

The conversation was brief enough and certainly to the point. Keough jotted down the names and addresses that Ramsden gave him. The first order of business, though, was to get to the office of Dr. Andrew Fortin and learn what he could about the man. "A package may have been sent to him, and that package needs to be destroyed. Whatever it takes." And the second order of business was a drive to Maine and Mrs. Whyte's mother's home in Auburn. "Post haste," were Ramsden's words, and Keough smirked at the use of the archaic speech. Yes, he would be there in just a few hours. Keough was to call Ramsden once his visit to Maine was complete; if necessary, Keough had the other names and addresses of Barbara Whyte's friends. A car rental agency was nearby and he'd make sure to report promptly. "And in your travels," Ramsden added emphatically, "I trust you will be certain that you have your weapon at hand."

So after his meeting with Murphy, Keough would be doing some traveling. He ordered a rental car for pick up at a downtown office, and then he'd be driving west, first to Fortin's office . . . maybe the Doctor's home, as well; then to Auburn, Maine. Later, he'd make his telephone report to Ramsden: Either the package was delivered or it was not. And either Barbara Whyte was at the mother's home in Maine, or she was not. Keough was patient and would learn the truth. After that, he'd probably be sent elsewhere.

Keough didn't particularly care for Ramsden. Found him brusque, condescending and pompous. If it wasn't for the enormous amounts of money he'd be collecting from the man, he'd just as soon be rid of him. Having spent several weeks in South Boston, Keough was aware of the anti-Brit sympathy of the American Irish. While the sentiment didn't dominate discussions in the local pubs, Keough heard them from time to time. John Murphy once expressed the opinion well in a conversation with Keough: When a Brit walks into a pub, he always acts as if he owns the place; when an American walks into a pub, he doesn't give a shit who owns it.

To Patrick Keough, Ramsden represented the worst of the Brits. There were Englishmen and there were Brits, and Ramsden was a Brit. As if Britannia still ruled the world. Keough didn't care who ruled the world as long as he enjoyed the benefits of a fine lifestyle, but he was dead certain that the UK was not even close to the top of the heap. Such was the delusional thinking of people like Ramsden, Keough mused, and he accepted it for what it was.

Charles Whyte was more of a puzzle. He'd met with Whyte just three times to give him updates on his progress. Whyte appeared to be a fine man, if a bit docile. Surprising to Keough was Whyte's utter lack of pomposity, and it set him in quite a contrast to their collective 'boss', so to speak, 'the most honourable high la-di-dah grand poobah of Nethercotswald', Sir Geoffrey Ramsden. Whyte was to funnel him the money in payment for his services, which, to Keough, was a fine thing indeed. Of great importance, though, Ramsden had given Keough the assignment of recruiting and training John Murphy, and most emphatically Whyte was to be kept entirely away from that part of the plan. For fifty thousand American dollars, Keough agreed to keep that part of the operation entirely to himself.

Late that afternoon, after his meeting with Murphy, Keough was on the Massachusetts Turnpike and headed west to pay a visit to Dr. Andrew Fortin.

Keough detested the afternoon traffic around Boston, and this was Friday. The Turnpike was clogged with commuters anxious to get home and start their weekends. He eventually reached the Natick exit. In other circumstances, the drive might have taken forty minutes; today, it was double that. He made a series of turns and headed towards the area of Wayland known as Cochituate and found Fortin's apartment on a heavily treed dead end street. The area was one of old Victorian style homes, probably late nineteenth century, and the one Fortin lived in was a gray and blue affair with scalloped siding. The house looked a bit down on its luck. It had two mailboxes perched at the edge of the road. There was a relic of a small pick-up truck in the driveway, and it, too, appeared to be on the downside of life. There were no other vehicles around.

Keough turned around at the end of the street and parked three houses away under the shade of an enormous oak. He pretended to consult a map while he kept an eye on Fortin's house through his rearview mirror. The neighborhood was quiet on this early Friday evening.

Keough considered calling Ramsden. There'd be nothing really to report, but he'd provide some level of comfort to the man. At least he was keeping an eye on Fortin for his boss. While he gave this some thought, he lit a cigarette and blew smoke out the window. His attention was suddenly drawn to an outside light that appeared at the second floor landing on the side of Fortin's house. A gentleman in a pair of tan slacks, green T-shirt and boat shoes descended the steps. To Keough, and at a range of perhaps two hundred feet, the man appeared to be in his mid-thirties. Medium brown hair, about six feet tall, perhaps less. Average build.

He climbed into the yellow pick-up, backed out of the driveway and drove down the street, passing Keough as he did. Keough wrote down the license number and could call Ramsden shortly; the man had contacts everywhere and would put that number together with the vehicle's owner in short order. At this point, though, Keough felt some level of confidence that he'd just caught a look at Doctor Andrew Fortin. When the pick-up turned left on to Main Street, Keough exited his vehicle and casually walked towards the gray and blue house. When he passed the mailboxes at the roadside, he noted that neither box had a name; only unit numbers. He assumed, properly that the 'B' unit was upstairs, which is where the man whom he assumed to be Fortin exited.

Continuing, he took the wooden steps to the second floor landing two at a time. He flipped his cigarette to the ground below and knocked once on the door, expecting and receiving no response. He contemplated the simple door knob lock and fewer than twenty seconds elapsed before he turned the knob and entered Fortin's space.

Not knowing where Fortin was headed nor when he'd return, Keough moved about the apartment quickly. He flipped through the few pieces of mail on the kitchen table and saw nothing resembling a packet of information that might have come from Barbara Whyte. It looked like a telephone bill and assorted junk mail. He set the mail down and entered the living room. Spare by anyone's standards, it still reflected some care and comfort. One wall held bookcases crammed with assorted works of fiction, plus an assortment of travel books. The bottom shelf appeared to hold only magazines. A small dining room table occupied one corner of the room. There was a small TV set and two stuffed chairs. A coffee table was bare except for a stack of coasters and an opened CD box. Keough picked it up; 'Time Out' by Dave Brubeck. The CD shelf on top of the bookcase held some Miles Davis, John Coltraine and a collection of Louis Armstrong, along with a boxed set of Beethoven. Keough shared the man's taste in jazz and classical.

The bedroom held a double bed, bureau and a bedside table with an opened book. Umberto Eco. Keough thought he might enjoy sitting down with Fortin one day and sharing a beer and a good discussion.

But no packet of incriminating information. Nothing to suggest that Fortin might be aware of anything concerning the disappearance or whereabouts of Barbara Whyte.

Then he saw the telephone answering machine. The indicator showed two messages, and Keough pressed 'play.'

"Doctor Fortin. It's Barbara Whyte. I need to see you. You're the only one around here I can trust." The voice sounded afraid and rushed. He could hear noises in the background, sounds of street traffic. More hurried breathing. *"I've got to go. I'll try you again later."*

So Fortin had been contacted. The message was received yesterday afternoon.

He waited for the second message.

"Hey Fortin. What's up? Any word from Barbara? Give me a call if you hear anything. Ciao."

It was a female voice, and the call came in about two hours ago. He could discern nothing else except for the very important facts that one more person was aware of Barbara's disappearance, that Barbara had, indeed, tried to contact Fortin, and that this female voice referred to Mrs. Whyte as 'Barbara', so this was not just a casual acquaintance. He wished the woman had identified herself somehow.

Keough picked up the telephone handset and checked caller ID. He clicked through the calls and found the number he was looking for and marked it down. He'd try to put the number together with a name later on.

Meanwhile, he decided that he's better make his exit. Fortin was gone for twelve minutes and he'd been inside the apartment for only eight minutes. Four more minutes to leave and return to his car; a total of only sixteen minutes, but that was long enough for Fortin to get to a corner store, buy a loaf of bread and return.

He flipped off the lights and closed the door, making sure that the lock was in place. He walked casually back down the street to his white rental car and noticed no one outside and no one peering from their windows. He had just entered his vehicle when he saw the aged pick up make the turn onto the street and head back to the apartment. Keough started his car and slowly drove away.

NINE

Fortin walked into his apartment and stopped cold. For some reason, not readily apparent, he sensed something was wrong. He turned on the lights and looked around. Nothing. But there was something that struck him as soon as he opened the door.

Then it came to him. Cigarettes. A former smoker, Fortin was a Lucky Strike unfiltered man. He thought if he was going to smoke at all, he might as well go for the gusto. And, indeed, he enjoyed it. He hadn't smoked more than ten cigarettes in the past three years, but he could smell the lingering effects of smoke when he went inside his apartment.

He set down the eggs and milk he had just purchased and picked up a carving knife from the block on the counter and went quietly into his bedroom. He flipped on the light switch. Nothing. He walked over to his bed. With a flourish, he flicked the covers off and looked under the bed. Except for a puff of a dust ball, there was nothing. He went into the living room . . . no place to hide here.

He scanned his bookcase and saw nothing out of place. The CD case on the coffee table, though, had definitely been moved. Before he went to the market for some fresh eggs and milk, Fortin had been listening to Dave Brubeck and reading through the liner notes. He remembered folding the notes over at the corner in a dog ear to remind him where he stopped. Now, the dog ear was flat. Somebody was here in the time he was out. Someone who smoked.

He checked his mail on the table. He couldn't recall the arrangement of the envelopes and magazines when he left, so he couldn't tell if they'd been moved.

He checked the bottom drawer of his bureau and lifted out a pair of old Levis. His small metal box was there with his important papers and two thousand dollars in cash. Nothing moved here.

"Do I call the cops?" Fortin thought that over. Sure, the police show up and he explains that his CD liner notes were moved and a smell of cigarettes lingered. That would be a class F what? Misdemeanor? No, he'd have no chance there. He sat at his kitchen table and considered his options. He came up with no good ideas but had a persistent sense that the invasion of his personal space had something to do with the Barbara Whyte situation. Whoever did enter his apartment must have done so in the brief period of time he was at the store. Perhaps fifteen minutes? Maybe twenty, even twenty-five? Surely no more than that.

He replaced the carving knife in its slot and paced the apartment. He was grateful that nothing was apparently broken or stolen, but gave no thought that whoever entered his apartment gained valuable information from his answering machine and phone handset.

He slept fitfully that night, more alert to every passing sound.

* * *

The only other people Fortin saw in his office building Saturday morning were the cleaning people. With little or no people traffic, they could polish floors and do their other chores without disturbing any of the tenants. Going to the office on Saturday was not a routine for him, but Fortin did so occasionally to either meet with patients or to catch up on paperwork. His footsteps echoed in the corridor and the stairwell. He checked his office, called his answering service, and found no new calls since the last time he checked.

He unlocked his patient file cabinet and removed the one for Francina Ficociello. She was scheduled in twenty minutes. Francina's file was not a thick one. He had seen her perhaps seven times, and most of their conversations centered on her late twin brother and how she was coping with his loss. He had found no reason to refer her to a physician but always kept that option open. Francina was, in his view, a healthy young woman who had some understandable difficulty grieving over her brother's death. While she hadn't been specific about why she wanted another therapy session, Fortin assumed that it was likely to revolve around the same subject.

He closed the file and left it on his desk, rising from his chair to look out his window onto the parking area below. He didn't see Francina yet, but he did notice another vehicle at the far end of the lot. It struck him as unusual only because it looked out of place on a Saturday morning. His battered pick-up and the cleaning staff's van were expected sights, but the white Taurus sedan was not. It was backed into a space at the far end of the lot and its driver appeared to be reading a newspaper. For some reason, the image caused Fortin to blink. There was something familiar about the scene; he couldn't remember how, but it was. He watched the driver who was smoking and flicking ashes out the window as he sat. He was trying to tie some loose ends together . . . perhaps seeing the car somewhere else . . . something was sticking and he couldn't figure out what it was. Then he saw the Turquoise Miata pull into the lot with Francina behind the wheel.

She pulled into a space at the near end of the lot and parked next to his pick up. Fortin watched her get out and saw that she was wearing shorts and a t-shirt. Some women, he mused, should not wear shorts and t-shirts. Their cellulite dimples and extra rolls of flesh did not embellish the view but distracted from it. Francina, he concluded, could wear them well.

Fortin cleared his head. He knew very well that he had absolutely no interest in establishing anything more than a doctor/patient relationship with this young woman, but he had to admit that her stunning face and voluptuous figure were troubling to him. Perhaps she needed to be seen by another psychologist, maybe a blind one. He clenched his eyes shut and waited for the door to be opened. He would survive.

Francina walked in and Fortin ushered her to a chair. She placed her small purse on the edge of his desk, and he considered that gesture for a moment. Usually, Francina held her purse close, as if for protection, a shield. Today, she appeared much more sure of herself, perhaps even aggressive. When she began the session, the reason became clear.

The cause for her visit was not, it turned out, her grief about her brother; she felt she was coping well, and Fortin sensed that she was correct in her self-assessment. The reason for her visit today was her anger at her father. Carlo, it seemed, expected Francina to work six evenings a week and six lunches. That totaled nearly seventy hours every week at the restaurant. That put a significant crimp in Francina's ability to develop and carry on a normal social life, but more than the extensive work schedule, Carlo also recently informed her that he was bringing over an assistant chef from his native Palermo to work with him. He made no secret . . . indeed did not anticipate any resistance from his daughter whatsoever . . . that he expected the new chef to (a) eventually take over the restaurant, (b) marry Francina, and (c) make many grandchildren for Carlo with his beloved daughter. Francina's color was high as she described the conversation with her father.

"That's absolute bullshit, Doctor. Look, what my father wants to do with the restaurant is fine with me; if my brother was still alive, I think he'd be looking to turn it over to him someday. It's the other stuff that's got me pissed off.

"This isn't the old country, and my father thinks I'm crazy to even think about seeing anyone else. He's yelling at me the other day that who I see is his choice. Meanwhile, I've already got a boyfriend. I don't know if I'll marry the guy, but at least I want to make the choice. And here's my dad telling me it's all set. I'm gonna be Mrs. Pasquale Massimo. Are you shittin' me?" She was fuming, and Fortin could almost see the smoke coming from her nostrils and ears. This was one angry young lady, and one with a reason to be.

"Look, Francina," Fortin began. But she cut him off.

"Doctor, there's no freakin' way I'm gonna marry this Pasquale Massimo. My dad showed me his picture. He's about five two with a little pencil mustache. He can't speak a word of English. 'He's a good Catholic Italian boy,' my dad says. Well B.F.D.! What if I wanna marry a freakin' pagan from Singapore? It's my choice!"

"I couldn't agree with you more, Francina, but you're getting yourself all cranked up, and that's not going to solve a thing. If you talk to your father in this state, you're only going to get him to blow his top, and then the volcano erupts."

"Believe me, I know. I told him I had no intention of marrying this guy Pasquale. And he has the nerve to tell me I can give him a good American name like 'Pat', like that's going to make all the difference. Look, I love my father. He's a good man with a huge heart, but I'm not going to sit back and let this happen because he thinks it's a great idea. That's just pure bullshit!"

Fortin considered the problem, rubbing his jaw as he did so. "Does your father know you've got a boyfriend?"

"He'd just shit! I wouldn't bring a boyfriend to meet my father right now. I did that once in high school and the kid was Irish. I thought my father would blow a gasket. That was bad enough, so I just keep my boyfriends away from him. If I ever decided I was getting serious with a guy, I don't know what I'd do, but the guy I'm seeing right now . . . when I even get a chance to get out of the restaurant . . . we're not ready for meeting Carlo right now."

"When is this Pasquale coming to America?"

"He's on his way next week. According to my father, I'm supposed to be all excited about this, and there's nothing I can tell my father that will change his mind. I almost quit the other day, but that would really leave him in the lurch, so I settled down and decided to ask you to see me. I need to do something and do it soon!"

"Francina, please listen to me." Francina was leaning forward and Fortin closed his eyes for a moment to stay focused.

"I'm all ears, believe me."

"Maybe Pasquale is a nice guy." She started to get out of her chair in rage at that suggestion. "Hold on, hold on. I'm just saying he might be a nice guy . . . for someone else. Not you, but someone else." He paused to let that thought sink in. "Think about this. Pasquale comes to America, does a good job as a chef, takes over the business, and marries some nice girl . . . just not Francina Ficociello. That's possible, right?"

Francina was pondering this with a furrowed brow. Her breathing was still rapid, and Fortin had to shift his gaze from the soft rising and falling flesh of her breasts. God, but she's a beautiful woman. Save me, Jesus!

"There's nothing you can say or do that will keep Pasquale from coming here or working in the restaurant with your father, right?" She nodded at that, her brow still wrinkled in deep thought. Fortin could see the gears moving. "So let him come. For all you know, he's not a bad guy, so you don't want to crush the guy like a bug. Just give it some thought."

"But what if my father's got him all prepped for the big wedding?"

"Think about it for a moment. He's not going to get married as soon as he gets off the plane. He's got to get used to the restaurant, learn the menu, work with your dad . . . all the stuff that keeps him occupied. So it's not going to happen right away."

"Right. He'll be working like a dog for a few months before he comes up for air."

"Where's he going to live?"

"My father already found him a little apartment in Framingham."

"So he's not going to be underfoot all the time, right?"

"Right." Francina was thinking things through now. He could almost hear the gears in her brain crunching through the possibilities.

"So give him a chance. Introduce him to people."

"Gina."

"What?" Fortin wasn't sure he caught what she said.

"Gina Maria Sabatino."

"Who's she?"

Francina explained that she and Gina had been best friends in grammar school. Similar backgrounds. Catholic. Daughter of Italian immigrants. But Gina's family was in jewelry and had an office in the Washington Street Jewelers' Block in Boston.

"She's this teeny little thing, probably a size one or a three. A few months younger than me. And Gina can wear a bikini that would bring every guy on the beach to his knees." Fortin could only imagine. He'd make plans to be there when it happened. "I think I'll give Gina a call. It's been about three months since we talked, and she really liked my brother. When he died, she was almost as devastated as me."

Fortin liked the way the conversation was going. In the end, Francina made plans to call Gina, invite her over, and then stop at her favorite shoe store. "I'm gonna buy me a pair of spike heels that's makes me a foot taller than that little Pasquale. If I fart, believe me, Pasquale's gonna be the first to know about it." She saw Fortin's eyes bulge a little. "I'm kidding! And when he sees me and Gina together, maybe it'll get his wheels in motion." The talking continued and Francina transformed from a raging bundle of anger into a determined young woman on a mission. When forty-five minutes had passed, Fortin wished Francina well and closed the door behind her, but not before watching for an extra moment as she moved down the hallway to the elevator. He went to her file and made a few notes and admired her from the window as she exited the building. He smiled broadly when he saw her walk to her car and take her cell phone from her purse. She punched in some numbers before she got into her car.

Fortin considered the session a success and turned back to his file cabinet. When he did so, he happened to see the white Taurus, still in its place, but with no one inside. Odd. Not so highly unusual that he'd have to make a note of the event. Just a little odd.

His eyes were distracted by the Postal Service truck leaving the lot at the far exit. He went down the hall and walked down the stairs to the first floor post boxes to check on the mail. When he pulled the door open to his post box, Fortin was surprised to see that his mailbox was more filled than usual. He pulled the latest issue of Psychotherapy Journal from the top and a single white envelope fell to the floor. He picked it up and proceeded to remove a large manila envelope from the mailbox. It bore no return address. Fortin closed the mailbox door, but his attention was focused on the brown manila envelope. Addressed to him in heavy black marker.

Fortin turned the packet over searching for some clue as to its sender. He closed his mailbox and turned to use the staircase to the second floor. He didn't like to use the elevator for a one-story ride. But his attention was drawn to a particular odor: cigarettes again. He glanced around and saw no one. Maybe he was dreaming all this. He'd heard of ex-smokers having these kinds of hallucinations decades after their last smoke, so maybe that was operative here. But no, he took another whiff. *This isn't my imagination.* Maybe one of the cleaning people smoked, but he doubted it.

Fortin returned to his office and placed the large envelope on his desk. He placed the magazine to the side and opened the single white envelope first. He was gratified to find a check for three hundred dollars from a patient, and he slid open the center drawer of his desk and placed the check inside. He finally turned his attention to the larger envelope.

He tore it open with his finger and slid the contents onto his desk. Clipped together were several pages of white paper, perhaps twenty or more sheets, Fortin estimated. The packet bore a handwritten note on top. He picked up the packet and read the note:

Dear Doctor Fortin,

I apologize for sending this to you, but I am not sure where else I might turn. The information doesn't make much sense to me, but I know that Charles has been acting very differently, and I'm certain it has to do with this.
These are notes I copied from a disc my husband brought home from the consulate. There are also some copies of some handwritten notes. He doesn't know that I saw them.

My husband was (scratched out) is basically a good man, but Geoffrey Ramsden has him under his thumb, and it's taking a toll on Charles. He won't tell me what's wrong, and was as angry as I've ever seen him when I told him that I saw some of his notes. That's not like him at all. He told me that we (Charles and I and our son) would all be in danger if any word of this got out.

I will be away for a few days, maybe more. My son is going to be with grandparents in northern England for a few weeks for his summer holiday, and that is a great relief with everything I am dealing with right now.

Please forgive me for involving you, but I don't know anyone else I can trust with this.

Barbara Whyte

Fortin slid the paper clip from the papers and looked through them. There appeared to be several copies of letters. All addressed to "C", presumably Charles Whyte. Plus some detailed maps and what appeared to be itineraries. He sat at his desk and began to read the first page.

"C: Latest message received and pleased you have met subject. Agree K. fits profile perfectly. Plans here proceeding. No added security expected. Equipment arrives next packet, traceable to events 03/09/88, your immediate attention required. K to dispose of his immediately after. Exact duplicate here and ready. Trust route is practiced and acceptable.

G. "

"G" would certainly be Sir Geoffrey Ramsden. The next one was as brief but somewhat less cryptic.

"C: Good to learn K prepared. Payment to K arrives next wks pouch. Also BritAir tkt for K in same. Route for London visit established shortly. Advise K security extraordinary, but certain that several options remain. I wish you luck. "Peace" charade comes to end. Ha! Sinn Fein leadership scheduled to meet PM this evening, and expect 'good feelings' all around. Phase One in Boston will provide the stunning left hook. If insufficient, London possible for Phase Two knock-out punch. 'Era of good feeling' will end quickly. It will happen.

G."

Fortin riffled through the pages. There must be twenty or more here, he thought. All from G to C. "K" was a riddle. He turned to the copies of the handwritten notes. Maybe there'd be something in there.

Later on, there were references buried in other text that revealed some added info.

"Keough: ready. Will make adjustments just prior." "$50K US to Keough." "Suggested Ritz/Newbury roof. Scope out sched. & will advise when confirmed" "Prob. Burberry's!!!" "Notify G."

In between were various jots, circles and random squiggles. Probably notes taken by Charles Whyte during various phone conversations. The notes didn't tell him much, but he at least felt confident that he could hang identifying names onto the initials. But what did it all mean? Why did Barbara send him the packet and then leave for parts unknown? So far, Fortin failed to see the "obvious reasons" that Barbara described in her cover note.

He replaced the materials in the envelope and placed the envelope in his briefcase. Maybe when he got home later on, he'd read through the rest of the notes and try to figure them out.

Patrick Keough watched Fortin from the cover of a doorway at the end of the hall. Keough was exhausted. He did get to enjoy a few pints when he got back to Boston last night, but it was the young lass that wore him out. He stumbled across her at Mickey's throwing darts with some friends. Her name, she said, was Terry and he guessed her to be mid twenties. He never guessed that she'd have an appetite for Olympian sex that nearly rubbed his willy to a nub. By the time he left her place, it was three in the morning he was still very tired and still very sore.

He watched as Fortin opened the mailbox and scrutinized the manila envelope. To Keough, Fortin appeared somewhat puzzled. If a package of information was involved, then this was most likely the item in question. He considered making a move at this point, but resisted the urge. Little was to be gained and there was a lot to lose. He'd keep his distance for now and let Ramsden know what he saw. The next move would be up to him. Meanwhile, he'd head now to Auburn, Maine to pay a quick visit to Mrs. Elizabeth Chicoine. He could get there and back in six hours and he'd still have plenty of time for a few pints when he returned to his apartment. And then maybe a good long sleep.

Thirsk is a small market town about twenty miles north of the city of York in north central England. At the edge of the rolling green dales to the west and the stark moors to the east, it has changed little over the past century. Its downtown market square still houses small shops and pubs catering to locals and the sheep and dairy farmers in the area. It was in Thirsk that Charles Whyte was born and spent his early years.

His parents still maintained a home a short walk from the market square. Now, Norman and Julia Whyte were enjoying the visit of their only grandchild, James. Thirsk was a safe town without the crime of the larger cities, and his grandparents felt comfortable with James roaming the neighborhood and exploring. This year, as in past years, James particularly enjoyed playing with his grandparents' two Border Collies. As if he'd never been away, the collies wagged their tails wildly when James arrived, and immediately went to their box of toys; they wanted to play fetch.

On a clear morning bright with sunshine, James led the collies to the field behind his grandparents' garden shed. The dogs were eager to chase after every ball and stick that James threw, each time dropping the retrieved prize at his feet, waiting for the next challenge.

A black Jaguar XJ8 pulled up across the road from the field and the driver sat for several minutes watching the interplay between the youngster and the collies. The scene brought to mind his own wonderful visits to visit his grandparents. James had certainly grown taller since last summer, he thought. Rangier and with more defined features, he still recognized James at once. He opened the car door and waved to the boy.

"Hello James, it's so good to see you." James stopped throwing and studied the man for some sign of recognition. Like most youngsters, he'd been taught very strictly not to talk to strangers, and he was sufficiently aware of the world, even at eight years old, to understand that this universe had plenty of sad stories about the things that bad people did to kids. He stood in place and watched the man approach him, coming to the decision as to whether he should stay or flee.

"It's me, James. I must say that you've changed quite a great deal since I saw you last summer, but I didn't think I'd changed quite so much."

Not yet convinced, James measured the distance to the back

door of his grandparents' house. "When you visited my house last summer, it was the first time you'd ever gone fishing in a boat. Do you remember that day?"

Now James recognized the man and started to move toward him, almost in a run. "Mr. Ramsden. I didn't know it was you at first."

Ramsden bent down and caught James in a hug. "It's good to see you, James. I heard that you were coming to England again. Are you enjoying your visit so far?"

"The dogs are a lot of fun. They never get tired of playing, and they're so smart. My Dad says that Border Collies are probably the smartest dogs of all. The big one is Ferlin. He's six. And the smaller one is Husky. She's only three." The two collies watched Ramsden carefully. Ferlin placed himself between Ramsden and the boy. Husky stood at James side. "Watch this, Mr. Ramsden." James lobbed the stick some distance into the field, but instead of taking off after it, the dogs stayed immobile. "That's weird. They usually go right after it." James couldn't understand the dogs' behavior. "They always race each other to the stick and the winner brings it right back and leaves it at my feet."

"I'm sure they do, James." Ramsden was aware that the dogs were keeping him in their sights. Neither dog's tail was wagging, and they were on full protective alert. "Well, I was in the area and I'd heard the news that you were visiting your grandmother and grandfather, so I thought I'd stop by and say hello."

"I flew into London and they picked me up. It was a real bumpy flight, but I got to see two movies."

"I used to visit my grandparents when I was your age. They were in Ireland, and it was only a short airplane ride from England. Many times, because it was a fairly short ways across the sea, I'd take a boat. That was always fun, and I once got to steer the boat with the captain."

"That must have been great, Mr. Ramsden."

"It was a large boat that carried boats and automobiles and even big trucks, so I thought it was just grand."

James turned his head when he heard his grandmother call. "That's my grandmother. Do you want to come with me to the house?"

"No, thank you. I have to leave, but I'm sure I'll be back this way soon, and maybe I'll have a chance to visit longer then. You take care of yourself, James."

When James left, the dogs trotted with him, Ferlin glancing back once in Ramsden's direction. Ramsden stared back at the dogs. To himself, he said, "Ferlin and Husky. How bloody appropriate. He walked to his Jaguar and drove off slowly, appreciating the almost total absence of traffic on the roads in this section of town. "Barbara Whyte," he muttered as he drove. "'A lonely soul within me cries. I acted smart and broke your heart. Now you've gone.' Barbara, Barbara, come out, come out wherever you are."

TEN

J anet Chapel reached Fortin on his cell phone just before
noon. "What the hell is going on? I called your house this
morning and got your machine. You working this morning?"

"Yes, as a matter of fact. I had a patient. Just one, but she
really exhausts me. Did you get my message last night?"

"Yes, I did. What's this about a break-in?"

So Fortin explained, and added his impressions about his
sensations when he picked up the mail today at his office. "And
there's something else. There was a white car in the parking lot
at my office this morning."

"No wonder you're all worked up, Fortin. You've got this
abnormal fear of white motor vehicles. I could write a paper
about this."

Fortin ignored the remark. "I'm almost certain that I saw
the same car on my street last night. The thing is, I saw the
driver smoking in the car last night, and I saw the driver smoking today. And then I smelled smoke in my apartment and
again in the lobby at the office."

"You know, in spite of everything, there are still plenty of smokers in the world, Fortin. The fact that you happened to see one yesterday and another one today, well that's not actually going to cause people to react with absolute amazement."

"Maybe I am reading too much into this stuff, but I really think it's this whole Barbara Whyte thing, Janet. It's got something to do with this package I received."

"So what's the story with this package? Are you in some kind of trouble?"

"I won't get into all the details, but Barbara Whyte sent me an envelope. Inside were a pile of papers and notes and emails that she copied from her husband's files. And a note. She asked me to hold on to them."

"What's in the papers that could cause so much of a mess? And what's her note say?"

"I've been reading through the stuff, and honestly, I only have a guess. It looks like her husband is tangled up in some kind of trouble. I'm just guessing, but it seems to me that there's something that he's involved in that just doesn't sound right. It's all in code and initials and abbreviations. I'm trying to figure it out, but I can't. I will tell you that Barbara Whyte's note that came with the package makes it sound serious. She's worried enough to send it to me and then take off."

"Strange. Nothing makes sense?"

"Just that whoever is sending these messages back and forth doesn't want the Northern Ireland peace talks to succeed. Beyond that, it's all guesswork."

"I don't like the sound of this jerk-o getting into your place last night. And if he's hanging around today, you need to cover your back. What do you say about staying at my place tonight? I've got the couch, and you'd be safe."

Fortin considered the possibility but suggested they meet instead for dinner and then go over the packet he received in the mail.

*   *   *

Liddy Chicoine was trying to focus her attention on finishing an afghan she'd been crocheting as a Christmas present for her daughter. She'd made three attempts to start but was interrupted by her own thoughts of Barbara and the predicament in which she found herself. She had hoped Barbara would have found some constancy and joy in her life, and until recently believed she had. Charles was a good husband and they enjoyed an interesting, if relatively modest lifestyle in Massachusetts. Her grandson James was a bright and energetic young boy. Liddy had hopes that she'd have more than the single grandchild, but her son, childless, was divorced and unlikely to remarry; her other daughter was a free spirit and not the settling-down type.

She had suspected that Barbara was going through a rough patch in her life, especially since her job at the school was gone. She'd also been alarmed at the changes in Barbara's appearance. She'd never been heavy, but now she was becoming rail thin. Barbara assured her that she was physically fine, and that she was seeing a therapist. This was not particularly comforting to Liddy, whose concept of psychologists was rooted firmly in the mid-twentieth century, in spite of her background and experience as a nurse: Only crazy people need a psychologist, and the best therapy for a rapid weight loss was plenty of meat and potatoes.

But Barbara's sudden and unexpected visit explained a lot. When her daughter drove away on Friday, Liddy knew that something much deeper than just a job loss was at work, and Barbara's marriage was fragile at best. While Liddy had always enjoyed Charles, there remained some level of discomfort that she attributed to his basic Englishness; he was not a sophisticate, and indeed seemed to revel in his visits to Maine and Barbara's extended family. It was more of an underlying sense that Charles was polished and formal; aloof might be too strong a word, but he never did seem to let his hair down in Liddy's company.

Now, though, a distinctly different Charles had emerged, someone caught up in some sort of plan involving guns and who-knows-what. It was more than Liddy could fathom. To herself she muttered, "I just hope Barbara can sort some of this stuff out, wherever she is."

Where would she go, she wondered? There were some possibilities: perhaps just hole up in a motel for a day or two; maybe to Liddy's brother's cabin at Worthley Pond, where Barbara spent several weeks every summer while she was a child; maybe to the home of a college friend. She tried once more to work on the afghan when the doorbell rang.

Standing at the front door was a tallish dark-haired gentleman in a blue blazer. "Mrs. Chicoine?" he asked. When she nodded she stepped back and allowed him in the foyer where the air was warmer than the dry Maine chill outdoors.

"Do you have a daughter, Barbara Whyte?" She nodded again, hoping from her belly that this was not a call about some horrific accident. "My name is Carl Morgan. F.B.I. I'm here because there's been a report that your daughter can't be located, and we've been asked to see if you've seen her or heard from her."

Liddy swallowed before responding. "Um, no. I haven't seen her. I spoke to her last week by phone. What do you mean 'can't be located'?"

Keough bypassed the question. "Do you know of a Dr. Andrew Fortin?"

This caught Liddy by surprise. "The name isn't familiar. Why?"

"I really can't say, Mrs.Chicoine. I've just been told to ask and make a report."

"Well who do I call about this? You're telling me my daughter has disappeared?" While trying to play the part of the mother distraught with such news, she silently hoped that Barbara was somewhere safe.

Keough didn't need more information than he already had.

"Mrs. Chicoine, I can only imagine how upset you must be, and I don't have the answers to your questions. I'll contact head-quarters and get back to you when I get more information."

Liddy waited at the front door while the gentleman went to his car, after which Liddy reentered her house, closed the door, and sagged against it. "Whew!" She prayed that Barbara would contact her soon, wherever she was, and let her know she was OK. "FBI my ass," she muttered under her breath. "Never of-fered an ID. That was a load of bullshit." Then, instead of wait-ing for Barbara to call, she immediately went to her phone and dialed Barbara's cell phone. She'd leave a message if Barbara didn't pick up. She needs to know what's happening here.

"This is nuts, Fortin. I'm no expert on foreign affairs but I do keep up with the news, and the peace talks in Northern Ire-land are real big news at the moment over there. They call them the Ulster Dialogues, and there are a lot of people who are hop-ing this brings an end to the violence once and for all. And this jerk looks like he wants to derail the talks and go back to square one. At least that's what I get out of all this."

They were seated in a quiet booth in the corner of the bar at Berkeley's, a seafood restaurant in Newton not far from the turnpike. Fortin was riffling through the pages of the packet looking for a particular item that caught his eye earlier.

"Here it is. Look at this part here. This is what bothers me." He pointed out the reference.

Import you stay with cons grp when POW arrives. K will be in area and ready for shot.

"So? What are you thinking? Whyte is with the consulate and the 'POW' is a prisoner of war. And K is . . . who did you say . . . some guy named Keough? Sounds like a photo shoot with a war hero, but I'm as lost as you are."

"But over here it says that Keough has to get fifty thousand American dollars, so it's not just a photo shoot he's talking about. It's something else. And what's he doing on the roof the Ritz? That's right at the beginning Newbury Street across from the Public Gardens."

"Burberry's is right across the street. A little too prep school for my taste, but if you like the plaid, it makes a statement."

"So what's this got to do with Whyte, and what does 'POW' have to do with anything?"

"Barbara Whyte must have assembled some more from this jig saw than we've been able to do so far. Why else would she think this is such dangerous stuff? She wouldn't run off unless she was pretty sure something nasty was going on."

"Fifty thousand nasty things could be one reason."

Janet looked at the papers again. "I'm looking at the money as part of a quid pro quo. It's payment in consideration of a contract, don't you think? I mean, if this K does one thing, then Whyte gives him the cash. If he doesn't, there's no payment. That's how I read it."

"I think you're right. But what?"

"I'll sleep on it. Let's get going and we can talk again tomorrow. Maybe something brilliant will come to one of us like a bolt out of the blue."

Fortin wasn't convinced. "Maybe we just can't figure it out. Maybe we really do need Barbara Whyte here to fill in the blanks."

Early the following morning, Keough drove to the end of Fortin's street and parked in the shade of an old maple. His conversation with Ramsden this morning wasn't a pleasant one. "Get the damned packet back!" As if all Keough had to do was stroll up to the door and ask. He watched and waited but knew he'd have to be gone soon enough. This was a quiet residential street and people didn't like the idea of strange cars appearing on their street with an obviously preoccupied gentleman sitting in it. Some nosy and concerned SOB would either come out of his house and ask questions or call the police to do the asking for him.

Nothing brilliant came to Fortin's mind during the night. When he awoke, he started the coffee maker and went to the porch to pick up the Sunday papers. It was a time that Fortin usually relished, sitting with a thick paper and a full pot of coffee. The day was glorious with the sunshine flickering through the leaves of the trees and Fortin inhaled a lung full of fresh air. He blew it out quickly when he saw a white Taurus parked down the street with a wisp of smoke coming from the driver's window. Without indicating that he saw the car, he took the paper back in and looked through his phone directory for a telephone number.

He knew that Barbara Whyte had been specific in her message . . . don't bring in any law enforcement . . . but Fortin didn't waste time. Seeing the Taurus once more made his mind up. He found the number and punched it in. The voice on the other end belonged to Jerome Wetman, a former patient and a police officer in Boston. After a few moments of pleasantries about how each other was doing, Wetman asked the reason for the call.

"It's early you know, and it's my day off. You're not calling just to say hello."

"Jerry, it's a little complicated but I'd like to talk to you about something. I need to keep this in confidence but it could be important."

Wetman was a homicide investigator who went through a nasty divorce two years ago, and Fortin helped keep him on track. Without Fortin's help, Wetman felt he'd either blow his brains out or his ex wife's. The detective was happy to extend an offer to help.

"Sure. If you want to meet this morning, how about the coffee shop in Newton next to the Flower Shop?"

Fortin rushed to get dressed and peeked through the curtains a few times to make sure the Taurus hadn't returned. In forty-five minutes Jerry Wetman was listening to the story. Fortin cautioned him.

"I have to ask you to keep this between us. I promised that I wouldn't go to the police, but I know I'm being followed and my apartment's been broken into, and I'm sure it's all connected with this."

"I can't promise anything about that, Doctor. If I think a crime's been committed, or if I think one might be committed, I can't just sit on it."

"Ok. I understand, so I'm going to try keeping this a little vague if you don't mind."

Without showing any of the material in the packet, Fortin described what he read and the problem he had deciphering what was really being described. "It's all in abbreviations and there's some of it in code. All I know is, there's some scheme to derail the peace talks in Northern Ireland and it involves someone over here."

"That sounds like something for the State Department, not some Boston cop."

"I know, but there's mention of the Ritz in Boston and Burberry's. Something is going to happen in Boston and it's all connected."

Wetman relented a bit. "Here's what I'm going to suggest. Show me this stuff. If it looks like there's something to it, that a crime is being planned, I'll do what I can to keep that from happening. That's all I can say. Who's the guy involved in the thing over here?"

Fortin hesitated. "I'd rather not give you a name yet. Look this stuff over first."

"You're dancing around on me, Doctor, but alright, let me

look it over." He spent the next half hour reading and scribbling a few notes on a pad of paper. He muttered a few times as he read and ended by passing the entire packet back to Fortin.

"Here's what I think. Not much. It doesn't look like there's anything violent happening according to this stuff, but it's so vague it could be anything. All I can do is keep my eyes and ears open. But for you, I'm going to tell you to get the Wayland police out to your place and tell them that you think your place was broken into and that you believe your being followed by a guy in a white Taurus." Wetman saw the resignation in Fortin's face. "OK, so you'll look like a nut case. Let me call them instead and tell them. They won't give me any shit and they'll at least drive by your place once in a while and maybe even catch up to this guy if he happens to be sneaking around the neighborhood again. No plate, right?"

Fortin nodded.

"Didn't think so." Wetman got up from his seat and shook hands with Fortin. "Watch yourself, and if you hear of anything else, give me a call. And, by the way, I'm seeing a lady from Everett. Nice girl. A little chunky in the butt, but can she cook!"

Fortin drove back to his apartment unsatisfied with his meeting.

Fortin went into a funk on the drive home and missed his exit from the turnpike. He drove to the next one and turned around, wasting nearly a half hour as a result of his error. When he finally reached his street, he was wary of finding the white Taurus once more. He pulled into the driveway and walked up the stairs to his back porch. The odor of cigarette smoke was obvious to him and when he opened the locked door, the odor was even more prominent. "Damn it!" he said aloud to no one. He scouted out his apartment quickly and noticed several items out of place this time. Whoever was here was looking through his bookcase and his personal papers and was less careful about putting things back. He left a message on Jerry Wetman's answering machine and then called Janet Chapel.

"This is really pissing me off," he told Janet, enraged now that he was being invaded almost at will.

"He's looking for the papers that Barbara Whyte sent, isn't he? He must be."

Fortin recounted his conversation with Jerry Wetman. "He didn't have any idea what this is all about either. I'm going to call Charles Whyte and tell him to call this guy off, whoever he is. I'll call you later on and let you know what I find out."

Fortin reached Whyte at home. "Mr. Whyte, I have no idea what you're up to, but someone has been following me and breaking into my house looking for some papers that Barbara sent me. I know you're involved in this thing, and I'm telling you to call the guy off or I'm going to call the police and let them deal with you."

Whyte was almost paralyzed with fear. So Barbara did copy the files and she sent the papers to her therapist. He suspected as much before, but was still stunned by the thought that key elements of the plan were in the hands of someone else. He would admit nothing about 'Shamrock' though, and tried to find a way to smooth things out. "Doctor Fortin, I'm so sorry about this. I don't know what got into Barbara, but she must have had some notion that there's some plot afoot. Of course, it's all rubbish. I don't know what to say."

"Please, Mr. Whyte, someone doesn't want me to have this package of papers and he's serious enough to be following me and breaking into my home."

"I don't know anything about that, Doctor. I'd like to speak with Barbara about this, but I don't know where she is at the moment."

Fortin lost his patience. This was denial he was hearing, and he didn't want to hear any more. "Are you going to call off this jerk or do I call the cops?"

Whyte lost his composure. "Please, Doctor, it's nothing, really. Please don't call the police. It would ruin me, and it could cause Barbara harm. Please!"

Fortin was intrigued. "Harm Barbara? What do you mean?"

"Please don't ask me any more, Doctor."

"There is a plan isn't there? Something's going on."

"Please," Whyte was pleading. "It's nothing evil or dangerous. Barbara has the entirely wrong idea. It's really nothing, and it certainly need not involve you at all. I wish I could explain this to Barbara."

"Get the guy to back off or I will call the police. Do it now, or I'll make the call, I swear."

"Doctor, please, I will do what I can, but understand that any effort on my part is unlikely to have any effect. If the police are brought in, I fear that everyone we love . . . and I mean both of us, Doctor Fortin . . . everyone we love will be removed, and you and I will never be able to prove a thing."

Fortin digested the words in silence.

"Doctor Fortin?"

"I'm listening."

"Please don't bring anyone else in on this. Please."

"I'll do what I think is best, Mr. Whyte. And you're going to call off the idiot who's following me and breaking into my place."

Fortin slammed the phone down.

He tried to calm down but his nerves were frayed. He decided to take a walk around the house, maybe check Todd's garden for tomatoes. Maybe his blood pressure would settle down.

That night, Charles Whyte slept barely a wink, so consumed was he with the maelstrom of shouting and demands from every quarter. At dawn, he made a frantic call to Ramsden and described his conversation with Fortin. Ramsden's rage was extraordinary. "Whyte, you may have ruined everything! What a stupid man I've brought into my confidence! We're just hours away from seeing Shamrock move forward, and you're doing your bloody best to blow the lid off."

Whyte was near tears.

"I'm going to deal with this from here. Please stay out of the way. Do not do a thing. And let me just tell you this, Whyte. There will be hell to pay for this!"

Whyte was getting accustomed to hearing telephones slammed. He had never heard Ramsden lose his temper so quickly or so violently. He could understand that his bungling did jeopardize the entire plan, but there was nothing he could do at the moment. Barbara was gone and he had no one to whom he could talk. He tried calling his mother-in-law on the off chance that Barbara was there. It didn't work before, and Whyte was near certain that Barbara would go to her mother's in such a crisis. But perhaps she's settled down. Maybe she's reconsidered. He called the number.

"No Charles. Barbara is not here. I told you before."

"Where is she, Liddy? I must find her."

"I'm sure she's safe, Charles. Please don't call any more. And please tell the fellow that came to visit me that I know he's not with the F.B.I. Carl Morgan, indeed. He's a fraud."

The telephone came down with a crash and Charles Whyte was quick enough to move the handset away from his ear to avoid permanent injury.

If Charles Whyte was frozen in place, Patrick Keough was running to and fro at an almost panic pace. "Stop this Fortin and do it quickly," Ramsden shouted into the phone. "I want him out of the way as soon as possible."

"Out of the way?" Keough wanted Ramsden to be entirely clear. There had to be no ambiguity at this point.

Ramsden enunciated every word as if to a recalcitrant child. "Stop-him-any-way-you-can." That was clear enough for Keough. "He knows too much and he's the biggest threat we have."

Keough had hoped to get in another hour of practice at the firing range, but he amended his itinerary and headed to Wayland and Fortin's house. When he arrived, he pulled into the same space he used before, some distance from the house and under the protection of a large shade tree. He exited his car and carried his weapon in a holster beneath his jacket. His pistol was loaded with one round in the chamber. One slight modification was the screw on silencer that he'd need in this situation. As he neared the house, he thought he saw Fortin sitting on his porch. He stayed under cover of the large maples and proceeded slowly in the shadows. Fortin, it appeared to Keough, was just sitting and thinking.

Keough decided that his best vantage point would be the tree just across the way. He began to move casually across the street when he heard a door open and a voice shout to him.

"Hello there. You must be new in this neighborhood."

Keough tried to ignore the elderly lady, but it was too late. She wanted to talk and Keough happened to have the nearest available ear. He decided to return to his car, park somewhere else and try again later.

The neighbor's voice caught Fortin's attention, though, and he watched as the tall man walked back to his car, the white Taurus that had been haunting him. He decided that he'd had enough and jumped into his beat up Nissan. Fortin raced down the street but the Taurus had already pulled into the main thoroughfare and was three cars ahead. At the set of stop lights, Fortin made some progress and trailed by only two cars.

The Taurus surprised him by turning into a side street. Fortin followed but the Taurus had already swung around and drove quickly past him. As it did, Fortin tried to read the license plate but it was already too late.

*   *   *

"Look, I'm sitting in the parking lot at the mall. I hate to ask you this, but I'd like to borrow your car for a while."

"What's up?" Janet Chapel was doing her best to write her presentation when Fortin's call came in.

"I'm being followed and I want to do some checking around. I need to drive up to Maine and my truck isn't in great shape."

"Are you going to look for Barbara Whyte? You think she's at her mother's?"

"Not sure where she is. But I'll bet her mother knows where she is. I called her and she was evasive. She's only three hours away, maybe less. I'd like to talk to her face to face."

"Well you can certainly take my car. It needs some miles put on it and I can always use a rental if I need to go somewhere. But I thought you were going to get the cops involved."

"I just spoke to Charles Whyte again and he told me that he did what he could to stop the nonsense but it's out of his hands now. He also told me that if I went to the police, the people who are in charge will make sure that everyone I love will be removed. That's what he was told as well. 'Everybody we love will be *removed*, and we'll never be able to prove a thing.' Those are his words."

"These guys sound serious. If I were you, I might consider staying put and forgetting everything."

"The only thing I've done is receive that package from Barbara Whyte in the mail. Even if they took it back, they know I know. And the police can't do anything with what I have. I already know that much."

"Look. I've got a call coming in a few minutes. As soon as I finish. I'll be ready to go. I'll pick you up at the Sears entrance in say one hour, give or take. You can drop me off back at the hospital and take my car. Hell, you can even stay at my place if you want."

"Thanks, but I need to do a little checking on this stuff and I might have to take off for a couple of days to do that. I might be putting a few miles on your car, if that's OK."

"I need to get some miles on this Saab before my lease is up, so go right ahead. For the time being, just stay out of sight for the next hour. See you."

Fortin hung up and looked around. He could go into the rest room and commandeer a john for a while. Not the most pleasant place, but suitable for now. Strolling as nonchalantly as he could toward the rest rooms, he passed a news stand and decided to buy a local paper. After all, an hour in a men's room stall required some diversion.

He entered the men's room, empty save for one gentleman washing his hands and exiting, and chose the last stall. He entered, set his newspaper and briefcase down and sat. In his briefcase were Barbara Whyte's patient file and the envelope she had mailed to him with the cryptic notes. Nothing to do now but read and wait.

Fortin checked his watch and folded his newspaper. It was time to get to the Sears entrance of the mall. On his way there, he passed a mall security guard in uniform. Fortin hoped his sudden sense of alarm wasn't transmitted to the guard. He paused in the men's department and bought three pair of under shorts and four pair of sox, paying with cash, and proceeded to the entrance where Janet Chapel was waiting in her Saab. He climbed into the passenger seat and, in moments, they were away from the mall and on their way back to the hospital and Janet's office.

"Look, Andrew, you've got a half tank of gas, a Rand Mc-Nally atlas on the floor of the back seat, and an envelope in the glove compartment with a thousand dollars in cash. Don't say anything. There's a Visa card in there you can use for gas, too. Nobody will say anything because everything is 'pay-at-the-pump' anyway. Just take care of yourself and don't use your ATM or a credit card. If someone's trying to track you down, that's a great way to find you."

Fortin knew enough to avoid arguing when Janet was in this kind of mood. Just obey orders and stay with the plan.

"I'll call Karen right away and let her know you have to be away for a few days. Family emergency. She'll call your patients. I'll check with a new psych on staff and see if he'll take the patients that absolutely have to see somebody right away. Otherwise, Karen will reschedule for the week after."

"But," Fortin began before he was cut off.

"I've seen your schedule, Fortin, and you're not exactly booked to the balls, so don't tell me we can't put off a few patients for a couple of days." Fortin just shook his head.

"Now, I've got a little cooler on the back seat with a two diet Cokes and a grinder. I hope you like Italian with everything. There's a sweatshirt in the trunk; it's real big on me and should be OK on you. You're going to call my cell phone every twelve hours starting at midnight tonight to check in. Let me know you're safe."

Fortin finally had a moment to speak. "I pulled three hundred from the bank yesterday, so I should be good for a while. And I love Italian with everything. Are you sure it's OK to use your car?"

"I've got a rental being delivered before I leave work later on. Probably a beige Ford something that some guy used to test smoke El Productos in for the last month. Don't worry about me. Worry about yourself for a change."

When they got close to the hospital, Janet pulled over at a gas station, pecked him on the cheek and hopped out. "I'm going to walk back from here. No sense walking into something stupid if you can avoid it." Fortin climbed out and gave Janet a hug and a kiss. She returned them and squeezed his hand. "You watch your back, big guy, 'cause the only other shrink I trust around here is Dr. Fishkind, and he charges twice what you do." Then she was gone, almost trotting back to the hospital in jeans, sneakers and a grey flannel sweatshirt.

Fortin put the car in gear and drove toward the highway. He planned to get to Newburyport near the New Hampshire border and then make some phone calls. He had a sense where he'd find Barbara, but wanted to be sure before he made another move. He kept his speed at the limit and paid close attention to the occasional state police cruiser that appeared.

When he did pull off the highway in Newburyport, he drove to a super market parking lot and located a pay phone. Through Information he secured the number for Elizabeth Chicoine in Auburn, Maine. Moments later, the phone rang and a cautious Liddy answered. "Yes?"

"Hello, Mrs. Chicoine, this is Doctor Fortin again. I'd like to meet with you if I could."

There was no response.

"My name is Andrew Fortin, Mrs. Chicoine. I'm a friend of Barbara's and I'm trying to reach her."

"I know. I know. I just don't want Barbara to be hurt. Why are you trying to reach her?"

"Mrs. Chicoine, I don't have any reason why you'd believe me, but I think Barbara is in trouble, and so am I. Have you heard from her?"

Liddy was almost ready to accept the caller's sincerity but reconsidered the stakes, especially regarding her daughter. "How do I know you're really who you say you are? There's a lot of lying going on around here."

"I'm asking you to trust me."

"Right. Trust you. What's her husband's name?"

Fortin was caught off guard. "What? It's, uh, Charles. Charles Whyte."

Liddy was quick with the follow up. "Any kids?"

"Yes, one son, James. He's about eight."

"What do you look like?"

"I'm white, about five-ten, about one-seventy. I've got brown hair with some gray in it. I wear glasses. I have a mole on . . ."

"That's enough." Liddy had a description of Fortin from her conversation with Barbara just a short time earlier.

"Look, Mrs. Chicoine, some guy has been looking for me, and I'm fairly certain that it has something to do with Barbara. I can be at your house in just a couple of hours."

"Call me in one hour at another number. Here it is." She gave Fortin the number of her sister-in-law who lived four streets away. She'd go there and wait for the call. Her sister-in-law, Stella Chicoine, was visiting her son in Pennsylvania at the moment, but she had a key. She broke the connection and went to the hall closet where she retrieved a jacket, hat and a pair of gloves. She'd be at Stella's house in plenty of time to gather her thoughts and prepare for the next call.

Fortin checked his watch and drove north into New Hampshire and then into Maine. He pulled off the highway in Kittery and drove along Route 1. There were several shopping outlets and plenty of public telephones. When the hour passed, he made his call.

"Hello?"

"Mrs. Chicoine, this is Dr. Fortin again."

"Look. I'm taking a chance but if you want to come here, I'll talk to you. I'll fill you in when you get here. Now, come to the address I'm going to give you. Do you have a pencil?"

"Fire away."

She gave Fortin the address and asked, "Do you know how to get here?"

Fortin had relatives in the general area but didn't know Auburn well. Liddy gave him exact directions.

"I'll be there in about ninety minutes."

ELEVEN

Fortin met Liddy at the address she's given him. "This is my sister's house. She goes away in the winter and I watch her place for her." She appraised Fortin as if she checking out her daughter's new boyfriend. "So you're Dr. Fortin. Barbara told me she was seeing a shrink, and I guess I get to meet him. I'm Liddy Chicoine." She stuck her hand out and Fortin responded. Her grip was sure and strong.

"Are you a psychiatrist or a psychologist?"

"-ologist, Mrs. Chicoine. I got my masters and doctorate at Texas Wesleyan."

"I got my R.N. at St. Joe's over in Standish. Know where that is?"

"Just south of Sebago. Near Limerick, Westbrook. I've been there many times."

"From Maine?"

"My family came from Maine before they moved to Massachusetts." Fortin understood the natural suspicion that Maine natives had of those who came from anywhere else at all.

"Well, what's up with Barbara? She's a real wreck. Can't

seem to focus. Paranoid. Losing weight. I think she's got a major case of depression going on."

Fortin was reluctant to go into details about Barbara's condition, but he had to agree with Liddy Chicoine's diagnosis. "I won't disagree with you, Mrs. Chicoine, but I'm concerned that she's put herself . . . and me, as well . . . in the middle of a predicament, and she could be in danger. Physical danger."

"I got that impression. She took off from here like a raped ape. That husband of hers is nice enough, but there's something about him I never really liked. Not a Caspar Milquetoast, exactly, but the guy doesn't have the strongest backbone in the world, if you know what I mean."

"I never met her husband, Mrs. Chicoine. What can you tell me about him?"

"Nice enough. Polished. All that Oxford stuff going on. Their crap don't stink like regular folks'." He suspected that Liddy Chicoine would be direct, no nonsense, when he first spoke to her on the phone. Now he was certain. "But he's weak kneed. Good father, don't get me wrong. He's conscientious, and he does spend a lot of time with his son. Takes him to ball games, plays catch. Reads to him a lot. But Charles doesn't think for himself. Pliable. Tries to be emphatic and purposeful, but it doesn't come natural to him."

"Where did Barbara go, Mrs. Chicoine?"

"No beating around the bush with you, is there, Dr. Fortin? Well, I spoke with Barbara a while ago while you were on your way here. She's safe and she's with family. I'll tell you where she is, but you have to promise me that you won't reveal it to anyone. If I found out you did, I'd have to hunt you down and kill you, and believe me when I tell you that I'd do it. It's just that I'm getting too old for that." Fortin had no doubt that Liddy Chicoine had the resolve to follow through; this was not an empty threat.

* * *

Sir Geoffrey Ramsden made the drive to Thirsk at dawn. He wanted to be ready as soon as James appeared. On the front seat were his newspaper as well as a large coffee and a scone. In a small container on the floor of the front seat, Ramsden had all the tools he'd need to succeed in his undertaking this morning: A bar of Cadbury chocolate, a fruit drink laced with Demerol, and a small single dose syringe containing three milligrams of Propofol. For the dogs, two lovely red steaks that he had injected with Demerol; that would hold their attention long enough. He felt confident that James would drink his sedating juice, and the concentration was sufficiently enhanced to induce drowsiness in just a minute or two. The Propofol would knock the kid senseless for perhaps two hours, and that was necessary if he wanted to keep the boy quiet on the ride back to the Ramsden estate in Cartmel. He'd need to get this into James quickly and there was some risk involved, but he felt confident that he could do so.

His cell phone was fully charged and he knew exactly what he'd say to Charles Whyte when the time came. As soon as James was safely asleep in the rear seat, he'd call and say: "Charles, please call your mother and father at once. Tell them that they should not look for James, even though they'll be certain he's in the back yard playing with the dogs. If they contact the local police, please be assured that James will not live to see the next sunrise." That would be it. Neat and tidy and the ideal insurance policy to keep everything under control.

Ramsden pulled into a side street, unfolded his newspaper and began read about the Prince of Wales and his upcoming journey to America. From this vantage point, Ramsden could easily see the back yard of the Whyte's home, and he'd be ready to move as soon as James came out to play.

There were few cars on the way from Auburn north towards Quebec. The sky was moonless and he still had four or more hours to go to reach his destination. Fortin tried a few radio stations with nothing to show for it but country western, a religious station and an oldies station. Little in the way of news. He did locate a few CD's in the armrest and was grateful that Janet had the good taste to have Sam Cooke's "Live At The Harlem Club 1963" in her collection. He remembered listening to Sam Cooke singing "Bring It On Home To Me" as a teenager and loving it; "Chain Gang" was a favorite among his peers because that's what they called the educational system of St. Jeremiah's school.

Fortin sensed early in life a strong connection to some spiritual presence in his life. A child of practicing Catholics, he was reared as a member of that church and never raised any question when he began first grade at St. Jeremiah's grammar school. He found the nuns there to be generally kind and honestly concerned with his physical, emotional and spiritual well-being.

Sensitive, rather quiet and perhaps more introspective than many of his friends, he progressed through school a better than average student, though not at or very near the top of his class. When he reached high school age, he knew that many of his grammar school classmates would opt for the public education system, but he never raised the issue within himself or aloud. He was not just content to extend his Catholic education, he welcomed the smaller classes and the sense of continuity it presented.

Perhaps the public high school offered better chemistry labs, more current textbooks and a far higher level of sports activities; it also warned of less personal attention and a greater acceptance of bad behavior; he viewed the benefits as slight comfort compared to the closeness he felt among his peers, and felt entirely comfortable with his school's idiosyncrasies. A friend who elected the public school route, and who introduced a particular poignancy to even his more casual observations, told him that he probably would do better to stay at St. Jeremiah's for he was "a good kid, and good kids aren't as valued at the public schools." Whether or not that was true, the remark stayed with Fortin and rang as true to him as if it was a divine revelation.

Sometime in his sophomore year . . . he would have been fifteen or sixteen at the time . . . he attended a class where a guest speaker caught his attention, imagination and even his soul. Father Gerry Callahan, a Maryknoll priest, discussed his experiences as a missionary in Africa and South America. The adventure he described, along with the horrors of violence, poverty and premature death, grabbed Fortin by the lapels and shook him to his core. He decided before the class was over that he needed to learn more and approached the priest. How did Father Callahan come to realize his vocation? (He was eighteen and just starting college when he met another missionary and began a conversation just like this.) Did his family encourage and support his life choice? (His mother did; his father had died earlier; and his brother and two sisters tried to dissuade him from enrolling in the seminary.) Did he ever have second thoughts about the choice he made? (Not often, but he knew the sacrifices he would make, accepted them, and immersed himself in an urgent and needed life task that left little room or time for questioning.)

Fortin left the conversation there and didn't raise the issue to the forefront of his consciousness until one of his teachers, Sister Mary Joan, approached him after classes a few days later without provocation and with a definite sense of purpose: "Andrew, Father Callahan mentioned that you expressed interest in the priesthood, and he asked me to give you this." It was a pamphlet on the Maryknoll missionaries, a full-color recruiting tool with a name and contact numbers on the back.

He accepted the pamphlet with a little embarrassment, for it was no longer just a personal and private question. He did indeed have an interest, and the priest had made a striking impression. Now, someone else knew there was something inside Andrew Fortin that sought at least clarification if not outright encouragement. He found this troubling and became wary of asking further questions. Simultaneously, he found himself being viewed by Sister Mary Joan and some of the other teachers as a potential "candidate", and he resented what he saw as an assumption that he'd enter the seminary.

That possibility had been in his mind, but he preferred it to stay right there, to be dealt with later, and not now. He was in the middle of his teenage years, mentally undressing the cheerleaders at football games, and not anxious to abandon the quest he shared with most of his male classmates: How to get Martha Visnoski (or any number of other females in his class) to let him feel her fabulous body, and maybe even get a return squeeze. That was his quest at the moment, and forsaking that kind of bliss for a life of celibacy was not running a close second.

It was later, at least a year later when a parish priest, Father Evans, approached him after morning Mass and asked to visit with him in the rectory. "You probably know that Sister Mary Joan talked to me about you. She told me you'd make a terrific priest." He said this rather solemnly, looking at Fortin directly in the eyes. "I told her I'd talk to you, but I thought it was too early. I can't say I know you very well, Andrew. but I'd guess that you've got more on your mind than whether or not you want to be a priest. Like, maybe, girls-college-girls-money-girls-car-girls. Am I right?"

Fortin just nodded. He was not prepared for this discussion, nor did he welcome it.

"If you're anything like I was at your age, talking about going into the seminary isn't one of your favorite things. I just want you to know that there are a lot of young men, like yourself, who have the seminary somewhere in their thinking . . . maybe not first, or even second or third . . . but it's there nonetheless. If it's something you really want to consider, if it's anywhere on your mind at all, I just want you to know that you ought to open yourself to the possibility and not discard it out of hand. Keep your mind open to it, and keep your heart open to it. If it's something you think you want to talk about, I'm always here. But I can only give you some practical information and maybe some guidance. The real conversation you need to have is with your conscience and with God. I can help, but I can't decide; I wouldn't want you to make that kind of decision because of any other reason than you welcomed the call. Is that fair?"

"Yes Father," was all Fortin could think to say.

"Okay then. If you've got a question, let's hear it. Otherwise get going to class. And stop by after school if you want to chat. Maybe around three o'clock?"

Fortin nodded and was glad to be released from the conversation.

He did return at three, having used much of his day forming some questions, and returned again several times over the months to follow. Eventually, he did choose to enter the seminary and did so after graduating from St. Jeremiah's High School. Some of his friends badgered him about the decision; a few others just drifted away as soon as they heard from him that he'd made that choice; not a single friend did anything more than wish him well, and he suspected that they hoped he'd grow out of the idea and return to reality. Never had he felt so alone.

Life at the seminary was filled with classes he felt comfortable with, and with discussion groups in which he felt far more uneasy. Unlike many of his fellow seminarians, Fortin was less inclined to open his heart to a crowd. His favored discussions were one-on-one affairs, not group interactions where he felt he had to scrape his conscience about the subject at hand just to appear involved. His colleagues, though, included many who used the group to either expound on a singular, usually shallow, subject of little common interest, or on topics that, to Fortin, seemed petty. Many, he learned over time, were gay. Few, to his chagrin, were the serious-minded young men of substance he expected to find upon his arrival.

Keough finally dropped off to sleep when the phone rang and woke him up. The caller was Ramsden and he was not happy with the developments Keough had to report.

"What do I have to do to get this job done properly? Charles has been compromised by his wife, for goodness sake. You can't even handle a simple break-in. Now you tell me you lost him entirely?"

Keough explained how he finally located Fortin's truck but not Fortin himself. He had no idea where he was. There one possibility left, but it was a long shot.

"Where do you *think* he's run off to?"

Keough wanted to slap Ramsden but kept his cool. Ramsden went on.

"You've got a big day coming up soon and I don't want to see everything bungled. If you can find this Fortin fellow, then do it. But don't let that interfere with your primary task. Get that done, and you must do it well."

Driving into old Quebec was like nothing else in North America. More European than most cities in Europe, he thought. The heavily walled city was a treasure of eighteenth century architecture, and he had not been here for a visit for nearly two decades. Then, the occasion was 'Carnival', the annual party celebrated in late January in the depths of winter.

Going to Canada was still an easy affair for U.S. citizens, and passport requirements wouldn't be in effect for at least another year. For people from New England, crossing the border into Canada was not much different from crossing the border between Connecticut and New York. But to Fortin and many others, the old city of Quebec was a magical place.

Fortin made his way along the Grand Allée and searched for Rue de la Chevrotière. It would be to his left, and only a quarter mile or so before outer city walls. He turned and found a parking space across from the convent. The convent was a great grey granite and red brick structure spanning the length of the block. At the center was a gabled entry and he climbed the stairs, rang the bell and waited. The door was opened by a tiny elderly sister dressed in the traditional black habit. She had a narrow wizened face and a broad close-mouthed smile. In his unpracticed French, Fortin introduced himself: "Ma Soeur, je m'appelle Andrew Fortin, et je viens à la recontre de Mere Marie-Jean."

"Oui, M. Fortin, venez avec moi et prenez une chaise ici. Je croit que Mere Marie-Jean vous attends." With a nod, she motioned to a green upholstered chair in the hallway. The nun reached for a black telephone, surely a relic of a prior age, and dialed a number. "M. Fortin, ma Soeur. Et il parle bien Francais."

Moments later, a middle-aged woman clad in a navy skirt and white blouse appeared at the far end of the hallway. Walking toward Fortin with broad strides, she extended her hand and greeted him in English in a strong voice with no trace of an accent. "Dr. Fortin. Welcome to the House of the Good Shepherd. I'm Mother Marie Granville, and I've heard a great deal about you."

"I hope it was good, Mother Marie."

"It was. Please, Doctor, come with me. We have a little bit of a walk ahead of us. And please call me Marie."

They walked to the rear of the building and ascended a narrow and rather steep set of stairs. "There are three more flights like this, so I hope you're in good shape."

"I'll be fine. Thank you."

As they made their away up the stairs, she said, "Sister Agnes tells me you speak excellent French, Doctor."

"It's been years since I've had a chance to speak it, but I grew up with the language in my home. It comes back to me when I have a chance to have a conversation."

When they reached the top floor, Marie stopped outside a doorway and rapped twice. "Barbara, it's me. And I have a guest. May we come in?"

The door opened and Barbara Whyte's appearance caused Fortin to do a double take. Pale to the point of ashen and thinner now than he'd ever seen her, Barbara Whyte was able to smile as she stood back and welcomed the pair into her small room. "Please, come in. I'm so glad you're here, Doctor Fortin."

Marie walked in without hesitation but Fortin paused and reached for Barbara's hand. She held it and began to sob. "It's alright, Barbara." He moved to her and held her closely as she sobbed. Marie reached for a box of tissue and held it out for Barbara.

She made an attempt to compose herself and smiled. "I'm such a mess. I'm just so glad my Aunt was here and could take me in. Everybody here has been wonderful."

Marie smiled and spoke. "It's not like it's crowded here, Barbara. Every sister here could have six rooms to themselves and there'd be plenty of room left. Come on over here and sit down."

The room held a twin bed, a small night stand, two sitting chairs and a narrow table between them. Marie took Barbara to one of the chairs and waited for her to be seated. Marie took the other chair and motioned for Fortin to sit on the bed. No one spoke and Barbara blew her nose. "Thank you, Dr. Fortin for coming. I spoke to my mother and she told me you were on your way. I just don't know what to do. You read the packet I sent you?"

"I did, Barbara. I don't understand it all, but it certainly seems like your husband is involved in something very dangerous. Have you heard from him?"

"No. I mean not directly. Marie called him for me right after I called England to check on James. It's James I'm worried about." Her eyes were filled, and Mother Marie finished Barbara's comments for her.

"Barbara sent James to England a few days ago so he could spend a few weeks with her in-laws. It's something they'd planned on for some time. But Barbara called England this morning to speak to James and his grandparents have no idea where he is. All they know is that Charles called and told them that James was safe and not to call the police or that James would be harmed. It's terrible."

Barbara continued: "He was playing with their collies in the back yard this morning, and when they called him in for lunch, he was gone. I found out what happened from Charles and James is OK, but Ramsden has James now . . ."

"Where is he? How do you know that's where he is?"

Barbara looked down at her hands as she answered. "Charles said he got a call today from Ramsden, and he told him that he arranged for James to be brought to a safe place. Those were the words he used: 'Safe place', as if there's anything safe about it. It's a kidnapping! Charles is beside himself, afraid for James, and Ramsden has all these demands. Ramsden let Charles speak with James, and he sounds fine; nothing's happened to him, but Ramsden has him secreted away . . . he won't say where. It all has to do with those emails and the papers. You read them. Ramsden has Charles in a vise and he's using James to keep everything quiet."

"And you can't go to the authorities." It was a statement.

"No, no. It's too dangerous for James. Ramsden has him, and there's no telling what he'd do if Charles was exposed."

"So what do you want to do? You just can't sit up here and do nothing!"

"I've got to go to England, find James, and get him away from Ramsden. Then, when he's safe, I can put an end to this plan that Ramsden has cooked up. Until then, it's too dangerous."

"But we know there's some kind of plot that Ramsden has in place. Maybe the FBI can get to Interpol or something and get James back."

"No. No police. If Ramsden feels threatened, there's no telling what he'd do. And he's got James."

"So where are you going to go once you get to England. How on earth will you be able to find James?"

"I need to get James away from Ramsden and I can't do that from here. I know a little about Ramsden. If my guess is right, then he's got James in either his cottage in Tunbridge Wells, or at his family's estate in Cumbria. The cottage is small, though, and it's in a village. There are a lot of other cottages close by, so any changes . . . like a young boy staying there . . . are probably going to be noticed. The family estate is my best guess. It's a big house up in the lakes district, well off the major roads. He could be doing anything there, and no one would ever know."

"But you need a passport. Do you have yours with you?"

Marie touched Barbara's arm. "Tell him what we talked about."

Barbara was gaining strength and determination as she spoke. Fortin could see that in spite of her fatigue and loss of weight, she was a bundle of pure resolve. "My passport is in a safety deposit box back home in Massachusetts. I never thought I'd need it. I can't get to it quickly, so my aunt will let me use hers. I'll wear a habit. With a little luck and a little makeup, I can get in to England OK. I have a reservation . . . or rather 'Marie Granville' has a reservation on Air Canada to London tomorrow night."

"And then what?" Fortin didn't have much faith in Barbara's plan so far.

"I know where his estate is and how it's laid out. Charles and I stayed there three or four times over the years."

Fortin considered this. But the thought of Barbara going to wrest James away from Ramsden did not set well. "I understand what you're trying to do, Barbara, but what kind of help are you going to have once you get to England. What if Ramsden resists, which he most certainly will? Charles is in enough trouble right now, and if you get hurt, what happens to James?"

Marie interjected. "I agree with you, Doctor. Barbara is right, and James needs to be safe, but she can't expect to do that by herself. She needs someone to help her."

Fortin studied the face of Mother Marie Granville. Strong features, determined jaw. A formidable woman with a sense of purpose. He could envision Marie leading the charge, armed to the teeth, into the midst of the action and against the odds; his money would be on this middle aged religious woman coming out victorious. Barbara, even with the steeled strength of a woman whose only child was at risk, presented such a delicate alternative. He knew Barbara's will was there; would she have strength to pursue Ramsden and bring her son to safety? Marie interrupted his consideration. "I have a thought, Dr. Fortin. It would involve a strong commitment from you, but at this time and under these circumstances, I must ask you if you would provide the help that my niece so desperately needs."

Fortin was almost bemused by the suggestion. "You can't be serious, Mother Marie."

"I'm as serious as you can imagine, Dr. Fortin. Barbara will need help, and she will need someone who understands the situation. You know that going to the police is out of the question as long as James is being held by this menace, Sir Geoffrey." Marie shifted herself in her seat until she was face to face with Fortin. "You tell me, Dr. Fortin. What else would you suggest."

"Even if I thought I could help Barbara get her son back, I need a passport. And I can't go dressed like a nun."

Mother Marie stared like a laser into his eyes. With the barest hint of a smirk, she said to him, "Bonjour, Père Laroque."

Père Gilbert Laroque was assigned to the parish of Saint Dominique, and had as one of his assignments the celebration of Mass every morning at the convent of the Good Shepherd. Only eleven sisters were currently in residence at the convent, and with the rare visitor, they began each day with Mass in their tiny chapel.

Born and raised in the small working class community of Beauceville, some fifty miles south of Quebec City, Père Laroque was a distant cousin of Mother Marie Granville, and in fact their families' paths had crossed often. Père Laroque and Mother Marie had become friends and relished their shared histories. But where Mother Marie was solid and sturdy both physically and temperamentally, Père Laroque was, in a word, mild.

This morning, Père Laroque and Mother Marie sat at a small table in the convent dining room after Mass enjoying a cup of coffee and beignets, when Marie began the conversation that would soon cause great alarm in the usually compliant Fr. Laroque.

"Father, tell me, you have been to the Vatican, have you not?"

"Oh, Marie, it was a wonderful experience. I was there twice. Once, six years ago, I actually kissed the ring of the Holy Father. I will always remember that journey."

"Gilbert, let me ask you for a giant favor. I need to borrow your passport and some clothes."

The priest nearly choked on his beignet and struggled momentarily to regain his voice. "What? But why on earth . . . ? That's fraud! It's against the law!"

"I can't tell you all the details, Gilbert, but a gentleman needs to go to Europe and he needs a passport. His is not available right now. I am asking you for your help."

"And clothes?"

"He'd be going as a priest, in disguise. You're about the same size and have similar coloring. He doesn't have a beard like you, but we can work on that."

"I can't do that, Marie. This is dangerous, and it's crazy."

"I understand how you feel, Gilbert, and it is a giant favor, but I am asking you as someone you know, and I hope you trust. Another 'jarrets noir'." She used the term 'black shins' to describe the local term for people from Beauceville. The small city flooded so often from the spring swelling of the Rivière Chaudière that the residents gained a reputation for living shin-deep in mud for months every year.

"I don't know, Marie. You are asking me to do something illegal."

"Well, it could be a matter of life and death, and there's an eight-year-old boy's life involved. I need your help."

Laroque tried his best to be assertive. "No, Marie. I am sorry, but I must insist." "I need them today, Gilbert. The passport and the clothes. This morning."

"I must think about this, Marie." Père Laroque picked up his long black wool coat from the chair and walked slowly and silently down the hallway. He was unenthusiastic about the arrangement and Mother Marie knew that he'd be ruminating for a while on the subject. She was confident, though, that he'd come through for her. Theirs was a shared background and local loyalties were strong. The priest, younger by a decade than Mother Marie, nevertheless had a common heritage. They knew the same people, had been baptized in the same church, and tobogganed down the same steep hillsides on the east side of the Chaudière River. Their families had survived the same floods and placed flowers at graves in the same cemetery.

Besides, Marie knew that Gilbert Laroque was, even if a bit docile, a man of basic goodness and conviction. He would spend some time ruminating and, she hoped, conclude that the crime of passport fraud was a small one compared to the matter at stake. He trusted Marie Granville and her judgment; he wished sometimes that he had as much command and confidence as she.

Within the hour, Father Laroque reluctantly delivered the passport and a complete set of clerical garb, including a black hat and long black wool coat. "I'm letting you have my old coat, not my new one; that was a gift last Christmas from my sister, and I'm not going to part with it." Marie smiled as she accepted the passport and the garments, giving the priest a quick peck on the cheek as she did. "You are a blessing, Gilbert, and I'm going to make sure you go straight to heaven. Do you want to meet the gentleman who will be impersonating you?"

"I'd rather not, Marie, if you don't mind. Coming here with the passport and the clothes was sufficiently difficult for me; I already feel like a revolutionary."

"I understand, Gilbert. Thank you."

"I'd like to say 'it was nothing' but I can't. I just hope you are making the right decision here, and I hope that the young boy is OK."

"He will be."

"If I thought you were going, I'd feel much more secure about that."

With some judicious makeup, a fake beard and artful application of some grey hairspray, both Barbra Whyte and Andrew Fortin became Mother Marie-Jean Granville and Père Gilbert Laroque. The resemblance, though not entirely accurate, was, all agreed, sufficiently acceptable that observers would have to pay close attention to spot the ruse. Fortin was a bit taller and heavier than the slight Père Laroque, and Barbara was somewhat thinner than her sturdier Aunt Marie.

"I'm happy to say that I keep all the personal possessions of the young novices in storage bins in our basement. When they enter our order they forsake all their worldly goods. Of course, some of them decide after a time that this is not the life for them, and they leave, taking their possessions with them when they do. You are now enjoying the benefits of an entire make-up kit once owned by Sister Claudia." Marie nodded to the younger nun who was now applying the matte powder that concealed the make-up lines. "Claudia was an actress and a newscaster for local television before she joined us here... when was it?"

"Eleven years ago, Mother Marie. Most of the things I have here came from my days as a make up artist for the Canadian film industry. It's big business, especially in Montreal and Toronto. Vancouver is huge, too." She spoke as she continued her work. "I also did a good deal of work for US television studios. They produced many TV series in Canada. It saved them a lot of money and it gave me a good business at the same time."

Mother Marie was fascinated by the transformation that was taking place. "The powders might be old, but they still work! You two look like a couple of serious minded pilgrims. In fact, Dr. Fortin, I think you look more like a real priest than the real Père Laroque, but don't tell him I said so."

Sister Claudia smiled and admired her work. "Eleven years away from it, but I think I did alright. What do you think?"

The pair studied themselves in a mirror and concurred.

Fortin said, "I was actually in the seminary for a time many years ago, so being dressed in a cassock and a Roman collar doesn't feel terribly out of place."

Mother Marie joked, "No wonder, Doctor Fortin. Perhaps you can hear confessions for us before you go? We might all need it."

The British Airways flight from Montreal to London's Heathrow had few empty seats in coach, and those were commandeered by passengers who'd spread out, ready to sleep during the seven hour flight. Barbara sat in a window seat, dressed in the full habit of the Good Shepherd sisters and gazed outside waiting for take off. Fortin asked the attendant for pillows and blankets and they settled in. Neither was hungry or anxious to watch a movie, and Fortin asked that they not be disturbed. He turned off the overhead lights and watched the lights of the city of Montreal.

Both were in a state of near exhaustion when the plane finally taxied down the runway and rose into the ink black sky. When the plane rose to forty thousand feet, Fortin managed to drop off into a half-sleep. Barbara Whyte simply stared out the window.

Finally, Fortin dropped off entirely and the first of his dreams began.

He'd been called by Fr. Evans one afternoon at his office. After a minute or two of phone chat to get reacquainted, Fr. Evans asked Fortin to drop by the rectory in the next day or so, and Fortin agreed. He knew that Evans' health had been failing, that he'd had a serious heart attack, and that he had taken a position as a nominal pastoral assistant at a church in Marlboro, just a few miles west of Fortin's office. He drove directly to the rectory after his last patient and found Evans asleep in his chair in one of the side rooms of the house. He was about to cancel his visit and leave without disturbing the priest when the priest awoke and asked him to sit with him.

"I'm sorry, Andrew, but I'm finding myself nodding off more than I'd like lately. Chemo and all that."

Fortin was not aware that the elderly priest was suffering from cancer along with everything else. "I'm sorry, Father. I didn't know." His complexion was grey and yellow, the skin hanging from the once powerful bones.

"So, I understand you're doing well in your profession and that you've helped a lot of people, and that's part of the reason I asked you here today." He rearranged himself in his chair, wincing in pain until he found a more comfortable position. "Close that door, would you, and grab a chair."

He studied Fortin's face for a moment with a searching look before he spoke. "I've always liked you, Andrew, ever since you first served Mass for me. I thought you were bright, quick-witted, and above all, compassionate. That's not a common-place combination, you know."

"Thank you, Father. I enjoyed our talks as well. You were a big help to me."

Evans brushed the compliment away and began. "I don't have a long time left on this earth, Andrew, and the chances are good that I won't see the end of the year. All this cancer is taking its toll, and I can feel my heart do some stuttering from time to time. 'Parts is parts,' they say, and mine appear to be all wearing out at the same time. By the way, reach into that cabinet next to you and get the bottle and a couple of glasses."

Fortin looked in the base of the side table and found a nearly full bottle of Johnny Walker Black and some tumblers.

"Pour us a couple fingers, if you don't mind." Fortin did so and handed the priest his glass. The priest held the glass up to the light. "God bless those Scots, Andrew. Give them some cold water, a lump of peat and a fistful of grain, and they know exactly how to make the best of the situation." After a sip and a sigh, he continued.

"I asked you here for a specific reason, Andrew. There's a good chance that I'm not going to be around very long. If you're a betting man, put odds on my never seeing next year.

Maybe even next month." He studied the amber liquid and rotated the glass slowly. He took another tiny sip before he continued, still looking deeply into the amber.

"There's been a rumor going around the Catholic Church that it's better to leave this life with a clean soul than it is with a soiled one. I sort of take that as true. And since my time is short, I'm taking that rumor a bit more seriously than I might otherwise do."

He looked Fortin square in the eyes when he went on. "There's also a rumor going around that confession is good for the soul, and if that's the case, it's probably wise of me to do those things that would be good for my soul. It's sort of like getting your car washed and shined before you bring it to the dealer to trade it in; whether or not there's a benefit to that, the process has its own rewards. So, in my own way. I'm asking for your help in cleaning up this old heap of a soul. Andrew, I want you to hear my confession."

The words caught Fortin off guard. "What? I'm not a priest." Fortin was sure that the priest was pulling his leg.

"Tell me something I don't know, Andrew. And I'm as serious as a heart attack. I want to say my confession and I want you to hear it." The priest repositioned himself in his chair and continued. "I've been thinking a lot lately about this, and I know that you can't hear my confession officially, but you certainly know the drill. All that time in Catholic school and then the seminary. You know it a lot better than some priests I know."

"It's not just the ritual, Father. You know very well that I can't give you absolution. I was never ordained. You need to be talking to a real priest."

"Andrew, I know the rules better than you do, so don't go telling me what you can do and can't do. And besides, I'm the one who's dying here, so I'm the one with the most at stake. I'm not doing this on a whim, Andrew. I've been praying and thinking about this for a while, and the God I know is benevolent and fair. I never went for this 'vengeful' God that you hear about. What kind of decent being would create something like the human race and then beat the crap out of them for eternity because they broke a rule like this? Honestly, would you want to spend the rest of perpetuity with somebody as hung up as that? I think my God is a being of more consequence than that."

Fortin listened to every word and read the earnestness in the priest's expression. He meant it. "So God is going to give you a pass on this?"

Evans chuckled at the choice of words. "In a sense, yes. For that matter, He's given me the authority to forgive you and grant you absolution, if you have trouble with this. 'Whose sins you shall loose on earth,' and all that. So as far as I'm concerned, I've covered the bases."

Fortin was not fully convinced by the priest's logic, but he was not one to dwell on ecclesiastic details. Here was a sane and sincere man with need to speak, and he was not going to deny him the opportunity. Fortin took a long sip of the scotch himself and waited.

The priest saw the acceptance on Fortin's face and began to speak. "Look, Andrew, we all come from places that we sometimes want to forget. Even when we want to remember some of those places, we usually only recall fragments here or there. But every one of those fragments is important, and those are what we use to reconstruct ourselves. Does that make sense?"

Fortin nodded in agreement but wasn't sure where this was going.

"I mean, there are times in my past that I remember clearly and others that are only dim memories, if they're there at all. But whether or not those memories are good or bad or somewhere in between, they are parts of who I am today. And, whatever brings those memories back . . . just simple thoughts or sights or even smells . . . just like Proust and his madeleines . . . they lead us to little clues about our past. They lead us, then, to who we are . . . and they even lead us to our future. I'm rambling, I know, but bear with me.

"Many years ago, as a much younger priest, I had an encounter with something . . . with someone. That encounter changed my life, and I think it changed it for the better. It was a woman I met who was kind, and gentle, and smart, and sensitive. She wasn't what you'd call a stunner, if you know what I mean, but she was eye-catching just the same. She had a freshness and a way about her that still brings my heart joy when I think of her. This woman didn't have an easy life by any means, but she managed to face life in such a way that she cherished every moment and seemed to find delight wherever she looked.

"I wasn't looking to become involved, and certainly not in any sexual way, but I truly enjoyed her company, and she would have told you, I believe, the same thing. In any event, she was alone, a widow, and she and I fell in love. There was no denying that there was a lot of lust involved as well. I have to say there was a passion and an energy that we shared. I'd be lying if I did not tell you that I thought she was lovely and that the moments we were able to be together were among the most beautiful memories I have."

He took another sip and closed his eyes before he continued. "We were lovers for a year and three months. Sometimes, we'd steal away in the middle of the day. For the most part, we just sat and talked. She was wonderful. I felt refreshed and renewed every time I was in her presence. She was a beautiful human being, inside and outside." He sighed and stared into space, as if reliving the scenes.

"But let's face it, Andrew, I knew . . . we both knew . . . that we were in the wrong. We talked about it at length and agreed that I ought to ask for a transfer to another parish. We both cried our hearts out, and I did. I asked the bishop to be sent to a mission in downtown Boston where my time and energy would be consumed with the street people and the drunks and the homeless. These were high maintenance people, and I loved the work. I dove into it head first. Over time, I overcame the urge to revisit the connection I had with this lovely woman, and eventually, I put the relationship behind me. It's been over twenty years. I didn't maintain contact with her, and that's just as well. I also never confessed it. Not to anyone.

"A few days ago, while I was at the hospital waiting get to hooked up to the bag of chemo, the tech, a woman of about fifty, was inserting the IV and I smelled the perfume she wore. I was lucky, because chemo tends to take your sense of smell away. I inhaled the aroma and closed my eyes, and was immediately transported to another time and place. I had a fragment of a memory, and that led to a clue, and I remembered all at once all the joy of the time I spent with the wonderful woman of my past. I asked the tech the name of the fragrance and it was 'White Linen' from Estee Lauder."

At once, Fortin recognized where the conversation, this confession, was going. "My mother."

"Yes, Andrew."

"I had no idea."

"Then I guess we were pretty good at hiding our secret, your mother and I."

"And that's your confession?"

"Yes. I'm acknowledging that I was at fault, and asking you, and God, for forgiveness." He studied Fortin's face. The news that his mother had conducted an illicit affair had surely stunned him. His brow was creased and the priest could tell that he'd given Fortin a great deal to digest.

"I was with my mother when she died. She never said a word."

"I learned of her death from the newspapers. I cried when I read the obituary."

"It was a beautiful death, if you can call it that. It's one we'd all want to have, if we had our choice."

"I'm glad to hear that, Andrew." The priest took another sip of his scotch, and drained his glass. "She was a bright light in my life, as I'm sure she was in yours."

Fortin reached for the bottle and poured another splash in the tumblers.

"Do you have any regrets, Father?"

"Regret isn't the right word. I have no regret about what we shared. We were both adults, and I really don't think I abused my position as a priest to gain your mother's trust or her love."

Fortin leaned closer and said, "But as a therapist, I counsel people all the time, and I do my level best to gain their trust."

"I'll bet you're very good at that, Andrew."

"But Father, if I took advantage of that trust, then I'd be absolutely out of bounds."

"You're right. If I wasn't your mother's official personal spiritual counselor, I was certainly in a position of some authority. In that sense, it was definitely an abuse of my status as a priest. But regret? No. Is that pragmatism? Am I just excusing myself for my bad behavior? Truly, Andrew, I don't think so."

"More than just the issue of violating a trust, did you violate your own promise you made when you took Holy Orders?"

"Absolutely! Yes I did. That's the other half of my sin, my regret, so to speak. So I can't honestly say that I'm sorry that we shared something special, or that I believe that I violated a trust with your mother. My sorrow is this: Our relationship could have seriously compromised your mother's self-image as time went on, and also I'm sorry about perpetrating a fraud upon my flock. They have a right to expect their priest to walk the walk."

Andrew interjected, "I can't speak to your flock, Father, but I can tell you that my mother lived life on her terms. She had periods of deep depression as long as I can recall . . . I can see that now . . . but those periods were there well before she ever met you. But she also knew how to take pleasure in life. She never lost her sense of humor, and she certainly didn't appear to be pining for a lost love after you were transferred."

"I know she talked about being a mother, and the fact that she needed to focus herself on that role, and that she wanted to set a good example for her kids. And I talked about my being a priest, and the fact that I had my own role in life. Both of our jobs were important to us. Denying ourselves the pleasure of our presence and our love was a huge price for both of us, but we were willing to pay it."

"And you want forgiveness from the son of this woman you loved?"

The priest nodded.

Andrew rose from his seat and walked to the window. "On one condition, Father." He paused and waited. The priest asked with his eyes what the condition might be.

"That I forgive my mother first. And then you."

The priest nodded and smiled. "Certainly."

TWELVE

When Fortin awoke much later somewhere high over the north Atlantic, Barbara was looking at him and almost smiling. "You were calling somebody's name."

Fortin yawned and stretched as well as he could in the cramped seat. "What was I saying?"

"For a while, right after you fell asleep, you were really serious. I couldn't make out any words, but you were mumbling something. Then a while later, you were almost smiling and saying 'Jessica" or "Jess." Is that someone you know?"

"As a matter of fact, yes. It was a long time ago."

"Well, normally it wouldn't make much difference, but remember, you're dressed as a priest, and here you are calling a woman's name." Barbara's smile broadened. "You certainly got the flight attendant's attention."

"Oh well, she'll have a good story to tell her friends. How long until we land?"

"Another two hours or so. You got yourself a good sleep."

"I think I needed it." His mouth felt like it was paved with sawdust. He signaled for a soft drink and turned to the newspaper he's brought on board. The headlines of the Montreal Gazette, one of the few English language papers in Quebec, dealt with tomorrow's trip to the US by the Prince of Wales. The first stop for the Prince was Boston. "I'll bet Charles has to be involved with this," he said, tapping the paper.

"That's what I'm afraid of. I can't figure everything out with Charles' notes, but I'm afraid that something is going to happen when the Prince gets to Boston. I want to believe that I'm putting too much significance on this whole thing, that I'm expecting something very sophisticated, something clever in those notes and codes. I mean, wives and husbands do it all the time in wartime, communicating to each other all sorts of facts that slip by the censors. 'I'm sorry that Aunt Betty has the flu; will write again soon,' might conceal the military intelligence that Sergeant Smith was being posted from Fort Hood to Kuwait next Saturday. The notes that I saw made reference to Burberry's on Newbury Street. I'm afraid something's going to happen there."

Fortin looked as his watch, still set on Eastern Time. "The Prince should be getting into Boston any moment."

Patrick Keough was dressed in a navy pinstripe suit, starched white shirt and burgundy silk tie. His black oxfords were polished to a mirror finish. The sky was brilliant and the air unseasonably warm for this time of year. He strode into the Ritz front door with a purposeful stride. A man on a mission. In his briefcase was the weapon of the day, the Beretta M501 sniper rifle that he brought for John Murphy, who, he was sure, was already awaiting his arrival on the roof of the hotel.

The weapon had been repeatedly tested and fired. Murphy was in awe of the Beretta's accuracy and had described it as a surgical tool in his last conversation with Keough. "I can pluck a hair from a guy's beard at a hundred yards and he'd barely blink." Murphy had adjusted and readjusted the sight to be absolutely accurate at one hundred yards, which was coincidentally not very different from the distance he'd need today. For in approximately thirty minutes, just after eleven AM, a passel of limousines would appear on Newbury Street, and the Prince of Wales would make the first stop on his U.S. visit.

The U.S. State Department furnished a good part of the security for the Prince's visit, and a dozen or more agents would be working today to keep the Prince safe. Keough looked out the window of the Ritz and saw two staff members already in position. They were easy enough to identify, dressed as they were and wearing dark glasses and a coiled earpiece. They were positioned near the front door of Burberry's awaiting the arrival of the Prince. Once the Prince arrived. they'd be joined by several others, all intent on keeping the Prince enveloped in a protective circle as he made his way into and out of the store. Four mounted Boston Policemen were also stationed near the store entrance, and they were extremely effective at keeping crowds under control.

As in past US visits, the Prince liked to visit the store and to say hello to the manager and chat up the staff. It was a wonderful photo op for the newspapers back in London. Then it would be a short drive to the Westin Hotel at Copley Place for a brief reception and a light lunch. Unlike past visits, however, this one would have a bit of excitement, courtesy of John Murphy and his Beretta M501.

Murphy and Keough had practiced their plans a dozen times so far. One shot from a crouch. Immediately disassemble and place weapon in the briefcase. Stay low and enter the stairway. Take stairs to eighth floor and proceed to elevator. Exit elevator on first floor and use Arlington Street exit. Turn left and walk to Beacon Street. Total elapsed time two minutes twelve seconds, give or take. Elevator delays could add up to an extra forty seconds.

There was one minor change in plans, but Murphy need not concern himself, Keough mused. Before he left his apartment in South Boston, Keough made a slight adjustment to the sight on Murphy's rifle. Just a single turn to the front of the sight and a half turn to the rear.

Keough entered the elevator and pressed the button for the eighth floor. He's take the stairs up the remaining flights to the roof and use the opportunity to make sure that his exit in a few minutes was not impeded by sacks of trash, workers, or whatever. But the way was clear and he slowly opened the door to the roof. Murphy had jimmied the lock when he arrived some time ago and left it ajar for Keough's use.

And there sat Murphy, Indian style on roof next to an air conditioning condenser, shielded from view by any other surrounding buildings. For this occasion, Murphy was dressed in a Blue Suit, white shirt and tie. He even wore black leather shoes. "You need to look the part, John," Keogh had cautioned at an earlier meeting, "and a black T-shirt and denim overalls won't get you into the front door of that hotel. So you need to look smart."

Murphy gave Keough a brief nod of welcome. Keough bent low, attaché case in hand, as he quickly approached Murphy. He squatted in front of Murphy and unsnapped the case. Without saying a word, Keough and Murphy examined the unassembled Beretta. Murphy smiled as if enjoying the presence of an old friend, stroking the stock with almost a caress as he snapped and clicked and screwed every part in place. He winked at Keough and belly-crawled twenty feet to the southwest edge of the roof where he slid his arm through the rifle strap and remained poised below the two-foot high parapet and out of sight. This was his spot, and from prior reconnaissance, the perfect location from which to rise and view the events below and across the street at Burberry's.

Seven minutes passed before they heard the police sirens and the resulting commotion on Newbury Street below. Another two minutes passed before the small motorcade arrived. Leading the procession were two Boston Police motorcycles followed by a black Rolls Royce limousine, the Prince's own. Following was a Cadillac limousine, this one most likely carrying a complement of security staff, and trailing were three police cruisers, one from the City of Boston and two from the Massachusetts State Police. The four Boston Police Officers on horseback took up their positions on the wide sidewalk. All the while, Murphy never looked back, but remained entirely focused on the task.

He knew his instructions. He was to remain hidden and below the parapet until the Prince completed his visit and made his exit from the store. The visit was scheduled to take no more than ten minutes. The Prince would exit the glass revolving door wave to the crowd, pause for photographs and then the limousine door would be opened for the Prince's departure. Murphy would use the outside crowd noise to determine when the Prince was preparing to leave. Then, with everyone's attention on the Prince, he'd extend his upper body to the top of the two-foot parapet, crouch, aim and the rest would be history.

The visit took fewer than the ten allotted minutes according to Murphy's estimate, and the crowd noise level began to rise. Murphy took a deep calming breath and raised himself to the top of the parapet, a small masonry wall about two feet high. He crouched and used his elbows to balance the rifle and capture the Prince in his sights. He watched the Prince shaking hands at the glass fronted store entrance with one of the shop workers. He made his exit, and, true to plan, paused and waved to the crowd.

He was in the crosshairs of Murphy's sights . . . a head shot . . . and Murphy silently counted to ten. The trigger action was swift and sure and the recoil was imperceptible. And at once, Murphy saw, to his horror, a shower of glass as the bullet smacked into the revolving doorway directly behind the Prince. The sound of the shot echoed in the concrete and granite canyon that was Newbury Street. It seemed to Murphy that a full second, maybe two, elapsed during which the scene remained frozen. Then the screaming began and the Prince was being hustled face first in the direction of the limousine.

Unbelieving, Murphy prepared to fire once again when he thought he saw Patrick Keough appear at his left, also crouched. As he struggled to keep the Prince in his sights, a task made difficult by the security personnel and police rushing him to the safety of his limousine, Murphy felt a sudden sharp shove at his back. The rifle fired wildly, its bullet chipping off a sliver of granite from the fourth floor of the building adjacent to Burberry's, and Murphy felt his entire body lifting over the edge. He had no time to react, no chance to consider what was happening, no handhold on which to grab, no foothold to maintain his position. In a fifth of a second, he began to cartwheel over the edge of the roof. Two seconds later, with barely sufficient time for the moan "Oh shit" to escape his lips, Murphy made impact, left shoulder first, in the alley below, just a few feet from the sidewalk where the crowd remained in its panic. The beautiful Italian rifle remained attached to Murphy and protected from the brunt of the impact by the strap. He never felt a thing.

Keough didn't wait for Murphy's body to make its way to the street level. His instructions were explicit and his planning was exact. As soon as he lifted Murphy over the edge of the roof, he was on his way quickly to the rooftop exit. The crowds below erupted in shouts and general chaos and the motorcycles blared down the street with the two limos and the following cruisers on their tails. The four officers on horseback made a brave attempt to calm their horses, secure the area and determine the extent of the injuries. Meanwhile, Patrick Keough strolled through the Ritz lobby and out the Arlington Street entrance. Three minutes and four seconds after Murphy fired the shot, Keough crossed Beacon Street and walked towards the MBTA's Park Street Station.

Richard Panel sensed something was wrong before anything happened. Alert to his surroundings, he was still on edge after the long flight from London. He was paying close attention to every move the prince made and every word the prince uttered. That was his job, and with paparazzi and reporters at every turn, there was no such thing as a casual remark or a careless gesture. He scanned the scene as he followed the prince out of the front doors of Burberry's. There was the official photographer, recording the scene; three other photographers huddled together directly in front, but a respectable twenty feet away, with cameras at work; they were probably independents hired by the European paparazzi for the prince's visit. At the end of the street were two remote television trucks. Their cameras were at a greater distance away, their reporters already having recorded their voiceovers.

Panel glanced up to the sky and saw the sun's refection in the windows of the Ritz across the street. The sky was a clear blue, the air much warmer than that in London for this early July day. When he did this, he thought he saw someone leaning over the corner of the roof high across the street. He would have guessed it to be a large person from this distance. For a reason he couldn't define precisely, he had the uneasy impression of something awry. Just then, the glass shattered behind him and over his head and he simultaneously saw a flash appear from the same direction. In the immediate ensuing confusion and the rush to seek cover and protect the prince, he caught just a glimpse of a human form flailing wildly as it fell.

This mental movie clip was immediately filed away in the panic that followed. The prince remained immobile, looking up at once at the shattered window. Panel gripped him by the arm and pulled him in the direction of the open rear door of the limousine. He was aware that he was manhandling British royalty, quite roughly as it turned out, but gave the prince a powerful shove when they reached the passenger compartment. Now, covering the prince's body with his own on the floor of the limousine, he tried to concentrate on the matters at hand. The prince remained immobile. The chief of security for the mission climbed in and slammed the door closed. With his pistol drawn and aimed up, he barked orders at the driver to "Move it! Move it!" The limo roared west along Newbury Street. In the front seat adjacent to the driver was the Prince's personal chief of security, shouting directions to the driver.

The street had been blocked to vehicular traffic for two blocks in preparation for the prince's visit, and a Boston police officer remained, lights flashing on his cruiser, standing at the intersection of Newbury and Clarendon Streets. Responding to the shouts from his two-way radio, he leaped into the cruiser, turned his cruiser to the left, pulled forward and remained in position, blocking traffic from Clarendon, as the black Rolls Royce limousine approached at speed. The intersection was clear, but he'd have to time his take off with precision. Accelerate too soon, and the cross traffic, unaware of the crisis at Burberry's, could be wiped out by the prince's heavily armored limo; accelerate too slowly, and the heavily armored limo would crawl up his cruiser's tailpipe and send him to eternity in a tangle of wrinkled metal. He held up his hand in a stop position to hold the Clarendon traffic and jammed his foot down on the gas pedal as the limo slued around the corner and stayed just feet from his tail. The cruiser led the limo, now followed by a motorcycle officer and another cruiser, across heavily traveled Boylston, St James and Stuart Streets, and veered to the right and the on-ramp of the Massachusetts Turnpike.

The instructions were clear and the entire public safety force in and around Boston was mobilized in moments. The VIP entourage was to proceed west along the Turnpike to the State

Police Troop E Headquarters. State Police, already on alert due to the Prince's visit, were dispatched to the highway to pull all traffic from the road and afford the Prince and the rest of the vehicles in the motorcade quick and unhindered travel. At Troop E Headquarters, the Prince would be brought to a safe room and a preliminary assessment should be available. The underground bunker of the Emergency Operations Center in Framingham could be reached in less than ten minutes if necessary.

Panel remained atop the Prince until he felt the security chief's hand on his shoulder. "How are we doing down there?" Panel looked up. "So far, there's no indication that there's any further threat." Panel rose to his seat and helped the Prince gain his own seat in the rear of the limousine.

"Your highness," the security chief went on, "we're heading to a secure location, but it appears that there's nothing to fear."

Panel tried to make sense of the past seven minutes as they headed west at one hundred ten miles per hour. He'd replay the events as he saw them and knew that he'd have his opportunity to share his impressions when he was later debriefed.

On Newbury Street, however, that sense was not shared by everyone. The streets surrounding the Ritz and Burberry's were closed off as dozens of police officers and emergency personnel did their work. Witness interviews were being conducted in the lobby of the Ritz, but the central focus was on the crumpled mass of bone and flesh that was once John Murphy on the sidewalk. The rifle, too gained the interest of everyone involved with the scene. Its polished stock, oiled barrel and powerful scope, protected as they were from the impact, lay across the victim's back. Yellow tape had been stretched across the area to protect the evidence and allow the investigators to do their work.

Detective Jerome Wetman was talking to his partner as they

approached the area where four uniformed officers stood guard around a sheet covering the corpse.

"I told you already, I asked for this case as soon as I heard where it was. There might be a connection to a guy I talked to the other day. Besides, can you see Bell and Cooper handling this? They were on tap to get this, but they could screw up a funeral."

Collins knew better than to interrupt.

"So I'm talking to this guy the other day and Burberry's and the Ritz come up in the conversation. Then all of a sudden there's a window blown out of Burberry's while English royalty is paying a visit, and a guy falls off the roof at the Ritz. Real coincidence, don't you think?"

Collins bent down and removed the sheet. Wetman had a notebook opened to a blank page and a felt pen at the ready. "Without the benefit of the Medical Examiner's preliminary evaluation," Wetman said, "I'm going to make my first assessment: He's dead. What do you think?" His partner, Collins, was accustomed to Wetman's irreverence in the presence of death and mayhem, but was much less given to his partner's levity. He stared at the body and the weapon.

Wetman went on. "Foreign made. Look at that beauty. The scope itself must be worth a grand or more."

Collins stood back up and answered in his baritone, "I'll go along with both of your guesses. No argument from me. What do we have so far?"

"Now, look, take this from someone who hasn't even been officially assigned to the case yet, but we have one Prince of Wales visiting this high fashioned raincoat store. He walks out, waves to his fans, and a weapon is fired . . . here's another guess: we're looking at the weapon in question . . . and the slug strikes the glass and shatters. There may have been another shot, although there's a hellacious echo in this canyon, and a couple people will say they heard four or five shots in a row.

The aforementioned Prince of Wales and his entourage rabbit out of here and Mr. Shooter-slash-Victim here goes plop where we now see him even before the limo takes off."

Collins just nodded and continued staring.

"So I figure we've got a guy who missed his shot, grew suddenly despondent, and committed seppuku in shame."

That, at least, got a small smile from Collins.

"Another scenario is he takes his shot . . . I'll even concede a second round, but it's unlikely . . . and misses. He tries to adjust his aim, or whatever, and slips off the edge of the roof, and here we are."

Collins nodded. "We're getting warmer. Are we sure the shooter was on the roof? Do we have anyone checking the hotel rooms across the street?"

"We've got two rookies doing the hotel check, but I don't think we'll find anything." Wetman's radio crackled. "Let me take this."

Collins took a step closer to the body and crouched down to get a closer look. The blue polyester suit was new. The shoes were hardly worn on the bottom. A bulge in the rear pocket of the pants might be a wallet. He'd wait for Wetman to return before he took a look. He'd also want photographs. This guy's not going anywhere, he thought.

Wetman appeared at his side and assumed the same crouched position. "That was from one of our rookies. They're not finished with the room checks yet, but the door to the roof was jimmied open. They even found one spent casing on the edge of the roof. There's also an open briefcase on the roof that was designed for a rifle to be broken down. Oils, cloths, extra ammo inside. I'm letting the room checks go on just in case, but this is a roof job."

"I think we've got a wallet here. Do we have a photographer yet?"

"Right over there." Wetman waved over a gray haired overweight man in a wrinkled blue shirt. Two cameras were hanging over his shoulders.

"Wetman and Collins both slipped on their gloves as the photographer started clicking away. The bulge was indeed a wallet, and the driver's license inside was that of a John Patrick Murphy, thirty-two, with a Charlestown address. Without doing a more complete analysis, Collins and Wetman agreed that this was their person. Wetman barked the license number into his two-way radio.

Collins felt around the pockets and found a small leather case. He removed it carefully and opened it up to find an array of lock picks. So that explained the jimmied door to the roof, Collins thought.

"The M.E. just showed," Wetman said. "Let's wait over here until he's done. I want to talk to that mountie over there anyway." Collins and Wetman walked in front of the shattered glass window of Burberry's. Another crew showed up with stanchions and drapes and enclosed the scene where the body lay while the Medical Examiner donned gloves and studied the corpse.

The mounted policeman stood next to his tall chestnut horse and acknowledged the presence of the two detectives with a nod. "Hey Jerry," he said to Wetman. "Is this one yours?"

"We're probably just sticking with that dead guy over there. There's bound to be all sorts of brass doing the whole coordination. So what did you see?'

"Not much. We're just here for crowd control and for show today. You can tell there's not a huge crowd. So I'm right here where we are now when the prince waves to some people and a shot is fired. The echo was strong, but it was definitely from above. The glass storefront shatters and the bigwigs run to the limo to take off. There was a second shot, I'm pretty sure, just when this guy you're looking at does this solo flight, arms waving around, and lands right where he is now. I didn't see exactly where he came from; I'm guessing the roof, because I thought to look across the street after a minute or two and there weren't any open windows across the street. I just saw him coming down fast."

Collins asked. "And there was nobody else on the roof when you looked up?"

"Nope."

"Thanks for the info," Wetman added, "and copy me with your report, if you don't mind."

"Sure, Jerry. So it's Murphy, right? John Murphy?"

Collins and Wetman both looked stunned. Wetman asked the officer, "How do you know? This guy been busy?"

"If it's the same John Murphy I know, then he's been in and out of small time stuff for a while. Some fights. Likes to get wrapped up tight and walk across the bridge on North Washington from Charlestown and insult our Italian friends in the North End. Not a good thing for a Townie to stir up a bunch of Italians with short fuses. Those guys, I swear, they do it for sport. This John Murphy, he brags a lot about his old man, him being I.R.A. and all that."

"What do you mean?" Collins was deeply curious at this turn.

"His father . . . I think his name is Roger or Rogan . . . goes back and forth to Ireland all the time. John claims his old man's a freedom fighter. He likes to tell war stories, like his dad is the last of the gallant heroes. Lot of rumors about sending money and guns from here to Ireland. That wouldn't surprise me. But John lives a little through his father, if you know what I mean?"

"Thanks," said Collins. "Thanks a lot."

To Wetman, "So where's our second guy? Where did he go?"

"Second guy? You're thinking like I am. This guy didn't jump; he was pushed. So we got a push-ee, and we need a pusher."

They made their way to the M.E. who was removing his

gloves when they arrived. "You guys didn't need me on this one."

"So no sirens on the way to the ER, huh?"

"No, Jerry. This guy is what we call, medically speaking, 'dead as a haddock'. We've got to do the autopsy anyway, but this man's got nothing left of his face, upper left torso, or even much of a neck. Sort of pushed all together at impact. Not that the guy had much of a neck, anyway. He was 'well-muscled', as we say."

"We think his name is John Murphy. A brawler from Charlestown. And it's 'deaf' as a haddock or 'dead' as a door-nail. You gotta little metaphor mixing going on."

"It's all those Latin words in medicine; I get confused, Jerry. In partial redemption, however, I will say that the poor fellow is indeed deaf. He can't hear a thing."

He picked up his black bag and continued. "Anyway, you're probably right about this chap. Those Celts are born to fight. My wife's a Flaherty, and her brothers are fairly typical. They can't stand too much peace, or they get all edgy and start to break into a sweat. This fellow here has fists like hams, and I'm guessing he's about 240. Look at his knuckles and his eye-brows; a spider web of little scars. He's had more than a few fistfights in his short life. Probably had his nose broken a few times in his life as well."

Collins said, "We'll look for the report when it comes in, but thanks for telling us what you could." The M.E. nodded and walked back to the police cruiser that brought him here.

Collins said to Wetman, "Let's take a closer look at this guy." The corpse was on its back, now, and the rifle lay on a sheet of plastic next to it. After a few silent moments, Collins said, "What do you say we take this rifle down to ballistics and see what they tell us? Hanging around here isn't likely to give us much."

"I'm calling the guy I spoke to the other day. He had some

strange paperwork that talked about some of this stuff and I don't like the coincidence."

Wetman's radio came back on. He took a few paces away and recorded the info in his notebook, returning then to Collins. "We're on the money so far. John Murphy it is. Dirty sheet, but not filthy. Looks like a bunch of anger management issues. And the word has already gone out: this guy's our case. It'll be official when we get back."

Collins marveled at Wetman's connections within the department.

Charles Whyte didn't even want to be there, but under the circumstances, he didn't see a choice. Ramsden had arranged to take his only son James from him and spirit him away to some unknown location. He was forced to participate in the royal visit festivities, and his heart and soul were elsewhere.

Now, White's face was as ashen as his surname suggested. Standing at the edge of the Prince's entourage at the event, he and other higher ranking members of the Consulate staff were barely forty feet away from the spot where the apparent shooter landed. The sound of the impact caused Whyte to turn in the direction of the sound, and he stood immobile at the scene. Only after the Prince was hustled into the limo and the car made its hurried departure did he reconcile the sight of the crumpled mass of flesh, the rifle, and what was supposed to have been a carefully scripted, ultimately non-injurious scheme. Death, even an accidental one as apparently this fellow had suffered, was not anticipated. The entire stratagem was to stage a contrived attack. Keough was to take the shot, miss, and leave his rifle, along with its history in earlier IRA scenarios at the scene.

Whyte had met Keough on a few occasions and had only recently handed over a satchel filled with fifty thousand dollars, all in twenties and fifties. He knew Keough to be tall and rather slender, yet here, on the pavement, was a much broader, burly man. This certainly was not Patrick Keough.

He wanted to get in touch with Ramsden right away, but the confusion after the shooting was followed quickly by the area being cordoned off. To Whyte, it looked like at least a score of patrol cars with dozens of police, uniforms and plain clothes, descended on the scene within six minutes. The process of being recorded as a witness and running through the questions and answers took over an hour. He finally made his way to Arlington Street and walked in the direction of the Four Seasons Hotel. There, the street was clear of police vehicles, and he hailed a cab to return to his office in Cambridge. In the Consulate upon his arrival, the staff was in a panic. This was the skeleton crew that remained behind during the royal visit to Boston. They all wanted to hear Whyte's account of the incident; at the moment, he was the highest ranking member of the consular staff on the premises, and they were desperate for details. They'd also been fielding phone calls from journalists as well as UK citizens.

Whyte rushed to his office and closed the door. Using the secure line, he punched in Ramsden's private number. Ramsden was almost gleeful when he answered his phone. "Smashing!" he said when asked if he'd seen any reports of the day's events in downtown Boston. Everything went according to plan. I can't wait until we hear from the Republicans denying any knowledge of the attack. It will make for some great sound bites."

Whyte interrupted Ramsden's rapture. "Yes, I'm sure. Sir Geoffrey, how is James? Tell me."

"He's just fine, Charles. I should ask, given the events of the day, what you've heard from Barbara. Where is she, Charles?"

"I have no idea, sir. You must know that."

"No, I do not. I was hoping that James being under my care

and supervision would have provided you with some greater level of motivation. After all, if she was aware of James' disappearance, I expect she'd be frantic with worry. But, rest assured, your son is as safe as a babe in his mother's arms. Did you know he fancies those expensive video games?"

Charles was in no mood to engage Ramsden in such a discussion and immediately jumped to the next subject: "Sir Geoffrey, something is not right. Someone died today. I saw the man myself. It was horrible. He fell and landed just a few yards away."

"I'm sure it added drama to the scene, didn't it. Have they identified the fellow?"

"Not yet. At least I haven't heard anything. There were so many police around, but all the news is still rather sketchy. But sir, it wasn't Keough. I know that for certain."

"I'm sure it wasn't, Whyte. There was a late development that caused Mr. Keough to modify his plans. There will probably be a release of some information later on, and I'm sure it will make some prominent people stand up and take notice."

"But there wasn't supposed to be any injury, sir. This is horrible, and it changes the whole dimension of the plan."

"Relax, Whyte. It's not as bad as you think. You'll see. The fellow that died was a man with a perfect background for our cause. I dare say, Boston will probably see a drop in its crime rate now that he's gone."

Whyte couldn't believe his ears. What was Ramsden talking about? He knew that there'd be a death? He actually planned this?

Before he could process the information, Ramsden went on. "Listen to me. We still don't know where Barbara's run off to. And we don't know what she might have told her bloody psychologist. This might be a great day for "Shamrock", but I still want to find out where Barbara is and what she's done with the information she has."

Whyte was careful to keep his contact with Barbara . . . the single telephone conversation with Barbara's mother . . . concealed from Ramsden. "I'm still searching. I don't think she's told anyone about what she's seen."

"I beg to differ, Charles. According to Patrick Keough, Dr, Fortin did receive a packet on Saturday. I suspect that it contains some very incriminating information."

Whyte was unaware that Ramsden had another set of eyes on the scene. "Even if she did send something, it was all in code! There's no way he could assemble the pieces and conclude that there was any kind of a stratagem involving the events today. Who saw all this? Was it Keough?"

"You're backtracking, Charles, and you're asking too many questions. As soon as we learn that Barbara has revealed nothing . . . or at least nothing of any importance . . . then James will be back at his grandparents' home safe and sound. It's imperative, though, that we learn Barbara's whereabouts so we can verify that everything is still protected from any scrutiny. You understand, I'm sure. We have made great progress today, and I'm convinced that the plan will bear fruit, but we must contain the problem."

Contain the problem? That could mean anything, and most of the possibilities were bad. "I want to speak with my son. I want to know that he's safe."

"In good time, Charles. Let's see what develops in the search for Barbara, and then we'll go from there. Meanwhile, I'm keeping the radio and television on waiting for the next shoe to drop. I'm sure it will be fascinating to listeners, especially those with a direct involvement with the Ulster Loyalist and Republican discussions."

The evening airwaves in the UK were interrupted within thirty minutes of the shooting. Word of the event traveled quickly. News analysts were already referring to the US as 'the

wild west', where 'guns are as easy to obtain as a box of chocolates'. The Prince of Wales was unhurt and out of harm's way,
and that was the good news.

By the early morning hours, the identity of the late John
Murphy was public knowledge, and his background on the
seamier fringes of society, and his paternal connection with
the IRA was news fodder on both sides of the Atlantic. Now
the analysts really ran riot. Here was a known criminal and
IRA sympathizer taking shots at the Prince of Wales.

In Belfast, a terse announcement was made by the chief of
the Loyalist delegation to the Northern Ireland peace talks.
Discussions with the Republican Sinn Fein were suspended
until further notice. A formal announcement would be made at
a later time. Protestant marchers donned their orange sashes
and held impromptu demonstrations. One group of toughs
overturned eleven cars in the Catholic neighborhoods, set two
Catholic churches afire, and beat a young man nearly to death
outside a pub in the Catholic section.

Ramsden sipped his Cockburn's port and smiled when the
news was announced.

In a pub in Gort, not far from Limerick, sat a stout curly-
haired man watching the television closely. When he first heard
the news, he was alarmed that the peace process might be jeop-
ardized; he was tired of the fighting, sick of the deaths and
burned out by the harm and destruction of the past decades.
His hair was nearly completely white, well ahead of his years.
His multiple scars that he once wore like badge of honor were
no longer sources of pride. One went through an eyebrow. Another crossed a cheek and the uneven stitching left him with a
twisted expression. His nose went west where it should have
south, and his heart was heavy with grief. When the name of
John Murphy was connected to day's events, he sank to his
knees. The publican rushed over and helped him to a seat in the

snug. "I need your phone, Kevin," he muttered when he was seated. The publican returned with a cordless phone and a full pint of Smithwick's.

"Here you go. Make your calls. And let me know what else I can bring you." He made frantic telephone calls across the ocean to friends and relatives, confirming his worst fears. Now, John Murphy's face was appearing regularly on television screens throughout Ireland.

He called the public over and returned the phone. "Thank you, Kevin. I'd like to use your room in the back if you don't mind. When Danny and Joe come by, would you tell them I want to speak with them?"

The curly-haired man waited alone in the private back room. Within the hour, his two friends entered, shook his hand, and took their seats. It was like a wake without the body of the deceased. He pushed the curls behind his ears. "You've never met the lad, but I'll tell you that my Johnny's not that smart," he said to his mates. "A good boy, but this wasn't Johnny's doing. He'd boost a car as quick as shake hands, but this? No. There's something else going on." He took a long draft of his Smithwick's. To his colleagues he said, "I'll need you lads to do some poking around for me."

In a conference room at the State Police Troop E Headquarters, two investigators sat in folding metal chairs on one side of a folding table. Richard Panel sat on the other side. The taller and older of the two investigators had a pen and paper on which he was capturing the results of interviews with those who were with the prince when the shot rang out. The younger and stouter of the two asked Panel, "Could you go over that once more? You saw somebody at the edge of the roof across the street?"

"Yes, I'm certain of that. It was a large sort of person."

"Male?"

"I think so, but I can't be sure. If it was a female, it was a large one. As I said, I didn't intentionally focus on the person."

"Go on."

"I saw a flash, and I assume it was the rifle firing. Simultaneously I heard the glass shatter on the storefront. Then there was a huge echo of the gun shot. That's when we all rushed to get into the car."

"You said something else was odd. What was that again?"

"Sometime after the shot was fired and we were scrambling into the back seat of the limousine, I glanced back up at the roof and I'm fairly certain that I saw that same large person coming off the edge. Then, his arms were waving around and he was falling to the ground."

"He was falling?"

"That's what I saw, but it seems to me he was pushed. I don't think he jumped off. He didn't just fall. He was propelled from the edge of the roof. At least that's what it looked like to me."

"Did you see who pushed him?"

"No. It was just a sense that he was pushed. I didn't see anyone actually do it."

THIRTEEN

The plane carrying the two religious visitors to London landed ahead of schedule in a light drizzle. They double checked each other's religious garb before wending their way in a line towards Customs. There was no sense whatsoever getting nabbed for a wrinkled wimple this far into the scheme.

They cleared Customs without incident and were passing a newsstand when Barbara stopped suddenly and pointed. "Look at that." Fortin bought the London Times and together they read the front page. In large letters: 'Attempt on Charles' Life in US.' In smaller letters beneath: 'Prince unharmed/ Shooter dies in Fall/IRA Connection Seen.'

"This is exactly what Charles and Ramsden were setting up in advance," Barbara said in a low voice. "You saw the notes and the emails. It makes sense." Barbara had already guessed at the seriousness of the plot that her husband was involved in, and Fortin had the same grave feelings. Now, as they read together, the references were clear: Newbury Street, Burberry's, the Ritz. Charles Whyte and Sir Geoffrey Ramsden had orchestrated an attempt on the life of Britain's Prince of Wales.

"We need to let the authorities know, Barbara. We can't just leave this alone."

"No! Not yet. As long as James is in Ramsden's hands, we're not going to tell a soul. There'll be plenty of time for that after James is safe."

"But they were calling Boston a 'left hook', and London was 'the knockout punch'. That means there's a second half of their plan, and it's going to happen here. We can't just sit back and watch."

"Yes we can, and we will. We're going to get James out of danger first, then we'll contact the police, or Scotland Yard, whatever. But until then, no word to anyone. You have to promise me that." His agreement was unenthusiastic but accepting. Barbara was balancing the events against the safety of her son; there was nothing that would make her shift her opinion under the circumstances. If he found himself in the same place, he guessed he'd do the same.

An hour after they landed, Barbara Whyte and Andrew Fortin, traveling as Mother Marie Granville and Father Gilbert Laroque, were sitting on a train in the London Underground system and heading to a hotel in Russell Square where they had early check-in. After they checked in to their adjoining rooms at the Hotel President, they met in the lobby, with Fortin still dressed in their religious garb and Barbara in street clothes.

Barbara Whyte bought a Michelin map of Great Britain and together with Andrew Fortin, they mapped out their plans. First stop would be Ramsden's house in Mayfair. They'd do this via the Tube. While they did not expect to find either Ramsden at home or James confined there, Barbara wanted to rule it out as a possibility. Fortin, dressed in religious garb, would go to the door and call on the owner for a donation to the Christian Relief Fund. Ramsden, if he were home, would certainly not be at the door to answer the call; he had staff for that. There just might be some indication from the Ramsden's staff as to his whereabouts. Unlikely, but there was that chance.

From there, they'd return to the hotel, pick up some clothes and head east and south to Royal Tunbridge Wells. Ramsden maintained a cottage there and used it as a quick escape from the city, especially on weekends. Barbara had visited the cottage and had spent a few weekends there with Charles. "He could be generous, and once or twice he gave Charles the key to his cottage in a wink-wink, nudge-nudge sort of thing. You know, take the young lass away for a day or two." Ramsden, again, would unlikely be there, but Barbara wanted to rule that out as well. "It's a small place close to the village center. I doubt if he'd be able to keep James there and out of sight, but it's near enough to London for us to check it out without wasting much time."

The third leg, and the one most likely to bear results, was the much longer drive north and west to the beautiful Lake District in Cumbria and the small town of Cartmel. That was the most likely location, and Barbara and Charles had also visited it and spent time there. "It's far from the road, a big house with tons of history and tradition. It was his parents' and his grand-parents' house before that. When Ramsden's father died several years ago, his mother moved to a small house about twenty miles away in Windermere."

Then they set out. As predicted, Ramsden wasn't at his Mayfair home. The woman who answered the door explained that Ramsden was away for a brief rest. "What with the events of the day in the states, I'm sure he's not getting any rest at all."

Fortin said he understood. "Probably gone to his cottage, I suppose?"

"Not sure where he went," she responded, not appreciating the comment.

Fortin apologized for interrupting and suggested he'd call again another day.

Royal Tunbridge Wells was a one hour drive from Russell Square, and they reached the village in mid afternoon. The cottage was shuttered up and no one was in or around it. By this time, Fortin was as hungry and as tired as he'd been in recent memory and he suggested that they take a break before they continued. Barbara urged that they achieve just a bit more distance. "Let's just get around London and start north. If we can make it to the M1 today, we'll have a good chance of getting to Cartmel by mid-day. In fact, let me drive if you're that tired."

Fortin willingly gave up the driving task. Having to concentrate on right hand drive and the left-hand traffic patterns of England took its toll, and he was happy to sit back and leave the chore to Barbara for a while. He checked his watch. It was nearly 4 in the afternoon.

Barbara took the motorway around London and caught the M1, heading north.

The drive was complicated by an enormous traffic jam near Luton. Barbara fiddled with the radio in their rental car and found a local station with a traffic report. The prospect of moving quickly was unlikely given word of a tractor trailer accident ahead. Given the late hour and the traffic, she pulled off the M1 and found a hotel in Harpenden. Tomorrow morning, they'd schedule an early departure so they'd be at their destination by mid-day.

The hotel was located near the center of the town and they ate dinner in a small restaurant nearby. Exhausted after their overseas flight and their full day, they returned to the hotel and their adjacent rooms where they both slept the sleep of the dead.

At 7:00 am the next morning, they were in their car and heading north once more. Traffic was moderate, and the weather was clear. Barbara calculated that they'd reach Cartmel by lunchtime. She was excited about the possibility of finding James and anxious to bring him to safety and away from Ramsden. She read updates on the attack in Boston from the pages of the London Times and noted that a definite IRA connection was established. John Murphy, whose father was a known IRA activist, was positively identified as the shooter. The fall from the roof was described, as was the Italian sniper rifle that was used. Police were speculating that Murphy must have lost his balance at the moment he took the shot at the prince and then fell to his death. Ballistic tests were being conducted and results would be available in another day or two.

After the paper, Barbara told stories about her time in England, the places she'd seen and the people she met. One of them was Ramsden's mother. "A striking lady. She was tall, elegant, and very real at the same time. Her husband was still alive when I first met her, but he was ill and eventually confined to a nursing home because of his health."

"Wasn't he a diplomat or something like that? I remember you mentioning that to me one time."

David Ramsden was a career employee of the government of Great Britain. Educated at Cambridge, he spent several years in various diplomatic posts. He never sought an ambassadorship, even with a stellar portfolio. Instead, he focused on serving on special projects and assignments throughout his career. "He was involved in settling the separation of Hong Kong with the Chinese, and spent time in every major capital. He was one of those people . . . we'd call him a "go-to guy" in the United States . . . that the Ministers turned to in foreign affairs. He knew everybody who was anybody and was usually brought in when things got sticky."

Barbara met him once and found him stuffy and rather cold. "He wasn't one of those gregarious types. I think that's why he never wanted to be an ambassador. Too much limelight for his style. At least that's the impression I got."

"What his wife like?"

"Expressive, warm, very outgoing. Just the opposite of her husband. She came from a well-to-do family in Ireland, somewhere up north. I think her father was a college professor."

"So is Ramsden more like his mother or father?"

"I think he loves the limelight, and he's certainly outgoing. Loves to talk. So probably more of his mother there. But there's an icy part of him that he lets show once in a while. He's been wonderful for Charles and his career, but there always seemed to be something under the surface that left me chilled."

They kept the conversation going for much of their journey. Fortin learned about the various colleges at Oxford, which always baffled him. And Barbara gave a detailed history of her travels around the globe as the wife of a member of the Foreign Service. She had met many of the leaders of the world at one time or another at various affairs, but yearned for a more simple life, especially with the events of the past few weeks.

"I get the feeling that Charles and Ramsden have developed a strange relationship. Ramsden is always there for Charles, but there's a quid pro quo. I never saw it before, but it's almost sick. It's almost like Ramsden barks and Charles obeys. I think Charles is a better man that that, but maybe I'm wrong."

In Boston, Detectives Collins and Wetman sat in a booth at Dunkin' Donuts and discussed the findings so far. Wetman was displaying his suspicious side, the side that made the hair on his arms rise up when anything made his job easier. "So the test comes back and it's ID'd as a weapon used in a hit over in Ireland. Years ago. Does that not sound too good to be true?"

"Maybe it's just your basic 'gift horse'." Collins was sipping his coffee and downing his second jelly donut.

"No, this is starting to smell. We got a dead guy who made the shot and who just *happens* to fall off the roof at the same time. He's a dumb but basically harmless punk who has a father who's semi-famous in the Irish Republican Army that this kid *happens* to idolize. The very expensive, rare Italian weapon he's using just *happens* to be tied directly to some IRA murders in Ireland. And this guy just *happens* to freakin' miss his target from across the street. Not to forget that the guy he was shooting at just *happens* to be the freakin' Prince of Wales."

"And we've got another witness who's pretty sure he saw the shooter pushed off the roof." Collins flipped through his notes. "Richard Panel. He's traveling with the Prince. I agree with you. This is smelling like a set up all the way. But why? And why go through all the trouble and miss the target."

Wetman stared at his coffee and said nothing.

Collins started to get up. "Come on. We've got to check back in."

"Hold on, hold on. Who did the ballistic tests?"

"Sue Benidt. She's the one I spoke to."

"If you've got her number, give her a call."

Collins checked his cell phone and made the call. "Sue? Collins. Yeah, I've got Wetman here and he wants to talk to you."

Wetman took the phone. "Hi, Sue. Look, on that Italian rifle . . . yeah, the Beretta . . . could you check the sight for me? I think it's way out of line. Maybe test fire it at the range from the longest distance. Yeah. See if it's way off. I'll bet it is. And can you call back? Thanks . . . and about last year's Christmas party, I just want to say I'm sorry. Had a little too much. Right."

He handed the phone back to Collins. "I sort of played grab ass at the Christmas Party, and hers was looking mighty fine. I forgot for a second who her husband was."

"She mentioned something about that when I spoke with her. She got over it. And her husband, the guy who used to play tight end for the Patriots? He did too. Don't worry about it. She's the best we got over there, and if she says she'll get back to you, she will."

Fortin reached Janet Chapel's private pager number and left a message to have her call back. Twenty minutes later, he picked up the phone in his room.

"So what's up? You were supposed to call every twelve hours, remember? Fill me in. You just arrived in Canada last time you called. So why am I calling you in England?"

Fortin gave her a summary of his travels so far. Tomorrow, the pair would try venturing onto the estate. The thought of kidnapping a youngster caused her enormous distress.

"That prick! I can understand why Barbara doesn't want to bring in the police, but this is a sign of one sociopathic bastard. Like Miss Kitty always said, 'Matt, be careful'."

"We're going to scope out the place when we get there and see if we can make our way in."

"Well, on this end, you've got some other problems. Somebody's looking for you and he tried to break into your place. That white Ford you told me about? Todd saw it on your street and called the cops on the guy. He was gone by the time the cops came, but Todd was freaking. I spoke with him last night."

"Any idea who it was?"

"Nothing. Todd didn't get a plate number, and there must be fifty thousand white Fords within twenty miles of here. But let me tell you the best part?"

"There's more?"

"Yours truly was followed to work this morning by a white Ford. It's creepy, let me tell you. He must have checked your caller ID and found my number all over the place."

On her way from her condo to the hospital, Janet spotted the car behind her. She made two unusual turns on the way to her office and the car remained, sometimes two or three cars back, but ever there. When she pulled into the parking garage, she had the presence of mind to jot the license plate number on a sheet of paper.

"Did you call the cops?"

"Better."

"How better?"

"Look, the fucker pissed me off, OK? So I called another enforcement agency to handle it."

"Like who?"

"Think about it for a minute. I work with Carlo as his unpaid wine expert, remember? He thinks I'm the second coming of Christ. And besides, he loves me. I mean really loves me. And he's got lots of cousins, if you know what I mean. And these cousins all have lots of vowels."

Fortin had trouble digesting this.

"So Carlo makes a phone call and all of a sudden this guy is followed by Joe Goombah and his little brother, and they find out that he's on a plane to London from Logan airport. Coming in tomorrow."

"So do we have a name or anything? Maybe he's coming after Barbara or me?"

"No way. He's used a fake name to rent the Ford . . . some guy who lives in Florida. And as far as I know, no one knows you or Barbara have gone to England. But don't worry about that. He won't be bothering you."

"What makes you so sure?"

"Like I said, Carlo has lots of cousins. Some are over here, some are back in Italy, and it's a very international enterprise he's connected to."

"So this guy is going to be trailed over here too?"

"You are a regular Dick Tracy, Fortin."

Word of the connection between the assassination attempt in Boston on the Prince of Wales and the murders by the I.R.A.

in Portadown hit the news too late for the morning edition, but the television coverage was saturated with the development. Every talking head with any connection whatsoever with the IRA, Sinn Fein, The Royal Ulster Constabulary, and other parties were recruited as "experts."

Rogan Murphy got the news by telephone at 4 in the morning. Through a convoluted series of Boston connections involving members of the Boston Police Department, the local Boston Mafia and the infamous Winter Hill Gang run by Whitey Bulger, the FBI's most wanted man, Patrick Keough was identified as Murphy's Boston connection. Enough people saw Keough meet with John Murphy at Amrhein's on Broadway over the past several weeks to provide a clear description. Keough was last seen getting on a plane to London. Some gentlemen would pick up the trail with Keough in London and keep their eyes on him. Apparently someone else was displaying an interest in Mr. Keough, and they were not at all of Irish descent.

"So who's doing the following over here? I want that bastard."

"There'll be two gentlemen . . . maybe from Verona, for all I know. They're going to keep their eyes on him and let us know what he's up to."

"How come they want this guy?"

"It's a complicated story, but it's enough to say that he pissed off the wrong person. That person had some friends and those friends have even more friends. There's a net going around this guy and he's not going to get too far without somebody knowing about it."

"Do I know these two 'gentlemen from Verona'?"

"*I* don't know them or I'd tell you. Some of these folks are not exactly forthcoming with that kind of information. But my guess is if you stay fifty feet behind this guy Keough, you're going to be walking side by side with these two guys."

By 5 o'clock, Rogan Murphy was on the road to Shannon

where he'd pick up an early flight to Heathrow. He was not going to be left out of this.

Collins grabbed his cell phone and listened. Wetman waited for the news. When Collins hung up, Wetman was already planning the next move. "So I was right, huh? It was off by a mile. No wonder he couldn't hit the broad side of a barn."

"That was Sue down in ballistics. Sue said the sight was in perfect shape. Not a ding on it, and nothing bent. So somebody did a little intentional misalignment. Probably the guy we know as the push-er."

Wetman considered the implications while he drove. After a minute, he turned to Collins and said, "What do you say we turn around at the next corner and let's pay a visit to my good buddy, Kavvy."

Kavvy was Wetman's nickname for Joseph Kavanagh, former state representative and South Boston's favorite son. With a reputation as a fixer, Joseph Kavanagh enjoyed a singular reputation in the neighborhood. He had slipped over and under so many indictments over the years that many still referred to him as "Slip", and that's what Wetman called him when they found Kavanagh at Cronin's pub.

"Well I'll be a Polish Pope, if it isn't my good friend Detective Wetman! Pull up a seat, my man. And what brings you to our fair little section of the city? Good news I hope?"

"You've got enough bad news today already. I'm looking for somebody."

"You've got that right. The Orange flags are being waved all over Derry, and here we are with nothing at all to do with it."

Wetman smirked. "I'll bet. You're as pure as the driven snow."

"Nothing to do with it, Detective. That's what I said and I mean it. Not that the continued healthy existence of British

Royalty is something I pray for, mind you, but this? Not one of ours."

"Let's say I agree with you. What can you tell us?"

Kavanagh made a wave with his beer mug and he led Wetman and Collins to a booth some distance from anyone else. In a voice low enough to keep the conversation from reaching other ears in the tavern he said, "John Murphy had nothing to do with this except for some bad judgment mixed in with hero worship for his Da. No, John never quite caught on with the movement."

"So what's the story behind the story?"

"You know John's father, Rogan, was . . . is . . . one of the toughest warriors we've ever had. John never measured up to his old man and he knew that. But he was sitting pretty the last time he was seen in the neighborhood. He's a 'Townie', and you know that the Charlestown branch doesn't always mix well with us on this side of the river."

Wetman said, "I know more about that than I want to know. Remember Danny McHugh? That was one of my cases."

Kavanagh directed his comments to Collins. "Young Danny McHugh was a Charlestown lad who had the misfortune of passing away just outside these very doors. Hyperventilation, I think."

Wetman interjected for Collins' benefit. "McHugh was hyperventilated with seven rounds from a nine-millimeter Glock."

"It was a sad day for us all," Kavanagh went on. "Taken from his family in the flower of youth. But you're not here to discuss Mr. McHugh. It's John Murphy you're asking for." Collins and Wetman both nodded.

"Well, young John started showing up at Amrhein's every few days. Course we know who he is. But he's always there waiting to meet some other fellow. And when they get together, they're both sort of hush-hush. Like some big conspiracy, know what I mean?"

Wetman was getting impatient. "Give me a name."

"I thought it was Herlihy or something, but I'm told his real name is Patrick Keough and he rents an apartment down the street, but I wouldn't bet on that being his real name either. He's old country, that's for sure. We've not got ears on the side of our head to miss the accents, do we? And then our young Mr. Murphy had a shortage of discretion, so to speak. Liked to brag here and there. How he was training with a fancy sniper rifle and could clip the wings off a pigeon at two hundred yards, that sort of thing. But he didn't, did he? Missed his target by several yards, I'm told. And he didn't have a little slip and fall, did he? No, we happen to believe that Mr. Murphy's demise was a direct result of Mr. Keough's actions. And when we went to find Mr. Keough he was already gone away. We even know where he lived, but he's gone now. On his way to London as we speak."

"How do you know all this?"

"Well, you know how much I admire the Boston Police Department and their skills of investigation. The only firm I know who might be better at the job is . . . well."

"Give me a break, Slip. We don't have all day."

"Now patience is a virtue that you should cultivate, Mr. Wetman. It would serve you well. Let me just say that two men with some strong family connections have helped us in our quest to find out the truth."

"Family connections. Like *family* connections?"

"Exactly, my dear Mr. Wetman. Of course, we have friends in a lot of unusual places. In today's world, it's important to make friends and keep friends. And when Mr. Keough alights from his plane in London, he's likely to find some other *family* members walking a few discrete steps behind him. It's safe to say that Mr. Keough's days are precious few. Let's say a prayer for the man's immortal soul." With a wink and a smile, he raised his glass.

FOURTEEN

Barbara Whyte and Andrew Fortin arrived on the outskirts of Cartmel in the early afternoon. Barbara scanned the scenery and tried to become comfortable once more with the area she'd once known. She asked Fortin to pull over and park while she regained her bearings. "It's been years since I've been here, but this is looking familiar. There's an old priory in that direction, and I think Ramsden's estate is about two or three miles from that. Let's turn right over there," she said pointing to the intersection just ahead of them. "I think I'll recognize the streets, but go slow."

Traffic at this time of year was thick though, and more than once Fortin felt compelled to stop on the side of the road and let the impatient drivers get by him. "Tailgating is a national sport here," Barbara noted. "They ride right up your tailpipe."

They proceeded along a long straight road with steep hills on the right. "There's a narrow road leading to the estate, and I think it's about a mile ahead." Barbara was leaning forward in her seat. "Some moments later, she shouted, "There! Just turn in here!" Fortin pulled into a small street, a lane really, that wound its way up the hills. It was unpaved but well graveled and well traveled. "Look, up ahead. There's the house. You can just get a glimpse of it on the side of that slope."

Fortin crept along the road and it became progressively narrow. "I'm going to pull off here. We just can't drive up, ring the bell and ask if James is there."

"I know," Barbara responded. "I just wanted to make sure I could find it. Let's turn around and find a place where we can hide this car and walk up. We can at least scope the place out and see what we think of it."

Fortin reversed direction. Stone walls appeared on both sides of the road until he found an opening onto a field. He pulled the car into that area and parked behind a stone wall and a cluster of trees. "How's this?"

"Great. Let's get out and take a little stroll."

"Barbara, before we go too far, we're going to stand out like sore thumbs. If Ramsden sees us, we're all in trouble."

"You're right. Let me think for a moment."

From their location, Fortin estimated the house to be about a quarter mile away. He made a suggestion. "What if we go back to the town center and pick up some hiking shoes and clothes? We're dressed in street clothes, and we can't go walking along here like we are. We need something to make us blend in so we don't make anyone suspicious. Plus, we haven't had anything to eat, and we need to eat. We can get lunch while we're there. Then we can come back and see if we can get close to the house."

That made sense to Barbara. "It will give me some time to sketch a layout of the place, at least as much as I can remember."

After they picked up some corduroy pants, pullovers, walking sticks, caps and sturdy hiking shoes, they stopped in at a local pub and Barbara went to work on drawing a layout of the house as much as her memory permitted. Meanwhile, Fortin went to the publican and asked about getting two rooms for the night. When he returned to the table, Barbara started to describe the layout. "There's a big entry foyer with huge rooms to the left and right, then a hallway to the kitchen in back. The stairs in the hallway go upstairs to the bedrooms. I think there are four or five of them."

Fortin raised a few questions. "Is there a basement?"

"I think so, but I've never been down to see it."

"How about a garage or other buildings? Like a shed?"

"There's a garage to the side, but it's not attached to the house. It's more of a barn. I'm trying to remember but I think it has at least three stalls. It's fairly big. I don't remember anything else. I mean, there are some arbors out back and some kind of gazebo or something in the rear garden. But I don't remember anything else."

"There a third floor, too"

"Yes, but I've never been up there either. Usually in these big old houses, those are the servants' quarters."

"Did he have any servants when you were here?"

"No. He always had a live-in maid in London, probably the one you met when you went there. But he didn't have anybody here."

"What about a living room, or maybe a TV room where he'd likely spend his time? He's probably watching the news about everything going on."

"I don't remember. There may have been a TV in one of the downstairs rooms, but I really can't remember ever watching television there."

Fortin looked at her drawing and studied it for a moment. "There's only this main entrance and one in the back?" Barbara nodded. "And where's the garage?" Barbara pointed to an area slightly behind and to the left of the main building.

"OK. Let's go change and meet back down here. Then we can go back and park out of the way, walk through the fields and get close to the house. And he knows you, so keep your cap on and wear your sunglasses."

Together they were on their way to the Ramsden estate.

BBC Television suspended its regular programming to focus attention on the events in Boston and the follow up reports about the suspected shooter and the weapon used. The Beretta rifle was indeed traced to a triple murder in Portadown in 1992, and the relationship of John Murphy and his father, Rogan, was explored in depth. Rogan had never been convicted of anything, but his role in several attacks over the prior two decades was the stuff of legend. Further, his Boston connections were examined, especially in light of several suspected arms shipments from that city to IRA members in the Republic.

Film crews were busy throughout Ulster with particular attention placed on Protestant marchers in Londonderry. Orange flags were everywhere, and the RUC could barely keep up with the firebombs and overturned cars. Ramsden was enjoying every bit of the coverage.

In the smallest of the bedrooms, he'd arranged a flat panel television and a comfortable sofa. Nearby sat two telephones on a polished mahogany table; one for his routine calls, the other attached to a secured and scrambled line. He'd poured a glass of Cockburn's to sip as he followed the news. James was secure in the basement, and he'd only just fed him when the special television reports began.

He detested the idea of kidnapping James, but given the limp wrested response from Charles Whyte to his demands that Barbara be located and silenced, he saw little choice. He didn't waste much time or energy considering the consequences and potential outcome; he was certain that neither Charles nor Barbara would bring in outside investigations given the effect it could have on the safety of their only child. No, he would likely release the child into his grandparents' care when the events in the US and the aftermath played out. Charles' willing complicity would assure such a high degree of security that Ramsden was certain that his Shamrock plan would not be exposed. The only other living and witting participant was Patrick Keough, and of his absolute silence, Ramsden was secure.

Of course, the scheme was dangerous, kidnapping being regarded as it was. But given the fact that not a single hair of the Prince was disturbed by the events in Boston, Ramsden was confident that Barbara could be made to see reason. The fact that Murphy fell to his death, well that was an accident, wasn't it. There were plenty of explanations for that.

Suddenly, the television flashed a crawling message across the screen: A special joint announcement by Loyalist Party head in Northern Ireland would be made shortly. Ah, thought Ramsden, finally a clear signal that any 'negotiating' with Sinn Fein would come to a close. This is what the entire project was all about.

He sipped from his balloon crystal of port and savored the sweet taste. Yes, sweet was the correct word for the moment. He glanced at his watch. It was past five and he was getting hungry. In the larder were some convenience foods he'd picked up and he knew there were plenty of choices. He'd made sure to have enough child-friendly foods for James, like pasta and cheese and baked beans with sausage. Every little boy liked those. But he also picked up some more adult foods suitable for a microwave. He didn't really enjoy cooking anyway. He just wanted some sustenance. He'd run down now and prepare something to eat. He wanted to rush back so as not to miss the announcement he'd been waiting for.

The sun was still high in the late afternoon and Fortin recalled that England, especially in the northern reaches where they were, would remain sunlit rather late into the evening given the nation's latitude. So relative darkness would not arrive for perhaps another two hours. Nevertheless, he and Barbara walked purposefully, as most hikers would, along the fields and back roads that crisscrossed the countryside. His new hiking boots were giving him a blister on his right heel and he tended to favor that as he walked. Barbara, on the other hand, would have walked through fire without complaint at this point.

Barbara suddenly came to an abrupt halt a few yards in front of him. "What is it," Fortin asked?

"Look! It's the top of his chimney. We're getting close."

"Then let's stick to the right side of this path to stay as far out of view as we can."

They kept their eyes fixed on the chimney and sidled along the right side of a gravel pathway that served as a one-lane farm road of sorts. In three minutes, Barbara came to a stop once more. This time, she lowered her voice. "Around the next curve, the garage will be in view. We have to be careful here."

"I think we'll want to go very slow for a while, maybe sit down over there near the clump of trees. I'd rather get there closer to dark than in this kind of light."

"Good idea, but let's get a little closer. There are plenty of stone walls and trees to hide behind along the way."

Now they took their time, taking slower steps and being more careful of the sounds of their footfalls. They made efforts to step on grass rather than gravel, even though they were still several hundred yards from the house.

After tossing a frozen entrée of beefsteak with a dubious brown sauce into the kitchen microwave, Ramsden set the timer and started up the stairs. It was then he thought he heard a noise. He stopped and cocked an ear. What was the source? He edged to the rear of the house and put his ear to the basement door. There was absolutely no way to escape the basement; he was sure of that. The three windows were barred many years ago, and they were too high from the floor for James to reach in any event. A bulkhead door gave access to the basement from the outside of the house, but it was locked twice; once from the inside with a padlock, and once from the outside with another. This door, as well, was secured with metal cladding and two keyed locks.

His ear pressed against the basement door, Ramsden held his breath and concentrated. No, it was only the soft sobbing of the youngster. Nothing with which to be concerned. He's made sure to have a television set and some video games for the boy's pleasure, and there was a small lavatory for his use. The basement was damp and a bit musty, to be sure, but this was not a lifetime sentence. A few days in the basement would do the child no harm. Ramsden straightened up and made quick steps back up the stairs to the television. He didn't want to miss a thing.

Fortin was leading the way now. The sun was setting and the half light of dusk was settling in. They could see the garage in plain view now, and the two doors were closed. In a few moments, they could make out the corner of the house. They were now within one hundred fifty yards. Then he felt a tug at his sleeve.

Barbara made a gesture with her left hand and leaned in close to whisper. "Let's go around to the left of the garage. We just have to make sure there's no one at the front windows looking out. We need to be sure he's here and not with any security."

Fortin nodded. If they went a bit closer and stayed low, they'd see the front of the house in full view. It would cut the distance they'd have to travel to reach the garage, and there were two large trees between them and the garage that could provide some cover. If there was anyone inside, chances are there'd be a light on somewhere inside. The chance they'd take in the semi darkness was the fact that they couldn't see inside any unlit rooms. But someone inside looking out would have the opportunity to see two figures, darkly clad, trotting across the front of the property.

Fortin paused under cover of some low lying branches to get a better sense of the house. He expected, when he heard the word "estate" applied to the property, that it would be a mammoth affair of brick or granite, with an enormous circular drive. Instead, he'd describe it as a very large house, partly fashioned of brick and standing on a granite foundation. The second story was of wood, and a third story with multiple dormer windows set into the roof surface, all of deep gray slate, reminded him more of the homes he'd seen in the Hamptons on the eastern end of Long Island. He could distinguish two chimneys with decorative brickwork poking through the surface.

The third story gables gave him the impression that the interior ceiling height would be lower than in the rest of the house, and Barbara's guess that this was most likely designed as servants' quarters was probably correct. Its multiple windows jutted out in every direction.

The second floor was built flush to the rest of the home's surface and featured tall windows and, from this distance, they appeared to have heavy drapes. The siding horizontal clapboard was painted pale yellow. The first floor, all brick, also held tall windows directly in line with the ones above. The front of the house had a porch-like structure. It was more of a gallery built the entire width of the house with a roof extending perhaps eight or ten feet from the front surface. It had a few chairs placed under cover, probably a good place to read a book or entertain visitors. Ivy grew up one side of the house to a height of perhaps ten feet. The basement appeared to be built entirely of large granite blocks. This was a solid house for someone with moderate wealth but smaller than he'd expected, perhaps fifty to sixty feet across the front and at least as deep.

The drive was circular but not grand, its surface of loose stone and gravel. The center of the circle contained a lush garden of flowers in all colors and heights. It appeared to be well tended and Fortin guessed that Ramsden had some hired help to keep the space in such beautiful condition.

Barbara tugged lightly at his sleeve, impatient to continue surveilling the property. In silence, he assented and they moved on. They neared the house with small careful steps and stayed as close as they could to the protection of the trees and shrubs that lined the pathway. This served as the main driving entrance to Ramsden's house, and if he decided to leave the house for any reason, they'd have to scurry quickly for cover.

Fortin stopped his progress and held up a hand. He whispered. "There's a light on inside coming from the back of the house."

"That's the kitchen."

"It looks like there's also some light on the second floor, but it's moving. It might be the light from a television set."

Barbara nodded agreement. Then she tugged at his sleeve. "Look at the basement window. Over on the right."

Fortin saw a faint light coming from the small basement window, but a light nevertheless. James. He looked at Barbara, whose attention was fixed on the same basement window.

"Barbara," he said. "See the first tree on the way to the garage? We'll go on three." Barbara nodded and watched as Fortin held up one finger, then two, then three. They trotted quickly to the protection of the first tree.

"Same thing. Next tree," he whispered and held up one, then two, then three fingers." In three seconds, they were now within twenty yards of the garage. "We'll go around to the left and stop. Are there any windows?"

Barbara shrugged her shoulders. She didn't know.

On Fortin's signal, they trotted the final distance to the side of the garage. There was, Fortin saw, one window at this end. He edged close and peered inside. A large car. Only one. In the shadows, it looked to Fortin like a Jaguar. He held up one finger and pointed. Barbara understood. This was a good sign.

From the protection of the garage, they sat down and commiserated in low whispers. Fortin began. "We need to see the back of the house. And I want to check out the basement. If James is there, I might be able see him"

"Can we get him out?"

"I don't know. It looks like those bars are set right into the foundation. We need to either get rid of the bars or get inside. But from what I can tell from here, those bars are secured to granite walls. Should we split up and meet back here?"

"I can scout out the back of the house to see what's there. I want to make sure there's only the one door."

"See if you can see any extra locks on the door. I'll try to get as close to the front entrance as I can and check it out. Then I'll see if I can get a look at the basement through the window."

"All right. But any movement, if either of us thinks we've been spotted, we scramble into the cover of the nearest trees and meet back up at the car on the main road."

They agreed to keep the close investigation of the house to five minutes.

On Fortin's signal, they split up, now in the cover of a deepening darkness and skulking like commandoes. Fortin stayed low to the ground and went directly to the front corner of the house where he pressed his body flat against the surface. He inched close to the front and peered as far as he dared directly at the front entry. It was comprised of a pair of large doors with leaded glass panels. Nothing unusual with the locking mechanism, and he could see no extra efforts at security. The problem he foresaw was the fact that the glass doors would make the entrant visible to anyone inside. They would have to plan carefully if they were to use this doorway to get in.

Then he moved into a crouch and then began to make toward the nearest basement window. He got into a prone position when he reached the basement and looked closely at the bars. They were secured by concrete into the granite surface of the basement wall. He tugged a bit, then somewhat harder. Not a bit of give. Then he peered inside. The glass was almost opaque with dust but he could see two bare light bulbs providing illumination from the basement ceiling, plus the glow of a television set. He could barely make out the sound and assumed that the glass was double thickness. He could not see any person, though, in the room.

He decided to check the basement window in the front and resumed his crouch to get there. Again from a prone position, he tested the bars with identical results. Looking in, he could see the television clearly now. And in front of the TV, he saw the shape of a young boy. He appeared to be using a video game joystick and the action held Fortin's attention. A few moments went by and the youngster threw the joystick to the side and rolled over, curled in a ball. The wails were unmistakable but brief. James was sobbing, but he was also heavily medicated.

Fortin regained his crouch and quickly reached the garage where Barbara was already seated and breathing in gasps. "What did you see," she asked. "Was Jimmy there?" Fortin nodded.

Fortin decided to leave out the scenes of James' condition. "He looks fine. He's in the basement. What about the back and the side?

"How was he? Was he OK? Was he tied up?"

"No. He's got a TV there and he was playing a video game when I looked in. He's all alone and he's just gone to sleep. We just have to figure out a way to get in there and get him out. What about you? What did you see?"

"Looks just like I remembered it. Big garden, gazebo. The back door doesn't look like it has anything more than a regular lock on it. There's a bulkhead door but it's got a huge padlock on it. Then I saw Ramsden. He's upstairs. That must be where he's watching television. I saw him come in and take a seat, the cocky bastard. I didn't see anyone else either, so he appears to be the only one there with James."

"OK. Now what?"

"Back to the car," Barbara said. "We're going to get James out of there. And now that we know where he is, we can work on our plan. Let's get going. I've got an idea."

Charles Whyte sat at his desk in the Consulate. The workers were buzzing all day long about the flurry of details that emerged. The report of the weapon's connection to the Portadown murders was the hottest topic. Most agreed that this would cause the break down of the Northern Ireland talks. That suggestion provided little comfort to Whyte who remained alone with his thoughts for most of the day.

Earlier, he tried contacting Ramsden to check on his son. Ramsden assured him that James was in fine condition and quite safe. "But if you truly want to assure your beautiful child's continued well being," Ramsden said, "you'll find Barbara and talk with her."

Ramsden insisted that the events were playing out precisely as he hoped they would. "Shamrock has been a great success, Charles, and we have only a single weak link, and that's Barbara . . . and if she's spoken with that Fortin fellow, then he's one more issue. We simply can't have that. What have you learned from our past conversation?"

Whyte assured him that he'd been trying repeatedly to reach

Barbara through her mother, her friends, and her relatives. He never let on to Ramsden that he'd traced her to Quebec, or that he passed on the news of James' disappearance."

"And your parents? What did you tell them?"

"I told them just what you told me to say. Not to call the police. That James was safe. That calling the police would only put James in grave danger. And that I'd explain everything to them soon. Look, sir, they understand that they can't tell a soul; they'd be harming their only grandchild. They're absolutely petrified."

"Good work, Charles. And please trust that James is quite well. He's not traumatized whatsoever. And once Barbara is found and we can reason with her, James will be back with his grandmother and grandfather. As I once heard expressed at a sporting event when I visited the US: 'No harm; no foul.' And as long as Shamrock continues along its path, there will be neither harm nor foul."

Rogan Murphy sat on a stool in a London pub near Covent Garden. Four stools away sat a tall rangy gentleman that Murphy knew to be Patrick Keough. Finding Keough had been easy. The description he'd been given in the phone call was precise. Following him had been a bit trickier. Murphy hadn't counted on being just one of three people trailing Mr. Keough.

When The British Airways flight landed and the passengers cleared customs, Keough was among the earliest to depart the airport. He had no luggage beyond a carry on grip, and he was processed early. When Murphy saw him stroll to the tube train and the Piccadilly Line platform, he saw two drop in line behind him, one on either side. Murphy gave them wide berth, staying close enough to watch Keough, but at a sufficient distance to stay clear of the two other men.

When Keough alit from the train at Leicester Square, the two men did as well, keeping their distance but definitely on

Keough's trail. Murphy exited from another door and watched and followed. Keough immediately located the left luggage section and produced a ticket. The attendant presented Keough with an attaché case. In another four minutes, he was strutting along London's streets with his grip in one hand and the attaché case in the other. Now, the four of them . . . Keough, Murphy, Mr. Tall and Mr. Short . . . were enjoying their draft beers in different sections of the pub.

Murphy used the mirror behind the bar to study the other two men. They were unknown faces to him, and they appeared to be professional. Perhaps the police? Murphy considered . . . possible, but not likely. Maybe Keough had bodyguards? No, they were keeping their eyes on Keough; if they were guards, they'd be watching everything else around him. No Keough was their target, just like he was Murphy's. He elected to keep watching and waiting.

Mr. Short was probably an inch or two shorter than Murphy and similarly built. Thick in the torso, they both had evidently enjoyed plenty of fine meals. Murphy guessed Mr. Short to be about forty five or so and perhaps of southern European descent. Dark hair going a bit thin on top with a comb over that he ought to reconsider.

Mr. Tall was a different story. At least three inches over six feet, he appeared to Murphy to be around fifty. His shoulders were slightly stooped and his eyes were darting left and right all the time. A tall Abe Vigoda came to mind. Most prominently, a scar stretched from the top of his forehead down past his nose and ending at his lip. The impression Murphy had was one of a Picasso portrait he'd once seen on a trip to Paris. Mr. Tall had flecks of gray in his thick wavy hair; again Murphy thought of southern Europe.

The publican asked Murphy if he'd like another and Murphy agreed, although the lagers here were less fresh and less inviting than those he usually enjoyed back home. "Here," the publican said, sliding the pint glass in his direction. "Enjoy this in relative comfort because the night's traffic is going to be atrocious. I hope you're not planning to drive anywhere soon."

"Why is that," asked Murphy.

"Big government deal going on, man. Haven't you seen the papers? Every Prime Minister and President from the free world has descended on us and the key roads are all blocked with security blokes. Big conference of all these people going on. Receptions, state dinners, the whole thing. Not that the roads are very good on any other day, but you're not likely to see traffic as bollixed up as it is today. A fine mess. Tomorrow will be just as bad. And you sir?" The publican had turned his attention to Keough and was asking him about a second pint.

When Keough waved him off and stood up from his seat as if to go, Murphy saw that Mr. Short and Mr. Tall stood as well. Murphy drank most of his glass in three gulps and kept up the parade.

Geoffrey Ramsden moved the plates of his leftover snack of kippers, crackers and pickles on a side table and turned the volume of the television up. The news presenter had just announced that the broadcast would be transferred to Belfast where a statement regarding the attempt on the life of the Prince of Wales would be made. Tempers had flared throughout Ulster as soon as the news reached Ireland that ties to the Irish Republican Army were found at the scene in Boston. Marchers were continuing to antagonize the catholic neighborhoods of the north; a priest had been pelted with stones by a group of thugs in Londonderry; the fire brigades throughout the area were being called in every direction to douse automobile fires; a pub in a catholic neighborhood in Antrim was firebombed and rescue workers there were being showered with rocks and stones whenever they attempted to do their jobs. Ramsden was thrilled.

The scene on the television switched to Belfast. A distance shot of Belfast City Hall, the stunning Edwardian stone wedding cake in Donegal Square, consumed the screen. An off-screen announcer welcomed viewers to the site of the important announcement and recited some of the events and discoveries of the past few days that led up to the statement tonight. The camera changed to a close up of the main doorway where a podium and several microphones were in place. Guards stood on either side of the great entrance. A small parade of dignitaries filed through the doorway and arranged themselves in a single row behind the podium. Ramsden knew most of the participants standing there and his sense of anticipation began to take on a cloak of doom. He stared at the television intently as the last two assumed their position side by side at the podium. On the left was Christopher McMichael, lead negotiator for the UK interests, and to his right stood Sinn Fein leader Adam Kelly. Ramsden heart sank at the sight of these two sober gentlemen. This was not what Ramsden wished to see.

McMichael started to read what he termed a "joint statement on behalf of all of those participating in the Ulster Dialogues". Ramsden had heard this sort of drivel before. "... disturbing events ... crucial time in our joint discussions ... pledged to peace ..." Ramsden sat in his overstuffed leather chair and absorbed the news, his stomach twisting at every conciliatory phrase. "... thorough investigation ... must not set back the progress ... appeal to the better natures of our people ..." Ramsden was reaching for the telephone before the statement was finished. He certainly didn't want to waste his time waiting for Adam Kelly to echo the same sop that came from McMichael. On the third ring, his call was answered.

"Yes?" The voice was calm and serious. Ramsden could hear voices in the background.

"You're watching this, Mr. Keough?" Ramsden's voice was

tight, constricted with the anger he felt at all the conciliatory phrases emitted from the television.

"I'm at the Dog and Duck in Soho. It's crowded in here; I'm going to step outside."

Ramsden waited until he could no longer hear the din of the crowd. "If you have not heard the news, it's all bloody peace and harmony in Belfast. It's absolutely revolting, I tell you. The Ulster Dialogues will continue."

Keough answered in a near monotone. "I was just watching the statement in the pub. But you're not calling me to discuss politics are you? I mean, learning my opinion of the situation is not the reason for your call, is it?"

"No, I suppose it is not. I just would like to vent my spleen, and you are not the appropriate person for that. I'm calling because the second phase of Shamrock is now in effect."

"I suspected as much. I'll take care of everything directly."

"Yes, please do so, because the longer . . ." But Ramsden was speaking to no one. Keough had already ended the call.

FIFTEEN

Sitting near the northern edge of the narrow lake, Ambleside was once home to William Wordsworth, John Ruskin and Beatrix Potter among others. Caroline Loughlin Ramsden had found a perfect, for her, cottage not far from the village center, yet affording her the quietude and room she enjoyed. Long a gardener, she had room to plot her rhododendrons and azaleas, and still had space for annuals and other plants. She especially enjoyed her herb garden with its gentian and sage and tarragon. At the family estate in Cartmel, she had plenty of acreage, but not the intimacy that her cottage in Ambleside offered. Since her husband's death some years ago, the Cartmel house was too large for her simple needs and required too much upkeep. Her son had been pressing to take over the house for his own needs for some time, and he used the home as a haven when he needed a break from his duties in London.

Cartmel was about an hour away by automobile and she enjoyed the drive along the winding roads adjacent to the lake. Even with the crush of tourists in the summer she still found the area to her liking. As the wife of a career diplomat, she'd seen much of the world, and still considered this spot on the planet the most attractive to her. In the middle of winter, she might have preferred a warmer climate, and indeed did visit friends in Florida and Belize when the opportunities were presented. But now, in the summer months, she could think of no more pleasant place on earth.

Today, she went to visit a friend and together they drove to Holehird Gardens, a lovely demonstration garden a few miles away. Afterwards, they enjoyed tea at the Brockhole Café between Windermere and Ambleside. This evening was exquisite. She sat on a garden chaise and sipped a sherry while the sun went behind the hills and the sky darkened. Later this evening, perhaps she'd spend some time reading and knitting. She had a television but found little on it to capture her attention. Tomorrow? She'd think about that later on. She had tentative plans to visit Ulverston and her cousin by marriage, Gwendolyn, who maintained a similar small cottage there. She had yet to firm that plan up. For now, she was content to simply live her life day by day.

At their hotel in Cartmel, Andrew and Barbara laid out their plans for tomorrow. Together they sat in Barbara's room and sketched what they remembered of the Ramsden house. "You're going to dress as a priest again, OK?" Barbara was assembling her thoughts. Ramsden doesn't know you, and he won't think it's terribly strange if a man of god appears at his doorstep."

"What about you? You can't be seen at all or he'll recognize you. Even in full dress nun's habit."

Barbara had figured that out and had her position all mapped out. She'd go shopping first thing in the morning at the sporting goods store. They would drive together to the lane near

Ramsden's house later in the day. Maybe early afternoon. She'd get out and sneak along the edge of the woods, taking the same route we took earlier today. Fortin would be assigned the task of walking up the lane in plain sight of the house and capturing Ramsden's attention at the front door. Ramsden wouldn't be inviting him inside, not with James tucked in the basement. More likely, he'd join Fortin outside in front of the house where they could chat about the financial needs of the church and his relative willingness to part with some of his cash.

"Keep him to the side and keep him talking. I've got to get to the front corner of the house from the garage."

"Then what?"

"Then you and I are going to walk in, take James, and leave."

"Oh, I get it. We just walk in, take James, and leave. Why don't I just levitate Ramsden, suspend him in mid air?"

"I'm not kidding. I'm just skipping the part where Ramsden is crumpled on the ground when we walk in."

"And he's going to crumple on the ground because . . . ?"

"I'm going to hit him on the side of the head. Really. I've got that part covered. You just have to be ready in case I miss. But I won't."

With a briefcase at his side and a fake press badge hanging from a chain around his neck, Patrick Keough strode through the outer checkpoint for the journalists' reception at Kew Gardens in advance of the international conference of the G-8 leadership. As with most such events, the real work of the conference was done well beforehand and all the details had been worked out by lower ranking diplomats from the several nations. A new international trade agreement would be announced tomorrow, and little was left for serious discussion between the leaders themselves. Instead, this would be the time for the ceremonial toasts, the lavish dinners, the pre-scripted press announcements and the highly crafted photo opportunities.

The Royal Botanic Gardens, or Kew, sits on the southern banks of the Thames about ten miles from downtown London. It is roughly three quarters of a mile by about a half mile and serves as a botanic repository and a public park. It has dozens of buildings and hundreds of display gardens. For the G-8 Conference, extra barriers were put in place so that entry to the grounds would be reserved solely for invitees.

Keough did not care what the subject matter of the G-8 Conference and its multi-national agreement was. He had a task to perform, and he intended to do it well. The phony press credentials were easy enough to obtain and allowed Keough entry onto the Kew Palace grounds. Reporters from across the world would be gathering at an enormous pavilion erected for the occasion. One day in advance of the conference, the reception gave the fifteen hundred writers, photographers and technicians an opportunity for camaraderie and good cheer. For such a group, free food, and especially the beverages to accompany the food, was a magnet. The crowd had a well-earned reputation for enjoying its alcohol. For the press, alcohol was an essential food group, a staple of their collective diet.

The central palace at Kew was surrounded by two sets of concrete and metal security barriers and no one, including the press, would have access to that area. No one would be allowed up close to the multiple presidents and prime ministers that would be in attendance for the next three days, and the security arrangements, as confirmed by Ramsden, would be extraordinary. But Keough didn't need anything else to secure the position that he required.

Keough, among all the many others here to cover the events, was shunted left, to the west, where buffet tables would be arranged in the journalists' pavilion and around the Palm House. Keough took his time walking in the general direction of the

Palm House. He neither expected nor wanted sustenance. The real members of the fourth estate, though, were eager to move forward, and made no apologies as they jostled him roundly on their scramble to get to the food and beverage lines.

Flood lights bathed the main pathway from the Kew Gardens entrance to the Palm House and Keough edged close to the far side of the path and stopped to light a cigarette. Keough meandered slowly ever closer to the dark edge of the pathway and made his move into the shadows. He crept along silently, avoiding the main pathways, and came to a clump of flowering shrubs where he knelt down and assessed his position. He opened his briefcase and removed a pair of night vision goggles, securing them with straps to his head. He scanned every direction and saw no aura of body heat.

A mound garden to his left concealed a path that led to the museum, and beyond that to the far corners of the garden. There, the Pagoda stood, facing the stunning vista that was a highlight for most Kew visitors. Keough faced at least a half mile walk in the moon-less dark to reach the low rise just south of the pagoda and the thick plantings of shrubs in the heath garden. There, he'd set up in privacy and relative comfort and await the morning. The Lion Gate, just a bit further to the south, would be guarded tomorrow morning from the outside by a single constable, and would afford Keough a quick exit from the grounds. He would be on Kew Road and away from the scene almost before the weapon cooled.

Rogan Murphy watched Keough approach the entrance to Kew Gardens and stop at the edge of the road where he removed an envelope from his pocket. Inside, from Murphy's distance, was what appeared to be an identification card on a cord. Keough slipped the cord over his head and went for queue that was forming at the entrance. If Murphy didn't stay close, he'd lose Keough on the other side and miss his chance to avenge the murder of his son. He watched the two other men on Keough's tale as they apparently reached the same conclusion. Once the prey was inside the gates of Kew Garden, they'd come up empty.

Murphy trotted across Kew Road and came to within twenty feet of the two other followers and only forty feet from Keough. Closing the distance was a chance he took, but he didn't want to watch Keough merely slip through his fingers. One of the other men, the shorter one, spoke to his companion and made a quick move to his left. Murphy watched, astonished, as the man approached a pair of camera toting young men in chinos and pulled them aside with more than just simple urgency. In thirty seconds, Murphy watched as a wad of pound notes changed hands. Then, with little objection, the two men handed over their identification badges. The short man hurried back to his companion, and in moments they were inside the gates and still on the trail of Patrick Keough.

Murphy cursed under his breath as he watched the exchange and the admission take place. He considered his options and concluded he had only one: Wait and watch.

The time was approaching ten o'clock and Fortin stood and excused himself from Barbara's room. "I think I'll go downstairs for a pint . . . maybe two or three . . . and think this plan over."

Barbara was not about to retire, as worked up over the promise of seeing her son freed, and she rose as well. "I could use a drink myself. My head's filled up and I need to clear it a little bit. Care for some company?"

When Fortin collected the ales at the bar and returned to the booth where Barbara sat, she was reaching into her pockets for some change. "I'm going to play some tunes on the juke box. Any suggestions?"

Fortin set the pints down and reached into his own pocket

for a pair of pound coins. "Anything by Queen. Maybe they've got 'We Are the Champions'. That'd sound good to me right now."

Barbara smiled and flipped through the list on the Wurlitzer reproduction and made her selections. George Michael's voice came over the speakers. Barbara resumed her seat and took a long sip. "You gotta have 'Faith'. That's the best I could do."

"I guess that fits as well as anything."

"Look, Dr. Fortin," Barbara was being serious, "do you mind if I call you Andrew, at least while we're over her."

Fortin smiled. "Sure."

"I'm getting to know you as more than just my therapist, and in this situation, calling you by your first name seems more natural."

Fortin continued to smile and stared at his pint.

"What are you thinking?"

Fortin took a deep breath and began. "I'm thinking that I'm probably not going to be your therapist when we get back. I've been watching you up close for a while now, and maybe I've gotten too close. Way too close."

"I'm not sure what you mean. Sure, we've been together on this whole trip, but what does that have to do with what happens when we get back."

Fortin looked up from his pint and held her gaze. "I mean, Barbara, that I'm liking what I see about you. A lot. A whole lot."

"Oh dear."

"Yeah. If I was a less honorable guy, I'd tell you I want to sleep with you tonight. But I'm not. So I won't say anything about that at all."

"I'm stunned, Andrew. Really stunned. And flattered." Barbara wasn't sure where she was going with this, but plunged ahead when the George Michael finished and Johnny Mathis began crooning "When Sunny Gets Blue". She could feel herself blushing as she considered Fortin's remarks. "One of my favorites of all time," she said. "Want to dance with me?"

The pub was only half full and there were no other dancers in the place, but Barbara and Fortin stood in the center of the dance floor and swayed to 'never knowing my right foot from my left.' Fortin held her close but not tight. Barbara leaned up and gave him a quick kiss on the cheek. "You're the sweetest person I've ever met, Andrew. Thank you for doing what you're doing. And thank you for thinking so much of me." She put her head on his shoulder and gave him a squeeze. When the music stopped, they returned to their seats.

An older gentleman at the bar leaned over and grabbed Fortin's arm. "Newlyweds?"

Fortin nodded, "No, but I wish."

The gent tapped him once on the shoulder. "Don't quit trying."

"What did he say to you," Barbara asked when Fortin took his seat.

"He thinks we're on our honeymoon."

The thought made Barbara let out a little whoop. "Was he listening to our conversation, do you think? Or did we just look that good together on the dance floor?"

She glanced over to the gentleman who was still looking their way and gave him a big wink. "Let's give him something to talk about." She rose from her side of the table and took a seat on Fortin's side. Their thighs were touching and she smiled when he tried to skootch in a little further. "So tell me a little about yourself, Andrew. I know you were in the seminary once, and that you're single and live alone in Wayland. But that's all. And you're probably between thirty six and forty one and went to college in Texas and love to cook."

It was Fortin's turn to be stunned. His mouth hung open. "How?"

"Friends, internet, paying attention. Your diploma on the wall tells when you graduated, so getting close to your age wasn't too tough. And asking judicious questions."

"Well what else is there to tell? You've got a pretty good picture of me already."

"Well, I'm sure that the seminary must have screwed you up a little bit. It screws up a lot of people. I'm a catholic too, so I know what the drill is. I've got a few relatives in religious life as you know, so I've got some idea of what goes on. And you've never married, but I don't think you're gay. And when we were dancing I got the distinct impression that part of you was trying to make a distinct impression, if you know what I mean."

Fortin didn't think his erection was that obvious. He considered her remarks before responding. "Sorry about that, but I have to tell you I find you very attractive . . . inside and out."

"Thank you. You know I've got a stretch mark or two under these clothes, and I've been 'around the block' with a few guys before I got married, as my mother would say. So I've got a few miles on my odometer."

"When I said inside and out, I meant that I'm attracted to you as a person as well as physically."

"I know what you meant, and it's very nice of you to say that." She put her hand on his and gave it a quick squeeze. "But you've got my life written down in a file. I want to hear more about you for a change."

"Well, I guess the seminary did have its effects on me, and maybe it did screw me up a little. It's a sheltered place. When I left, I tried to get into being not-a-priest and in some ways, I succeeded. In other ways, I just continued being who I was and what I was. It's why I went on to be a therapist."

"But here you are, sitting in an English pub with a married woman. And you made a move on that married woman. And it's all over something that has nothing to do with you. I wouldn't have guessed you to be risk taker, but you sure are taking risks now."

Fortin described his thoughts when he decided to follow up on the mysterious package of coded correspondence that Barbara had sent him. "I knew something was seriously wrong, and that maybe I could help. It was easy enough for me to reschedule my appointments . . . I don't exactly have the busiest office in the building." He took a deep draft before going on. "I felt you were in danger, and I liked you. *Like* you. I didn't want to see you get hurt."

"My mother likes you. She said she could tell she was dealing with a decent and honest guy. Those are her words, by the way."

Fortin only smiled. He liked Barbara's mother right away.

"Here's my thoughts. A lot of people are observers, almost voyeurs. They don't *live* life as much through their own actions as much as they do through others. Maybe that's why you're a psychologist . . . you see life through other people and their problems. It's something vicarious. I know you've traveled quite a bit, and I'll bet you've got a fancy digital camera. Am I right?"

Fortin nodded, suddenly uneasy with the conversation. "You travel, and you witness things, witness things as other people *live* those things. Does this make you uncomfortable?"

It did, but Fortin just nodded and said, "Go on."

"I see similar things in my husband. He wants to be at the center of things, but he can't. So he gets some degree of excitement by living life through Geoffrey Ramsden."

"Does that make me like your husband?"

"No, not at all. You see, I don't think Charles *can* live life directly. I mean, I've tried, but it's just not part of who he is. He's a good looking guy and has a good job and we've seen a lot of the world. And he's a good father. That's all terrific. But to actually make his own decisions . . . the big ones, I'm talking about . . . that's just not him.

"But you're different. I've had a chance to watch you and listen to you. You observe and make suggestions. You listen and offer advice. I suppose that's what you mean by continuing to be who you were after you left the seminary. You are a 'priest' in the broad sense of the word. You have something inside you that wants deeply to help people. But you also have the ability to live life yourself. That's something Charles doesn't have. Frankly, I was surprised that you had that in you; I would have guessed you to be more risk-averse, more like Charles. But you're not. At least not right now. You've taken some enormous risks here." Barbara saw that Fortin was objecting to the description, but she waved him off. "Wait. Hold on and hear me out. It was *you* who decided to follow up; *you* who drove up to Maine to find out what you could do to help. And then you put on a cassock and fly all the way to England to keep helping me and helping James. That's not something everybody does."

"Ok. I get your point. And I am uncomfortable."

"Well, as long as I'm on a roll here, let me share two other observations."

"I'm not sure I can take it."

Barbara smiled and took a healthy gulp from her glass. "I'm going to guess that your mother was a strong person who had a lot of influence on you. Not just the motherly things. And I don't mean that you didn't love your father, but I think you really, really think your mother was absolutely great."

"OK. I won't disagree with that. After my father died, she raised us alone, and she had to overcome a lot of adversity to do it. Not that she wasn't strong before my father died, but she was always up to the task. What's your next observation?"

"I'm not through with this one yet. My point is, I've watched you and seen how you interact with different women. Dr. Chapel, Mother Marie, my mother. And me, at least right now. You like strong women. You like to be around strong women. And you'd never be happy with one of those lovey-dovey coo-coo things. You need to find yourself someone who's strong and assertive and confident." She let out a burp and said, "Excuse me, Andrew. I'm getting so worked up, I'm making rude body noises."

She continued. "The other thing is, you *need to be seen* as a concerned, compassionate human being. It's not just something you think is a good idea; you truly believe in your core that you need to be compassionate and caring. It defines you. That's why you chose to be a therapist. And thank god, it comes natural to you. You are a wonderful person, Andrew, and I hope I'm not telling you something you haven't heard before, because you deserve to hear it."

Fortin sat silent, absorbing the comments from his 'patient' who was more perceptive than he ever believed. "Maybe I'm not as introspective as I ought to be."

Barbara just looked at him and shook her head. "You're a guy." She let that sink in and finally broke the silence with, "I'm going to get us a couple more beers. Then we've got to get to bed. It's going to be a tough day tomorrow."

In the basement of Ramsden's house, James was shouting, "Let me out of here!" He had climbed the basement stairs and was banging on the door to the kitchen.

Ramsden, drunk on sherry and still angry with the reaction he'd been watching all night on the television, became furious and raced down the stairs to the basement door. Get away from the door, James. I'm coming down."

"I want my mother and father. Let me out of here."

Ramsden released the dead bolt and flung the door open. He

grabbed the young boy by the collar of his polo shirt, almost lifting him off the ground. With his other hand, he gave James a sharp slap across the face. He held the boy by the arm and roughly forced him down the steps. When they reached the basement floor, Ramsden flung the boy on the bed and James cowered, holding the tears back from the pain of the vicious slap.

"You're going to stay here and be quiet James. And if something goes wrong because of you, I want you to know that you'll never see your father again. No one will. And if you still keep it up, I'll make sure your mother joins him. And your grandparents as well. You'll never see any of them again. Do I make myself clear? You'll have no one. Nothing. They'll all be gone. And all because you couldn't control yourself. So stay here and shut your mouth." In a moment he was up the stairs and slammed the door closed, making sure the lock was thrown.

Patrick Keough had established his position well. In a thicket of shrubs, he had scraped the ground clear and had a perfect line of sight to the target, an area just in front of the pagoda. He'd be unseen. Late tomorrow morning, when the honored visitors arrived, there'd be nothing to obstruct his view of the target. Of greater importance to him was the proximity of the exit, just yards behind his position. Once he had done his work, he could easily slide out of his position and make his way, under cover of the shrubs and trees, to the gate and the safety of the crowded streets.

For this evening, he'd simply have to get some rest and wait. With no one around, he was safe from prying eyes. His briefcase held the weapon with which he'd become so familiar on the firing range. Screwed to the barrel was a silencer and inside the clip were eight rounds of frangible ammunition, though he was confident he would use only one round. Upon impact, the bullet would fracture into thousands of pieces traveling at sub-sonic speed and never effect an exit would. Supremely lethal. In his pocket, he'd stowed some snacks he'd taken from the plane, so he had little to do now but wait until morning.

In the morning, as soon as the sun rose, there would be security personnel in the area. If he wanted to practice his escape, he'd have to do it now. He walked from his position to the gate and scanned in every direction. Nothing moved. Keough returned to his lair and removed the night vision goggles and placed them back in the briefcase. Then he checked his watch. The Timex expedition was a bargain at less than forty dollars, but it had a backlit dial and a built in stopwatch. He lay down on the carpet of leaves and mulch and pretended to take aim and fire. He pressed the stop watch to start and backed quickly and silently out of the shrubs. Three seconds, four, five. In eleven seconds, he was at the gate, locked on the outside but allowing him to push the mechanism from the inside and escape. He'd returned to his firing position and tried again. He'd like to keep this part of the task to something under ten seconds.

Once more, he performed the drill. Aim, fire, back out from position. Three seconds, four, and to the gate in ten seconds. By staying in a crouch and hooking left around a large walnut tree, he shaved a full second from his time. He'd try once again.

Just as he reached his firing position, he felt something grab his leg in a vise grip. He went down with a thud. He was flipped over by another pair of hands and tried to kick his way free from his attackers. That's when he was punched repeatedly in the abdomen and kneed in the groin. Someone had him from behind and held him upright while another delivered the blows. Keough did his best to wrench himself free when he heard a snap and felt a sharp pain in his right shoulder. His arm had been pulled out of its socket and perhaps broken. Nevertheless, with a final thrust of a leg, he thought he could strike his frontal assailant, fall over to the ground and roll. Maybe then, he'd be able to scramble free and take his chances on an escape. Darkness prevented him from seeing clearly, but he hoped there were only two to fend off.

He swung his leg up sharply and tried to place the blow on his assailant's jaw. Instead, though, his leg was stopped mid air by what felt like a fence post. That's when the blows came furiously and he felt himself blacking out.

Detectives Collins and Wetman sat on a park bench in Copps Hill in Boston's north end. They'd just completed interviews of two of the neighborhood's citizens, Rodolfo Fagioli, also known as 'Rudy Beans', and Carmino 'The Moose' Langone. Both were affable types given to hearty laughs. Neither admitted to any knowledge of any wrongdoing related to the attempt on the life of the Prince of Wales beyond what was reported in the press, although they knew former state representative Joseph Kavanagh, at least by name and reputation.

"You are definitely in the wrong neighborhood if you want to know about Joe Kavanagh," offered Langone, to which Rudy Beans roared his laughing agreement.

Wetman pressed the pair, asking about trailing a certain gentleman to Logan airport. "So who asked you to follow this guy Herlihy or Keough or whatever his name is? We have you identified as being at the airport at the international terminal when he arrived there. Who sent you?"

"Detective," Langone responded, shrugging his shoulders as if insulted by the question, "we were going to Santarpio's for a pizza the other day and we missed out turn, that's all. So we got out and asked directions." Langone could hardly contain himself.

"And I suppose you don't know anything about anybody following this same guy over in London," asked Wetman.

"Detective, if we did, what does that mean to us? We can't even get our wives to do what we want, so how am I going to get somebody over in England to do something like this?" Beans was beside himself.

Collins and Wetman just shook their heads and left.

"You knew before we got here that we wouldn't get anywhere with these guys," said Collins, enjoying the brief rest in the park. "They didn't commit any crime, and we really didn't have much to go on."

"I know," spat Wetman. "It's just that Langone really pisses me off, and Rudy Beans thinks he's such a riot. I'd like to give that guy a nice warm cup of Shut the Fuck Up."

"Did we get anything from Interpol?"

"Nothing beyond the fact that Rogan Murphy was tracked to London from Ireland. He bought a ticket from Shannon to Heathrow and got in before Keough's plane arrived. Not much to go on."

"I guess I'd rather be somewhere else if I was being followed by Rogan Murphy and two goons like we just met. Murphy must be one angry man."

Rogan Murphy was pacing the sidewalk near the main press entrance to Kew Gardens when he saw the two other followers carrying what appeared to be a drunken Patrick Keough between them. "Sorry, sir," one of them said to a guard at the entrance. "Poor bloke had too much to drink on an empty stomach. We'll make sure he gets home."

Murphy watched as the shorter one attempted to hail a cab. He noticed that the briefcase that Keough had carried in was now at his side. It was now or never.

"I need to talk to you." Murphy was speaking to the taller of the pair who remained propping up Keough. The man didn't acknowledge Murphy's presence. "Please," Murphy was almost pleading, "this fellow killed my son. He just got in this morning from Boston, and I want some time alone with him."

A taxi pulled up and the man hauled Keough along and tossed him into the rear of the cab. He and his companion conferred briefly and the short one winked and motioned for Murphy to hop in. Together, they were all headed to a warehouse in the east end.

Before retiring for the night, Fortin made a phone call to Janet Chapel. It was a long conversation, and Fortin was exhausted after recounting the events of the day. "If I ever stopped to think about what we were doing, I'd fall over in a swoon."

Janet Chapel was more direct. "You can get your tit in a wringer, and who can you call? There's nobody there you can count on; nobody knows you're there; you're in a foreign country with a bogus passport. This will all look great on the eleven o'clock news."

"We're going to try to get the kid out of there tomorrow, and if we can, we're out of here."

"And under whose name will you be coming back? And to which county will you be returning?"

"First things first. We've got to get the kid out before we think about anything else."

"Details, right?"

"This is an unusual situation for me."

"You sound a little depressed. Are you feeling OK?"

"Maybe. I think I've just gone through the toughest psychoanalysis session ever."

"Do you mean Barbara Whyte?"

"Yes, except I was the patient, not her. She sort of hit several nails on the head. It's a lot of information for me to process, and I'm just thinking about it now."

"So how does it feel, Sigmund?"

"She's provocative. I'll say that. She's also very direct. Reminds me of someone else I know."

"Wow, I need to speak with that woman. Did she really get you upset?"

"More uncomfortable than upset. See, I've felt myself growing pretty close to her over the past few days, and I wasn't expecting that kind of response."

"You're practically living in the woman's shorts right now, so don't beat yourself up about it. It's no wonder you're more interested in her after seeing her fight this battle. Watching her would tend to inspire anyone. She's a strong, smart, attractive person with few illusions, and she's got her only child at stake. But, wait a minute. Did she say anything about liking strong women?"

"What is it with you? As a matter of fact, yes."

"I knew that."

In the adjacent room, Barbara made two phone calls. The first was to her mother, reassuring her that she was safe and that she hoped to get James away from Ramsden soon. Liddy Chicoine drew small comfort from the conversation. "Why try to do this yourself, Barbara. The man is a kidnapper, and maybe a lot worse, if he had that young man killed in Boston. Don't try to do this by yourself."

Barbara insisted, though, that the risk was small, that she'd already scouted the property and that it was two to one as long as she was with Fortin. "Besides, Mom, I still have a husband and James still has a father. If I blow the whistle, I'll lose my husband and James will lose his father. This can come to a stop, and Charles can still save his family."

Liddy wasn't convinced. "The man is letting you fight his battles. He should be the one over there fighting for his son and bringing a stop to this nonsense."

"But he can't. If he wasn't at his office in Boston, Ramsden would know something was wrong and we could lose James. I want Charles to stay where he is. Mom, I have to go, so I'll call you tomorrow."

Her second call was to her husband. She tried the house first with no answer before calling his office. Charles was there, and to Barbara's ear, in a dangerous state. She could not remember his voice so low or monotonic.

Barbara didn't reveal her location and asked several questions to begin the conversation. "Charles, first of all I want you to know that I am safe. What have you heard from Sir Geoffrey?"

"But where are you? I've been looking everywhere."

"That's not important at the moment. I'll just tell you that I'm doing my best to make sure James is safe. Tell me what you've heard from Sir Geoffrey."

"It's awful, Barbara. He's threatened me and everyone in my family . . . James, you, my mother and father. He's insane, Barbara, and I don't know what I can do."

"Stay where you are. Tell him anything. Tell him you know where I am and you're going to talk with me about the whole scheme. But tell him something. He needs to know that you've got the situation under control."

"But Barbara, he has James."

"Charles, I'm doing my best to take care of that?"

"But how?"

"Just make sure you let Ramsden know that you've reached me and you're confident that nothing will be exposed. Let him think that his 'Shamrock' scheme is safe with me. We need to keep him from doing anything to James. Do you understand, Charles? Will you call him?"

"Where should I tell him that I found you?"

Barbara's frustration with Charles was growing. He could be dense at times, unable to think for himself. She saw it earlier, years earlier, and rued the day she accepted the trait. "Tell him I went backpacking or camping, whatever. Tell him you found me at Worthley Pond at the cottage. That will sound good. But I called you and we spoke, and he has absolutely nothing to fear."

"I'll call him right away."

SIXTEEN

In an abandoned warehouse near Bethnal Green on London's east side, Patrick Keough sat immobile and resolute. Lashed securely with thick marine ropes to a plain metal chair, he was surrounded by three men, all apparently considering the value of keeping him alive.

One, known only as Victor, stood behind him, looking at the back of Keough's head. "I say we just gut him and float him down the canal. He's a nothing to us."

A second, Tony, was much taller than Victor and simply pared his fingernails with a small blade. He said nothing.

Rogan Murphy cocked his head at Keough and asked. "I'd like to have a conversation with the gentleman first if you don't mind. He may be nothing to you, but he murdered my son."

Tony took a step back and motioned to Murphy that Keough was his for the moment, to do with as he saw fit.

"Mr. Keough, what was my Johnny to you? A nothing? A cipher in your plan?" Keough, one eye half closed with swelling, stared straight ahead.

It looks to me like you just needed the appropriate individual, preferably dead. From what I've been able to hear, the rifle they found on John was used many years ago in an IRA attack. Now, I happen to know a few things about John Murphy, and I can say with a high degree of certainty that John didn't have any access to that sort of weapon. It was an Italian sniper rifle and hard to find. So I'm going to leap to the conclusion that John and that weapon were put together for a reason. Am I right?"

When Keough didn't respond, Murphy applied the heel of his hand to Keough's forehead. "I remember using this same hand to drive a bloke's nose right into his brain. I thought he'd die right away, but the poor fellow just went blind and crazy. I think he's still in a hospital somewhere. They feed him soft food and he drinks through a straw. Has to wear nappies, poor chap." Keough looked straight ahead and kept his jaw clamped tight.

The warehouse had tall windows affording a wealth of light into the nearly empty space. Murphy walked in a circle around Keough who remained resolute in spite of the bindings securing him to the chair. Murphy swung his left hand in a long arc and caught Keough across the cheek and bridge of his nose, so hard that he ended up on the floor. Victor heaved him back up into a sitting position, telling Keough, "I think the man's serious. I'd talk to him if I were you." Keough remained focused straight ahead.

Murphy crouched down low and looked Keough square in the face. "Look at these scars. Look at this face. I've seen a few battles and lost a few of them. But I kept coming back, Mr. Keough. I believed in what I did, so I took my punishment, licked my wounds, and girded my loins for the next battle. I wonder if you have the same determination."

Murphy stood up and turned to address Victor. "I think he

considers himself a real hero sitting here without saying a word. I might be mistaken, but I think I suggested a conversation, and mine is the only voice so far." He crouched down again to face Keough. "So why not chat me up a bit. Why did you murder my son?"

No reaction. Murphy tried once more. "Was this Boston thing your idea or were you hired to do the job by some other bloke. You strike me as a professional, but not so smart that you'd be the brains behind this scheme. So who did the planning? Whose idea was it? And who in hell told you to turn my boy into a dead body in the process? Who was it?"

Tony watched Murphy's attempts and turned away, walking to another corner of the building where he rooted around several crates until he found what he sought..

Victor slapped Keogh on the top of the head. "You have a few minutes right now where you can exercise your voice, Mr. Keough. In a few minutes, you're not going to have much choice."

Keough smirked and remained silent and steadfast.

Murphy looked over at Victor. "I'm afraid Mr. Keough wants to remain silent." Murphy turned to Keough and made a violent vicious jump directly on Keough's instep. He heard bones break followed by a low growl from Keough. "Ah, at least he has the human ability to make noise. I was beginning to wonder." Keough had his eyes squeezed shut, trying to absorb the pain. "Now we'll see what you're made of, my man."

Tony walked back and held a coil of an extension cord. With his knife, he calmly sliced off the receptacle ends and peeled back the insulation from the black and white wires. Saying nothing, he twisted the braided wire into points. Keough watched him with growing anxiety. Tony worked meticulously, pausing occasionally to admire his handiwork. He spread the wires apart and walked to a wall receptacle.

Murphy watched, eying Tony and Keough's reactions. "As

much as 240 volts, Mr. Keough. Make a grown man want to piss his pants."

When Tony returned, the two exposed wires now held spread apart. He motioned with a nod for Victor to step back. Tony took Victor's place behind Keough and with calm precision touched the wires to Keough's neck. He counted to three and removed the wires. Keough lurched and bawled in pain. An odor of burning flesh wafted in the air. Seconds passed and he regained his composure. The look of determination never left his face.

Tony withdrew and stood ready to apply the next jolt. Keough closed his eyes in preparation and breathed deeply. This time Tony went for the ear. Keough squirmed and howled. His breath was coming in short gasps now.

Victor, now standing with Murphy, said "Looks like a real bitch, Mr. Keough."

Murphy smiled and added, "It's starting to smell in here, isn't it?"

Victor shrugged his shoulders. "He doesn't smell like shite just yet, but that could change very quickly."

Murphy added, "I think we should perhaps consider the testicles next. What do you think?"

The next morning, after a hearty full English breakfast, Tony, Victor, Rogan Murphy and Patrick Keough were on their way up the M1 heading towards Cartmel. Keough wasn't very hungry. When they finally retrieved the information from Keough, the man was a slobbering mess. They stripped him of his clothes, hosed him down with cold water, cinched his ankles and wrists and wrapped him in several blankets. Now, stuffed in the trunk of Victor's Volvo, Keough remained trussed like a turkey as the car motored along Victor held his speed at the legal limit so as to avoid the discomfort of a police stop and the discovery of their cargo. "Safest car on the road, Rogan. Best impact protection of any vehicle. Collision warning system. Even has a blind spot camera built in to the rear view mirror. Turbo diesel for efficiency. I'm telling you this is one fine automobile."

The conversation consisted of such things during the drive. It was a companionable journey, given that the data they'd derived the night before from Keough gave them all the information they needed for the day's work. After a few more judiciously placed electric pulses, Keough became a font of information. "Sir Geoffrey Bloody Ramsden" was Keough's first phrase, and he repeated it often over the next hour. The entire 'Shamrock' plot, the early involvement of Charles Whyte as the intermediary while Keough trained and recruited John Murphy in Boston, the delivery of the Beretta sniper rifle, the sham assassination attempt on the life of the Prince of Wales, even 'Phase Two' and the plot to assassinate the US President's wife: It all came out in dreadful detail.

"This thing will do a hundred thirty and you'd never know it," said Victor, still extolling the virtues of the Volvo. "Twelve freaking speakers, can you believe it? I don't know why I never bought one before. I guess I was always a Mercedes man."

Murphy chatted while they traveled of his activities in the IRA and how he'd tired of the mayhem and the sadness and the lost and damaged lives. A strong supporter of the Ulster Dialogues, he was hopeful that time and togetherness would ease the distrust on both sides. "This next generation, they don't know anything about Michael Collins and 'Operation Harvest' and "Bloody Sunday,' and that's a good thing. The potato famine is old news, and there's no going back to fix it. It's like trying to fix the Battle of Britain by killing every German. We can remember the bad times, that's important. But we've got to consider our collective future on this little planet and move forward. All the rest is just romance, don't you think?"

From the back seat, Tony, who'd been admiring the weapon

they'd captured from Keough the night before, added, ". . . Once in the dear, dead days beyond recall, when on the world the mists began to fall . . ."

Victor looked at Tony in the rear view mirror. "What the fuck is that?"

Murphy answered for him. "It's *Love's Old Sweet Song*, and Tony is so right. Those are the dead days. Dead and gone. Damn it, Tony, you are so right."

They proceeded to the M6 and headed north, stopping at a Road Chef for lunch. They'd been on the road for three hours and needed to stretch, fill the tank and get something to eat. In forty minutes, they were back on the highway. Victor checked his watch. "We'll be there around three. Any idea what we're going to do when we get there? I mean, I doubt if this Ramsden fellow is just going to invite us in."

Murphy had been giving it some thought. "Keough said he was up there, so we can be fairly certain he'll be at home. I figure we'll knock him up and see what gives. If he doesn't greet us properly, we can just set his house on fire."

Tony was absorbing everything in the back seat. In his uninflected baritone, he said, "Keough told us he had a young boy inside."

"Right, Tony. So maybe we try something else like breaking in through a window or just ramming his door down. After all, it's not a social call."

Victor offered an opinion. "I think it might be best if, when we get there, we assess the situation, maybe walk the premises, get a clear idea of the mission."

"The mission is to fuck the bastard over." Rogan Murphy was emphatic. "He arranged the premeditated murder of my son. This is payback time."

"Ok, Rogan. That's a given. But we have to formulate a plan. Get the lay of the land. By the way, if that Keough guy has pissed his pants in the boot, he's also going to be a dead man."

* * *

Caroline Loughlin Ramsden looked at her watch. She'd accepted an invitation to visit her cousin by marriage, Gwendolyn, in Ulverston and spend the night, and she was packed and ready to go. She hoped to be there by four in the afternoon for tea, but if she left now, she could stop at the Village Shop in Cartmel and buy some sticky toffee pudding as a gift for Gwen. It was one of her favorites and Caroline thought she might even pick up some Montezuma's chocolates while she was there. At their age, she and Gwen could indulge their sweet teeth without outside criticism.

While she was in the vicinity, she just might stop by the family home to say hello to Geoffrey, if he was in. Going to Cartmel would be only minutes out of her way, and she enjoyed seeing the old homestead, whether or not Geoffrey was there. She had fond memories of the home and the area, especially the annual grand carnival at the edge of town that was held as part of the horse racing days. She hoped Geoffrey was enjoying the home as much as she did, but with his travel schedule and responsibilities, he was likely to be anywhere.

Caroline Ramsden had little contact with her son and for that she blamed herself. He'd been especially bright, precocious to the point of being distinguished academically at a very early age. Given her husband's formidable position in every government in which he had served, however, she felt compelled to support him, and that meant frequent absences from home and from Geoffrey. Her parents were saviors in the early years, and they were never less than overjoyed whenever Geoffrey spent time with them, which was often. He loved her parents and they him, and when her father resigned his professorship and her mother sold her bakery, they were able to spend even more time with Geoffrey.

When their brutal, horrific murders occurred, Geoffrey was inconsolable. Caroline had always understood that her father was engaged in a dangerous circumstances and she and her mother had hoped that his retirement would lead him to be perhaps more circumspect in his choice of avocations. But Ian Loughlin was a stubborn man who had principles. In the violent world of Irish politics, that was a perilous combination. Further, Caroline's mother was no less committed, if more circumspect in how she professed her beliefs.

Their murders, accomplished on a bright summer day in Ireland, as bright and as sunny as this day in England, stunned the nation. The fact that Geoffrey was at his grandparents' home when the murders occurred had scarred him as well, and much more deeply.

Geoffrey became much more purposeful, more serious, more brooding as time passed. Caroline lamented the change in several conversations with her husband, but he, recognized as a most perceptive negotiator when the stakes were international and the parties were men of enormous egos, power and influence, failed to see the changes in his own son. He dismissed Caroline's concerns as simple excessive empathy. "You're being overly maternal, Caroline. The boy is resilient, as all children are. He needs to be with other boys his own age. He will get over it, Caroline. He's strong."

Over Caroline's objections, Geoffrey was sent to an elite all boys preparatory academy. He did seem to enjoy it, she thought with some consolation, and he was an achiever. But he was never the same. She'd lost him.

In his adulthood, Geoffrey went on to achieve even more. A noted professor, he parlayed his intelligence and talents into a career in Parliament, and today was one of the leading politicians of the nation. Some considered him a future Prime Minister. Caroline would not disagree with that assessment but she stayed far away from the news of the day. After years of being in the midst of the power brokering world of high politics, she craved her solitude and her simple pleasures, like her garden.

She would like to know more about her son, but he was almost unknowable, at least as much as a mother would like to know her son. Her relationship with her son remained polite and kind, but she sensed a void in her son, something missing or damaged, a deep scar that had never properly healed.

As she stowed her overnight bag in the boot of her Vauxhall Vectra and began her drive south, she hoped that Geoffrey would be home and that she'd have an opportunity to visit with him, however superficial the exercise might be. She checked her fuel and decided she'd stop in town for petrol before getting too far on her journey.

Barbara Whyte and Andrew Fortin reviewed their plan over breakfast. After, secure in their respective responsibilities and timing, they found a shop in the village that sold, among other sporting accessories, cricket bats. Barbara Whyte hefted a few before she selected the one she wanted. "I actually played cricket a few times when I lived here," she told Fortin, "but my real love then was tennis. I had a vicious serve, but I don't think a tennis racket will supply quite the degree of impact I'd like to make on Sir. Geoffrey."

The returned to the pub and went to their rooms. Barbara changed into some outdoor clothes while Fortin retrieved his priestly garb. He'd change in the car so as not to attract attention in the village center. They still had at least two hours ahead of them before they planned to leave for the Ramsden estate, so they sat in the pub and had tea, trying to rehearse in their minds how events would unfold later on.

Fortin understood his role. Engage Ramsden in conversation about the financial needs of the church at the front door. But what if he didn't answer the door? What if he simply stayed upstairs in his study and decided not to come down? Fortin recognized that he would not likely be invited indoors because an outburst by James in the basement would cause alarm. But what if Ramsden simply didn't step outside? What if he stood framed by the front doorway? That eventuality would disrupt Barbara's attempt to stun Ramsden . . . "stun", as in clobber with a cricket bat. He sat perplexed.

Barbara, for her part, was concerned with remaining hidden from view. There was some cover, but was it adequate? What if she was seen by Ramsden, skulking between the trees and the garage or the garage and the house? She had a thought and expressed it to Fortin.

"I think I'll go up to the property well ahead of you, say about fifteen or twenty minutes."

"Why?"

"Well, if he does happen to see me moving from the cover of the trees to the back of the garage, I'll still be far enough away from him that he wouldn't necessarily recognize me. But he might call 9-9-9 . . . that's 9-1-1 to you and me. We'd at least have some warning and could get away without disrupting everything. But if no police show within a few minutes of my getting to the rear of the garage, and we know we're relatively safe."

"Good thinking, but let's keep at ten minutes. That will give you enough time to get there before I start walking up the lane. I've got some concerns too. What if he doesn't answer the door?"

"Just keep at it. If he doesn't appear, we regroup and try again."

"OK. And if he does answer the door but he doesn't step outside?"

"Yeah. That would be a problem. Fortunately, it's a nice day, so if he doesn't step outside, then you might step back and say something about how beautiful the weather is and make sure he has enough room to come out. If he doesn't, just try to get him facing you so he doesn't see me coming up behind him. Stand to the right so he's got his back turned to the corner I'll be hiding in."

They spent the next hour deliberating and pondering and bouncing ideas and contingencies off each other. When Barbara looked at her watch, it was 2 o'clock and they decided to get moving.

Sir Geoffrey Ramsden was on the telephone most of the morning. He was anxious to appear fully engaged in the usual business of government while he was waiting for further news of Shamrock's second phase. Before nine o'clock, he'd spoken with two cabinet ministers, and by ten o'clock had a conference call with two others. In between, he took a call from Charles Whyte on his secure line. Charles must be at the Boston office at this early hour.

"Charles, tell me the news."

"It's Barbara, sir. I've reached her. She's in Maine at a cottage where she stayed as a child. She's coming home soon, sir, and all is well. We had a long discussion, and I have to say, sir, she's most agreeable. I don't think there's a thing to worry about." Charles sounded enthusiastic as he broached the news.

To Ramsden, Whyte sounded too exuberant and such good news made him suspicious. "And when will she be home, Charles."

"I think tomorrow. She sounded wonderful and I believe it's only a question of her depression. Melancholy, you know, since she lost her position at the school. All seems perfectly well. I can't wait to see her."

"That's wonderful news, Charles. Can I speak with her? What is her phone number at this cottage?"

There was a much longer pause than necessary, thought Ramsden. "I'll ask her to call you, sir. She's on the road and she told me she'd call me sometime during the day. I'll ask her to call you then."

A sham, Ramsden knew, but he played along. "That's good news, indeed. I'll look forward to her call. Meanwhile," Ramsden went on, changing the subject, "I'm sure you've seen the news from Belfast. The Ulster Dialogues are going to continue. Bloody conciliation all around."

"Yes, sir. Very bad news for Shamrock."

"Such collegial gentlemen." Ramsden mimicked the announcement in a high pitched voice: "Terrible events. Shocking, absolutely shocking. But our dialogues must continue. We must find the means to push forward in the spirit of peace and reconciliation. Blah-di-blah. Peace. Progress. Living in harmony."

Ramsden regained his composure. "I wanted to retch when I saw them making their announcement. They simply have no idea of the treachery that sits quietly in the room as they pat each other on the back. Hail fellow well met. It's such a bloody sham and people are tripping over themselves to bask in the limelight of perfect and lasting peace. But the last laugh will be ours, Charles. The last laugh will definitely be ours. Plan B is set in motion, as I'm sure you would expect."

This was news that Charles did not want to hear. Participating in a faked assassination attempt was one thing . . . especially when the death of John Murphy resulted and made matters much worse. But Phase Two was arranged as the real thing from the very start. No intentional misfiring. These would be real bullets striking real flesh. Whyte never liked the idea from the first time Ramsden described it, but he was certain then that the event involving the Prince of Wales in Boston would be sufficient to accomplish the objective.

Whyte had no response. "Are you there, Charles? Because I cannot reach our mutual friend, and the second phase is scheduled to occur momentarily. I would have thought it would have happened already. But no word whatsoever."

Now Charles could feel Ramsden's frustration coming through the line. " I haven't heard any news, sir."

"Well, I'm waiting for a message soon that the task was performed as planned. The coup de grace, so to speak. Our initial sortie was successful, but the fatal result did not ensue. The successful completion of the Phase Two mission will most certainly guarantee our success. I must go now, Charles."

"But sir, how is James. Is he OK?" Charles was left staring at a telephone in Boston. Ramsden had hung up.

SEVENTEEN

Ramsden kept the television turned on all day and grew increasingly impatient with the news out of London. The leaders of the free world appeared from time to time in the telecasts, but no news from Kew Gardens. Ramsden considered calling his London office to have them check: Did the wife of the US President visit the Gardens as planned? He decided to wait rather than raise questions that might be re-membered later. He wanted no connection whatsoever with the events scheduled to occur as part of Phase Two, even though he had a speech prepared and rehearsed that he would deliver as soon as possible after the event.

The President and his counterparts were scheduled to attend a full day of meetings at Kew Palace, and at noon, his wife was scheduled to visit the pagoda and the Japanese Gateway at Kew Gardens. A formal tea was set to begin at 1 o'clock at the Queen's Cottage at the northwest corner of the property, so he stared intently at the TV set waiting for an urgent broadcast. How would it be phrased? "The wife of the US President was fatally shot at Kew Gardens in London during a conference of world leaders." Some variation would do, as long as the words "wife of the US President" and "fatal" were included in the announcement.

Ramsden had no doubt that Keough was the perfect man for the job, and he'd proven his worth in Boston. This was certainly a different case, but Ramsden was secure in the sense that the only way to stop the Belfast talks once and for all was to bring international outrage to bear. The IRA received its greatest support, financial and otherwise, from the US. The sitting president was of German and Italian descent, but his charming wife, born Eileen Sullivan, was the daughter of Irish immigrants, a fact that appeared in several of the president's speeches. Her violent demise would cause an outcry of such proportions that the old enmities, now dying in the Belfast talks in a spirit of empty conciliation and appeasement, would be rekindled and the flames would touch both sides of the Atlantic.

Ramsden paid no heed to the substance of any other news of the day. He tried to picture the scene at Kew in his mind, the frantic call for emergency medical treatment, the ambulances, the security vehicles, the utter mayhem. To Ramsden it was a beautiful scene to imagine. But no call yet, no announcement. He checked his watch.

His reverie was broken by the sound of banging pipes and the screams of young James in the basement. Ramsden had ignored his routine and was paying for it now. He wanted to bring a light lunch to James by 11 o'clock along with a juice cocktail of grape, cranberry and apple, liberally laced with Diazepam. The combination had worked so far and the effects on James were generally beneficial. He was generally drowsy, slept often, complained rarely, and was generally compliant. Now, the effects of the earlier dose had probably worn off and Ramsden hurried down the stairs to prepare the lunch and the accompanying beverage.

When he went into the basement with the boy's lunch, James was crying and sitting on his bed. Ramsden truly didn't want to harm the boy, but he would brook no outbursts. Visitors to the estate were rare, and certainly none had been invited, but he wanted no distractions. If all went well, James would be back with his parents soon. If events did not go well, that would present another decision sequence to consider. Ramsden set the grilled cheese sandwich and bag of potato chips on the small table he placed in the basement for just this purpose. Next to it, he placed the cup of juice, appropriately enhanced.

Ramsden returned to the second floor and sat in front of the television. Still no news. In fact, the latest report indicated that a major announcement on international trade would be made by mid afternoon. The Prime Ministers of the UK and France would be joined by the US president and the president of Italy. This might be good news for the economic community, but it was horrible news for Ramsden and Shamrock's Phase Two. It could only mean that the president's wife would be sipping tea at the moment at the Queen's cottage on the Kew Gardens estate. Bad news indeed.

Ramsden grabbed for the phone and called Charles Whyte who answered on the third ring. "What's happened? Is there any news on your end?"

Whyte was still flustered from his earlier conversation. "Nothing. There doesn't seem to be anything happening. Sir Geoffrey, please, how is James. I must know."

Ramsden dismissed any thoughts of the boy. "He's fine, but where could Keough be? I haven't heard a word. I would think he'd call, even if it was bad news."

"I can't imagine sir, but I have no idea. There was a meeting here this morning as soon as I arrived and I've been unable to catch any events on the television."

Ramsden cared little about Whyte's busy day. "And where is Barbara's phone call? I've heard nothing at all from her."

There was a pause before Whyte responded. "I spoke to her last night, sir, and asked her to call you. She has your number. I'm sure you'll hear from her soon."

"Certainly, Charles. I don't believe you, but I'll humor you for the moment. Barbara has yet to call, even though you tell me she's aware I have James. How odd. I would think she'd be on the phone at once. But never mind." He hung up.

Charles sat staring at the telephone. He was near despair, frightened for his son, desperate to be assured of his safety and not at all concerned with the progress . . . or lack of it . . . with Shamrock. He felt twisted and hollow inside, despondent and doomed. He had no excuse for his recent involvement with Ramsden and Shamrock except his own weakness and his misplaced respect for Sir Geoffrey Ramsden.

"What was I thinking when I agreed to this," he asked himself? "Did I actually believe that I'd be rewarded with a better position? I've been a willing pawn, that's all. A conduit. I have no influence on the man. I'm losing my wife and my child over this and for what?"

Whyte had been at the consulate since three in the morning, unable to sleep at home and anxious to be near his secure phone line to Ramsden. He looked drawn and disheveled, unable to focus on matters at hand and drifting into a nether world during conversations and meetings. His condition caught the attention of his colleagues, and more than one had suggested he go home and rest, perhaps even see a doctor. "You look horrible, Mr. Whyte, his assistant said when she saw him early in the day. "Is everything OK? Are you feeling well?" He dismissed the concern with a wave.

His phone rang again, this time not the secure line, and he picked it up. "Charles, it's Barbara." Whyte almost blubbered in tears at her voice. "What have you heard from Ramsden? How is James?"

"He doesn't tell me much. According to him, James is fine,

but he didn't believe me when I told him we talked, or that you agreed to say nothing. He insists that you call him. Can you do that? I think it might help."

Barbara wasn't ready for this. Fortin would be waiting at the car for her to appear. She said, "Can you transfer me to him from your phone?"

"Can't you call him directly? I'm afraid, Barbara, very afraid. The second part of our plan was supposed to happen today, and so far we've heard nothing?"

"What 'second half'?"

"Barbara, there was supposed to be a second phase today in London. The Boston phase went as planned, but it didn't halt the talks. So this was supposed to be the big blow. But something happened. It didn't take place, at least not that we know. We're in the dark."

"Can you transfer me to him over your phone?"

"Yes. I think I can. It would be like a conference call. I'll have to keep my line open. If I hang up, then the call will disconnect."

"Then do it. Just listen in. Don't say anything and let him think the call is coming in from me. When the call is over, then you can hang up."

Charles dialed and pressed the conference button of his phone. When Ramsden answered, Barbara began.

"Hello, Geoffrey. Charles said you wanted me to call you. Here I am."

"And where is that?"

"At my brother's home. In Maine. I'm on my way home to Massachusetts. Geoffrey, how is James? Is he alright?"

Ramsden's anger was in check and he spoke in smooth controlled tones. "James is just wonderful, Barbara. But tell me, did Charles tell you why I wanted to hear from you?"

"Yes. It's OK. I've said nothing to anyone and I don't intend to. I just want to know that James is safe and that you won't harm him."

"You have my word, Barbara, as I assume I have yours. I would not want to see anything happen to him . . . or to anyone he loves, like his grandfather and grandmother. You understand?"

"Completely, Geoffrey. I want James released at once."

"In due time, Barbara. There's very little in the way now for our plan to succeed. Of course, if it fails, I can't control what will happen." He hung up the phone. Charles did as well, and Barbara was left, like her husband only minutes before, stunned and staring at a disconnected telephone.

"There's the exit coming up." Victor made the turn and asked Murphy to check the distance.

"Only a few miles and we'll be there. This could be an interesting afternoon for all of us."

Tony made a rare remark. "I hear Keough in the trunk. He's kicking around."

Victor wasn't pleased. "If that bastard does anything to this car, he'll wish we dragged him here tied to the rear bumper."

Murphy added, "His bladder must be ready to burst in there. He's been tied up and wrapped up for six hours in the dark. We'll let him out in a few minutes and he can get some air."

Barbara hurried to the car where Fortin had his cassock and roman collar laid out in the back seat and ready to go. "I just spoke with Ramsden. I called Charles and he made the phone connection. He says James is fine, but his plan has gone awry and I don't trust what he'll do. We've got to hurry."

Fortin was in the passenger seat and began to change on the way to the estate. "Let's not get too hasty. We've got a plan and we're comfortable with it. Let's just do what we planned to do."

Traffic was getting heavy on the way to Ramsden's home. Tourist season added cars and busses to streets and lanes that were never designed for anything other than slow moving horses and buggies. When they reached the lane at the foot of the hill at Ramsden's, Barbara pulled in and parked behind a stone wall. The car wasn't completely out of sight, but it was unlikely to draw anyone's interest. "We're here," she said when she removed the key. "I'm going to head up to the house and you're going to wait for ten minutes before you start walking up. Are you ready?"

"The good father is ready. Here's your weapon." He handed her the cricket bat. "Good luck. And if you get spotted, you're going to come back here right away." Barbara nodded and began edging her way along the path. Fortin looked at his watch. Time to rehearse his approach and wait.

Caroline Ramsden placed the package of sweets in the rear seat and climbed in. She always enjoyed her stop at the Village Shop in Cartmel and was pleased when the clerk recognized her from previous visits. She checked her watch and saw that she had sufficient time to stop in at the family estate before heading to her cousin's home.

Fortin checked the time once more and saw that the time had come. He walked in the middle of the lane and momentarily saw the roof of the Ramsden house appear over the trees ahead of him. Another two or three minutes and he'd be there. There were no sounds of sirens or alarm, so he assumed that all had gone well so far for Barbara. He approached the front of the home, passing the gardens that were in full bloom. He guessed that Ramsden had a gardener on hire and couldn't imagine Ramsden himself doing the work.

He approached the front door and searched for the door bell. In the center of the right hand door was a metal handle that he assumed must be the bell for there was nothing else apparent to him. With a twist, a bell sounded loudly.

Ramsden was startled by the noise, not expecting anyone. His estate was sufficiently out of the way that casual visitors were rare, and solicitations rarer still. He pulled the drape away from the window and saw no vehicle in the driveway. "Unusual," he said aloud to himself. He couldn't see the front door from the second floor window and deliberated whether he'd even answer it. Then it rang again. "Persistent bugger," he said. He decided he'd better answer, if only to dismiss the visitor.

On the way down the stairs, he paid close heed to any noises from the basement and was pleased at hearing none. The Diazepam had done its work, he concluded and James was probably sound asleep. As he approached the front door, he checked the closed circuit camera system in the hall closet and saw that it was a priest standing there. The picture was too blurry to make identification and he was unsure why such a visitor would appear. He opened the front door with no hesitation and placed himself squarely in its frame. Fortin and Barbara had guessed correctly; there'd be no way of gaining access to the inside of the house with James still in the basement.

"Well hello, father. What might I do for you today?"

Fortin saw that Ramsden had the bearing of a man in charge. Tall, erect, assembled and prepared. His smile was radiant and warm, no hint of suspicion.

"I'm so glad to see you at home, Sir Geoffrey. I was told that you are not here often and I bless my good fortune."

Ramsden held the priest firmly in his gaze, still not opening his door wider for the priest to gain entry, but more importantly, not stepping outside where Barbara would have clearer access to the back of the man's head. "And what brings you out on this beautiful day, Reverend?"

"I'm afraid I'm in charge of soliciting funds for the good charities of the Cumbrian church council. I was told that you are someone of uncommon generosity, both financially and in terms of your most precious time." Ramsden remained in the door frame and Fortin stepped back.

"I must say, I didn't expect this beautiful weather and these flowers. They're spectacular."

"You're American, Reverend?"

Fortin was prepared. "Laroque. From Canada originally. Yes, just visiting some friends when I learned of the fund raising campaign, and found that some extra hands would be a benefit. So I'm on vacation, actually, and doing God's work at the same time." Fortin was seven feet, at least, from Ramsden, but the man refused to step away. If Barbara was in position, she must be anxious about the lack of movement. "Tell me, Sir Geoffrey, what do you call those flowers over there? I don't think I've seen such things in New York where I'm from."

Finally, Ramsden made some movement to the outside. Fortin tried to appeal to the man's vanity to get him further away. "I think they may be some form of stocks and maybe those are cosmos, but your gardens are spectacular. I've never seen anything quite like them."

Ramsden answered, "I'd like to spend some time with you on the subject of English gardens, father, but I'm afraid I'm in the middle of an important telephone conference. I'll be very pleased to make a contribution if you could contact my secretary. I'm afraid that . . ."

"Oh, I understand fully. It was rude and presumptuous of me to come up here expecting you to jump at the chance to give me money. Certainly I'll call your office. I'm sure we have the number on file. But perhaps, if you'd be so kind to just tell me the name of those bright purple flowers?"

Ramsden was getting impatient. He wanted to return to the television to find out what was happening . . . or not happening . . . with Keough and Phase Two, and he didn't want to have a screaming James in the basement make his presence known. He just wanted to get the priest on his way.

"It's those tall ones in the center, can you see them? If you could tell me, I'd be so grateful and I'll be on my way."

"Which ones, where?" Fortin pointed. "Why, I believe those are . . ." Thwack. Thwack. And Ramsden lay crumpled on the stone driveway.

Barbara held the bat high for a third strike. Fortin held his hand up. "Enough, Barbara. He's out cold. Let's get him inside and you can watch him. I'll go downstairs and get James."

Barbara took the feet and Fortin lifted Ramsden under the arms and they placed him on the floor in the entry hall and closed and locked the door. Fortin watched as Barbara kept her bat poised for another strike in case Ramsden began to come out of his unconsciousness. There didn't appear to Fortin to be much chance of that happening very soon.

Barbara motioned down the hallway to the rear. "The door to the cellar should be in the kitchen in the back of the house. I'll wait here." Fortin walked to the rear of the house noting the grand rooms on either side of the hallway. A broad set of carpeted stairs led to the second floor from the hall and Fortin looked for a door that might lead to the basement. He reached the rear of the house and saw a large kitchen and what appeared to be the remnants of past meals still on plates. He tried one door and found a pantry stocked with food and cleaning supplies and tried a second door that turned out to be a closet housing mops and brooms. The third door had a lock on it and Fortin thought this might be the basement door. He tried it but the lock was set and held fast. He returned to Barbara in the front hall and told her that he needed a key and to check Ramsden's pockets. She extracted a set of keys from his trousers and tossed them to Fortin, still keeping close watch on Ramsden.

Fortin returned to the lock and tried several keys before finding the right one. He heard the tumbler slide and then opened the door. The light in the basement was faint and Fortin was careful descending the stairs. He noticed a television was on but no noise coming from it. Apparently a video game was on, but no one was playing. It was then he spotted James, curled up in the corner of a bed on the far side of the large room. He went over to him and shook him but received little response. James was either in a deep sleep or unconscious from drugs administered by Ramsden. James flexed his hands open and closed but remained largely inert. "C'mon, James, we're taking you home." Fortin lifted the boy to his shoulder, and for the boy's diminutive size, he was dead weight. He moved to the basement stairs with the precious load. Then he heard the call from upstairs.

"Come quick, Andrew. He's beginning to stir and there's someone else coming up the driveway. We've got to get out now."

Fortin grabbed the railing with one hand and held James to his body with the other, taking the stairs carefully. He was halfway up when he heard the gunshot.

Victor pulled the Volvo into the lane leading to the Ramsden home. Murphy commented, "Someone's got a car parked over there. I hope the fellow's alone."

"Keough said he was," Victor said. "I don't trust the bastard though. We'll see when we pull in."

They parked in front of the home in the circular drive and all three exited the vehicle. "Let's see how Mr. Keough is doing, shall we?"

Murphy was on high alert as Victor opened the trunk. "Be-jeesus, man." Victor stood back from the car when he lifted the lid. "Have you taken a shit?" He lifted Keough half way out of the car and asked Tony to help. "He's taken a shit in my car!"

Together, Tony and Victor rolled Keough out of the car and he thudded to the driveway, still bound and gagged. "I told you to be careful back there," said Victor with a cuff across Keough's ears. Victor pulled Keough to a standing position and told him to hobble along. "You're not tied up so tight that you can't take some baby steps. Now move!"

Tony withdrew the beautiful weapon that he's taken from Keough and held it at his side as the quartet approached the front door. "Let's ring the bell and introduce ourselves."

Murphy twisted the door bell and heard the ringing from inside. There was no answer and Murphy gave the door knob a try. It didn't budge. He tried ramming the door open with his shoulder, but all his weight didn't move the door an inch. Tony suggested that everyone stand back as he aimed the pistol at the door. The report was deafening and door splintered. He fired once more and the door splintered again, this time allowing Murphy to kick and push the door open. The sight that greeted them was something they hardly expected.

Barbara Whyte let loose with another swing of her cricket bat and clubbed Ramsden on the side of the head. She drew blood with this smack. Fortin was still not upstairs and she called to him to hurry. Her attention was given over to a noise in the front yard, probably a car. She heard muffled conversation and doors being slammed shut. "Hurry, Andrew. We've got to get out of here now!"

Fortin was doing his best to reach the top of the stairs when a gunshot rang out, and then another. He stayed on the basement stairs and shouted. "Barbara, are you alright?"

When he didn't get an answer, he used all his energy to scramble with James on his shoulder, to the top step and the kitchen. He placed James on the floor gently and leaned around the corner of the kitchen and peered down the hallway. There, he saw Barbara, still clutching the bat. Three men stood at the broken front door and one was holding a large pistol aimed at Barbara. A man with curly white hair was the first he heard speak.

"What do we have here? Is that the honorable Sir Geoffrey Ramsden on the floor, miss?" Barbara just nodded. Then Fortin saw that another man, bound and gagged, was slumped at the door frame, and he looked vaguely familiar. Murphy continued. "Please put down the bat, miss. We're not here to harm you. We are, indeed, here to harm this fellow, but it looks like you've beaten us to the punch, so to speak. Good work."

"My son," was all Barbara could manage.

"I see," Murphy said. You're the mother of the child that our friend here kidnapped. Is he here? Is he safe?" Barbara nodded to the back of the house and Murphy's eyes were drawn to Fortin, still peering from the back of the house. "Is that fellow with you?"

Barbara nodded. Tony by now had lowered the weapon. "Well let's go see what has transpired, shall we?" The group walked to the rear of the house and left Ramsden and Keough where they lay. Fortin stepped to the middle of the hall and said, "The boy's here, but he's been drugged. He won't wake up."

Barbara hurried to her son and stroked his hair, holding him close to her as she wept with relief and joy, mixed with concern for her son's continued stupor. "We need to get him to a hospital." She kissed the boy's forehead and saw that his eyes were fluttering, trying to open. "James, it's me, your mom."

Victor was first to offer assistance. "I've got a large car, so we can take him to a hospital, but he seems to be coming around." James' eyes were now more open than closed and he returned his mother's hug with one of his own. She lifted him and sat down on a kitchen chair, still holding him close. "I've got to contact Charles and tell him James is OK. Where's the phone?"

Victor looked around the kitchen and saw a cordless phone in a cradle at the end of the counter. "What's the number? I'll ring it for you."

Barbara started to recite the number when a sudden noise from the front hallway grabbed their attention. Tony stood nearest the hall and said, "Ramsden's moved. He's not on the floor."

Before anyone could react, Ramsden's voice bellowed from the reception room along the hallway. "That's correct, my friends. So if you'll drop any weapons right now, that would be most appreciated. I happen to be holding a wonderful little rifle in my hands, and I assure you I know how to use it."

Tony refused to cede his weapon and the group in the kitchen stayed out of sight of the hallway. The exit door from the kitchen to the rear yard was on the far side of the room, however, and getting out of the house meant passing directly across the hallway entrance and in sight of Ramsden. Tony crouched down on his chest and jutted his nose into the hallway to see if he could see Ramsden. A rifle crack took part of the doorway and Tony scrambled back into the kitchen. Victor looked at the open doorway to the basement. "Any exit from down there?"

Fortin answered. "Nothing. The basement windows are all barred."

"That window then," Murphy said, suggesting that they open the sash and escape that way." The plan appeared to be the only one affording the group any degree of safety and Murphy slid the window open, punching out the screen when he did so. The lady goes first, then we hand the boy to her."

Tony kept his pistol ready in case Ramsden decided to make a move in their direction. "If I were you, I'd think twice about climbing out the window. I'll be able to see you quite well, and

I am a fabulous shot with this rifle." Ramsden's voice was closer now and coming from the other side of the house. He'd moved across the hallway into another room, positioning himself so he could command a view of the hallway as well as see people escaping from the kitchen window without having to leave the room.

Tony, holding the only weapon in possession of the group in the kitchen motioned to Victor that he'd try to approach Ramsden from the hallway. "Keep making noises at the window and that will keep his attention." Then he slipped off his shoes and made for the hallway in stocking feet. Victor continued ripping the screen out and speaking in a voice that suggested that they'd try the window escape, even with Ramsden watching. Ramsden was less gullible than they hoped, though, and was positioned at the room's entrance with his rifle raised and sighted when Tony began to move. The crack of the rifle shot caught everyone else by surprise and Tony fell back into the kitchen, rolling out of Ramsden's line of fire. He'd taken a slug in the left forearm and it dangled uselessly at his side. He gave the weapon to Victor and held the wound closed with his good hand. Barbara grabbed a towel and applied pressure to stem the blood flow.

Victor shouted back from the edge of the hallway entrance. "Good work, my man. Now you can sit back and take us at will. Even the woman and child. You are such a brave bastard."

"Shut up! If Keough hadn't screwed up his assignment today, the boy would be free and you'd all be walking around without a care."

"And his assignment was to shoot an unarmed woman. That's the honorable cause?"

"No less honorable than the ones for which we're fighting."

Murphy asked, "And who are they that you're up against?"

"You're Irish. I can tell from your accent. You should certainly know what terror your people are capable of inflicting on the world. Plenty of dead women and children as well. That's the Republic for you."

"So this is all about hating the Irish?"

"For good reason, for extremely good reason. You murdered my grandparents in cold blood and right in front of my eyes. There. You remember the 'Harvest'?"

"Yes," said Murphy. "Late fifties. Some violence, but it died out after a while. It was only a few years later that the fighting began in earnest."

"It was during Operation Harvest that your colleagues decided to slay my grandfather and grandmother in their cottage near Rostrevor. Sliced up. Their house was like an abattoir. That's the kind of people who think they can take away another piece of the Kingdom. And it's all a sham."

"Geoffrey."

Ramsden turned with a start and poised his rifle on his shoulder. He'd nearly taken a shot when he saw that the voice was his mother's. How long had she been standing there?

"Geoffrey. What's going on?"

In the kitchen, Fortin asked Victor to see what was happening. He heard a woman's voice coming from the front of the house. Victor peered around the corner, took note and reported. "An older woman. She's standing near the front door and talking with him."

Barbara went over to the hall and repeated Victor's move. In a low voice she said, "It's Ramsden's mother, Caroline Ramsden. She must have just pulled in."

Ramsden called to his mother, "Get over here, Mother. They'll shoot you!"

"Who, Geoffrey? I've been listening to you shouting back and forth, and I can't believe my ears."

"How long? How long have you been here?"

"Long enough to hear you talk about the murder of your

grandparents, my mother and father. And much more, Geoffrey. But who are you shooting at? And what's this business about a man named Keough and shooting at a woman? Did I understand that you ordered such a thing?"

"This," Ramsden said, pointing at the still trussed Keough, "is Mr. Patrick Keough. He had a rather simple task and he bollixed it up. Now here we are. Please, mother, get out of the hallway."

"No, Geoffrey. I think not. This is going to come to a stop. You have no earthly idea, do you?"

"What are you talking about?"

"About Operation Harvest and your grandparents. You think it was the IRA, don't you?"

"Of course it was. I was there. I saw the two men come up to the door and then they stabbed both of them. Calm as can be. Not a shred of emotion. Absolute evil incarnate."

From the kitchen, Barbara called out. "Hello Mrs. Ramsden. This is Barbara Whyte, Charles Whyte's wife. Please tell Geoffrey to put away the rifle."

"Yes, Barbara, I remember you well."

Ramsden was shocked to hear Barbara's voice coming from insider his house. "But I just talked with her a short while ago . . ."

"Sir Geoffrey kidnapped my son, Caroline, and I was just coming to retrieve him. It's all about a plot that Sir Geoffrey calls 'Shamrock'."

"Shamrock? What is this 'Shamrock', Geoffrey?"

"You've seen the charade in Belfast, Mother. The world is sitting back watching as the participants step all over each other making nice. What the world doesn't see is that the IRA and its so called sympathizers are simply doing an end run on the empire. It has to stop, Mother, and merely stating the obvious has proven less than worthless. The world has to be shocked enough to pay attention to the pretense of peace. It's no peace at all."

Ramsden's voice was becoming more shrill as he went on.

"It's one thing to actually take all the steps necessary to stop the violence. It's entirely another to stand in front of the microphones and mouth platitudes. That's all they've done for the past century. And I don't intend to stand idly by and watch the rest of the world give its blessing!"

Barbara called out, "Ask him about the recent visit to Boston by the Prince of Wales. That was a set-up from the start by Sir Geoffrey, and my husband was the unwitting servant to a murder."

Ramsden looked up at his mother whose eyes took on a pleading quality. "You had something to do with that, Geoffrey? You were involved in an assassination attempt on the life of the prince?"

"Of course not, Mother. There was never an effort to harm him. It was only to add the necessary drama to the scene in Belfast. The shot was deliberately misfired and the only damage was one broken pane of glass."

"But Geoffrey, a man died there in Boston. Was that your plan as well?"

"The man was a minor local thug. The world is safer without him."

"The man was my son!" Rogan Murphy called from the kitchen. He was a young lad who never committed a violent crime. Ever. And you consider him expendable in your cause? You're demented, man."

Caroline remained standing in the center of the hallway. She looked at her son with a combination of sadness and disbelief. "And what was this about a Phase Two, Geoffrey? Tell me."

"You'll never understand, mother. If we'd succeeded, the peace talks would have been brought to a halt and a little bit more sanity would creep into the whole Irish controversy. But this fellow," he went on, indicating the bound Keough lying on the floor, "failed miserably."

Caroline stepped over to Keough and removed the tape over his mouth. "And what do you have to say about this? Is this all true?"

Keough nodded. "I was ambushed last night just as I set up. In Kew Gardens."

Victor called out, "He was all set with a weapon when we found him. He was actually planning to stay the night there so he could be ready to shoot his target today."

"And who arranged all this," Caroline asked Keough?

Keough uttered one word. "Him."

"My son? My son set this up? And who were you supposed to shoot?"

Keough was rasping, his lips dry and blistered. "The American president's wife. It was his plan."

"So, Geoffrey, the idea was to actually kill the first lady of the U.S. And that was supposed to bring a stop to the peace talks in Belfast? Is that the idea?"

Ramsden ranted. "Of course it would! Don't you see? If she was killed not long after an attempt was made on the Prince's life, the talks would end in turmoil and the process would cease once and for all. It was an elegant plan, and it would have worked! Both sides would have distrusted the other. The Ulster Dialogues simply couldn't continue. It would have ended the entire sham!"

"And, I suppose it would avenge the deaths of your gran and your granda?" Is that what this was for?"

"Don't you see, mother? When they were killed by the IRA, they were martyrs, and the pretense that their deaths would simply be forgotten . . . not to say anything about the others who were slain during all the troubles . . . why, their deaths would have been for nothing!"

Caroline studied her son. He was acting like a feral animal, almost frothing with anger and hatred. Where was the bright young boy that she had borne? When her husband insisted that

Geoffrey be sent away to school, she lost him forever. Surely, she'd had contact with a young man and later with a celebrated professor and even later with a noted MP and advisor to the nation's leaders, but her son was truly someone else. She did not want to ever acknowledge the fact, but her son, the clever lad she had known, had died with her parents that sunny day in Rostrevor in 1958.

"It's time, Geoffrey, for you to understand what this is all about. You are so insanely in error, so painfully unaware. It's time, Geoffrey. Please put your rifle down."

EIGHTEEN

Ramsden was reluctant to release his grip on the rifle, but he did place it at his side. His mother drew a chair from the sitting room and parked it in the center of the hallway where she sat.

"I need to explain some things to all of you. I need to do this. It should have been done long ago. So please, hear what I have to say."

Those in the rear kitchen paid close attention, much more at ease and attentive to her every word. And then she began her story:

Caroline's Story

The priest walked down the narrow street with a cautious eye. At his side, clutching his hand, the little girl, seven years-old and all arms, legs and freckles, was aware that this was not a time for play. Like the priest, she was careful of the strangers they passed and wary of every blind corner.

Wearing a Roman collar, cassock, biretta, a full beard and glasses, the priest presented a not unusual sight in the neighborhood except to the little girl. She'd never seen him in such an outfit. The pair turned and walked along a cobbled sidewalk, fewer people on this street. The day was gray and cool, an early morning in the city and in a neighborhood she'd never seen before. The priest said, "Mind yourself here. We're almost there and you need to be quiet when we go in. There's a room on the side and I'm told you can stay in there while I'm busy. You have your book, eh?"

"Yes," she said, holding up the children's picture reader.

They stopped in front of a heavy black wood door and the priest rapped four times, then twice, then once. A few moments passed and a latch was thrown and the door opened a crack. The darkness inside kept her from identifying the person who answered. She did hear the voice. "Ah, Doctor, it's you." The door closed briefly and the little girl heard the chain slide. The door was reopened, now much wider and the priest ushered the little girl inside. "I almost didn't recognize you. Ah, a wee guest as well."

"My wife is at the shop and I didn't want to leave her alone. I hope you don't mind. She can stay in another room and read. She's really no trouble."

"We'll sit in the back room, and I'm sure she'll be fine." To the girl he said, "And what's the lass' name?"

"Caroline," she said.

"Well Caroline, there's a seat over there and you can read by the light through the window. I'm sorry I can't turn on any lights for you right now. Can I make you a nice lemon squash?"

"That would be nice. Thank you." When she looked

around the room she saw she was in a pub. The man went behind the bar and mixed up the beverage and presented it to her. To the priest the man said, "And you, my good man of the cloth, can I perhaps draw something for yourself?"

The priest nodded assent. Caroline went to a front table and sat, placing the book and the lemon squash on the table in front of her.

The priest and the man went through a door to a back room where she heard other male voices in deep discussion. When the door closed, she opened her book and began to read from her book. The first story she chose was *The Wind in the Willows*. She could still hear some voices rising and falling, but could make out nothing distinct. She wondered at the content of the conversation, especially after the discussion she overheard last night at her home. She'd been in bed but unable to sleep when she heard her parents arguing.

"Ian, it's so dangerous there. Why do you have to go?"

"Because no one else will. It's important to keep talking, Margaret, and right now there's only silence."

"But you'll be recognized. They'll tear you to pieces."

"That's a bunch of malarkey. No one's going to set on a priest in that neighborhood. Especially one that has a beard and doesn't bear any resemblance to me."

"And what about Caroline? I have to open tomorrow morning and I'll be all alone until ten. You can't leave Caroline here alone."

"She'll be fine with me, Margaret. No one's going to be harmed. Please trust me."

"And who are you meeting with? I've heard those streets are filled with IRA types."

"Maybe, Margaret, but I'm meeting with some men of

reason. Kevin Doyle will be there and so will his cousin Marty. Mickey Dolan and Billy Shaw will probably be there as well."

"And for how long?"

"Margaret, we'll be back home before the pubs open, believe me. Kevin is letting us meet in his back room and he want's me out of there by ten fifteen, so we'll be home not long after you get in from the bakery.

"Ok, then. But I want you to be careful."

The scene was repeated a few more times, and the "priest" had conducted many more visits to the same people in the same neighborhood over the next several months. Eventually, some calm was restored and if there wasn't true peace, there was at least some degree of tolerance and certainly less violence. Years later, some backsliding had taken place. Some thugs, most from the border regions to the south, had incited some attacks in a period known vaguely as Operation Harvest.

The operations were largely confined to the border districts where the IRA made several attempts to stir up trouble. There were few successes in Operation Harvest and the IRA was in disarray.

The government of the north, and later even in the south, responded to the violence by instituting a rule of internment without charge or trial. The morale of the IRA was shaken but the resentment that caused the unrest was never properly addressed.

It was during this period that the mysterious "priest" became active once more. He made contact with the IRA and worked closely with them to find ways to keep discussions going, even if the process was too slow for the Catholics who suffered most. But the priest insisted that there was some progress, however slight, and that no one had yet died as a result of a barbed tongue. The priest was older now, but his words were still taken to heart. In spite of the conflict and the oppression by the Protestants in the north, there was some slight progress, and the priest considered this a worthy accomplishment.

For whom did the priest serve as an intermediary? He acted on his own and traded on his influence as a learned and respected university professor. He had friends in high places, as one might say, and could make the concerns of the Catholics known to those in power without the attendant bloodshed that would certainly have occurred in a direct confrontation. He met with members of the political leadership in Belfast and several leaders of the Protestant religious community. Everything was done in private, as it had to be so. The Catholics in the north and its supporters in the south felt that the progress was too slow. Too, the Protestant majority would have been as equally violent if they thought that face to face official discussions with the Catholics were being conducted.

That's when the word reached the wrong ears. Reverend Brian Folsom was the loudest of the complainers. He made it known from the pulpit and from his public speeches that any concessions to the "apostates" and "Romanists" as he called them, were to be considered violations of God's laws.

> "We hear rumblings about 'peace' and how 'ecumenism' is a valuable tool to secure that peace. Some of this even comes from the mouths of our own priests!" he would shout during Sunday services.
>
> "Let me be clear that ecumenism is not of God. On the contrary, ecumenism is energized by a demon of false religion and makes it "the cage of every un-

clean bird". It is the vile work of darkness and a crime against our Lord Jesus Christ.

"Romanism you must remember is contrary to the very word of God. Every Protestant minister swears at his ordination to uphold the Westminister Confession of Faith that says there is no head of the church but the Lord Jesus Christ and that the Pope of Rome is the Antichrist, a man of sin and the son of perdition.

"Those who claim that we should make peace with the Romanists are either being dishonest or else they perjure themselves, for as Protestants we have all sworn to believe this same Confession of Faith. Just what impact does it have upon a people when some prominent members among us are guilty of swearing to believe one thing but, in fact, believe and practice the very opposite?"

It was Folsom who let it be known to some of the less benign members of his flock that Ian Loughlin was seen consorting with Catholics; that those same Catholics were known to be members of the IRA; and that Ian Loughlin and his supporters needed to be taught a lesson.

On a lovely day in 1958, two men pedaled their bicycles along a path that led to the whitewashed cottage owned by Ian and Margaret Loughlin. They never knew that their grandson was at their home, on holiday, nor that he was present for their visit.

"Lies! That's a damned lie! They were slain by the IRA. They even left their signature scribbled on the wall in blood." Ramsden was beside himself with anger. He strode across the room brandishing his rifle. "It's a lie! I saw the two men and they killed my granda, and then they killed my gran. I saw it all. I was up in the tree just over the doorway. I told you that!"

Caroline maintained her calm during her son's outburst. "I'm afraid it's not a lie, Geoffrey. Your gran and granda were murdered by their own. It's true."

"It cannot be! My granda and gran were Protestants. They took me to services every Sunday. I was there!"

Ramsden pounded his fist on a table near the entryway. "It would have worked, you know. It would have stopped the whole thing. 'Ulster Dialogues' indeed. Nothing but a bunch of deceit and dishonesty wrapped up in three piece suits and cordial handshakes."

Caroline said nothing. She held her son's gaze and could only have pity on him.

"They came to the door as calm as could be and stuck them like beef at a slaughter. No emotion. Just stabbed them where they stood!"

Rogan Murphy was the first to speak. "You killed a young man for nothing, Ramsden. You wanted to avenge their deaths, and you had it ass backwards. You're a miserable cur, Ramsden, and you're a fool. A stupid bloody fool."

Caroline said to her son. "It's over, Geoffrey. You can't go on like this. Kidnapping, murder. You're a better man than that."

Barbara called to Caroline and Ramsden. "We're going to walk out the back door now. We're going to take my son and we're going to leave."

Ramsden lifted his rifle and shouted a response. "You'll not leave!" There was desperation in his voice and it cracked as it rose. "You'll not leave! I'll shoot you and you'll die right where you are. All of you. I won't let you leave!" But Caroline walked to him and placed her hand on the barrel of the rifle. They locked eyes. Caroline slid the weapon from his grasp and walked to the hallway, opening the breech and removing the remaining cartridges, spilling them on the floor.

She left the rifle and returned to her son, holding him closely as he began to sob.

Barbara Whyte walked across the kitchen and opened the back door of the house. Directly behind her, Fortin, still in cassock and collar, carried James. Tony and Victor stayed with Murphy who still wanted to confront Ramsden face to face and personally and painfully avenge the death of his son. But they held him by the arms and Victor spoke. "You've got to let it go, Rogan. You can't bring him back. Killing the man will solve nothing. Let him be shamed if it's revenge you want. It will break the man when the police arrive, and they surely will when we call them."

Tony placed his one good hand on Murphy's shoulder. "Victor's right, Rogan. Let it go. That man inside has just looked into his soul and he's found there's nothing there. Let him be broken and let him live a broken man."

Rogan Murphy relaxed his arms as they made their exit.

Barbara was still frantic over James' continued lethargy. "He's beginning to stir, Barbara," Fortin said. "We should get him to a hospital to be checked, but he's beginning to wake."

Victor came over to check on the boy. "Was that your car at the bottom of the lane?" Fortin nodded. "Then let me drive you to the hospital. No sense in walking all the way back with the boy. Come." To Tony and Murphy he said, "Would you call 9-9-9 and talk to the police when they arrive? Keough is still trussed up as well." Tony nodded.

To Fortin Tony said, "Strange isn't it? It's not very often we get to be on the reporting end of a crime."

James was nearly awake by the time they reached the local hospital and was delighted to see his mother holding his hands and kissing him. He didn't appear to exhibit any lingering effects from the medications Ramsden had been feeding him, but the doctors suggested he stay at the hospital for at least one, perhaps two nights to be certain. Unwilling to leave his side, Barbara decided to stay at the hospital through that first night.

Andrew Fortin returned to the house and was met by several members of the Cumbrian police force. The process of sorting out the story was a long one and Fortin spent most of the night sitting on a hard metal chair in Ulverston. To an assortment of constables, including the Chief Constable who'd made the drive from Penrith to oversee the investigation, he told his convoluted tale. Still clad in full R.C. regalia, he described the journey to Canada and the flight to the UK using another man's passport. Rather than lie, he thought, it's better to simply tell all and avoid having to retrace any fabrications.

Assistant Chief Constable Derek Woods conducted most of the interview. To Woods, a giant of a man who spoke in short bursts, almost snorts, Fortin retraced everything from the cryptic email messages to the rescue of James at the Ramsden home. He was incredulous when Fortin described the disguises and make up used to effect a successful trip from Canada to London, and made copious notes regarding the involvement of Mother Marie Granville and Père Gilbert Laroque. "Major crime, you know." (Snort) "Entering via false passport and/or identification. Hell to pay." (Snort)

Fortin didn't care. His concern was directed more towards the lack of questions surrounding the involvement of Sir Geoffrey Ramsden in the Shamrock plot. Neither ACC Woods nor any other official asked specific questions regarding Ramsden, and to Fortin, they seemed to dismiss the mention of the honorable MP in any discussion.

"Do you think we came here because Ramsden was a nice fellow?" Fortin was getting sarcastic with Woods.

"Fine gentleman, Sir Geoffrey. Fine man." (Snort) "Brilliant."

Fortin made several attempts to direct the attention of the

police officials to Ramsden and the entire Shamrock plan. Nothing seemed to change the opinions of the police squad until the early morning hours when ACC Woods and his colleagues met with Caroline Ramsden and later with Barbara Whyte. Barbara never wavered in the retelling of the tale and gained a degree of ferocity when she insisted that the Chief Constable himself discuss the matter with her. Her relentless contention that Sir Geoffrey Ramsden was the architect of the diabolical plot eventually did bring the Chief Constable into the discussion and no attempt by him could divert Barbara's fierce attention. "Did you speak with his mother? Did you?"

Chief Constable D. Linley Hare was built like a steel drum and was just as stolid in his calm assurance that "the matter of Sir Geoffrey would be looked into."

Barbara lost what composure she had left. "With all due respect, Chief Constable, we're not talking about a man whose nerves are simply a bit frayed. Sir Geoffrey Ramsden is off his fucking rocker. He's a murderer, and he's plotted to kill the US president's wife! How much more fucking nuts does the man have to be before you think it's a matter worth more than a little sedative for the man's nerves?"

"Mrs. Whyte, there's absolutely no reason to go on like this, is there? Sir Geoffrey is being interviewed and I spoke to him myself, didn't I? Obviously the man is extremely tired. A most diligent man, he is. He's worn to an absolute frazzle." Hare almost harrumphed at the thought that Ramsden could be behind such a stratagem as Shamrock.

"Have you spoken to his mother, Caroline Ramsden?"

"She's resting. We'll let her gather herself and talk with her in the morning. In the meantime, miss, we have several matters of concern here." Hare studies a clipboard over his reading glasses. "False identification. Passport fraud. Most serious, isn't it? And what do you have to say to that?"

A knock on the door of the interview room caught their attention and CC Hare rose and answered it. To his surprise, and in Barbara's view his chagrin, Caroline Ramsden entered the room and took a seat. Hare could not have been more gracious.

"I'm so sorry that you have to participate in all this, Mrs. Ramsden, but there are so many loose ends to tie up and so many allegations that require corroboration. Most serious charges have been made, and believe me, we intend to sort this all out post haste."

Caroline was serene as she listened and took a deep breath before she began. "Mrs. Whyte. I'm sure, has described the events of yesterday. My son has, I'm sorry to say, deluded himself into believing that he must do everything in his power to disrupt the Ulster Dialogues, the peace talks in Belfast that are going on as we speak. This included ordering the murder of a young man in the U.S. plus the attempted murder of the U.S. first lady. My son also kidnapped and drugged a young child. I don't know if you've heard all the details from everyone else to this point, but that's the thrust of the issue. My son did all of these things and he's now in a state of physical and emotional collapse. He needs psychiatric care. But the facts are as I've just stated."

Hare was silent for an extended period. "Mrs. Ramsden," he finally said, "You're saying that Sir Geoffrey ordered a murder?"

"Yes I did. And if you were listening to everything I said, he did much more."

"But nothing, to my knowledge, has happened to the president's wife. In fact she was on the telly last night with her husband at a formal dinner in London, wasn't she?"

"Attempted murder, Chief Constable. I said that, did I not?"

Barbara interjected, "And childhood abduction." Hare glowered at Barbara.

"She's correct. My son kidnapped a beautiful eight year old

child and held him captive in his basement in Cartmel. Shot him up with anesthesia and dosed him repeatedly to keep him sedated. It's all true. And he threatened several others with his rifle yesterday as well, but I don't believe we have to add to the confusion you are already displaying, Chief Constable."

Hare nodded, unsure whether he'd just been insulted.

In an adjacent room, Constable Harry Leek was doing his best to take notes. Across the table sat Rogan Murphy along with Victor and Tony. Tony's arm by now was bandaged and in a sling. Victor did most of the talking and his delivery was rapid fire and without interruption. Murphy, unfortunately, had a lengthy criminal history that caught the attention of Leek and others. No crime had been perpetrated by Murphy, though, except for his participation in carrying Patrick Keough from London to Cumbria in the trunk of a car.

Victor and Tony, Murphy became convinced, were not nearly the given names of his new colleagues in the adventure. Murphy had met many men like this pair over the years, and none of them held such pristine histories as these. Nothing at all was on file, and Leek grew increasingly convinced that the trio would have to walk free. He wanted corroboration from a higher authority and called on ACC Woods to confer in the hallway outside the door.

"We can't just let them go, can we? I mean, they're obviously men of criminal backgrounds, but I can't find anything with which to hold them further."

Woods agreed and Tony, Victor and Murphy returned to Victor's Volvo and began the long drive back to London.

Patrick Keough lay confined to a hospital bed with his right arm in a cast and gauze coverings on much of his head. His eyes were swollen shut. Intensive interviews were not yet permitted by the medical staff, but to the investigators who had an opportunity to visit, Patrick Keough would likely remain mute. A fingerprint check had revealed nothing as well as a thorough background check including a check of his passport and other documents. It was, to Chief Constable Hare, as if he never even existed.

The nurse assigned to Keough disliked having her routine interrupted by having a constable stationed outside Keough's door. "He's not going anywhere with those wounds and his arm in a sling. You may as well tell your boss that it will be at least tomorrow afternoon before he can even talk, his lips are so swollen." Indeed Keough still bore rope burns and raised welts across his back and chest. Victor, Tony and Murphy had not been gentle. The physicians also noted burned flesh on his neck, scalp, and even his testicles, and could ascertain no apparent reason for them.

Late in the day, given the reports given by everyone else involved, CC Hare determined to conduct an interview with the man who was described as the "trigger man" in the assassination plot on the life of the US first lady, and the actual murderer of one John Murphy in the city of Boston. CC Hare had already been in touch with the Boston Police and had a long conversation with officers Collins and Wetman about the facts surrounding the death of John Murphy. When the physical description of Mr. Patrick Keough was disclosed, all were convinced they had their man. Collins and Wetman were surprised the man remained alive given their conversation with Kavanagh in South Boston. "We were sure he'd be dead meat," said Wetman. "The guys we're talking about don't fool around."

After agreeing to watch for an order of extradition to the US, Hare decided he'd give Keough one more chance to explain himself. Hare was still shocked that Sir Geoffrey Ramsden could be implicated in such a plot and was sure that he could attach much of the blame on Keough acting alone and without Ramsden's direction. He drove to the hospital with his ACC and demanded over the protests of the nurse that he be given access to Patrick Keough at once and in spite of the physical suffering the man was enduring as a patient. The nurse gave her grudging assent and led the two officials to the door. They nodded to the constable on duty and strode in only to find a window open and the thin drapery fluttering in the breeze. Hare raced to the window and looked to the ground below and slapped his leg with Keough's file folder. Keough had disappeared.

Barbara Whyte and Andrew Fortin returned to the pub hotel and collapsed in a snug away from the crowded bar. They each drank their beer in silence and ordered another before they began to speak. Barbara's in-laws made the drive from Thirsk and picked up James. Barbara and Fortin were advised by the police to remain in Cumbria for another day for additional questioning. Meanwhile the police would deal with the issues of their fraudulent passports and illegal entry. Caroline had been permitted to leave and elected to complete her journey to her cousin's home where she could compose herself and her thoughts. She too would be subject to many more additional questions regarding her son.

Ramsden remained in the Ulverston lock up where he insisted to anyone who'd listen that the charges were trumped up and that he ought to be pinned with medals rather than treated as a criminal.

Fortin was the first to speak. "I called Janet. She's mad as hell that she wasn't here to smack the guy that broke into my place and followed her around."

Barbara described her own phone call. "I spoke with Charles. He's probably going to be arrested before this is finished."

"I'm so sorry."

"He knew it had fallen apart when Ramsden took James. But he says he wants to cooperate with the police, and maybe that will help him. After all, he knew about the gunshot when the prince was in Boston, but he also knew that it was meant as a drama, not to hurt anyone. He never considered that Ramsden had arranged for John Murphy to be tossed off the roof and killed."

"You're right. What are you going to do now? After they finish with us?"

Barbara looked into her half empty glass. "Probably stay here for a while. We're both supposed to meet with someone from the US Embassy and the British Home Office tomorrow to sort out the passport issue, but under these circumstances, I think we'll be OK. I'll stay with James at my in laws for a while before heading back. You can probably leave right away as soon as we get that cleared up. Your practice has got to be suffering with you away."

"I'm sure there'll be some busy days when I get back, yes. But I'm grateful that things worked out here without James or you getting hurt."

Barbara put her hand on his sleeve. Remember what we were talking about the other night? You said you might want to sleep with me?"

"I remember it as clear as a bell."

"Well, I truly appreciate that. If you weren't dressed like a priest, I just might have jumped your bones tonight."

Fortin looked down, having forgotten he was still clad in the black cassock. "I guess it started feeling natural. Maybe too natural for my own good."

Barbara smiled at him and spoke with her eyes. Yes she loved him and she would have slept with him. "And as for being a voyeur, just watching life as it passed along right by, let me correct myself. You jumped in when I needed you most, and you risked your life for me. But I think maybe you can't be my therapist when we get back. Too close."

"I'll be sorry to lose you as a patient, Barbara." He meant it.

NINETEEN

The next day was filled with stenographers, tape recorders and lawyers. The questions were repetitive and detailed, as if the intent was not to gather evidence as much as it was to cause Andrew Fortin and Barbara Whyte to stumble, thereby exposing the entire episode as a bad dream and restoring a sense of equanimity throughout the nation. The questioning was conducted separately so that neither knew the precise responses of the other. In the end, though, telling the truth proved its value as a virtue and the interrogators never caught either party in any significant contradiction of the other.

Fortin's questioners on behalf of the UK police were bigger brass than he encountered the day before. He sat on one side of a long metal table and faced three interrogators. A stenographer sat at another table that also held a tape recorder. To Fortin, the scene had all the makings of a bad movie.

A lunch break that included an assortment of dry sandwiches and soft drinks was abbreviated by the arrival of Scott Edwards from the US Embassy. Edwards wasn't pleased to hear the details of the pair's surreptitious entry into the UK.

"You realize the seriousness of the offense, don't you? You used someone else's passport to secure entry into a foreign country. You intentionally disguised your appearance in the commission of a fraud. You failed to report a conspiracy to murder, a crime of which you had knowledge, and you also failed to report a second conspiracy to commit a crime in the UK against the spouse of a U.S. official who just happens to be the President of the country. And that's before the UK folks at Immigration deal with you." Fortin and Whyte could see that the next few hours with Mr. Scott Edwards would be difficult ones.

By four in the afternoon, Andrew Fortin and Barbara Whyte were thoroughly exhausted and elated when they were told they could leave for the day. "There will be more interviews in the morning," they were told, but Edwards was sufficiently impressed at the end of his investigation that he assured them that he would do his best to expedite the process of obtaining at least temporary passports when the questioning was completed. "There will likely be some depositions you'll have to sit through as soon as Ramsden is formally charged," Edwards went on.

Fortin asked, "What if he's not charged for another two weeks? Does that mean we can't leave until then?"

"No. The depositions can be taken later and you can come back here at that time if there's a need. Every statement given to the crown so far is consistent. Based on what I'm told, I don't see Ramsden being allowed to leave a secure medical facility for a long, long time. The crown has a list of charges a mile long, and Ramsden isn't going to be walking around free for many years." This was pleasant news to the pair as, until that point, no mention had been made by anyone else that their sagas would result in any criminal charges against Ramsden.

Caroline Ramsden was allowed to leave as well, but she chose to spend time visiting her son. Still ranting about the "noble mission he'd undertaken on behalf of the empire," Ramsden was spluttering in his cell. His eyes were deep set and dark and Caroline read his appearance as signs of madness. He certainly wasn't the calm, urbane man that the English populace had come to know. So far, word of the plot and Ramsden's direct involvement were still officially wrapped up tight but Caroline assumed that the press and the television crews would descend soon enough. The fourth estate thoroughly enjoyed a good fall from grace, and Ramsden's was a spectacular tumble.

Fortin went to the bar and ordered two ales as soon as he and Barbara returned to the pub. When he returned to the table, Barbara was staring into space. "What are you going to do now?"

"I'm going to Thirsk to spend some time with my son and my in laws. I'm going to have to stick around anyway so I'll stay with James." She took a long draft. "He's looking great now and I'll head over there as soon as the questions are done tomorrow. How about you?"

"Heading back as soon as they'll let me go. If things go well, I can be home tomorrow night." He was feeling enormous relief at the prospect of returning home and getting back to a normal life. He could see that Barbara's ordeal was far from over. The successful release of James did not put an end to her distress. "Have you spoken to Charles?"

"Charles?" She looked wistful. "I spoke with him." There was a pause before she continued and Fortin read Barbara's expression that the conversation with Charles did not provide her with any respite. "He's already been interviewed by the Boston Police. There are no formal charges yet but they took his passport away. He can't go to his office anymore; the Consul told him to stay away until the situation gets settled. Charles knows he's out of a job. It's a question of going to jail over there, or getting deported and going to jail over here, or maybe both." She took another sip of her beer. "He has a lawyer. He's going to need one." Barbara reached into her purse and found some British coins. "How about if I find a tune on the jukebox that we can dance to?"

She found Bonnie Raitt's "I Don't Want Anything To Change" and they moved slowly to the melancholy sounds. Barbara held on tight and placed her head on his shoulder, nestled in and protected. When the song ended, she looked up into his eyes and repeated the last lines of the song . . . *I don't want anything to do with what comes after you . . .* kissed him deeply, a soft but urgent kiss. "Please, Andrew, take me upstairs now."

Fortin took her by the hand and walked with her to his room. When he closed the door, she put her arms around his neck and pressed herself to him as she kissed him and nibbled at his neck. "I want you to make love to me," she whispered, and his hunger for her was equal to the challenge. Their lovemaking began slowly with tender kisses and soft caresses. He explored her body with his hands and mouth, feeling an intense warmth develop inside her. When they joined, they maintained a relaxed rhythm, looking deeply into each other's eyes with each thrust and probe. They both wanted the moment to last forever, but their pace developed an insistence that carried them to places unknown. They came in a heated rush, and they stayed locked in an embrace. When he rolled away, she clung to him and snuggled like a child and began to fall asleep. "I love you, Andrew. I love you."

He stroked her hair and she looked childlike as she fell into a slumber. "I love you too, Barbara. I do."

When Fortin awoke, Barbara was already gone. He dressed, showered and went downstairs where he found her slathering cream on a scone and sipping her coffee.

"About last night," Fortin started, but she waved him off and offered a forlorn smile.

"It was what I wanted." Barbara spoke in a low voice. "I used you, Andrew. And do you know what? I liked it. My emotions might be running around like crazy, but I'm not letting guilt about last night get in the middle." She smiled when she continued. "I wouldn't trade a single minute of last night for anything. Thank you."

Fortin took a sip of his coffee. "I'd like to say that I deserve all the credit, but I want you to know that I was incredibly turned on by you. I didn't exactly beat you off with a stick."

"You're right. In fact, your 'stick' was wonderful. The only regret I have is that I didn't sleep with you before." Barbra winked at him and continued to drink her coffee.

In a low tone, Fortin said, "I wish things were different, Barbara. I don't want to see you hurt any more."

Barbara reached across the table and put a hand on his. She squeezed it when she spoke. "I'm not very religious, but I did promise to stay by his side even when things got rough. But I truly think Charles will just walk away. He's broken. You should have heard his voice." She reached for the right words when she went on. "He has no spirit inside him. But I really don't think he's nearly as crushed by what could happen to us . . . to Mr. and Mrs. Charles Whyte as a couple . . . as much as he feels let down by Ramsden. In the end, I don't think he fully understands yet how much of his life was really a marriage to Ramsden, or at least the ideal of Ramsden, versus a marriage to me.

"He . . . Charles . . . he fell in love with a pipedream. There was never anything real about it, was there? Oh sure, there was James. He was real, and I suppose at first I was real. But Ramsden . . . ah, Ramsden, he was the reality of Charles' life."

Fortin was struck by her argument. "And Ramsden, he built his life around something no less of an illusion."

Barbara nodded assent. "True. The man's mad. He created this entire persona, this entire career, this life, all based on something as false as could be. 'Sorry, Geoff, but every single thing you've built your life around is utterly false.' Can you imagine the abyss he must have looked into when we were all in his house? And his mother standing there directly in front of him recalling the events of her youth and giving lie to his whole sense of purpose. I almost felt bad for the man."

"It doesn't change the fact that he killed a person for his dream, as unreal and as much of a mistake as it was. There was no excuse for that. And remember that he had absolutely no qualms with arranging the deaths of more people in support his fantasy."

"And presidents and prime ministers actually declare war for similar illusions, and *thousands* of young people die trying to kill people they don't know well enough to hate."

"But we hope as a people that we pay heed to the truth before we convince ourselves to accept the great lie."

"But we don't, Andrew. Maybe I'm too cynical about everything right now. In our case, we just had the good fortune of seeing Caroline walk through the front door, and she just happened to tell a story that changed everything. But what if she didn't happen to come by when she did? What if she had died some time past? What would there be today to align things as they should be?" Barbara reached for a tissue and blew her nose. "The whole plot might have worked in Boston and the peace talks could have ended. There'd be no more Ulster Dialogues. More people would eventually die. Charles and Ramsden would have cause to celebrate, wouldn't they? I shudder when I think of it."

"But there must be some scruples in the man. I can't see you having married a man who had nothing good inside. Charles must feel terrible about James having been in the middle, for example."

"Absolutely. That hurt him deeply. I don't know. I don't know what to think. I want to believe that Charles could have been a good father, but he's lost himself in his ideal, and now that his ideal is shown to be just a babbling tattered rag of a man, he's at sea. There's nothing of Charles Whyte left."

"Does he have somebody he can talk to?"

"You mean like a therapist?" Fortin nodded his head.

"No. That's not something Charles does. Maybe some day, but he doesn't have anyone right now."

They both sat in silence and then waited outside for their ride to the Ulverston constabulary and the day of questions that awaited them. When the van arrived, she turned to him before climbing in. "I meant what I said last night, Andrew. I love you."

Detective Jerry Wetman looked over his notes before addressing Charles Whyte and his lawyer. "Mr. Whyte, I don't think the District Attorney is going to want to prosecute you for the murder of John Murphy, but that's going to be his call. I happen to believe you when you tell me that you didn't know anything about Murphy's involvement. What will happen for sure is that you're going to have to stick around and give some depositions about Geoffrey Ramsden and Patrick Keough, and we're going to seek extradition of both of them from England. That may never happen, and even if it does it's going to be a long time. They're going to prosecute over there and if their courts move as fast as ours, well we'll all be old men before they end up in front of a judge in Boston."

Collins added, "We're going to recommend that after you're deposed, if the DA is fully satisfied, that the charges against you be dropped. The fact that you knew about an assassination attempt is a serious thing, even if it was scripted to be faked. I don't see how that's going to get the DA all worked up. The fact that you had prior knowledge of an attempt that was going to be made on the president's wife, now that's a different story. I'm guessing that the DA is going to do a hand off to the UK courts on that one. Again, that's entirely up to him. There'll probably be some civil matters as well, but your lawyer will talk to you about that. I understand you've been advised to stay away from the consulate over in Cambridge."

Whyte nodded.

"Then I'll suggest you just go home and wait to hear from the DA about depositions. He'll probably deal through your lawyer."

Wetman rose from his seat and opened the door. "You can go now, Mr. Whyte."

When Whyte and the lawyer left, Collins moved some papers into a neat pile and began placing them in a folder. "Stupid sonovabitch. What a dumb thing to get involved with." He stood up from the table and prepared to leave. "He's a broken man. You can see it in his eyes. I talked to his lawyer before we sat down and he said he thinks the guy's suicidal."

"He won't. He doesn't have an ounce of determination left inside him."

TWENTY

Andrew Fortin found a row in the rear center of the plane where he could stretch out and sleep. The last several days were as intense as he could ever imagine a set of days to be. He wondered if this was like war, where intense and sustained emotional and physical experience could run together into such a packet of bewildering data that sorting it through could takes weeks or months or even years. "Shell shocked" was the old term; PTSD was the more recent diagnosis. He decided he didn't want to rush into his own self therapy and instead chose two nips of Johnny Walker Black neat and a long sleep.

His dreams came quickly and, as often was the case, his childhood was their focus. He saw his mother, pretty, alone and smiling. She transformed into the pain-ravaged sickly woman he knew later in life and relived the memories of her long illness and eventual death. He had always imagined that her illness would somehow prepare him for her demise, and that his grief and guilt, if they followed, would be clear-edged and more defined. He also imagined that he'd eventually pass through those feelings, that they'd become finite and permit him to recall, if not relive, the pain of losing her.

Instead, he found himself experiencing repeatedly old conversations and events that did nothing to diminish the ache nor permit the tenderness to heal. He was working at Leonard Morse Hospital in Natick near the end of his mother's life, a member of a group therapy team that dealt with the more distressing cases of depression and suicidality. At times, as he listened to patient complaints, he found himself disassociating with the experience and with his expectations, becoming placid and noncaring in a sea of anguished souls. As a catholic and former seminarian, guilt was not a completely foreign sense. He went through an extended period of self-loathing, and criticized himself for ministering to his own needs and not those of others.

Fortin woke from his dream state in a sweat in spite of the blast of cold air that burst from the airliner's ventilation system. He went to the rest room and splashed cold water on his face, returning to his seat and asking for one more nip of scotch, this time on ice.

Some people awake and recall their dreams with vivid clarity and Fortin was one of those. He tried to find the string of one conversation that replayed itself, the one he'd heard from his mother at his grandfather's funeral. "Your father is nothing at all like Pepère Jack, and I think that's good. I don't think you're anything like your Pepère either, if that's any consolation." Fortin sipped at his scotch and wondered.

Andrew's father was a different sort of man than Pepère Jack. Thicker around the middle and with none of the sharp elbows and knees that he remembered. Bill Fortin was less intense than Pepère Jack as well. While Andrew's memories of his grandfather were colored by the man's old age and general good nature, he'd heard some stories . . . most of them from Aunt Alice, his father's eldest sister . . . that painted a different and less flattering portrait. Pepère Jack plowed his small holding behind an old and failing horse, Pete. At the horse's advanced age of twenty-three, he was generally at his best when ridden gently around the fields by the Fortin passel of children. Dragging a plow across the stony hill of the family farm drained Pete quickly, and his stamina was such that all his concentrated strength would barely help the plow break ground. Frustrated, Pepère Jack threw the plow to the ground, withdrew his jack knife and sliced Pete's lips on both sides behind the bit, then whipping the horse to pull its hardest, finally walking away and letting the old horse stand alone and bleed mightily in the field. Soon after, in spite of tending by Aunt Alice and other siblings, Pete succumbed and died a painful death of starvation.

Andrew, when he heard the story, wondered if that was what his grandfather meant: "You're the only one that's like me." He tried to reconcile that event with his own feelings about senseless cruelty and felt simultaneously confused and saddened.

Bill, on the other hand, was a gentle man, less garrulous than his grandfather, and perhaps the gentlest of all his brothers and sisters. Unlike his brother and two sisters, Bill was the only one who didn't drink, except for an occasional beer; this contrasted vividly with the rest of the clan. Andrew's mother once mentioned in passing that Korea had changed him. Before being sent over as a twenty-year old, Bill was as likely as his friends to be pounding down shots and beers at the Lithuanian Club: "If you couldn't get a drink at the Lithuanian Club, no matter how old you were, you just couldn't get a drink." But even then, his mother related, Bill was more likely to be sitting at the edge of the group and not at its center.

Andrew was sixteen when his father told him stories for the first time about his experiences in Korea. Andrew etched three of them in his memory, naming them the Deaf Story, the Turk

Story, and the Dead Kids Story. "I was in the service for less than three months when I found myself sitting on a hillside with a squad of kids in the same predicament as me. One day I'm changing tires at the Esso Station; next day I'm carrying metal ammo boxes up a mountain in heavy sleet and shooting at shadows that we thought were North Koreans or Chinese." The mortar fire was non stop. After three months there, his father lost all his hearing. "I have some of it back now, but that's why I still can't hear a thing on my left side."

Andrew wasn't sure what prompted his father to tell the stories so many years after the actual events and he never raised that question to him directly. Maybe it was the news of the day about the illegal guns-for-oil scheme and Oliver North. Whatever the reason, Andrew sensed that his father held feelings of deep distrust about his government.

"We were all supposed to rotate sentry duty at night. It was dangerous, and a lot of kids got nailed at night by enemy snipers. The snow and the cold were incredible and we were dressed up as if we were waging war in North Carolina. The brass had no idea what was going on at the front." In his father's group were several Turkish soldiers.

"It was a United Nations mission, they told us then, so we had men from Australia and England and everywhere. I'd never seen anything like these Turkish guys before, though. They were crazy, and they actually volunteered for sentry duty. At daybreak, they'd come back to the camp and undo their belts and let these gray lumps fall to the ground. They were the ears of the enemy soldiers they killed during the night. It was like a contest for them. They'd sneak up on the enemy, stab them, and slice the left ears off before letting them drop down to the ground dead. One guy had seven ears on his belt loop one time."

But the worst of the stories involved the young Korean boys who seemed to treat the military compounds like their own little village. They'd hang around for favors like chewing gum and candy. But the most valued rewards were the dimes and quarters they'd earn from the GIs for odd jobs they'd perform, like picking up litter and washing the jeeps. "We had a train that delivered supplies to the main camp every seven days and the tracks ran right through the center of our little area. A bunch of rednecks in camp thought it would be great fun to have races where the last kid to cross the tracks in front of the train would get fifty cents. That was huge money for those kids, and their families lived for a week on a lot less. So every seventh day, a bunch of kids would stand behind a line as the train made its way into the camp. Then they'd race the train and cross the tracks right in front of the train. The most desperate kids were crushed to death when they were run over by the train. It didn't make any difference to the rednecks or even the other little kids. They'd just drag the bodies into the woods after the train went by. And the last kid to cross the tracks without getting killed got fifty cents. It happened like that every seven days. Fifty cents and one dead kid every seven days."

Eventually Fortin flopped across the row of seats, comfortable with the memories he had of a compassionate father and accepting of those of a cruel grandfather. Both saw hardship in their lives, and one chose to inflict it in return. He once again railed at the spirit of his grandfather for the suggestion that he, Andrew, was most like him. He fell asleep and knew that the scene would surface again someday in his dreams.

The days immediately after his arrival found Fortin back in his office and seeing patients. Janet Chapel had worked miracles to make sure that every patient whose appointment with Fortin had been postponed had access to another psychiatric assistance, meaning herself in most cases in spite of the jarring effects it had on her own grueling schedule. She called him early one morning to vent.

"You've got some crackpots in your patient files, Fortin. I'll give you that. Where do you find these people? One guy likes to dress up like a baby and get spanked?"

"C'mon Jan, where's your tolerance? Odd as it may sound, Janet, these people are out there. You took plenty of abnormal psych classes. Your esteemed colleagues refer most of them, and should I remind you of a few you've referred yourself?"

"Most of my flesh and blood therapy patients are children who haven't been quite so bent by life experience as some of yours seem to be. I mean, there's that woman who just can't get over the death of her dog. Alright, that's understandable."

"I know what you're going to say."

"But the freakin' dog died eleven years ago! Get another puppy! There's no end to the 'its' this woman doesn't get. But OK. Enough. It was a pleasure to work with them. I mean that. They all think you're the balls, if that's any help. I almost puked when one woman couldn't stop gushing about how wonderful you are. Jeesh!"

"All kidding aside, Jan, I'll bet it was interesting for you. This is the other half of the 'medication and talk' therapy that we do. It probably brought back a lot of memories for you."

"It did, but I think I'll stick with pediatric psychiatry and the pharmacology aspect. It suits me better. Thinking of which, I need my Saab back some day."

"Father Laroque is actually driving down with it this weekend. I figured I owed him a little bit, considering the fact that he let me be him. I'm trading him his clothes for your car and he's going to spend a few days in town courtesy of me."

"Like you can afford it?"

"Look, it's not that bad. It's only a couple of days and he's not a bad guy. Plus, I need to brush up on my French and he told me he'll only speak French to me while he's here."

"Sounds like a real treat. Three days with a priest in Wayland."

"So when are we going to have a chance to break bread?"

Janet's smile could almost be heard over the telephone line. "I thought you'd never ask. How about tomorrow, say seven o'clock at my place."

"Whoa, you're going to do the cooking?" This was a switch since Janet didn't usually offer to be chef for a night. Her forte was the fruit of the grape and that's what she usually stayed with.

"See? You're not paying attention. Just show up and don't bring the wine. It's all taken care of."

Fortin considered the conversation again after he completed the call. I wonder what she meant, he thought to himself.

His first appearance before a magistrate was kept quietly buried in an otherwise non-newsworthy court agenda. In spite of the efforts to keep the events out of the press for as long as possible, the news of Shamrock and Sir Geoffrey Ramsden was now everywhere. Adding fuel to the banner headlines, Ramsden shrieked loudly of the righteousness of his efforts to sabotage the Ulster Dialogues. Caroline sat in the first row of the gallery and observed as her son, now confined to a wheelchair due to the medications that were being administered, raged about the cause of a truly united kingdom. The Prime Minister had been apprised of Ramsden's deeds over the past few weeks and wished not to be seen anywhere in the vicinity.

Ramsden had lost weight and his eyes were sunk deep into his skull. In just a week, his hair had become like straw, thinner and more brittle. The chief prosecutor did his best to suggest that Ramsden be secreted to a mental health facility but the judge had yet to rule on the request. No one connected to the case wished to extend the public display of a man gone mad, especially those who had some political obligations to Ramsden for past favors.

At the end of the day, Caroline visited her cousin and stayed the night. Caroline commented to her cousin on the events of the day after Ramsden's loud appearance before the bar. "His friends are abandoning him like rats from a burning frigate and I can't say I blame them. Geoffrey has become poison to them."

Meanwhile, Caroline secured the services of an estate agent to make inquiries about disposing of the Mayfair property as well as the Ramsden home in Cartmel. She was already approached by her son's barrister about a directed of power of attorney and she expected those documents to become effective soon. Neither property had a mortgage so the entire proceeds would be available to help pay Geoffrey's bills, legal and otherwise. If her son continued to remain convinced of the rectitude of his Shamrock plan, Caroline had no doubt that her son's mental state would translate into a prolonged commitment to psychiatric care.

"I will miss the Cartmel home," she told Gwendolyn. "It has some fond memories, but I think now that the bad ones will overshadow them."

Boston's Logan Airport international terminal was crowded when Charles arrived. A low pressure area had formed over the north Atlantic and temporarily closing some airports in northwestern Europe, including England. The resulting back up on both sides of the ocean caused substantial flight delays and Whyte's British Air flight from Logan to Heathrow had yet to arrive on its inbound flight. He looked at the flight status board and resigned himself to an extended wait.

Now without a job, Charles was returning to England six weeks after the horrendous Shamrock episode. Those weeks were spent in relative solitude except for the many hours when he sat at a table before attorneys on both sides and uttered his depositions. He spent much of his time either gathering his things and packing them; the balance of his time was spent drinking heavily.

As soon as he did arrive at Heathrow, representatives of the Crown would be waiting to escort him to Brixton, a few miles south of London, where he'd be the guest of the Queen at Brixton prison. There, he'd undergo interrogation as investigators and prosecutors reached a determination as to his immediate future. News of the Shamrock scheme remained big news in the UK and the entire world and Charles Whyte's name was known to play a significant role in its formulation and execution. Whether he'd be remanded for trial or released, Whyte recognized that he'd be hounded by the press for months. His parents had been successful in fending off reporters who squatted in front of their home in Thirsk demanding a story, but only because the local constable saw fit to gently but firmly harass the reporters into looking elsewhere for a story. He didn't want to deal with the crush any more than Charles' parents did.

He spoke with Barbara several times and understood her anxiety to return home with James and continue her life. He also understood that a separation and likely divorce proceedings were called for. Barbara would contact a family law attorney when she returned and the process would begin. The process would not be contested by Charles.

The P.A. announcement was heard over the din of the crowd . . . The British Air flight from Heathrow was just landing. He knew that refueling and servicing the plane would take some time so he settled in with a copy of the London Times and waited.

Janet Chapel's condo had plenty of space for seating six for dinner, but when Fortin arrived he saw that everything was set up for a buffet. "How many people are you having for dinner, Janet?"

Janet stepped out of the kitchen dressed in black slacks and a white silk blouse. Her hair was pulled back with ringlets at each ear. Drop dead gorgeous, he thought. What a loss for maledom. She walked over and took his jacket, giving him a warm hug and a kiss as she did so. "Enough. There'll be enough for dinner. And don't be so nosy."

He could detect wonderful aromas coming from her kitchen and started to walk in that direction when Janet stopped him. "Stop it. Just sit over there and have a glass of wine. Montepulciano d'Abruzzo tonight. Tell me what you think of it."

He poured an ounce into his glass, swirled it around and breathed in. "Very forward."

"Like the person who bought it. I thought it only appropriate."

"Some spice."

"Right once again. Just like yours truly."

"And very earthy."

"Gr-r-r."

He took a sip and swished it around in his mouth before swallowing. "Smooth, a lot of jam and plum. Good balance." He took another sip. "It has a wonderful finish."

"Fortin, if the job of sommelier at Carlo's wasn't already taken, you'd make a good one. Excellent description and right on the money."

"I usually look for a good gulping wine when I shop. Maybe you should keep your job at Carlo's."

"I had no intention of giving it up!"

A voice rang from the kitchen, a familiar one. "Who just said Carlo's?" Francina Ficociello stepped out of the kitchen with a ladle in her hand. She gave an enormous smile to Fortin before she ducked back into the kitchen.

"Francina" he said to Janet? "She's doing the cooking?"

"She's got some help in there, but she's very good in the

kitchen. And keep those lecherous eyes off her tits. I saw you drooling."

Fortin couldn't respond. Janet was right.

"Who else is in there with her?"

"Well, for a start, there's my buddy Patsy Massimo."

"Isn't he . . . ?"

"He's Carlo's new assistant chef, and the guy's incredible."

"Is he . . . ?

"You mean with Francina? No, that didn't exactly work out, as you probably guessed. Francina tried to fix Patsy up with her friend Gina . . . what a little honey she is . . . but it turns out that Patsy's, well . . ."

"Don't tell me."

"A three dollar bill. Justice, huh? Carlo gets this guy over here to wed his only daughter and it turns out he only wants to play hide the salami with other guys. He and Francina are best buds, but she's not going to bear his little bambinos. But this guy can cook!"

Fortin was at a loss for words.

The doorbell rang and Janet walked over to answer it. When the door opened, Fortin caught sight of his friend and former patient Detective Jerry Wetman. "Hi Doc," he said to Janet. "Hi Doc," he also said to Fortin when he came over and shook his hand. "Welcome back to the U.S. of A. How's everything across the pond? I heard you had an interesting trip?"

Fortin's attention was distracted by the enormous man standing behind Wetman. "Oh, this is Collins. He, er, works for me."

"Hello Doctor Fortin, Jerry's told me about you. You are one lucky man to get back in one piece."

"Collins is actually my partner," he whispered to Fortin.

"I've seen the name on the reports and in the papers. It's good to meet you."

From the kitchen came a procession of Francina, followed by a short fellow wearing a chef's hat, and then a slightly taller person, a Sicilian goddess. Francina made introductions all around. Patsy wore a smile as wide as he was tall. A cherub. His sister was the goddess, Maria, a more mature but no less attractive version of Francina. Janet motioned everybody to the dining room table where she handed everyone their plates and silverware.

"Dig in, people. And grab a seat on the balcony. It's a beautiful evening and we'll catch a great sunset in about fifteen minutes." Fortin felt a bit overwhelmed and Janet sensed it.

"C'mere for a sec." They stepped to the side as the guests, including Francina, Patsy and Maria, made the parade to the feast that graced the table. In a low voice, Janet said, "Francina had the idea and we talked about it last week. Patsy can speak four words in English, which is four more than Maria, but she doesn't have to say a word, does she? Is she hot or what?"

"What a stunning work of art."

"She's thirty four and her husband died about three months after they got married. Some accident with a sheep, God strike me dead if I lie. And the way she's been checking you out, I think she likes you."

Fortin looked over at Maria who coyly looked down. Fortin wondered, what am I getting into?

Eventually, full plates were all carried to the balcony where Janet had arranged several small cocktail tables. Everyone had a glass of wine as she proposed a toast. "To Andrew Fortin, mental health professional and international crime fighter. We welcome you back safe and sound."

Fortin stood and provided a response. "First let me thank all of you for being here." He could tell that Maria and Patsy were grinning but not understanding the first word. "I am grateful to all of you, and it is my pleasure to be back here in America with all of you."

The meal was fabulous and Fortin was the last to leave. "I feel awful about all those dishes. Are you sure I can't help you."

Janet waved him off. "Just know that you have friends and that we all care for you. We think the world of you and want to express our love when we can. Just seeing you smile was terrific." She kissed him and handed back his jacket. "And if I ever suggest that you take off and that I take over your practice while you're gone, please just shoot me."

Six months later

Rogan Murphy stood clutching a single rose and stared at the plaque. On it was engraved "John P. Murphy' and the years of his birth and death. Not thirty years old. Murphy bent low on one knee and laid the rose across the grave, uttering lines from an old prayer and finishing with, "May the good lord, Johnny, hold you forever in the palm of his hand."

He started to rise and was helped to his feet by Victor. Tony stood on the side and made the sign of the cross.

They were dressed for the weather in long wool coats and scarves. Victor put his arm over Rogan's shoulder and suggested they say their farewell to John and move on. "The boy was doing his best, Rogan. He wanted to be just like his old man, his 'Da' as you'd say. And from what we've heard, he never felt a thing. He was gone when he hit the pavement."

Rogan brushed away a tear. "Let's go. My friends will be waiting for us."

The trio drove in a rental car to South Boston and parked on a narrow street near the Gillette factory. Rogan led the way to Cronin's and waved to several patrons as he made his way to a booth in the corner. Joseph Kavanagh was holding court with two young men when Murphy arrived. He stuck out his hand to Kavanagh who dismissed the two youngsters with a wave of the hand. "Kavvy, I want to say thanks."

Kavanagh stood up and gave Rogan Murphy a bear hug. "I thought you'd be by this afternoon. I've been waiting here for you."

"The grave, the marker. I can't repay you."

"Ah, and we had Monsignor Ford do the Mass at Saint Monica's. It was beautiful. We had quite a contingent there in honor of your son, and we even had many from Charlestown make the trip, which says something about you and your family."

"I can't thank you enough, but . . ."

"This is what we're here for, isn't it? To help each other in time of need? And who are your two companions?" Kavanagh would stand for no more discussion about the costs involved in burying John Murphy.

Murphy made the introductions. "I've heard wonderful things about you lads. We are grateful for your help in getting some justice for the ills that befell young Mister Murphy. Please sit down. Can I offer you something to drink?"

Kavanagh signaled the barman who stood at the table awaiting instructions. "Two pints of Guinness and two Smithwick's. My friends and I have developed scorching throats and we need some medication, chop-chop."

One drink apiece turned into eleven and Kavanagh was impressed with the ability of the two non-Irish guests to keep up. "They're from England, Kavvy. They know their ales." By nightfall, the bar was crowded and noisy with customers, many of whom came to express their condolences to Rogan Murphy. Even Rudy Beans and Moose Langone stopped by and spent some time with Victor and Tony. It was a true Irish wake, except for there being no corpse in the room. And like most Irish wakes, this one involved a few fisticuffs that Kavvy made sure took place outside the confines of Cronin's. "The Celts, Tony, but we're a bellicose tribe, are we not?"

Tony raised his glass to salute Kavvy. "Aye, but that's the truth." By this time, Murphy and Victor were passed out.

Across the rolling hills and into the fertile fields of the valley, sunlight played in the leaves of the ancient olive trees. Branches that twisted, dark and gnarled, in every direction were heavy with their fruit.

The tall man adjusted the brim of his woven hat and squinted to see in the distance. A few puffy clouds held no ill omen; the harvest would begin tomorrow. He turned to his foreman.

"Domani, Franco."

Franco nodded in agreement and accepted a cigarette from his boss. "Si, signore. Domani, et grazie." They stood together silently and smoked, relishing the scene of near perfect tranquility. Tomorrow at dawn, the same area would be a beehive of workers and machines, and the olive presses in the barn would begin to hum. The man's cell phone rang and he turned and walked away as he answered and began his conversation.

Franco noticed that the man's limp was now just a memory. Just a few months ago, he wondered if the boss would even survive. But the man was resilient and determined. He had a few more scars, but he had survived. The phone conversation was over and the man returned.

"Franco," he began. "Una altra emergenza."

Franco would once again have to manage the harvesting process on his own. His boss was being called away, as he had been so often in the past. "Capisco, signore. Capisco."

Worthley Pond sits in a valley in East Peru, northwest of Auburn Maine. A small pond, it is surrounded by camps, most now converted to year round homes. In the summer, the pond is filled with swimmers, water skiers and anglers. But in winter, visitors get to enjoy the pond virtually alone.

From a round metal chimney piercing the roof of a white cottage on the south side of the pond, wisps of white smoke signaled the presence of visitors. Inside, Barbara Whyte turned up the flame of the propane fueled range. "I'm going to heat up some beans and hamburgers. Is that OK with you?"

Andrew Fortin stood up from where he worked, stoking the fire in the pot bellied stove and adding more wood. "Sounds great to me."

Fortin closed the latch on the stove and walked into the kitchen where he took a seat at the table. "I'm going to have to stay awake most of the night to make sure the fire doesn't burn out. If I don't, we'll be popsicles by morning."

"I intend to do my best to keep you awake, Andrew. I consider that part of my mission."

She poured two cups of coffee from the pot and joined him at the table. "This place brings back memories of when I was a child."

Fortin smiled. Barbara was almost in a dream state. "This little cottage was always crowded with cousins and aunts and uncles. It's nice to see it quiet; it gives me a chance to see everyone in my mind without too many distractions." She looked at Fortin and continued. "I remember thinking as a child that you only needed to take one breath up here for every two you took back home. It feels that way to me."

"And after this weekend?" Fortin didn't want to distress her, but they did need to talk about this.

She put down her cup and put her elbows on the table. She was ready to get serious.

"After this weekend, I'm going back to my job teaching. Is that what you mean?"

"You know very well what I mean." When Barbara returned

with her son, she was prepared to move back to Maine and start fresh when a call came from Monsignor Lambert that a position was available at St. Francis and would she like to come back? She jumped at the chance. James could stay in the same neighborhood, play with the same friends and attend the same schools.

Fortin was in his office two days ago when her call came in. Would he like to come to Maine for a few days? She had the keys to the family's cottage and James would be staying with Barbara's mother in Auburn. Fortin didn't agree at once but considered the ramifications before assenting to the plan. She gave him directions to the lake and they'd meet at the little store on Worthley Road at the head of the lake.

"After this weekend, after this weekend . . . I don't know just yet, Andrew. I really don't. I just know I wanted to see you."

"And Charles?"

"The papers are being processed. We'll be officially divorced in another month or two. Besides, Charles isn't going to show up, if that's what you're thinking. He's still in Brixton prison and his trial won't begin for another ten or twelve weeks."

"I'm not worried about Charles; I'm worried about you."

"And, just so you'll know, I'm seeing another therapist. She's in Framingham. Doctor Margaret Mary Maggio. Know her?"

"I know of her. A psychiatrist."

"That's her. And I'm doing fine. I just needed . . ."

"What?"

"Is this the third degree? Do I have a light bulb over my head?"

Fortin cracked a smile. He *was* making this sound like an interrogation.

Before he could say anything, she held up her hand in a

'stop' motion. "So I spoke with my mother. She likes you a lot, by the way. Did I say that already? And she knows I need a man. I mean: She-Knows-I-Need-A-Man!"

"How does she know this?"

"Because I told her. And I told her I needed *you*, and that I wanted *you*, and that she should take James for the weekend and spoil him rotten, and that I should take you away to the cottage and beat you into submission, and she likes you, by the way, did I say that already?"

Acknowledgments

I owe a great debt to many people who contributed to getting this work completed and published. Take Greg Larrison, for example, a great friend, a voracious reader, and someone who is not afraid of putting me in my place. He read an early draft of this book and gave me valuable feedback and criticism that improved the work. Sue Benidt is a careful reader and experienced copy editor who picked up several inconsistencies in early drafts. A woman with a highly organized mind and sharp wit, she pointed out flaws that, when corrected, moved the book forward. An editor par excellence.

Suzanne, my wife, puts up with all the drafts and is my inspiration. Without her encouragement, ideas, patience, love, and thorough editing, I could not have brought this book nearly as far.

Like most works of fiction, there are shreds of certain actual people, places and events that appear on these pages. For example, "Harvest" was an actual IRA bombing and shooting campaign waged in the border countries from 1956 to 1962. It was eventually called off by the IRA because it lacked broad support. Rue de la Chevrotière in Quebec does exist, and there is an old Bon Pasteur convent there. Most of the place names are real, but their geography is modified here and there. In the end, this is a novel, and by definition it is just a story that arose from imagination. Any errors are mine alone.